My Skin Begs You Please

(a '90s Universe novel)

LETA BLAKE

An Original Publication from Leta Blake Books (LB Press)

My Skin Begs You Please
Written and published by Leta Blake
Cover by Dar Albert
Formatted by BB eBooks

First Edition, 2024

Print Edition
ISBN: 979-8-88841-036-3

Other Books by Leta Blake

Contemporary

Will & Patrick Wake Up Married
Will & Patrick's Endless Honeymoon
Cowboy Seeks Husband
The Difference Between
Bring on Forever
Stay Lucky

Sports

The River Leith

The Training Season Series
Training Season
Training Complex

Musicians

Smoky Mountain Dreams
Vespertine

New Adult

Punching the V-Card

'90s Coming of Age Series
Pictures of You
You Are Not Me
Only You

Winter Holidays

North's Pole

The Mr. Christmas Series
Mr. Frosty Pants
Mr. Naughty List
Mr. Jingle Bells

A Boy for All Seasons
My December Daddy

Fantasy

Any Given Lifetime

Reimagined Fairy Tales

Flight
Levity

Paranormal & Shifters

Angel Undone
Omega Mine

Horror

Raise Up Heart

Omegaverse

Heat of Love Series
White Heat
Slow Heat
Alpha Heat
Slow Birth
Bitter Heat

For Sale Series
Heat for Sale
Bully for Sale

Audiobooks
letablake.com/audiobooks

Discover more about the author online

Leta Blake
letablake.com

Gay Romance Newsletter

Leta's newsletter will keep you up to date on her latest releases, sales and deals, future writing plans, and more from the world of M/M romance. Join Leta's mailing list today.

Author's Note & Content Warnings

General warning: *My Skin Begs You Please* is an incredibly intense book, and the story, while powerful and meaningful, won't be a good fit for everyone. Please proceed with caution and look over the extensive list of warnings below.

Content warning regarding activity between the main characters: BDSM, graphic kinks throughout the book, choking, high-level impact play/beatings, humiliation kink, and multiple instances of bodily fluid play.

Content warning applicable to main characters separately: graphic sexual assault, stalking, graphic physical/sexual violence, rape, incest/child abuse, graphic homophobia, suicidal thoughts, emotional abuse, mental illness, hate crime, HIV.

Content warnings applicable only to side-characters: domestic abuse, fisting.

Necessary Spoiler: This book contains **NO character death,** and both heroes achieve a happily-ever-after *together.*

Disclaimers: The medical advice and the beliefs regarding the transmission of HIV in this book are period appropriate, however, they are not accurate. Please ask a medical provider about the current findings on transmission of and reinfection with the disease.

In addition, any sort of breath play can be hazardous and even deadly. Please do not take the portrayal of the act to be an endorsement of safety by the author.

Dedication

For M
May you be living well

Prologue

Autumn 1991
Luke

I HADN'T PLANNED to take on another boy. Not right now anyway. Maybe not ever.

But somehow here I was, barefoot in just a pair of jeans, standing in my basement dungeon with a fidgety, snarling, and naked submissive kneeling at my feet. The boy looked as if he might get up, grab his clothes from where they were folded on the chair in the corner, and run away.

I *hoped* I could be what he needed, but I wasn't sure. He wasn't either, as was evident by the angry, doubtful glances he sent up to me before jerking his eyes to the concrete floor again. He shifted from knee to knee.

"Do you know why you're here?" I asked, reaching out to slide a hand over his silky, white-blond hair, down his freshly shaven jawline, to tilt his chin up so he was forced to meet my eyes.

"Yes," he bit out.

"Tell me."

"I'm here to get hurt."

My lips twitched and so did my dick. "Yes, but what else?"

His eyes skipped away from mine. I gripped his chin, and he swiveled his gaze back up again, gulping quickly. "I don't know," he whispered.

That sexy, wavering uncertainty crept over his features again, giving me a glimpse of the creature he truly was beneath his tough exterior. He pushed his hard shell to the surface again, covering the softness up. "I mean, I don't know, *Sir*."

"Good. Remember you can call me Sir, Master, or…" I smirked. "If you're feeling especially needy, Daddy."

He closed his eyes, and when he opened them again, the flinty hardness was back. "Yes, Sir."

"And I'll call you Mitchell."

He stiffened, trying to jerk his chin out of my grip. I held him fast, tightly enough I could leave bruises. It'd been a long time since I had a boy fight me at all. It was an intriguing and arousing challenge.

"No, Sir," he said. "I'm Minty."

"The name your mother gave you was Mitchell."

He swallowed again, clenching his jaw, before muttering, "How do you know that?"

"You put it on the form I had you fill out for me, remember? Along with all the kinks you thought you'd enjoy, and questions about your health and past kink experiences. Did you forget?"

"It also asked me what name I prefer to be called, and I put down 'Minty.'"

"Sir," I reminded him.

"I put down 'Minty,' Sir," he gritted out.

He was still thinking of running from me. It was there in his tense shoulders, his toes turned under to push into the floor and rise, the expression on his face. It wasn't because he didn't want the pain I planned to give him, but because he didn't know if it would be enough.

My lack of compromise with his name during a scene was the start of *the enough* he truly wanted. He just didn't know that yet.

"Here are your options: I call you Mitchell, and we go on with

this scene today, or you can use your safe word—poodle, correct?—
and we end for today with no hard feelings. We'll talk it out so I
understand why this is a hard boundary for you and, in a few days'
time, after we've let this settle, we'll renegotiate another meeting."

"But why, Sir?" His trembling lips were plush. Perfect for cock-
sucking. I hoped I got a chance to feel them on my dick today.
"Why does it matter what you call me?"

"Because Mitchell is what I *want* to call you," I told him.
"That's all that matters. I could call you Shit Stain, and you'd agree.
Understood?" I gripped his jaw again, squeezing until he winced
and tears rose. I wasn't sure if they were due to how rough I was
being, or if he really objected to the name. He had his safe word.
We'd see if he used it.

"Yes, Sir," he said, deflating as soon as he agreed.

"Say it," I ordered.

"What, Sir?"

"Your name."

The boy's face wrenched through a series of emotions, each
more vulnerable than the next, and then he whispered, "I'm
Mitchell, Sir."

"That's right. When you're here on your knees for me, you're
Mitchell."

I released his jaw and slipped my hand into his hair, gently at
first, but I recalled that tenderness wasn't what Mitchell wanted,
and it wasn't what he needed either. So, I clenched a handful tightly
enough to sting, bringing the tears back to his eyes.

"Don't move," I whispered. "Stay very still."

His gaze held mine, a challenge rising in them the longer I kept
him stationary and did nothing, said nothing.

When the challenge dissipated, submission taking over his features, I pursed my lips and spit a glob of gooey saliva onto his face. I
aimed for his left eyebrow and didn't miss. "There. That's more like

it. You're a filthy cocksucking whore, aren't you, Mitchell?"

"Yes, Sir," he whispered, keeping his eye closed against the spit that slid down to coat his lashes. His breath came in sharp pants and a red blush spread up from his pale chest to his neck and into his cheeks, making them shine with heat.

"Let's try this again. Why are you here?"

"To get hurt, Sir," Mitchell whispered.

"And what else?"

"I don't know."

This confession was followed by a whimper of unease as I tightened my grip in his hair. With my free hand, I smeared the glob of saliva all over his face, down to his lips, and then back up into his hair at the temples.

"You're here to be used," I said. "To be my bitch. My fuck toy. My dick's slave."

His breath stuttered, and I noticed the erection now straining between his legs. He'd been mostly soft until I'd spit on him. Humiliation was key then, just as my friend Barry had suggested in our initial discussion of Mitchell. Humiliation, rough use, and daddy issues stood out clearly amongst many other demons that called to and tormented him.

"You're HIV positive," I said.

"Yes, Sir." His voice was so low that I strained to catch the words, and an expression of shame passed over his features. I understood. I'd struggled with that too. It was bullshit, I'd decided though, to feel shame over what came down to bad luck. But for Mitchell, shame was essential for the game between us. It was part of why I refused to use his preferred name. He came to me so he could feel unmoored, uncomfortable, and disrespected in a consensual and sane situation instead of the insane ones he'd been putting himself in before now. If I agreed to call him Minty, he'd feel respected and, deep down, he didn't want that.

"Yes, Sir, what?" I pressed. He needed to say it. He had to get used to saying it.

"I'm HIV positive, Sir."

"That's right. You are."

He trembled all over now, his cock straining up, his torso flushed, and his one open eye going glassy. My saliva was already drying where I'd smeared it on his face and mouth.

"I am too."

He blinked his eye open, the clumped lashes making it look like he wore mascara—which I knew he sometimes did, but he'd arrived today barefaced. "I already know that. You told me before."

I gripped his hair and tugged it, jerking his head. "How do you speak to me?"

He gasped. "Sir! I'm sorry. Please, Sir, you're going to pull my hair out." His whine trembled alluringly in the air.

I felt the first sadistic pulse hit, and my lips curled into a smirk as my cock began to fill. "You beg nicely," I said.

When some of the fear doused in his eyes, I reined in my urge to praise him. "But not nicely enough."

I slapped his face. He gasped in pain, eyes flying wide and a surprised cry wrenching from his throat. I hadn't slapped him hard enough to bruise him. He had fine, fair skin, though. It wouldn't take much to leave a mark. This first slap might even linger as a red stain for hours. I was curious to see how long.

"Say it again," I demanded, unzipping my jeans and pulling my hard cock free. "The right way. And thank me for correcting you."

"Yes, Sir. Thank you, Sir." His voice was breathless. "You—you told me you were HIV positive already. Before, Sir."

He looked dizzy, as if he were already dropping into subspace, which was unexpected. From what I understood, he got off with the men who abused him, but he didn't fall into subspace or fly with them. I got the impression he often kept control of the scenario throughout. Or kept whatever semblance of control could be maintained while getting the shit beaten out of him and being fucked ruthlessly—egging the assholes on to do it harder, pleading for them to hurt him again.

My own breath hitched just imagining it. Not out of fear for his life—the way it would have for any non-sadist—but in arousal. The truth was I'd like to take him like that. Fuck him like I hated him. Beat him while I did it until we both got off screaming.

Afterward, I'd soothe him and bring him down to a safe, comfortable place in my bed…

But that kind of abuse wasn't sane or healthy. It was a fantasy no one should live out, not without a lot of clear rules and boundaries in place. But, perhaps, if Mitchell and I were compatible enough, we could stage something close to that brutality, something that would scare him deeply, but not risk his health or life. It'd be fun to try. I hoped I'd get the chance.

Releasing his hair, I wrenched his jaw open and spit into his mouth. "Swallow it," I said.

He did, eyes wide, and chest heaving with his breaths. A drop of pre-cum formed at the tip of his cock, and my aching dick brushed against my stomach when I leaned down to spit into his mouth again. "We."

Spit.

Mitchell dutifully swallowed.

"Are."

Spit. Swallow.

"HIV."

Spit. Swallow.

"Positive."

Spit. Swallow.

I thumbed his mouth open wider, pressing down on his lower teeth, and then aimed my cock at his pink, glistening tongue and wide-open throat.

"Do you know what that means?" I said, keeping his mouth firmly open so he couldn't speak to answer me. "It means I can do this…"

I hesitated for a moment, giving him time to use his safe word before I penetrated his mouth for the first time. But he didn't. He just opened wider for me, and I shoved in. "Without a fucking condom."

Christ, his mouth was good. He knew exactly what he was doing. Gripping my thighs hard, he sucked, licked, kissed, and gulped me down like he hadn't had a cock in his hungry throat in a hundred years. But I knew damn well from our friend Barry that the kid hadn't let his HIV status slow him down when it came to his love of cum guzzling.

After pushing my jeans lower, giving him more room to work, I let him go to town on me. I gripped his hair roughly in one hand and tweaked my own nipples with the other. As I drew close to climax, I pulled him off, and he gazed up with a hazy, aroused expression, keeping his mouth open in case I wanted to plunge back in. Perfect.

"Do you know what else being HIV positive means between us?" I asked him.

He licked his red, suck-swollen lips, and rasped, "No, Sir."

"It means I can also do this." Using my grip on his hair, I forced him around on his knees. He cried out in pain, surprised by the sudden manhandling. I forced his head down to the ground, knelt behind him, and lifted his hips up as I aimed my cock at his hole.

The skin on his back shimmered with sudden sweat, and his ass cheeks quivered with goose pimples as I pushed my way through the tense muscle of his tight anus. He'd lubed beforehand, as I'd instructed him to do when we made our plans to meet, but I wouldn't have stopped even if he hadn't. Still, the slick had grown tacky since he'd applied it, making my entrance less than gentle. Mitchell panted and clenched his hands into fists, but he didn't move away from me. In fact, he pushed back, forcing me deeper and faster into his hot, velvety ass. Fuck, he was eager.

I slapped his hip hard. "Be still. I'll decide how fast I get into my nasty little cum dumpster. Because that's what you are, isn't it, Mitchell? Daddy's dirty cum dumpster."

Mitchell went perfectly still, immobile almost, and I smirked. The buzzy sensation of power and domination that I loved like nothing else in the world arced through me. Sliding in deeper, I threw my head back, enjoying the delicious grip of his hole and the control I was exerting over him.

"Poodle."

I froze, shocked to hear the word that ended our play. As quickly as I could, given how tight he was, I pulled out.

Mitchell winced, whispering something over and over.

I hitched my jeans up and quickly knelt down to where his head was still pressed to the floor. His breath came in shallow gasps that I'd taken for arousal, but I now saw they were his attempt not to cry. He shuddered as I bent low to hear what he was saying.

"Poodle," he whispered. "Poodle, poodle."

Part I

September 1991
Two Weeks Earlier...

Chapter One

Minty

"Y OU'RE GOING TO get yourself killed."

I poked a straw into the McDonalds' shake Barry had bought for me after he chased me down on the Strip, determined to convince me to talk with him. Not even thirty minutes ago, I'd run from our local gay club, Tilt-a-Whirl, in a blind rage after being confronted by my so-called friends about my recent romantic and sexual choices, and Barry still thought he could save me.

"Did you hear me? Killed."

"I don't have a problem with that," I said, though it wasn't entirely true. I was terrified of dying, but now that I was HIV positive, I knew it was just a matter of time until I was worm food anyway. And the only thing that obliterated the fear *that* brought up in me was pain. And degradation. And hard use. And being beaten up.

Allowing me to exchange one kind of terror for another.

"I think you do have a problem with it," Barry contradicted me, seeing right through my b.s. the way he always did. "And I can help you."

"Oh, you've got a cure for HIV stuffed in your back pocket, huh?"

"No, I have a friend who hurts people professionally."

I blinked at him. "A Dom or something?"

"A Dom *exactly*." He ran a hand over his shiny bald head. "Look, I've been friends with you a few years now, and I know you pretty well."

I shrugged. I wasn't going to give him the pleasure of admitting we were close like that, but yeah, my Tilt-a-Whirl gang—Windy, Antonio, Barry, and Robert—were my closest friends. The best person in the whole world, Daniel, would always be my *best* friend, of course, but he'd been busy and distracted lately. His mom's drinking made his life hard, and there were his little siblings to look after, and now he had his new boyfriend, Peter...

"I think you need pain," Barry went on. "You always got a lot out of the spankings Renée used to give you on stage in her act. So, I'm not against you getting hurt, if it's done in a safe, sane, consensual way with someone who gives a shit whether or not you live through it."

"My current lover gives a—"

"Cut the crap."

I gazed out the window. The lights inside McDonalds were bright against the night outside, and the cars zoomed down the Strip with little care for the pedestrians around them. I sucked the milkshake in, watching a straight couple cruise down the sidewalk, their hands in each other's back pockets, looking so perfect it was like they'd stepped out of a hair commercial for gender-neutral shampoo. A fresh scent by Calvin Klein.

"I'm scared," I admitted when I'd swallowed down half the shake. "What's wrong with that?"

"Nothing," Barry said, reaching out to take my hand. "It makes sense to be scared."

I could feel eyes on us. We stuck out even amongst the college kids who crowded McDonalds every night avoiding their school-work. They'd wonder about me being here with Barry simply because he was Black and I was white, and this was the South. But with me being dressed the way I was—in a tutu, makeup, and looking femme and glitter-covered—they were going to keep on staring at us for an entirely separate reason too. Several girls giggled behind their hands, and I distinctly heard speculation about how I was a fairy who must like big, Black dicks.

Cool. Racism, stereotypes, and homophobia all for the price of one milkshake.

Though I *did* like big dicks of any color, the bigger the better. I loved it when a dick hurt as it fucked into me, when I was stretched to the point of pain, and how that pain felt like power.

It was difficult to explain, but when a man was inside me, I felt like a god. Especially when they didn't *want* to want me, when they hated wanting me. In those moments, I was a beautiful, *irresistible* god who could take whatever those assholes dished out and still make them come harder than they ever had—against their will and despite their self-loathing.

Power.

A posse of frat guys came in, and I pulled my hand out of Barry's. I liked pain, but not six frat guys' worth of it, and I didn't want Barry to get into a fight with them just because he was being nice to me. Not after I'd already been a massive asshole to him and everyone else tonight.

"I like it when they hate it," I said. "What do you not understand about that?" I'd explained as much back at the club. I knew he'd heard me.

"You might like this kind of pain too."

I rolled my eyes. "What? Some old leather daddy wielding a crop and telling me to giddy-up?"

"More like a handsome thirty-four-year-old tying you down and whipping you until you cry and beg, and even then not stopping."

I swallowed. That didn't sound like a bad time. "But he'd like it, wouldn't he? He wouldn't hate himself while hurting me." I shrugged. "Ultimately that's my kink. *That's* what I like best."

Barry gazed at me solemnly. "Do you like it when they hate *themselves* for wanting you? Or when they hate *you* for making them want you?"

I sucked at the milkshake again, the cold, thick liquid sliding down my throat. I glanced over to where some of the frat guys had taken a table near us. They were talking about game stats for some sport, I wasn't even sure which one, but at least they weren't paying us any attention at all.

"I'm not sure," I admitted. "I like both."

"What if you could have ungodly amounts of pain? So much that you hate *them* for giving it to you? Or you feel like they *must* hate you to be dishing it out so hard?"

I rolled my eyes again. "What do you know about pain?"

"Before I met Robert, I had a Dom for a while. He's the one who trained Luke, the guy I'd like you to meet."

I sputtered. "You had a Dom? *You?*" I'd never imagined Barry like that. He was big and broad, and always strong and in charge. I couldn't visualize him submitting to anyone, much less letting them hurt him.

"His name was Jerome, and he was damn good at what he did. It didn't last long. I discovered I wasn't into it. Shortly after I ended things with him, I started working on the cruise ship."

"Where you met Robert." Suddenly I wondered. "Does *he* spank you? Bust your ass?"

"Robert wouldn't dare."

"Wouldn't he?"

Robert—or rather his alter-ego Renée—had spanked me plenty of times as a titillating part of her drag act at Tilt-a-Whirl. She called me her Naughty Boy and cracked her hand on my ass until I cried. I always loved the pain of it, and the humiliation of it too. Sometimes it was exactly what I needed to keep my head from going to bad places.

But I couldn't imagine Barry being into that.

He snorted. "Only if he wanted his own ass busted."

"And *does* he?" I was fascinated. This was much better than talking about what I needed and how I should get it.

"Sometimes. Look, Minty, I want you to at least meet with Luke. Do an interview."

I smirked. "Is that like an audition? Would he whip me and see if I looked pretty enough when I cry?"

"No. He's a professional."

"What's that mean?"

"He'd review the kinks he offers and see what, if any, you want to try, and which, if any, you want to strike from the plate of options. He'd ask you to fill out some questionnaires and talk to him about your sexual history, what you like about pain, and when you like it the most. When you don't want it at all. He'd be thorough. He'd likely have you sign a contract with him."

"A contract?" I asked, stupidly.

"It's not especially typical for people in the BDSM world to have actual written contracts, but in a situation like this—where you're both strangers from the start—it can make it easier to jump right to the pain play."

Pain play. I chewed my lip, thinking it over.

"What if he can't hurt me enough? What if he tries and I can't be satisfied?" I glanced toward the frat guys, each so like the other with their thick necks, beefy hands, and the same horny vibe that let me know any one of them would let me suck them off in the bathroom—

But they'd have to beat me up afterward to prove they weren't gay.

"What if I need that?" I tilted my head slightly toward them.

Barry's lips flattened. "You might. But I think if you give this a try, you'll be surprised by how little you'll want or need that kind of roughness from those kinds of boys."

"I don't know," I said, sitting back and slurping the last of the milkshake, the cup rattling as I tried for more.

Barry leaned forward and took the empty cup from me. "It can't *hurt* to meet Luke."

I grinned. "But then what would be the point?"

Barry rolled his eyes and, for the first time all night, I laughed.

Luke

"THIS KID ISN'T right in the head," I surmised, after Barry explained the situation.

Sitting in the passenger seat of his Dodge truck, I bit into the Wendy's burger we'd picked up from the drive-through. I only had an hour's meal break before I was due back at Knox Supplies & News, an adult toy store and porn shop with a child-safe, misleading name to satisfy the neighboring businesses.

I was working the third shift this week, aka the busiest shift. With the commissions I received from larger sales, I earned a lot more when I worked through the night, but it fucked with my sleep schedule like crazy.

Barry worked at Tilt-a-Whirl, and also at the University of Tennessee Library, and he understood sleep deprivation. He sometimes went straight from one job to the other, closing the club to open the library just a few minutes later. I didn't know how he did it, but he never seemed challenged by it.

He always came across as calm, collected, and in control.

Which was why I was listening so closely to his plea for me to "handle" this Minty kid. For the first time since Jerome had introduced me to Barry all those years ago, he sounded uncertain, worried, and I'd even say scared. As a sadist, I recognized every tenor and tremble of fear in a voice. I lived for it.

"So, what do you want me to do?" I asked, after Barry once again outlined the situation and the urgency of it.

"You're good at pain."

"I'm great at it," I agreed.

"And you don't mind degradation."

"Not my favorite way to play, but I can do it for a sub who requires it."

"He needs it," Barry said. "He won't stick around if you're soft with him, that's for sure. He'll go right back to courting death with those assholes who truly despise him and aren't just pretending to hate him for the orgasm."

"Mm." I chewed a bite of hamburger thoughtfully, tossing a fry into my mouth. "But what's in it for me? Aside from what will probably be some great sex. I'm a pro. I get paid for this and he's broke, or so you say. Are *you* going to pay for it? Or is Robert?" I shook my head. "Is this some kind of desperate, kinky, birthday present for this kid?"

"I'm asking you to do it as a favor." Barry's breath hitched, and I knew he was getting ready to throw down a card he was embarrassed to use, and I also knew exactly which card it would be. "As one of Jerome's students for another."

I chuckled. "I knew you'd drag his ass into this."

"He did train you and me both."

"Two failed subs of his is more like it," I said, laughing again. "You dropped out, and I became a sadistic Dom instead of his kneeling, sweet boy."

"He had to see it coming from both of us," Barry said. "And just because I dropped out doesn't mean I failed. I learned a lot from my time with him—stamina, endurance, how to control myself when I want to lash out. Tons of things. I bet you learned a lot too."

"Oh, everything I know, just about." I popped in another french fry and slurped my Coke. "I'm in between boys right now."

That was a lie. The truth was I wasn't Domming professionally *or* for fun at the moment. As a nearly exclusive top—who'd made a few unfortunate exceptions in recent years—my HIV diagnosis made it hard for me to play the way I wanted to, especially with any HIV negative subs. And I didn't want to advertise for pos guys only. It seemed grotesque, like fiddling as Rome burned down or dancing on graves.

It wasn't that I was never going to Dom again, or that I refused to use condoms, or that I would never seek out a pos guy to play with; it was just that I hadn't made peace with my illness yet. I was only six months into this diagnosis—T-cells strong, condition still good, and I felt completely healthy—but just knowing I was infected was a weight I wasn't used to carrying. To be a good Dom, I needed to be all there. I had to be willing and ready to carry someone else fully for the duration of the play and the aftercare. I hadn't had that kind of energy in me since the diagnosis.

After I'd ended things with my last boy, Benji—who, thank fuck, was still HIV negative at the time and presumably still was— I'd taken a break from the kink scene to get my affairs in order. Affairs. What a way to put it. Before the diagnosis, that word had meant something *fun*—typically with a man who wasn't trying to tie any strings. Because he was already attached to a very oblivious wife.

Now the word meant making wills, writing out final wishes, completing end-of-life paperwork, deciding what to do with my home, the contents of my dungeon, and my bank accounts. Thirty-four years old, and I was contemplating issues I'd assumed I had more than forty or fifty years to consider. That was before AIDS, before I even knew the term HIV, before I'd lost friends and lovers and play partners, and even my favorite bartender.

If I were a different sort of man, I'd think maybe the disease was a punishment from God. Not for being gay, because that was bullshit, but for being unduly happy here on earth, for fucking and sucking like His creation was nothing more than a 24/7 bacchanal. For years after I achieved adulthood, I'd lived carefree, cum-soaked, and happy as hell.

But all that was stripped away, bit by bit, loss by loss, until playtime became edged with fear, and I'd dreaded as much as I'd longed for the release that came from dominating a cum-hungry submissive. My diagnosis was the final straw that made me step away from it all.

And backing away had been responsible. Necessary.

So, no, I hadn't planned on taking on another boy any time soon, if ever.

But I would be lying if I said I wasn't intrigued by Barry's request. The boy he was putting on my plate was pretty—if Barry was to be believed, and he wasn't a liar—positive, and a pain slut. It also sounded like he was a very bratty submissive in need of a firm hand. Just my type.

"The boy wants to meet me?" I asked.

Barry laughed. "No."

I lifted my brows. "Then why are you talking to me about him?"

"He doesn't *want* to meet you, but he's interested. I know him. If I tell him he has an appointment with you at a certain time, he'll show."

"Why?"

"He's curious," Barry said. "He's also scared of himself. He might not admit he wants help, but deep down he does, and when he finds out what you can give him, it'll be hard for him to walk away. Even if some part of him does still crave what he gets from those assholes who use him and beat him recklessly."

"Ah, so you want me to get him addicted to the pain I give him, and then what? Tell him he can't have it if he starts letting those boys go at him again?"

Barry smirked. "You act like that's not what you'd do if he were your sub anyway."

I laughed. He was right, of course. I'd never let my boy treat himself that way. As much as I adored hurting my subs, their bodies were *mine* to abuse and no one else's. Not so long as they had a contract or verbal agreement with me.

"One last question."

"Shoot."

"Why's he doing this? Why does he need it?"

Barry frowned, seemed to consider his words carefully, and then said, "You know what they say about the shiniest people covering up the worst pain? That's always been him."

I noticed how Barry's eyes darkened when he went on, "Well, until recently. Now he's not bothering to cover his pain anymore. No more sparkles, no more shine. It's like he's been swallowed by his own shadow."

"Since the diagnosis?"

"Yeah."

I pondered that. "All right. Tell him Tuesday, four o'clock, at Knox Supplies & News. We can meet in the back office before my shift."

Barry nodded, and I hoped I didn't regret my choice. This Minty kid would be my first boy since I'd dropped Benji, and I wasn't convinced it was a good idea. But if I was ever going to take on a sub again, this one certainly sounded intriguing.

I always did have a thing for the difficult cases, and maybe this could be a way for us to "rage, rage against the dying of the light."

Before it—and we—blinked out for eternity.

Chapter Two

Minty

I'D BEEN INSIDE Knox Supplies & News plenty of times, of course. I'd bought every dildo, butt plug, and sex toy I'd ever owned there. But I'd never been inside during the middle of the day, when it was still light outside, and anyone could see my car out front. Good thing my mama lived and worked in Kingston, forty-five long minutes away, or I'd have been too terrified to park my truck outside in case she drove by.

I wished I'd brought Barry with me as backup. He'd offered, and I'd laughed him off, but now that I was standing outside the gray, square, one-story building, getting ready to see a man about hurting me, I wished I hadn't.

I didn't even know what Luke looked like. Probably some thick muscle pig. That was the usual type, wasn't it?

What did I know, though? I talked a big game, but when it came to sex, although I'd had a lot of it, it was usually in rather conventional ways. Dick in one of my holes until climax was achieved. If I was in the mood for pain—which was all the time lately—I'd get an asshole, bully frat boy to hit, slap, kick, and hate on me, but none of this fancy shit with contracts, and whips, and a professional Dom or whatever. It had never appealed to me before.

I wasn't sure it appealed to me *now*.

I put on some extra cherry lip balm, though my lips were perfectly well-hydrated, and stuck it back in my hip pocket with my keys before straightening my shirt's pink spaghetti straps and heading into the shop.

The door opened onto the familiar, fluorescent-lit showroom. A middle-aged woman with blonde hair cut into short, punk rock, messy hanks stood behind the counter looking bored, chewing gum, and reading *Spin* magazine. Paul Westerberg was on the cover clutching a guitar and wearing glasses. His chunky brown hair wasn't dissimilar from hers, and I wondered if she knew it. Meanwhile, "Holiday" by Madonna piped in overhead.

The woman glanced up. "Can I help you?" she asked, leaning her elbows onto the counter on either side of the magazine. "Looking for something in particular?"

The rows and rows of dildos, pocket pussies, vibrators, cock rings, porn VHS tapes, and more called out to me. I could walk around like any of that was what I'd come for, maybe even buy a new butt plug—I'd been wanting a bigger one, hadn't I?—and just never mention this Luke guy at all. Or I could turn around, leave this plastic-scented place, get the hell out of that exposed parking lot, and just pretend none of this had ever been discussed.

"I'm, uh…I'm looking for…" I swallowed hard, and she stood up straight, curious now that I'd started talking.

"S'okay, baby, spit it out," she said. "I've heard it all before. Nothing to stutter over."

I blushed. "I'm not embarrassed," I declared. Or at least I wouldn't have been if I were there for toys, but I must have seemed absurd, red as a beet and denying it.

"I mean, not about that. I'm not here for—" I cleared my throat. She was starting to look concerned. "I'm not here for sex toys. I'm here for Luke."

"Oooooh." A knowing expression passed over her features before being quickly tucked away. "He's in the back. I'll ring him."

She picked up the phone, pressed a single digit, and ran her eyes over me as she waited. "Yeah, hey. Got a pretty thing out front here to see you." She laughed. "Uh-huh, pretty *and* nervous."

"I'm not," I said, lifting my chin.

"Says he's not," she went on, laughing some more. "All right. Sure." She hung up. "He'll be right out. Said you should look around, see if there's anything here you like."

Was it a test? Was he going to buy some toy for me and… what? Use it? Today maybe? To see how I handled that sort of thing? Was I supposed to demonstrate submission by doing what the woman behind the counter told me to do? Was I supposed to refuse her and just stand here like an idiot watching her read?

"Okay," I said, finally, turning from the counter and moving down one of the aisles of massive fake cocks. She didn't pay attention to me much after that, just glancing up occasionally to ask if I had any questions about a particular model or toy.

I did not. I wasn't even really looking. Though the extra-large butt plugs were as intriguing as they were terrifying. I wasn't sure I could ever manage to get something so enormous inside me, though I didn't hate the idea either.

But I should. I should hate that idea. There was something wrong with me that I wanted pain more than I wanted pleasure these days. I hadn't always been like this. Once, not very long ago even, I'd been almost past the worst of my self-destructive urges. But now…

I *knew* what was wrong with me, of course. That fucking diagnosis. It'd thrown every good thing inside me off kilter, and I'd gone spinning back to my old ways of coping. The memories I'd tried so hard to bury surfaced most nights in my sleep, and I woke with sticky sheets and shame that could only be beaten out of me or fucked free.

I was thinking about that shame and staring at the colossal plug when I heard his voice for the first time. It was dark, deep, and gave me shivers immediately.

"I see you have enormous ambitions," Luke said from behind me. "That's a plug to work up to for sure."

I swallowed and turned around, greeted first by a chest that wasn't as broad as I'd expected, and then a slim neck that was almost pretty. I tilted my head up, up, and up and found his calm, narrow face peering down at me. Dark blond hair—or was it light brown?—cut all shaggy around his handsome face. He had to be at least six-foot-one, and I was barely up to his nipples. I was glad I'd worn my prettiest top and a slim-fitting blue jean skirt. At least I knew I looked good as he scanned me from head to toe and back again.

"Are you transsexual?" he asked. "I want to call you by the right terms."

"Would it matter if I was?" I asked, genuinely curious whether he'd still hurt me if I were a girl and not a boy.

"Not really."

"Well, I'm not," I said. "I'm a very pretty boy with the correct priorities in fashion, and that's all."

"It'd be okay if that ever changed," he asserted so calmly that I almost didn't understand him.

"It won't."

He shrugged. "That's fine too. So, let's talk."

"Here?" My gaze darted over to the woman at the counter.

"No, in the back office. Cherise doesn't want to hear the details, do you?" he called out the last two words.

Cherise didn't look up from her magazine. "Sure do not, Luke."

He grinned. "All right then. You okay with coming in the back room with me?"

I thought about it a moment.

Seeing my hesitation, he said, "We can always talk outside in my car, or your car if you prefer. Or we could go grab a fast bite at Gourmet's Kitchen. Up to you."

"The back room is fine."

"Great. It's simpler that way."

I followed him past more raunchy paraphernalia and into the office space of the building. It wasn't spacious, especially since there was stock back there, but there was a desk and two chairs, and a computer with a green screen and some various numbers next to a blinking cursor.

"Have a seat," he said, indicating the chair across from the desk.

I took it, the hard plastic cold against the back of my exposed legs.

"So, you're Minty, and you like pain," he said, like that was a normal opener.

I answered with the truth, though my stomach was a churning vat of acid. "Yes, I am, and I do. Kind of. And you're Luke, and you like giving pain."

"You can call me Sir."

A thrill went up my spine. I hadn't expected to like that, and yet I very much had. "Oh."

"As Barry told you, I'm Luke Montgomery, but when you and I are together, 'Sir' is the correct mode of address."

"Okay…Sir."

"Let's talk."

An hour later, I was stumbling out into the orange glow of sunset with shaky knees and a rushing feeling in my veins, almost like a drug.

We'd talked, sure, but it'd been more like a business deal or a purchase.

He had a stack of papers for us to discuss—the contract Barry had mentioned, and a pages-long list of kinks. We went through that at length, with Luke asking me if I knew what each kink was—

and if I didn't, he explained it to me. He then told me to consider whether I was willing to experiment with it or not. Some were a definite yes, some were an automatic no, but he told me we didn't need to fill the forms out right now.

He said he was an exclusive top, and my HIV positive status was of no worry to him because he was positive too. He told me that's why there were options on the list for going bare. It was up to me if I wanted to include cum play in our time together.

"You don't need to decide today," he'd said. "There's no rush to this. Take the papers home. Think about everything. Research the kinks at a library if you need to. Talk to Barry. Call me to ask questions. I'm happy to go over any part of this again. Whatever it takes for you to feel safe and ready. Or, if that never happens, I'm all right with that too."

Safe and ready?

Remembering his phrase, I rolled my eyes. Safe wasn't what I wanted to feel. If anything, I wanted to feel at risk. Always.

I rolled my truck's windows down, letting the breeze flow over me, cooling my hot skin. I should tell him. Let him know right now I was never going to get what I needed from him and exactly why that was. I was wasting his time and my own, pretending I could be hurt in a "safe" way and be satisfied.

Gathering my nerve, I got out of my truck and went back inside. I walked right by Cherise and straight into the back room. Luke looked up in surprise, but he kicked back in his cushioned office chair and crossed his legs at the ankle, a smirky smile blooming on his face as I shut the door behind me. I leaned back against it, breathing heavily, before I thrust the sheaf of papers out toward him.

"Decided already?" he asked, not reaching out to take them.

"Yes," I said.

He raised a brow.

"I mean, yes, Sir. I've decided you can't help me."

"Why's that?"

"Because you want me to feel safe before we start, and I don't *do* safe, Sir. That's not what I want from you or from anyone right now. I want fear, pain, and hurt. I want to forget I'm dying. I get off on knowing the man who's fucking me hates me, hates wanting me, and *hates* coming for me. I love that. You won't give me what I need. You can't."

"Can't I?" he asked, standing and stalking toward me, his expression darkening. "You think because I'll enjoy fucking you that I'll be soft for you? That I'll make you feel loved and wanted?" He shook his head, putting one hand on the door and the other across my throat.

I panted, my cock thickening in an instant. He stared into my eyes until, intimidated and horny, I looked away from his gaze, swallowing hard.

"Think about it," he said, pressing slightly against my throat, a tease of the kind of pressure I wanted. "Maybe I'll surprise you. Whatever you decide, call me."

He released his hold and moved me bodily away from the door, opened it, and shoved me out. "We're done now," he said, and shut it in my face.

I blinked, breath hitching and legs trembling.

In a daze, I stumbled out to my truck, not even saying bye to Cherise again. I sat there holding the papers in my hand, staring at them like an idiot until the sun vanished and evening fell.

As I turned the key in the ignition and drove away, doubts circled my mind.

Luke could never be enough. He couldn't give me what I needed to escape my own mind and the helpless terror that awaited me there. I was going to die. There was no way around that for me. Everyone knew AIDS was a death sentence, and I surely wasn't going to be one of the lucky ones who got years of reprieve before the Reaper came for them. When had I ever been lucky?

So, no. Luke and his contract, and his whips, and his sexy voice couldn't save me. No one could.

I didn't deserve to be saved anyway.

Chapter Three

Luke

THE LAST FRIDAY of the month meant dinner at my parents' house up in Johnson City. Mainly because the last *Saturday* of the month, I went to visit my sister Betsy at Riverwoods, her special-needs living facility on the Cumberland Plateau. Mom always made a meal she knew Betsy liked so I could take the leftovers over to her the next day.

Betsy had been born with Down Syndrome, and she'd lived at home for most of her life. But when she was in her mid-twenties, my father had suffered a stroke, and with the increase in caregiving responsibilities, my mom had fallen apart. Everyone, including Betsy, had decided it was time for her to get outside help.

Riverwoods was an expensive option, but one that Betsy was thrilled with. She'd long wanted to have more independence, and she saw the boarding facility as a huge step away from being reliant on our family. They'd helped her get a part-time job, and she was happy there. She'd even found a boyfriend, a fellow Down boy that made her light up whenever she talked about him, and who'd been very sweet when I insisted on meeting him. Not a sadistic bone in that kid's body.

Unlike Betsy's older brother.

When I arrived at my folks' place, I'd tried to put aside my thoughts about the bratty young man who'd sat across from me yesterday, fighting his instincts to run. But as I stirred the spaghetti sauce and Mom put the final touches on Betsy's favorite dessert— almond bars—I couldn't stop my mind from going back to him.

It'd been hot seeing all that push-and-pull warring within such a tasty form. I could only imagine how much fun that tension would be in a scene. His lithe, pale body naked and trembling for me. Fear in his eyes, shaking with the urge to get away, with lust overpowering it all. Making him sweat. Making him sing with need. Making him scream. Making him come.

We could be good together. If he'd give in and let me show him just how dark I could go, I'd rock his world.

"Penny for your thoughts," Mom chirped, pulling out a chair at the old, comfortable kitchen table and indicating I should leave the sauce alone and sit.

"Ah, it's nothing."

The wood grain was familiar beneath my fingers as I obeyed, tracing the pale outline left long ago by a cola can. I was twelve, and my father had swatted my ass for letting it sweat on my mother's nice table.

"You've been so broody the last few months," Mom said, taking over the stirring and casting a glance over her shoulder. "Is there something you haven't told me?"

Ever since HIV had made the nightly news, my mother lived in terror that I'd contract it. She knew I was gay, and she knew I slept around. She *didn't* know about my professional Dom practice, she'd never met Benji or any of my prior boys, and as far as she knew, I'd never been in love.

As far as I knew, I hadn't either.

There was one guy, really early on in my life, a football player at my high school with whom I'd shared three sleepovers. Alex Trent. He was six-one, blue-eyed, hard-bodied, and ignorant about gay sex. He'd fucked me raw with only spit for lube, and a sock stuffed into my mouth to keep my cries of pain from reaching his parents' ears. In my innocence, I'd sworn it was love.

It wasn't.

He turned into my worst bully soon enough, terrified I'd spill the beans. But I'd never told a soul about what we'd done in his room during those late nights. How he'd initiated it. How I'd sucked his dick, and how I'd let him into my body in a way I'd hardly let anyone else since.

I wondered where Alex was now. If he was still fucking guys, and if he might be positive too. Or dead.

There'd been just two other guys after Alex. Jerome, of course, and then one that I really shouldn't have let fuck me—a stranger visiting from Atlanta. I wasn't even sure of his name.

Shivering, I tried to shake off the unwanted thoughts of him— tall, handsome, with a great smile and a persuasive voice—and memories of how high I'd been, rolling on X that night. I still wanted to blame the drug for making me lose my inhibitions and my judgment, but the truth was there was no one to blame for it but me. I'd been the one to take it.

"Honey?" Mom asked. "*Is* there something you haven't told me?"

I realized I hadn't answered her. "No, Mama, of course not."

Mom put the big wooden spoon down on top of a paper towel to absorb the mess. She sat next to me and took hold of my hands. "Then what's wrong?"

"Nothing." I lifted her fingers and gave them a kiss. I didn't want to burden her with my diagnosis. I was still healthy, and there was no reason for her to be scared for me, not yet.

"Is it money?"

"Things are tight," I admitted.

Finances were always tight now. I'd made the majority of my disposable income from professional domination, and I'd stopped doing that. I still helped out with the cost of Betsy's facility, which left me with very little at the end of the month. Plus, now that I had this diagnosis, I was also putting aside funds in case I ever needed to start on AZT. The drug was ridiculously expensive, but it was the only treatment option available. The only glimmer of hope.

"But I'm all right," I hastened to reassure her when her brows lowered.

"Then what's all this moodiness about?"

I decided to give her a portion of the truth. "I've been working a lot of third shifts. Trying to sleep during the day and staying up all night is making me come a little undone."

"If you'd get a respectable job," my father's slurred voice came from the doorway. He stood there with his cane, one side of his face drooping and the usual disappointed gleam in his eye. "You'd be better off. It'd get you away from all those perverts who make you think you're queer—"

"Dad, I've told you. I'm gay."

He rolled his eyes and tried to blow a raspberry as if what I was saying was absurd. Spittle dotted the front of his shirt from the effort. "No one's gay, son. That's just a lie to make sissies out of real men."

I glanced at Mom, but she shook her head and patted my hand. I could either choose to go down this path, point out how unhinged his statement was, or I could just let it go and preserve the peace for dinner. For my mom's sake, I knew what I had to do.

Besides, there was no reasoning with him after the stroke. The pieces of his brain that exercised restraint were damaged, and now he leaned into the dark prejudices he'd previously repressed... or hidden. He no longer had any sense of shame or worry that he might hurt anyone else with his words.

"It's spaghetti night," Mom said, rising from the table and helping him over to his chair. "Your favorite."

Dad released an argumentative sound, but refrained from denying it. He let her tuck a cloth napkin around his collar and prepare his serving for him—noodles chopped into tiny bits like he was a baby because he couldn't do more than scoop with a spoon these days.

I said nothing more, simply getting up to move in synchronicity with Mom as we got the plates and bowls out, pulled the bread rolls from the oven, and set out the parmesan and extra sauce.

"Bless this food to the nourishment of our body, and use our bodies for thy service, amen," Mom intoned, bowing her head over her plate.

Dad released yet another argumentative noise, but dug into his food without speaking.

"How's Betsy?" I asked. Mom went to see her twice a month, leaving Dad with a volunteer from their church. That way Betsy had visitors three weeks of every four.

It said a lot about my relationship with my father that she never asked me if I had time to stay with him. I'd have made any excuse I could think of, even if I did have the time. Leaving aside my father's rampant homophobia, there were still very few things we saw eye to eye on.

"She's her usual happy self," Mom said with a big smile. "She's taking a sewing class off campus. They bus her and a handful of other residents over to this fabric store where they have ten sewing machines available. She's learning to make dresses." Mom indicated the blue floral one she wore now—a breezy thing with a built-in shawl over the shoulders.

"She made this one for me. Can you believe it? To think we were worried she'd never be able to take care of herself," Mom said with a soft tut before taking a bite of spaghetti.

"She can't," Dad said around his food, his mouth lopsided as he chewed. "If she could, we'd be a hell of a lot richer."

"Richard," Mom scolded.

"It's the truth. But I'd take two Betsys over this one any day of the week," he indicated me with his spoon. "Worthless pervert."

I put my fork down. I'd only taken a few bites, but I'd lost my appetite. I hated that his words stung. Part of me knew he wasn't my dad—not the man who'd raised me and loved me, not the man who'd kept his peace when he didn't agree with someone, a man who'd thought before he spoke.

That dad was dead, and this was the man the stroke had left behind. Angry, hateful, prejudiced. I didn't understand it, but the doctor said it was due to the location of the damage—the frontal cortex? I didn't get the science of it all, but what I knew for sure was the man who'd taught me to throw a ball and wax a car and change the oil, and who'd seemed to love me unconditionally, was gone.

This was the person my mom, Bets, and I were left with now.

"Richard," Mom said, sharply. "You won't talk to your son that way."

"He's no son of mine," he whisper-slurred, shoving in another messy spoonful, getting sauce all over his chin and lips.

"I'm sorry, sweetheart," Mom said to me. "It looks like it's going to be one of those nights."

I knew sometimes Dad was worse in the evenings. I'd even suggested we switch to a Sunday brunch, but Mom didn't want to miss the after-service activities at her church. I hadn't pushed back because I dreaded getting up before noon after pulling an all-nighter at the store, and I knew how much she needed the fellowship of her friends. Still, our evening meals were becoming more and more fraught as time passed.

"It's fine." But I couldn't just sit there and take it tonight. I was too tired. "Maybe I'll just go ahead and pack up some of this for Bets and hit the road."

Mom's shoulders sagged. "I was hoping you could stay a while after, so we could listen to music together."

I glanced at my father, watching him make a mess with the spaghetti. Mom was tired too, and caring for him took a toll. Was it too much for me to stay and give her a little attention? To listen to music with her and let her relive the past, a time when her future had looked brighter?

I leaned over to kiss her cheek. "All right," I whispered. "You can choose the album this week."

Her eyes grew damp. "Thank you."

"Don't thank me, Mama. It's nothing."

But as Dad belched and fixed me with another glare, we both knew that was a lie. It was something. And it was all I had to give her these days. Maybe even ever. Because if I got sick…

I shut that thought off.

If there was any justice in this world, Mom would never know about my diagnosis, and I'd be around to distract and soothe her for a long time to come. She'd been a good mother to me and Bets, and after all she'd been through with my dad, I only wanted to be a source of happiness for her.

I had to hope for a miracle. Surely those still existed in the world.

"I was looking through my old vinyl records earlier and chose a few out. We'll have fun," she said with a shy smile.

I nodded and squeezed her hand. "We will."

"Faggot," Dad muttered.

Minty

MY ASSHOLE HURT like a motherfucker as I sat down on the hard rocking chair across from the sofa in my mom's living room. I'd paid a visit to my "lover's" dorm earlier in the day, and I had the pain to prove it. Bruises on my hips. A bite on my shoulder. Kyle had hurt me horribly, and I'd left feeling high as a kite.

But along with the after-bliss crash came thoughts of the kind of pain Luke had offered me. Fuck, he'd been so hot, shoving me against the door, his hand on my throat… Could it be enough?

I didn't think so.

I clenched my asshole and remembered the rush of fear as Kyle throttled me, the hate in his eyes, and his seething rage as he'd come so hard he bit his lower lip until it bled. Ever since I'd enticed him to follow me to Tilt-a-Whirl a few weeks ago, he'd been more brutal than ever. His hatred more concentrated and intense.

I turned my attention away from the rough-sex memories derailing my brain and focused on the present. Mom sat on the sofa opposite, glowing with joy. She was always so happy when I came home. I knew I should visit more often, but there were reasons I stayed away. My HIV diagnosis being just one of them.

The *other* being that while the trailer was cozy and warm, and it smelled like my mom's soft perfume, it was also full of bad memories.

At least I'd never *lived* here with my father. We abandoned the old house we'd shared with him not long after "the incident," as my mother called it, or "the rape," as I did. For years we'd stayed away from my dad as best as we could. That'd been easy enough while he was in prison, but once he was released…

I shivered, remembering.

He'd found us.

And the last time he found us, I'd been here…

I shook off the blaze of rage and hate that threatened to engulf me again, the way it always did when I thought of him and of what he'd done.

Of what I'd done.

Whatever the case, this trailer was now home, and given my shortened life-expectancy, it would be my last one. Mom would probably live here for the rest of her life too. It was the best she could afford, and she'd decorated it just the way she liked—country-chic with gingham and lace fixings. Trashy, really.

But we were trash. So, it made sense.

Mom worked at the local diner, which didn't bring in a ton of money, but years ago she'd made friends with Marlene McPeak—my best friend Daniel's mom. That had been a few years after Daniel's father died, and Marlene had needed help with her younger kids. Mom had been happy to step in. It was her Christian duty, she'd said, but aside from that, I think she truly loved being needed by someone.

After their bond had been forged, Marlene helped pay my mom's bills from time to time. Eventually, she bought us this trailer for three-thousand dollars when we'd unfortunately lost our lease on the two-bedroom rental house we were staying in. She'd gifted it to Mom as a thank you for assisting her during her many alcoholic relapses. That was a secret even Daniel didn't know because I'd promised to never tell him. He thought my mom had bought the trailer with her saved-up tips from the diner.

Hilarious.

As if she could have ever earned enough tip money from the gut bombs served at HeyDey Burgers to buy anyplace livable.

The trailer was decent, though, and Mom felt safe here. But I'd always dreamed I'd get a job with TVA one day in river ecology, and I'd buy her a real home—a nice, big house of her own.

Dread curled in my gut.

Now none of that would happen. Now I was going to die, and she—

"Baby," Mom said, interrupting my horror spiral. Her eyes shone brightly. "Have I showed you what I found at KARM?"

She leapt up from the stained, cream-colored sofa we'd had since the "before times," as we called the years when we'd lived with my father, and I averted my eyes from the brown spot she'd been sitting on. The bloodstain hadn't come out. I'd scrubbed and scrubbed, but it remained. I'd always thought we should have bought a new sofa. But we hadn't.

Mom held up her latest acquisition from the local charity store. A black pot with a spindly spider plant drooping within, set snugly wrapped up in a tangle of cord and beads.

"That's atrocious," I proclaimed.

"Hush, you." Mom stood on her tiptoes and lifted the pot by its horrendous macramé holder so that it dangled in front of the window over the sofa. "Now I just need you to hang that wall hook I asked you to bring. Did you remember it?"

I nodded. With every way I'd failed my mom lately, I wasn't going to let her down on the little things. Of course I'd brought the hook. And a hammer and nail too. "It's in my backpack." I gestured to where I dropped it by the door as I'd come inside. "I'll hang it for you after dinner."

Mom kissed my cheek, and the scent of her floral perfume rushed over me as her long, blonde hair draped around my face for a moment. Then she grabbed my hand and tugged me toward the trailer's small kitchen area. "Talk to me, baby, while I finish up in here."

The scent of chicken soup bubbling in the crockpot was rich and warm, and I watched as she checked the status of the rolls she'd put in before I arrived. "Nearly done," she declared before dropping into one of the chairs at the tiny, battered, two-person table. I gingerly took the other one. "Tell me everything," she said with a grin. "What's happening in your life?"

She'd been so excited for me to start back to college for my senior year. She knew I loved my classes and my friends, but she had no idea about the dark turns my life had taken in recent months. I planned to keep her ignorant for as long as possible.

"The usual. Going to classes. Dancing at Tilt-a-Whirl. Hanging out with friends."

Lies. All lies.

I hadn't been going to Tilt-a-Whirl or hanging with friends much lately because *I was HIV positive.* My mind had been far too taken up with panic over that—or clouded over with the aftereffects of rough sex with a guy who hated my guts, despite churning them regularly with his dick—to want to party and have a good time.

I flashed to Kyle's expression as he'd shot his load into me, the rage followed by the pleasure and the complete surrender. I'd broken him again. Made him need me, made him feel things no one else ever had.

And he'd punched me in the stomach when it was over.

It still hurt to take a deep breath. Christ. Kyle was a handful.

Such a teddy bear, that lover of mine. I cracked a smile.

Mom tilted her head, curiosity joining her natural optimism. "What's got you grinning like the cat who got the cream?" she asked.

It would never occur to her to think anything bad was going on. She'd never even fully accepted the horror of our past, and now she lived with the belief that after all that, we were owed only a happy future. She always said everything would be roses and fairy dust from now on. "You've paid life's dues in pain, baby boy. Now you'll be paid in only joy."

Life didn't seem to agree with her. Not one little bit.

"Something good must be going on to get you smiling like that," she prompted again.

I smiled brightly at her, counting on her not noticing that my joy was only skin deep. "I'm just thinking of your birthday in November. I've got a great surprise for you."

Didn't I just?

In fact, I'd gone to the clinic to get the test as her gift. She'd been asking me off and on for the last year, the specter of HIV being the only thing that made her doubt the happy future she saw for me, and I'd wanted to reassure her. But there was no way I could say, "Happy birthday! I got that test you wanted and, hooray, I'm dying."

"Oh, a great surprise?" Mom's blue eyes twinkled. She was so innocent in her own way. It was no wonder my father had so easily captured her in his nasty net. "A trip to see Biltmore House?"

I made note. Biltmore House. Easy enough. That was now the new plan. I'd been considering a gift certificate to my friend Jennifer's hairdresser, but this was a better idea. "What kind of surprise would it be if I told you?"

Mom rolled her eyes and patted my hand. "Just don't put yourself out too much money, sugarbaby. Your education is way more important than an overpriced trip to a giant house."

"A trip to Biltmore House isn't going to ruin me," I assured her.

Though I didn't have a job right now, and my cash from *Cream My Face*—an art performance piece I'd done twice for cash tips— was almost gone. I'd have to figure out a way to save enough money to get tickets for Mom and me to enter the house, plus pay for the cost of gas to Asheville and back.

But I'd find a way.

I always did.

Maybe Kyle would give me some money if I threatened to tell his friends about the things he did to me in his room. That'd either work out perfectly or end up with me dead. Some might call that scenario a win-win.

"Baby?"

"Yeah, Mama?"

"You seem so…" She moved her hands around softly, like birds fluttering. For a moment she looked fragile and haunted, the way she had after the rape, and the way I'd promised myself I'd never give her reason to look again. "…far away. Are you sure you're okay?"

"I'm just tired," I reassured her, taking hold of her hands and squeezing them. I put on a perky smile. It felt foreign on my face, but I forced it to shine even brighter. "My classes are hard this semester. They get harder the closer you get to graduating, you know?"

"Right," she agreed. Her head tilt told me she wasn't completely convinced, but she wanted to be. "If you're sure?"

"I'm sure." I powered up my grin, and her shoulders relaxed.

"I love you so much, sugarbaby." She brought my knuckles to her lips and kissed them. "You're the whole world to me."

"I love you too, Mama."

Her brows lifted hopefully. "Will you spend the night? We could watch a movie. Your choice from all the VHS tapes we have."

I blinked rapidly. The idea of sleeping in the bedroom here wasn't one I could stomach. The last time I saw my dad, two years ago, we'd ended up in there…

It'd been…

And I'd…

I grimaced. I hadn't stayed the night since. "Can't. Sorry. I need to study for an exam I have on Monday."

"Oh? It's okay to say you'd rather go dancing with your friends."

"No dancing this weekend. Too much to do."

The oven dinged. The rolls were ready. I helped her dish up the soup, and then held her hands across the small table as she said grace over our meal. Every time she said the word "Jesus" or "Lord," I clenched my sore anus and let the pain and memories of Kyle's wild surrender to orgasm remind me of my power. I was strong, formidable, and brought straight men to their knees.

Our Lord Jesus had no dominion over me.

Only HIV had that.

Five hours later

I COULDN'T BREATHE.

Black dots swam in my eyes.

I'd been choked out twice already, and I thought this time Kyle might really kill me. His pounding of my ass was fierce, and I'd lost my erection after coming hard very early on in the torment.

I'd left my mom's house and driven straight to campus. Kyle hadn't answered when I knocked at his dorm room, so I'd set up camp outside his door. When he arrived, flushed with alcohol, and handsome in that terrifying, brutal way of his, he'd been furious to see me waiting there.

"What if someone saw you?" he growled, hauling me up from the floor and shoving me into his room before locking the door behind us.

Then he'd started. Slaps. Punches.

I hadn't lifted a finger to defend myself, even though he'd transmitted every strike in advance. With my Aikido training, I could have deflected most of his attacks before they landed. But I never even tried because I needed what Kyle did to me. I craved it.

Tonight, though…

Maybe we'd gone too far.

Clarity descended around me. I could die right now. Kyle could end my life. He was so lost in his hatred and lust that I didn't think he was going to be able to stop himself. My head ached, and my eyes bulged as he increased the pressure of his hands around my throat. My chest throbbed. I scrabbled at his fingers, unable to suck in a breath.

I worked my asshole around his cock, trying to make him come, trying to get him to end the madness before I went unconscious again. But he wasn't anywhere near the edge. He was drunk, and he'd already come in my ass earlier in the day. He could make this go on and on, and I could die beneath him and—

The world went dark and fuzzy at the edges. The roar in my ears swallowed all other sound.

Darkness.

Coming to, I focused on his face above me. Kyle stared down at me as he continued to pound my ass, having never stopped even when I was unconscious. His expression was demented. No more words left his lips. No more curses. No more nasty names. Just sharp exhales of breath and sheer loathing escaped from him as he took my body, his hands on my throat stealing my air again.

I relaxed, stopping my useless scrabbling at his fingers. Surrendering to him entirely, I let my power go. I let him fuck me, choke me, and withhold my breath.

I greeted death.

Hi.

Blackness took me.

Again, I came to.

Orgasm shattered through me as I gasped for air. He throttled me again.

I went out.

I struggled, burst with pleasure and sensation, and then passed out again as he squeezed my neck.

Again.

And again.

Death never took my hand and led me out of Kyle's room. She just caressed my face sweetly, and then shoved me back into the brutal violence of my life.

When I came to consciousness a final time, I was alone, cum dripping from my asshole, and a huge wad of spit sliding down my face. I stood on wobbly legs and dressed myself with shaking hands.

Kyle was nowhere to be seen. He'd fucked me, choked me out, and left me for dead.

Staring at myself in the mirror above his dresser, I took in the handprints on my neck, the streaks of dried tears on my cheeks, and wondered how long I'd been out and where Kyle had gone. I swallowed, and my throat ached, feeling somewhat swollen inside. Dangerously so.

You're going to get yourself killed.

Barry's words circled in my mind.

Yes, I was. Did I really want to die?

You think because I'll enjoy fucking you that I'll be soft for you? That I'll make you feel loved and wanted?

Luke's promise-filled voice whispered though my brain, offering me a way out.

You're the whole world to me.

Mama's soft voice, sweet and earnest.

I was all she had now, and I *was* going to die on her soon—that was inevitable—but no matter how much I deserved it, maybe it shouldn't be like this. Not like this.

Shaking and exhausted, I limped out of Kyle's dorm building and made my way across campus toward my own. The moon was full. My throat was tender. I felt so tired and so full of longing. I needed someone. Anyone.

No, not anyone.

I needed someone who could handle me.

I still had Luke's contracts in my room, along with the results of my most recent STD tests from the Health Center.

After keying open the lock, I sat down at my dorm room desk and took out a pen, read over the papers again, and checked off everything—every single kink—without even considering if I really wanted to try any of them or not.

I stared out the window for a moment, watching the lights of cars go by. Then I signed the forms.

"Okay," I whispered to myself. "Okay then."

Maybe I *wasn't* ready to die yet.

Luke

RAIN STARTED FALLING on the way home from my folks' house, wetting the streets and making the early autumn night feel heavy.

Mom had managed to keep me later than I'd wanted. We'd left Dad in front of the TV set, and then she and I crashed on the floor of the sunroom, surrounded by the plants she loved to grow. Karen Carpenter's voice had floated around us through the big wall-mounted speakers I'd put up several years ago.

We hadn't talked much, just listened, but I knew how much Mom needed me now. She had no one else to depend on, except the folks in her church, but they weren't going to lay on the floor, holding her hand, and listen to old vinyl records for hours on end.

Next to me in the car, the sound of the CorningWare rattling in the bag was an unsettling companion. I wished Karen Carpenter's voice could blanket over me now, soothing away the anxiety that lingered in my bones after another bad encounter with my father on my way out the door.

But, alas, I didn't even own a cassette deck in this car, and the radio receiver was busted. It wasn't the only broken part of the old Buick I drove. At least I had new tires and felt reasonably assured that the engine had another twenty to forty thousand miles left in it.

Money was becoming a problem. I was probably going to have to start doing 1-900 number phone sex work again before long. I didn't make as much at it as Cherise did—the demand was higher for women—but there were plenty of subby queer men with cushy office jobs who liked to be bossed around via telephone line at night and on the weekend. I was good at it. Got plenty of tips. It was just boring, and sometimes I hung up the phone feeling scuzzy.

Something that almost never happened with in-person D/s play.

My thoughts drifted back to that Minty kid. He couldn't help me with my money problems, but he would be so pretty at my feet. I could just imagine how red his skin would blush with lust or from targeted strikes of my hand or flogger. He'd be so fucking sweet all beaten up and covered in my cum.

In a consensual way. Of course.

I hadn't heard from him, though, and I was starting to doubt that I would. Barry was confident I just needed to give him time, but he was also anxious for Minty to kneel for me sooner rather than later. Every day the kid stayed away was a day Barry worried for his life.

I worried some too, even though I barely knew him. There'd been that undeniable fire in his eyes, followed by such angry submission when I pushed him against the door of my office. He was more than just a twink with a hard-on for pain. He was a mess.

I loved messes. And I especially loved cleaning them up.

The rain patter on my car's roof halted when I pulled in beneath the carport. The night was chilly, and I could smell a hint of wood smoke from a neighbor's fire. Autumn would fade into winter soon enough, with its gray, cloud-heavy skies, and this rain was just the start of it.

Inside, I hung up my coat and toed off my sneakers. Carrying the bag of food into the kitchen, I stored Betsy's meals in the fridge for tomorrow. Bets loved Mom's spaghetti, and I looked forward to seeing her smile when she realized what I'd brought.

I couldn't shake the lingering tension from the final interaction with my dad. It was like talking to a monster wearing a beloved face. Heartbreaking. I had no idea how Mom handled it day in and day out. And, God, the stuff he'd said to Bets before she'd moved to the facility…

Cruel things.

Betsy had laughed them off. Somehow, she'd taken his personality change post-stroke better than any of us. "He's not our father," she'd say to me with that small impediment that marked her speech. "He's someone else now, and he's mean."

Simple.

But Mom told me that Betsy had cried a lot at first, saying she missed her daddy. It was just for me that she played brave, Mom claimed. Even though I was the older brother, and I should have been the brave one for her instead.

I'd barely settled in on my sofa with a bag of chips, determined to get my mind off things by flipping through cable TV channels until I found something compelling enough to make me stop, when a knock came at my front door.

It was a quiet but firm sound. I wasn't expecting anyone, and I almost ignored it, but it came a second and third time, so I peeled myself from the green sectional and passed through the hallway to pull open the front door.

The night had settled in dark and hard, and so had the rain. It came down in buckets and rushed down the street. The front porch light was pale, almost as pale as the soaking wet boy in front of me.

Blond hair slicked against Minty's forehead, glistening wet in the low light. His blue eyes were shadowed to obscurity beneath the hood of his jacket. Minty looked like a scared, half-drowned kitten. He opened his jacket, pulled out a sheaf of papers, and shoved it at me. The contract.

My blood rushed. I licked my lips before speaking. "This is unexpected." I made a show of glancing at my watch. "It's nearly eleven at night."

"You're awake," he stated.

"You could have called first." I ticked a brow up. "Manners, and all that."

"Your address is on the letterhead," he said, shaking the contracts and what looked like his STD results at me. "I didn't want to wait, and I didn't want to call. I'm ready. Now." He sucked in a breath. "When can we start? Tonight?"

I stared at him, noting the way he trembled all over. He had a manic gleam in his eye. He wore loose jeans and a sheer, lavender, women's blouse beneath a soaked jean jacket with a built-in sweatshirt hoodie. My gaze lingered on the livid marks on his neck.

"Come in," I said, guiding him into the hallway. "Put your shoes there."

He did, shaking so hard he almost fell over as he toed them off, foot-to-foot.

"Jacket," I reached out my hand for it. He handed it over. I hung it on the rack beside my own coat. "This way."

He followed me without question deeper into the house. I led him to the kitchen, sat him at the table, ignored his confused expression, and turned to put a kettle on the stove. Somehow the moment seemed to call for tea, but I didn't keep any in the house. I did have some discount decaf instant coffee, and it would have to do.

While Minty sat in impatient, shivering silence, I made us both mugs.

"Well?" he asked, as I took the seat across from him at my round wooden table. "Can you hurt me tonight?"

I sipped my coffee and gestured for him to do the same.

With an annoyed grimace, Minty took a swallow. "This is gross. Worse than the stuff at my mom's diner."

"Yeah, it's crap." I sipped some more. "Drink up."

Narrowing his eyes at me, Minty took another taste, and then another. The shaking in his body slowly calmed, but I could still see his pulse thundering beneath his bruised throat.

"Who did that?" I said, indicating the handprints around his neck.

"My lover."

"Mm." I drank my coffee. "Did you consent?"

Minty shrugged. "I didn't fight back, so that's as good as consent, isn't it?"

"Not really."

Minty's jaw clenched. "Look, can we just skip the bullshit? I want pain. You like to give it. I need it now. Tonight." He glanced around. "Where do you do it? In your bedroom? The basement?"

"I think you've already had some pain tonight."

He snarled. "I want more."

"And if you don't get more?"

He slammed the coffee mug down. "What do you want from me? I signed the papers. I gave them to you already. I have the STD tests. I just need—" His voice cracked. "Please. I really need it."

I took another taste of my coffee again before rising. I stood in front of him, close enough that he had to tilt his head way back to keep his eyes on mine. "There's no way in hell we're doing a formal scene tonight, but if you need some pain to stabilize you until we can meet and do this properly, I can do that."

"Then do it!"

I slapped him. Hard enough that his head swung to the side, and when he looked up at me, a handprint blared across his pale cheek. Tears stood in his eyes. "Again," he whispered.

I shook my head. "You're not the boss here, little bitch."

I grabbed his wet hair and tugged his head back, forcing his gaze up to mine again. I stepped forward into his space, forcing his legs to spread so I stood between his knees. "I am."

He sneered, and my cock hardened so fast I felt dizzy. Such a brat. Christ.

"You know what a safe word is?"

"Yes."

"Yours is poodle."

He blinked at me. "Why?"

"Because you remind me of one. All bark. No bite."

"I bite."

"Sure you do."

On the table, in a neat little pile from where I'd used them to string up my laundry over the stove the day before—my dryer had gone out well over a month ago—were a heap of plastic clothespins. I picked one up and showed it to him. "Any objections?"

Glaring up at me, he held his peace.

I clipped one onto his earlobe, and then a second on his other ear. He hissed, but he didn't move or jerk away. Opening the buttons on his blouse and spreading it wide over his pale chest, I felt my cock thud as his pink nipples appeared. He had almost no chest hair, and what was there was light and blond. I tilted his chin up.

"Sensitive here?"

He sneered. "Yes. Very."

I smirked, and confirmed again, "Any objections?"

"Do it," he gritted out.

I laughed. "Oh, you're such a little shit. I'm going to break you so hard when we do a real scene."

I pinched his nipples ruthlessly to get them to peak, and then added the clothespins. He couldn't contain his squirm and whimper as each clamped down on his sensitive nubs, though he clenched his jaw and didn't make a sound.

"Now," I said, pushing a hand into his wet hair again, smoothing it back from his flushed face. "Drink your fucking coffee. And call me Sir."

Minty's expression flashed with resistance before he softened slightly. "You want me to drink my coffee, Sir?"

"Yes." I gestured to the clothespins. "Those stay on until you've finished every drop."

I sat across from him. "And until I've finished mine too."

I took my time, drinking slowly, taking long pauses between each swallow, enjoying the view as the burning pain dug into his chest muscle and spread over his skin. I grinned as his breathing escalated. He flushed all over. Sweat popped out on his forehead.

Still, Minty didn't speak. He sat there, drinking his coffee, nipples trapped in the clothespin clamps, two more dangling from his earlobes like ugly plastic earrings, and he endured it. The red mark on his cheek diffused out from a handprint and turned into a simple, red shine that made his other cheek look pallid in comparison.

"Feel good?" I asked with a chuckle.

He grunted.

"Answer me."

"No, Sir. It does *not* feel good." Each word was bitten out with a hint of rage.

I smiled and rose. "I think I could use a second cup. You?"

Minty shook his head, a gleam of alarm showing in his eyes. I loved the brightness of it, the hint of desperation. Gorgeous. I was going to love seeing more of that the next time he came around. Which would be soon. Very soon. I looked forward to having him down in my dungeon so I could really take him apart.

"Let me review these STD results," I said, casually adjusting my cock before I sat back down at the table with a steaming fresh mug. "How recent are they?"

"Three weeks ago."

"How many guys have you fucked or sucked since these?"

"One."

I nodded, considering.

Minty went on, "He doesn't fuck other guys. Just me."

I lifted a brow. "How do you know?"

He smiled with a snarl that made my gut flutter. "Oh, I know."

"Girls?" I surmised. "He also fucks girls?"

"Probably." He shrugged, and the pull on his clamped tits made him gasp. His eyelids fluttered before he met my gaze again. "Yeah, he probably fucks girls."

"Girls get STDs too, you know, and they can spread them."

"I can get a new test, Sir, if you want, but—"

"No. It's fine."

Not getting another test was a risk I probably shouldn't have taken, given my HIV status and the possibility of immune compromise, but I'd taken much higher risks in the past. I wasn't a saint. I never had been. I wasn't going to pretend to be one now.

"Do you want to see mine?" I asked. "I have a set from a few months ago. I've fucked no one since."

"I don't care, Sir. It's not something that worries me."

It should. Still, his position was relatable. I pulled the sheaf of contract papers toward me and began at the top, sipping my coffee after every page or so, making sure I made no real progress.

Minty groaned, squirming.

I laughed. "You've checked off every kink. Did you even read them over? Think about what each of them entailed? Research them?"

Minty's jaw worked, but he said nothing.

"That's a no then." I tutted. "I don't see scat in your future. It's only on there to weed out incompatible partners. Be honest, do you really want to play with my shit? Or yours?"

He shook his head, wincing at the pain from his clamped earlobes.

"No, I didn't think so." I crossed it off. "And you've specifically written 'no kissing.' Interesting. Is there a reason for that?"

"I don't like to get kissed when I'm being hurt. Kyle never kisses me."

"Kyle is?"

"My lover."

"Right. Your 'lover.'" I lifted a brow and swallowed some more coffee, filing away his words for later, and going back to the list. "Oh, here's a fun one, though. Cage play. I think putting you in a cage sounds very satisfying. And you've got piss play checked off too. I could go for that. Mm, I could hose you down from my dick while you're all caged up. Could work. We'll see."

Minty whispered something.

I cupped my ear. "I couldn't hear you."

"It's hurting." He quickly added, "Sir."

"Good catch." I smiled. "And, yeah, it hurts a lot when you've got sensitive tits. People with less sensitive ones don't get nearly so riled up by clamps. You're lucky." I paused, letting that sink in. "Believe it or not, this isn't the worst of it. Just wait."

I peered inside my cup and then showed it to him. "I still have a lot to go. How about you?"

He tilted his mug to me. Empty.

"I see. Well, be patient. This is just a first taste of my kind of pain. This is low intensity. The things I'll do to you in the future will hurt a lot more than this. I see you checked off whips. Excellent."

"But will they scare me?" he blurted. "Because I don't feel scared right now."

"Oh, you will," I told him. "Before long, tonight even, you're going to be scared."

He huffed, rolling his eyes. "Clothespins can't hurt me."

"They're hurting you right now, aren't they?"

He gritted his jaw, not answering.

"That's a yes. But you know what hurts the most?"

He shook his head.

"When you take them off." I cackled. "I can't wait to see your face." I reached out to pat his hand. "Don't worry, boy. Just wait."

Minty chewed his plump bottom lip. "Sir."

"Hmm?"

"Can you please just fuck me? It'll get my mind off things."

"Not tonight," I said, though my dick was absolutely appalled by that answer. "Tonight is just to keep you steady until we can make an appointment for a scene."

I turned back to the checklist. "Shame kink, spitting is okay, hmm…fuck machine? Wow. I have to say, if all this accurate, playing with you is going to be a dream." I paused. A check mark beside a few words caught my eye. "Cum play, raw fucks. You're positive, and I'm positive, so… I agree that's all right for us."

I hadn't come inside a playmate since I'd first learned about AIDS, or rather since I'd first accepted that AIDS was a real illness and that it was predominately a gay one. I had, however, had someone come inside *me*. The results of that encounter were not just regrettable, but probably deadly.

"Sir?" Minty asked.

He was shaking now. The deepening pain was starting to undo him. I could see it by the way his eyes had gone glossy.

"Wait," I told him. "I've still got half a cup left."

"Fuck."

I chuckled. "Next time, I'm going to make you scream. Like that idea?"

"You'd better," he bit out.

"You don't think I can?" I shaded my tone with danger.

"I have my doubts." Minty's bruised throat bobbed as he swallowed convulsively. I wondered if his asshole was injured. Probably. He had a crazed, just-been-rough-fucked energy beneath his desperate need.

"Hmm." I drained my cup in one big swallow, stood, and wrenched the clothespin from his right ear. He screeched, his hand coming up to cradle the lobe like I'd cut it off. His now-sharp gaze leaped to me with betrayed horror, as if I hadn't warned him just how bad it was going to be.

"So," I said, sitting down again. "I guess that proves I can make you scream."

I turned back to the contracts. "I've already struck scat, and I'm striking knife play…" I did and then signed beneath his name. "This is all renegotiable. If you decide you don't like something later, or want to add something in, we can. It just requires a conversation."

"Sir!" he gasped, still holding his ear. "I'd like to come while I'm here."

I tutted. "I don't think so. Orgasms are at my discretion when you're with me, and I'm guessing you already came tonight. With someone else."

"It wasn't good, Sir," he panted. "He choked me out at the end."

I pondered that, gazing at his throat. "You know, this contract you've signed states you won't have intercourse or play with anyone except for me for the duration of our agreement. In baby words, that means you won't fuck or get fucked by anyone else. Period. No exceptions."

He pressed his lips together, but nodded sharply.

"If I don't let you come tonight, are you going to break this contract? Right from the start? Will you go to the asshole who did this—" I stood again and moved between his legs, sliding my fingers over his throat. "Make him fuck you, make him hurt you?"

Minty seemed to consider it, and then, like it was incredibly hard for him to say, he whispered, "No, Sir. I'll keep my word to you."

I plucked the clothespin from his left ear.

He wailed and probably would have hit me or kneed me in the balls if I hadn't grabbed his leg and arms, holding him in place.

"Fuck!" He threw his head back. "Jesus, fuck! That hurts." He twisted to get away, but I held him fast.

"Mm-hmm." I bent to breathe by his reddened ear. "If you can come from pain, go right ahead. But if you can't, then you'll have to wait until the next time we're together. No jerking off either. You'll wait to come for me. Only for me."

His breath hitched. "I need you to hate me," he muttered. "Can you hate me a little?"

I bit his tender earlobe, and he convulsed. "You disgusting pain slut. You want to hurt? I'll make you hurt."

I tugged both clothespins from his nipples, and he went off beneath me like a siren. Hurt wailed from his throat, and when I reached down to rub his nipples to increase the torment, he shoved me back, rising from the chair like fury embodied.

He kicked me, his foot landing hard on my hip.

As I fell back against the opposite kitchen counter, Minty's eyes flew wide. "Oh, fuck. I'm sorry. I'm *so sorry*. Fuck. I didn't mean to—"

I stood up straight. My hip ached, but I got my head together quickly. "That's impressive. Don't do it again. Control yourself no matter what I do to you. Got it?"

Trembling, he nodded. "I'm sorry, Sir."

"Sit down."

He dropped to the chair again. Tears ran down his cheeks, snot started to leak from his nose, and he wiped it with the back of his hand.

He was a mess in so many ways. My responsibility as a Dom was to see him through this, to de-escalate the scene, to give him aftercare and keep him safe. There was no way I could let him drive home tonight. Aside from the fact that I'd just fucked with his head, he was beaten and bruised from the asshole he'd gone to before me. Even without the mild pain and degradation play we'd just performed, he wasn't in his right mind. I needed to help him into a safe mental place now.

"Steady?" I asked, as I approached with my hands out.

He nodded.

"You're staying the night here," I ordered. "On my sofa."

He blinked up at me. No excuses or rejections.

"In the morning, you'll leave and go to school, or work, or home. Wherever it is you're supposed to go. I'll go to my work. Later, we'll talk on the phone, plan a scene, and in a few days' time we'll meet up again." I ran my hand down to touch his throat. "In the meantime, you'll stay away from the jackass who did this to you, and you'll heal up. That's an order. I don't want my boys covered in bruises that aren't from me."

Minty's round, blue eyes grew hopeful for the first time. He licked his lips, and when he spoke, his voice shook. "Yes, Sir. I'd like to wear your bruises, Sir."

"That's right. Until the day I tear this up, or you do," I said, lifting the contract. "You'll wear only my bruises."

He nodded.

"Good." I got him a glass of water, watched him drink it down, and then I pushed a bag of chips into his hand. Not the best aftercare food, but not the worst either. I sensed he wouldn't respond well to an overt attempt at caretaking, and I didn't want to undo the progress we'd made tonight. He was trusting me to help him, to make him feel the things he needed to feel in a safe and consensual way.

I was relieved Minty didn't fight me when I led him into the living room and over to my sofa. He let me guide him to lie down on one side of the sectional, and he watched as I took up my spot on the other end.

"Eat the chips," I said, turning on the TV.

The sound of his crunching and the opening strains of the

theme song to *Cheers* cued the end of our session for me. I relaxed as the two of us watched reruns long into the night. We didn't talk much more, aside from him asking where the bathroom was, and then returning to curl up beneath a crocheted blanket I passed over to him.

Around two in the morning, he fell asleep. I turned off the TV set and went upstairs to my bedroom.

Struggling to drift off, I kept thinking of his shout of pain, his violent rage when he kicked me, and the complex problem of his need for being hated on. I calculated and schemed and made future plans to hurt him. As I imagined scenarios, I found myself hard again. I didn't jerk off, though, preferring to hold on to the edge.

When I finally succumbed to unconsciousness, it wasn't restful at all. Dream-me was full of buzzing arousal and sadistic glee as, for hours on end, I dreamed of making Minty break.

Luke

WHEN I WOKE the next morning, I walked downstairs to find the living room empty and so silent I thought for sure Minty was gone. But when I padded into the kitchen, he was standing by the stove looking disheveled and nervous.

Holding a bowl of batter and brandishing a ladle.

"Um, good morning, Sir," he said with a flashy smile that was as beautiful as it was false.

"Good morning. What are you doing?"

He flushed, but went back to dolloping scoops of batter onto an oiled frying pan. "I'm amazing at pancakes. Back when I had a job at this great grocery store—Nature's Foodway—"

"I've heard of it."

"Well, in exchange for a blow job, the night manager would give me all the out-of-date box mixes and canned stuff for free." He shot me a glance. "You know, instead of throwing them out."

I stared at him. He was babbling. It was sweet. "Whoring yourself for brownie and cake mix. Are you always that easy?"

"Of course." Another flashy smile.

This one seemed almost half-genuine. I wondered what the real thing looked like.

"He wasn't bad, though. He liked fucking my mouth, and, because I let him, he wanted to do nice things for me." He shrugged, going even redder. "I liked that."

I lifted a brow. "I thought you *didn't* want the men you fuck to be nice to you."

"This was *before*," Minty said, waving a hand dismissively. "He was middle-aged, cute, and chubby. He was completely in love with me." He transferred pancakes from the pan to a plate. "And I swear on my mama's future grave that his dick tasted like sunshine and rainbows."

I leaned against the doorjamb, crossing my arms over my chest. A smile lifted the edges of my lips. "What does sunshine taste like?"

"Lemon frosting."

"And rainbows?"

"Lucky Charms."

I almost laughed, but he kept on babbling, ladling out more batter for another round of pancakes. "Best tasting dick I ever sucked. Hand to God." He raised the ladle and paused, thinking. "Maybe he rubbed it with some sort of flavored oils?"

"Or out-of-date lemon frosting?" I suggested, stepping away from the door and coming closer to watch him make the pancakes.

"Maybe. But what about the Lucky Charms taste?" He seemed to genuinely consider the problem before sighing in disappointment when no answer appeared. "Anyway, my favorite pancake mix Ruben—that was his name—ever gave me was a fancy-pants organic brand called California-Suncakes. It cost like six dollars on the shelf. No one ever bought it because that's bonkers, right? No matter how good it is."

I nodded, watching as the pancake pile grew on the plate.

Minty flicked off the stove and transferred the pan over to the sink. "So, I told him to always save it out for me, and he always did. He was so sweet."

"Sweet in exchange for you deepthroating his dick," I reminded him.

"No, I mainly just licked and sucked him the usual way. The better to taste him, you know?" Minty winked. I felt my own smile grow too. "Besides, he was hard up, so it didn't take much for him to spunk—which, by the way, did *not* taste like sunshine or rainbows." He grimaced. "It was bitter as fuck." Another sigh. "I'd still be there getting my free out-of-date goodies from that fine feast of man-flesh, but they fired me."

"For blowing the night manager?" I hazarded a guess.

"Could be," he said, thoughtfully, scrubbing out the pan. "Could be for offering to suck off a customer, though."

My lips twitched into a smile. He grinned back at me, a shiver-inducing, shiny thing that felt almost real this time. Darkness still lingered in his eyes, untouched and untouchable by the superficially hypersexual conversation he was spilling out, but the smile at least was genuine.

"Anyway, I can't vouch for *these* pancakes," he concluded, gesturing to the steaming stack on the counter by the stove. "You just had Aunt Jemima mix, which isn't exactly gourmet, but a pancake's a pancake. Hard to do badly."

"Especially for someone who's amazing at making them."

He looked bashful, but shook the ladle my way, almost losing a fat drop of batter to the floor. "Don't make fun of me."

"I'm not."

He moved the ladle and bowl over to join the pan in the sink, plated some pancakes, and slathered them with butter and honey before handing them my way. "Here. Thanks for staying up all night to take care of me."

I took the plate from him and sat down at the table. He dropped down across from me with a stack half as large as mine. We both dug in. The pancakes were, as promised, fucking delicious.

"These are good," I said.

Minty looked up at me, his eyes wide, the smile fading on his lips. I watched as he battled out the various reactions going off like bombs in his mind. Pleasure at the praise, swiftly followed by doubt and anger, and even, very briefly, rage. Wow. His head was a mess, and it'd only taken a single sentence to make it that way.

With his throat flushing and still mottled with another man's bruises, I made up my mind. No matter what, no matter how long it took, I was going to crack this kid open. I was going to hurt him like no other person ever had, and he was going to kneel at my feet, beg me for more, and thank me afterward.

And *my* reward for all that work and devotion? Well, I was going to get to see the true heart of him. With a kid as gorgeous, conflicted, and confusing as Minty, what sadist wouldn't want to see that? And it seemed I'd get morning pancakes too. A total win for me.

I hadn't had many wins lately, and neither had he. Eating pancakes, watching him squirm at my praise? It was the most normal I'd felt in a very long time. That was worth something to me. More than words could say.

Chapter Four

Minty

"YOU MADE PANCAKES for him?" Barry smiled, leaning against his rake. The pile of brown leaves he'd scraped together from his and Robert's small back yard rustled with wind. The autumn sun was a glare against his dark, bald head.

"I know," I said, shaking my head. "I woke up on his sofa, and he was still asleep upstairs. I didn't know what to do." I fluttered my hands around—so like my mother when she was nervous. "Like what's the etiquette? Escape without a word? Leave a note? Send flowers?" I paused, remembering. "It was so quiet at his house, except for some dogs barking down the street…"

I rubbed my hands over my face. I was still exhausted. After two rounds of violent sex with Kyle, followed by the emotionally intense pain play with clothespins at Luke's, I'd slept like the dead, passed out cold on his sofa.

But once I'd woken up, all the usual fears had risen relentlessly. I had HIV. It would turn to AIDS soon enough. I was going to die an ugly, painful death. Everything I'd fought to get over, all the awful shit I'd overcome, was for *nothing*. I'd suffer and die without ever being truly happy. Sure, I faked it well enough—or I had—but I'd never felt it deep inside. I didn't want to die. I didn't want to get sick.

The fear was an exhausting, endless mental battle that I'd endured ever since the doctor first told me the results. And it dragged up every last crappy thing from my past too, making all of them roar in my memory like vicious, uncaged animals just waiting to devour my sanity.

"I'm surprised you didn't just leave," Barry said, sweat dripping down the side of his face.

"I almost did." I gave him a cheeky grin, the kind that used to come so easily only six months ago. "But then my mama whispered through my brain saying, 'Baby, a man always loves pancakes.'" I lightened my voice, trying to sound like my old self, the one everybody knew and loved. Could Barry hear the effort it took?

"Not that I hadn't *already* impressed him with my performance last night." I batted my eyelashes. "No doubt he's in love with me now."

"No doubt." Barry's voice was calm and steady. He raked a yellow leaf into the small pile of brown ones. "You don't have to pretend with me, you know."

I swallowed hard, looking at the grass. "I'm not pretending."

"You've been pretending for a long time, but I see you."

I pressed my lips together, trying to decide if I was going to argue with him. He wasn't wrong. Over the last few years, I'd used drugs to escape the past, spun out absurd fantasies of love, and more. I lived on the surface of things so no one would suspect how much horrible shit there was underneath my shiny veneer. All just to keep from ever thinking about what had happened to me. It wasn't that I'd been insincere in recent years—it was that I'd been *sincerely* determined to run away from my history and never look back. The HIV diagnosis had made all that effort feel pointless. That was one reason I'd been avoiding my mom and my friends.

I met Barry's sturdy gaze. He'd stopped raking again and stood just gazing at me, no judgment or fear on his face.

Relief swept through me at being with someone who didn't

need me to shine a distracting light away from the gross shit at my core. Tears pricked my eyes. I cleared my throat, determined not to cry. "So, yeah, I made pancakes for him. I wanted to say thanks for…for getting me out of my head. I was in a bad place when I went over."

"I'm sure he appreciated it." Barry went back to raking, gathering brown and orange leaves together. The wind shifted and the scent of wood smoke drifted over from a neighbor's house. "I'm also sure he enjoyed what you did together."

I remembered the heat in Luke's eyes as he watched me squirm in the chair, his cruelly-placed clothespins making me hurt and ache all the way to my core. The pain had been peculiar, growing and growing as time passed, but the discomfort of the clamps paled in comparison to when he removed them.

"Maybe." I didn't bother trying to turn on my shine again. I just didn't have it in me to power it up anymore. "But it's not like we'd made an appointment. I just showed up, and he took me in and—" I cleared my throat again. Would Barry believe I was allergic to the leaves if I claimed *that* was why I was getting choked up?

"He made you understand why I thought he could help you," Barry deduced.

"Yeah. I think I get it now."

"Glad to hear it."

I went on, not wanting to linger on that. "Anyway, he had Aunt Jemima brand pancake mix, and enough eggs and butter. He didn't have any maple syrup, but he had some honey—the kind with the piece of honeycomb still in it? I love that kind. When I was a kid, I'd chew the wax." I twitched anxiously. "So…yeah. I made him pancakes."

I leaned against the tall oak Barry was working beneath, the bark biting into my skin. It was warm enough to wear short sleeves, and even though I was in what I called boy-drag—cowboy boots, jeans, and a Pixies concert tee I'd found at Repeat After Me—I still felt feminine inside. I didn't always—that's why I wasn't transexual—but today I did.

There'd been something about the way Luke took control of me, hurt me, calmed me, and then put me in my place on his sofa, that left me feeling soft. Like I was a rose, and the pain he gave me had stroked my petals open, exposing my tender center. The breakfast we'd shared, the smiles and laughs, and the sweetness of the honey made *me* feel sweet.

Suddenly, a flare of anger twisted in my gut. Fuck him. He should have punched me in the face instead.

"Hey now," Barry said, dropping the rake, sensing the change in me. "So, you made the guy pancakes? No big deal. A Dom likes it when his subs show gratitude. I'm sure he appreciated them."

I shrugged. "Fuck him, really."

Barry's pierced brow lifted. "Why's that?"

"I don't know. He…" I scrubbed a hand over my face. "He was *nice* to me. Told me the pancakes were delicious. Laughed at how I blew Ruben at the grocery. Smiled at me. It made me feel…" I gagged a little. "All fucking gooey inside."

Barry's eyes grew tender. "Just two months ago, our sweet Minty loved the idea of being in love," he reminded me. "He'd *wanted* to feel gooey inside."

"That Minty of two months ago was an idiot. He still thought he had a long life left to live," I reminded him back. "This Minty of *now* knows he's dying, and it's going to be painful, and it's gonna be ugly. There's nothing romantic about it. I'll never have gooey or nice."

And I *hated* myself for being scared and even more for *deserving* all of it.

If Barry knew what I'd done…

If everyone knew what I'd done… They'd all agree. This diagnosis, this horrible future I was faced with was all my own fault. It was my karma. There was no way I could fake and shine my way free of *this* nightmarish reality. I had this sickness now, and it would make sure of that.

So *fuck* pretending. *Fuck* being shiny. And, yeah, everyone else should hate me too.

Especially the guy who was supposed to hurt me.

"Having HIV doesn't mean you can't have sweet moments between now and…" Barry's lips twisted down. He couldn't even bring himself to say it. The sun glinted off his bald head. A bird chirruped from the tree. "You can still have the sweet moments," he repeated gruffly.

"No. I can't."

"Why the fuck not?"

"If I feel sweet like that, I'll get weak."

I needed my anger. Didn't he get it? Without all this anger and rage, I was powerless. I was just a soft, dying faggot with no hope, no future, no love, and a rotten soul. With it, I was at least powerful and strong. I was a miracle who could take a beating and rise up with rage to embrace the pain and convert it into my own glory. I was a god who could make straight men come against their will, a magician who could take their hate and alchemize it into orgasms, into pleasure.

"Listen to me, asshole. You *liked* making him the pancakes," Barry said, pulling me into a gross, sweaty hug. He smelled like garlic and onions. I pretended to fight him off, but gave up quickly, letting him hold me. "You liked being his sub. This could *work*. Don't fuck it up. Luke and you—this could be special."

I shook my head. "I don't think he'll be enough."

"Just give him a chance."

"I am."

"Good."

When Barry released me, I stumbled over to pick up the rake. There were a few more leaves I could add to his pile. I focused on that instead of the trembling of my chin and the tears that wanted to surface.

In a year or so, give or take any number of months, I would be gone, and Barry was going to keep on living, raking leaves and teasing Robert. They were going to move into their shiny new house out in the countryside and rake the leaves from different trees. Leaves that I'd never see. That was how AIDS worked. It was absurd and aching and *terrifying.*

Barry came and took the rake from me, putting a stop to my attempt to add a shadow to the pile.

"I'm supposed to meet with Luke later this week for a real scene," I whispered, almost hoping he didn't hear me.

Barry's brows lowered, and he sucked on his teeth thoughtfully. "Do you know what he's got planned for you?"

I shook my head. "We talked about it, and he told me all the things he was considering doing to me, but honestly it was just a bunch of noise."

"You should have let him know you weren't able to concentrate."

I shrugged. "Nah. He was eating the pancakes I made him, and he seemed…excited. I agreed to everything because he swore I'd like everything he did. Or hate it, I mean." I grimaced. "Which is really the point." I clutched his arm. "God, Barry, I really need to hate it."

"Or do you really need to feel hat*ed?*"

"I don't know anymore," I admitted, still clinging to him. "This is a bad idea. I should go see Kyle."

"No. Not that asshole."

"He's not an asshole. He's my former lover," I corrected, powering up my shiny, protective façade. It was still too hard, though, and not worth the expense of energy, so I dropped it again. I dug a toe into the ground. "He still doesn't know that I won't be coming around anymore. He'll be expecting me at his dorm soon."

"Fuck him."

"I do. Or I did, I guess." I bit into my lower lip, trying to explain. "Imagine, Barry, fucking someone who makes you come so hard you see stars and your knees buckle, and you feel like your heart's going to explode with pleasure. But then you hate yourself for how amazing it is. You tell yourself you'll never do it again. But you can't stop thinking about it, about *him*, and so you hate-fuck him, and you come *so damn hard* again. Every time it's better. Just imagine that."

Barry wiped a hand over his face. "Fucking hell."

"Then imagine the guy who makes all that happen for you just goes away." I tutted softly. "He'll be looking for me."

"Minty..."

Another sigh ripped free. "I *know*. I promised Luke. I signed a contract."

Still, one last brutal fuck would be *so good*. It'd clear out all the demons, just the way it had when I'd gone to Kyle after going to my mom's and seeing the bloodstain...

Remembering the first time on the sofa...

Remembering the last time in my room...

Kyle had shaken all that foul stuff free from my mind. He'd been so violent. He choked me out over and over, and I let him... I wanted it. I needed it. But what if I'd died?

And that was the crux of the whole thing, wasn't it?

Barry was wrong that any part of me was still the Minty who'd dreamed he might be worthy of romance and sweetness, but I didn't want to *die* just yet. I wanted to graduate. I wanted to see the spring flowers. I wanted to go to the ocean one last time. If Kyle killed me, I couldn't do any of that.

"Whatever you're thinking, just stop."

I met Barry's gaze and reminded him, "I signed a contract."

"Good." Barry's one word of praise hit me like an arrow, and I remembered Luke had used it too. But he'd said it in that sensual voice of his that rubbed at me like sandpaper—good and rough, awful and sweet.

"I just hope Luke fucks me hard and mean enough that I *can't* make him pancakes the next morning," I said with a sigh. "Or this isn't going to work out at all."

I heard the heaviness of my words. In another place and time, I'd have said the same thing, but with a bubbling lightness that made everyone laugh. Where was my easy mirth, my joy, my sparkle? With that HIV test result, crumpled up in the trash and sent to the dump.

Trash. Like me.

"Oh, Luke will work you over," Barry promised. "And if he doesn't, I'll beat you up and fuck you myself."

"Ew. Gross." I shrank away from him. "No. You're like a dad to me."

"I'm thirty-two."

"Yeah? You seem older."

"Fuck you, kid."

"Sorry, but no can do. Not interested in getting fucked by my dad. *Again.*"

Barry's eyes darkened at my joke, and he didn't laugh. I did, though. A high peal that cut through the air, swallowing another chirrup from the bird above. The sharpness of it felt good ripping from my still-sore throat.

Barry didn't budge.

"C'mon," I insisted. "That was a good one."

He shook his head.

I scoffed. "If I can't joke about being raped by my dad, then what *can* I joke about?"

Barry's eyes teared up, and he grabbed me in another hug. I pushed at him, struggling to get free, but eventually I gave up, going limp in his big arms.

"It'll never be funny," Barry growled in my ear. "Not even a little. I'll kill him if I ever meet him. I swear to God."

"Well, don't go to prison for me," I whispered, my voice sounding thick with tears. "Besides, I'm going to kill him myself. I'll be the one who gets to wear the orange jumpsuit."

The sound of the back door banging caught my attention, and then Robert was there in his tiny running shorts and white tank. His long, dark arms wrapped around me from the back.

"If this baby needs so much love, I figure he needs mine too," he said, his voice giggling in my ear. "Let's love him to death, Barry."

"I think he'd like that too much," Barry responded, starting to let me go.

I grabbed him back. "No, I wouldn't. I'd hate it. I'd hate it *so much*. Stop."

It was a lie. I felt so safe squeezed between these two men, the whisper of a breeze racing around our bodies, and the early autumn sun pouring down on us while the oak tree creaked overhead.

Swaying in a three-way hug, I closed my eyes and, for a moment, let myself have what I used to crave. Love.

Because soon I hoped to get hated on the way I deserved.

Chapter Five

October 1991
Minty

I T'D BEEN FIVE days since I went to Luke's house with the contracts and endured the clothespin torment, slept on his sofa, and made him pancakes in the morning like some kind of whipped pussy.

I wasn't whipped—at least not yet, though I hoped to be soon—but while I waited, I'd already decided if Luke couldn't handle me, I'd just go back to Kyle. I could feel the urge to get under that man again like a rope around my balls pulling me toward danger, toward pain and power.

God, I loved that power. The power to make Kyle come.

Earlier, I'd taken my time getting ready, and I had to reapply my pink lipstick three times due to my shaking hands. Now I wore a green skirt that swung loose around my knees—the easier to access my junk and ass—and a pink blouse that I'd picked up while out shopping with my friend Jennifer from Psychology class.

I'd chosen it so I'd look sweet and feminine, as well as to challenge Luke's ability to hurt me the way I needed. If I looked soft and pretty, would he go easy on me? We'd find out.

I finished the outfit off with white Keds and socks with pom-poms at the ankles in an attempt to feel cute and young and innocent. The dirtiest part of me still longed to feel innocent again.

Right now, though, I felt anything but. I felt evil and horny with sweaty palms and a shivery gut.

"You've seen the house," Luke was saying. "Or at least the main floor." He waved toward a flight up. "Those go to the master bedroom and bathroom. It's that dormer you can see from the front yard."

I didn't care about his bedroom or the layout of the house. I'd been wrestling anxiety and hope, and an awareness that I was a perverted demon all day long, and this cozy crap was the last thing I needed.

"I don't typically take play partners up there, but—"

Was *he* nervous? Was *he* rambling? Shit.

"—I like everyone to understand the arrangement of the—"

"Sir," I interrupted. "That's all fine. I don't really give a shit where your bedroom is. I just want to know: where are we doing this?"

A strangeness descended over Luke's features. It wasn't a dark expression, not quite cruel either, but it *was* predatory. As if he were taking stock of me and seeing every last weakness he could exploit, and I'd just handed him a new one.

"In a hurry to get your ass beat?"

"Yes." I gulped at the flash in his eyes. "Yes, Sir, I mean. Yeah."

He took me in for a long, swollen moment. My heart pounded. I thought I'd made a mistake, that he'd deny me.

Instead, he crossed his arms over his chest, nodded, and muttered, "Fine then. Strip. Now. Let me see what's on offer."

We stood at the foot of the stairs up to that master bedroom I didn't give a hoot about. I darted a glance into the living room, but I saw nothing there to support the kind of play I'd been promised.

Play—ha, what a word for what I wanted to do.

Staring into Luke's eyes, I saw something I didn't want to see there. He *wanted* me. He wanted to get inside me, and breed my ass, and he *wanted* me to agree to come back to his house when it was over to do it again. I could see it all in an instant.

He didn't hate himself for wanting any of that either.

Fuck.

An anxious giggle welled and nearly broke free, but I swallowed it down with the disappointment. There was no way this was going to work. He'd never actually scare me.

Discontent settled inside. Along with it, anger.

With a snarl, I pulled off my clothes, dropping them in a heap at my feet. I smeared my lipstick tugging the pink blouse off over my head instead of taking the time to undo all the buttons. Naked, I raised my hands to the side. "Well?" I asked. "Like it?"

His brow popped up. "Excuse me?"

I bit back a groan. Did we have to play this game in such a lame way? Couldn't we just be honest and fuck? I'd get off, he'd get off, and I could go back to Kyle to get what I needed—and what Kyle needed too if we were all being honest about it.

"I said *excuse me*."

"Sir," I spit out. "Do you like it, Sir?"

"What do you think?"

"I think you do, Sir. I think you want to fuck me, Sir." My dick stirred, and despite feeling certain this encounter wouldn't provide me with what I needed to give up Kyle, I was still beyond ready to get fucked.

Luke sneered. "You *would* think that," he said, eyeing me all over. "But all I see is a slut who's too pale, too skinny, too eager to come, and way too fucking sure of himself." He turned away from me. "Don't worry. We'll fix that."

The door beside the stairway, which I'd assumed was a closet, opened to reveal the way down to the basement. "Pick up your clothes," he ordered.

I hesitated, but only a moment.

"Fold them."

I held the bundle in front of me, my cock deflating. "Now?"

"Did I say later?"

With difficulty, I folded my clothes without dropping them, using my chin to hold edges as I worked. When I had a pile in my hands, he nodded. "Go," he said, motioning me toward the staircase to the basement. "Get down there. Put your clothes on the hardback chair in the corner. Wait for me. When I join you, I'd better find you on your knees."

"And if I'm not?"

"You will be."

I wanted to argue, to laugh in his face, but I held it back.

I started down the stairs, my legs shaking, and a hot shot of excited fear raced up my spine and tingled my brain. What was I going to find down there? A truly scary dungeon? Implements of pain and bondage equipment? Would Luke's basement be terrifying enough to save me from myself?

At first glance, my hope intensified. The finished basement was like many others I'd seen in my life except it had a concrete floor with a drain in the middle, and instead of a TV set and a sofa or a lounge chair or two, there was a full-size bed, a night table with a lamp, a lounge chair, a bathroom, and a half dozen or more large contraptions that were obviously designed for torture. Sexual torture.

I stared at them one by one. A table with straps and a section that slid away so a person's balls, cock, and ass could be easily accessed. A bench with more hooks and straps which could be used to immobilize a sub while exposing everything that mattered. A Saint Andrew's cross. A series of cages from quite big to worryingly small. A wall displaying instruments of all kinds, most notably whips and paddles and chains. There was some kind of machine with a thick dildo attached at one end.

How much had all this cost him to put together? How had he afforded it? Who spent that kind of money on these sorts of tools? More importantly, what kind of pain could they wring out of a person? And what sort of man got off on causing it?

A cold-blooded sadist.

The futility of the situation hit hard. I wasn't about to make Luke feel things he didn't want to feel. I wasn't about to own him the way I could own Kyle just by licking my lips while holding eye contact. Luke wasn't going to come inside me screaming with rage and trying to kill me.

He was going to hurt me, get me off, and *he* was going to get off doing it.

It just wasn't the same.

I was the helpless one here, not him. He wasn't going to resent me for the joy his orgasm brought him. *Fuck.*

I gritted my teeth as I heard the door at the top of the stairs open and close again. I remembered what he'd said. I was supposed to be on my knees.

Part of me wanted to see what would happen if I didn't greet him from my place on the floor. But a bigger part of me wanted to comply. Both to see what came next and, in a weird way, to get it all over with as fast as possible.

Since it was clear this wasn't going to work for me—I was still going to need Kyle or someone like him—this was just going to be a fucked-up orgasm dressed in some pretty nice pain.

Let's do it, I encouraged myself. *Get hurt, get off, get out.*

On my knees, I didn't feel godlike or powerful like I did with Kyle. Not with the concrete coldly digging into my knobby joints, and the air in the room feeling still and oppressive on my skin.

As I waited to hear his footsteps descending, the silence pushed into me. It was a relief when Luke came into view, wearing just his jeans. He was shirtless, barefoot, and hard. I could see the outline of his cock pushing against his zipper. His lips drew into a curved line when he saw me waiting on my knees like he'd asked.

He looked fucking smug.

Hatred rose. It burned in my heart. This asshole was going to hurt me, and I was going to *let* him, and he *knew* that I'd come from it. He knew *he'd* come from it too. He was far too fucking sure. This must be how Kyle felt. No wonder he hated me so much.

I shifted from knee to knee, considering what to do. I could run. I could leave. I could just say the safe word and get the hell out of here. I could, but…I wouldn't.

Because while this wasn't going to be what I needed, I found I still wanted it. I wanted to hurt. I wanted to endure. I wanted to prove to Luke that he couldn't break me, or make me his pet submissive, or be what I needed.

I had to show him he was wrong.

They were all wrong.

"Do you know why you're here?" Luke asked, reaching out to slide a hand over my hair and down my jawline to tilt my chin up, forcing me to meet his eyes.

"Yes," I bit out.

"Tell me."

"I'm here to get hurt."

His lips twitched like what I said pleased him. I gritted my teeth. I didn't *want* to please him.

"Yes, but what else?"

I slid my gaze away, but he jerked my chin, forcing me to meet his eyes.

I whispered, "I don't know."

What did he want me to say? What did he need me to confess? It didn't matter. This wasn't about him.

I pushed a hard shell of emotional armor to the surface of my skin, lifted my chin, and spoke with confidence. "I mean, I don't know, *Sir*."

"Good. Remember you can call me Sir, Master, or, if you're feeling especially needy, Daddy."

Daddy. I closed my eyes against the nausea that rose up, and I fought the always-ready memory of my father on my back. I let out a shaky breath. I was here with Luke. Nowhere else. I'd agreed to this. I was safe.

Far too fucking safe, in fact.

"Yes, Sir."

"And I'll call you Mitchell."

No. I stiffened, trying to jerk my chin out of his grip. But Luke held me fast, gripping me hard enough I could feel bruises forming.

My heart pounded. The room spun. I felt dizzy.

Shit. I'd wanted to be afraid, but not like this.

I insisted, "No, Sir. I'm Minty."

"The name your mother gave you was Mitchell."

Mitchell, the name my *father* had given me, the name he'd called me the day of the rape. The name I loathed.

I swallowed again, clenching my jaw and muttering, "How do you know that?"

"You put it on the form I had you fill out for me. Along with all the kinks you thought you'd enjoy and questions about your health and past kink experiences. Did you forget?"

"It also asked me what name I prefer to be called, and I put down Minty."

"Sir," he reminded me.

"I put down Minty, Sir," I gritted out.

I could go to the corner and grab my clothes, ending this bull-shit now. Turning my toes under, I felt the cold concrete on the pads of my feet and nearly pushed up to standing. But I held out.

My heart was pounding, and it only ever thudded like this right before I knocked on Kyle's dorm room door, or right before he shoved me into a campus bathroom and took me hard and rough against the sinks.

I was scared.

Luke was scaring me and, so far, he'd only used words.

I stayed put.

"Here are your options—I call you Mitchell and we go on with this scene today, or you can use your safe word—poodle, correct?"

I nodded.

"—and we end for today with no hard feelings. We'll talk it out so I understand why this is a hard boundary for you, and in a few days' time, after we've let this settle, we'll renegotiate another meeting."

End it? Now? We'd only just begun, and I was finally feeling the rush of fear. Still, I couldn't bear being called Mitchell. It was a name soaked in bad memories.

"But why, Sir?" I asked with trembling lips. "Why does it matter what you call me?"

"Because Mitchell is what I *want* to call you," he said with a satisfied smirk. He loved that I hated it. I could see that much. The power that I'd had over Kyle, he now had over me. It wasn't the same alchemy at work, but it was still heady, and I was afraid and not ready for it to be over.

He went on, "That's all that matters. I could call you Shit Stain and you'd agree. Understood?"

He gripped my jaw again, squeezing hard enough that some tears rose. It was going to have to be Mitchell or nothing, and there was no way I was going home now. Not when things had finally started getting good.

"Yes, Sir," I said, deflating as soon as I agreed.

"Say it," he ordered.

"What, Sir?"

"Your name."

Fuck. He wasn't going to let this go. He'd discovered a painful place inside me and, like the sadist he was, he was going to press on it good and hard. It took all my strength to gather the words. "I'm Mitchell, Sir."

"That's right. When you're here on your knees for me, you're Mitchell."

He released his grip on my jaw and slipped his hand into my hair far too gently at first, but then he grabbed a handful of it, clenching so hard that tears leapt back into my eyes. I gasped.

"Don't move," he whispered. "Stay very still."

I gazed up him, saying nothing, doing nothing, feeling the way he owned me and this moment. *I* was nothing. I was no one but Mitchell, the HIV-positive shit stain, the whore boy whose father had—

I swallowed the thought down.

Luke pursed his lips and a glob of gooey, shiny spit hung from his lips for a long moment until it fell, splattering on my eyebrow. I closed my lid against the inevitable hot, slick slide of it down to my lashes.

"There. That's more like it," Luke said. "You're a filthy cock-sucking whore, aren't you, Mitchell?"

"Yes, Sir," I whispered. My breath came in sharp pants, adrenaline rushing in my veins. The room spun. The name felt like a slap. I went hot all over.

"Let's try this again," Luke said, his voice oozing with smug nastiness. It wasn't quite hate, but it was getting closer. "Why are you here?"

"To get hurt, Sir," I whispered.

"And what else?"

"I don't know." He tightened his grip in my hair, and I whimpered.

With his free hand, he smeared the pooled saliva all over my face, down to my lips, and then up into my hair at the temples until I was coated with his juice, sticky and slimy with it.

"You're here to be used," Luke said. "To be my bitch. My fuck toy. My dick's slave."

My cock pulsed, and pre-cum slipped from the slit. I felt it slide down the side of my cockhead and start a slow, honeyed trail down to the floor. I hadn't realized I'd grown hard again, but apparently I had—probably around the time he spit on me and called me Mitchell. I shivered at that.

"You're HIV positive," Luke said.

Shame like a splash of cold water hit me, and I whispered, "Yes, Sir."

"Yes, Sir, what?" Luke pressed.

"I'm HIV positive, Sir." I wanted to vomit saying it, and yet my cock was straining hard now. I felt myself sinking into a place that was thrumming with lust, shame, horror, and hot need too, a place where orgasm was held just out of reach.

"That's right. You are." Luke's voice grew grittier, and I felt it in my balls like a vibrator. "I am too."

I wanted something more. I didn't know what, but I wanted him to hit me already or spit on me again. I spoke impatiently. "I already know that. You told me before."

Luke gripped my hair and tugged it, jerking my head back. "How do you speak to me?"

The pain was sharp and fast and I feared he'd pulled out a handful of my hair. Tears welled in my eyes, and my cock pulsed greedily. A flare of fear went off inside me, shiny and bright. This was good. *This* was what I needed.

"Sir! I'm sorry. Please, Sir, you're going to pull my hair out." Deep down, I craved to see his hand come away from my head with a bloody hank of blond.

His lips curled into a smirk, and his cock seemed to push even harder against the front of his jeans. "You beg nicely," he said.

Ugh. I didn't want him to call me good or to praise me. I wanted him to smack me. Tell me I was a cunt to be used. Choke me out like Kyle would, or just roll me to the floor and start fucking into me already. What was he delaying for? Why was he making me wait?

His eyes went cold. "But not nicely enough."

The slap rocked my head back, and I cried out. Fucking hell, that hurt, and with him holding my hair, the wrench on my scalp was agony too.

I loved it.

"Say it again," Luke bit out, releasing my hair to unzip his jeans and release his hard cock. "The right way. And thank me for correcting you."

His dick was thick at the head, and already wet with pre-cum. My mouth flooded with saliva. A yearning to taste him filled my mind, loud like the buzz of bees on a hot summer day.

I *needed* to lick his cock. I had to get this right. What if he put it away again? What if he dragged this out further?

"Yes, Sir. Thank you, Sir." I felt breathless. "You—you'd told me you were HIV positive. Before, Sir."

I was dizzy, and the world opened up around me in a weird, gorgeous way. I'd experienced it only a few times before when I'd surrendered to Kyle's choking, let him have control over my life and death. Each time, I'd floated away into a sea of painful pleasure that had little to do with what Kyle was doing to the rest of my body, and everything to do with a flood of internal chemicals that made me feel high.

Only this time, I felt more like I was flying. I could almost sense a breeze on my skin, and I was aware of every sensation on my flesh—from the drying spit on my face, to the pain in my knees from still kneeling on the cold floor, to the thud of my pulse in my dick. But it was all beautiful, peaceful, sharp, and perfect.

Luke was going to hurt me, and I was ready.

I existed only for this purpose. He needed to give it to me. I needed to receive it.

I *needed* it.

Luke wrenched open my jaw and spit into my mouth. His saliva tasted bitter and a little gross. I swallowed it down at his command. Luke's hum of satisfaction was laced with cruelty as he gathered another wad up into his mouth.

"We." Luke's spit landed on my tongue.

I dutifully swallowed.

"Are."

Spit. Swallow.

"HIV."

Spit. Swallow.

"Positive."

Spit. Swallow.

Luke thumbed my mouth open wider, pressing down on my lower teeth, and then aimed his cock at my wide-open throat.

"Do you know what that means?"

I hoped it meant he was going to throat-fuck me.

He held my mouth firmly open so I couldn't speak. "That means I can do this…"

He hesitated for a moment, and I opened wider for him, groaning as he shoved all the way in.

"…without a fucking condom."

Fuck, his dick was thick. It was meaty and perfect, and I closed my eyes and gripped his thighs hard as he pulled back out. I went to work sucking, licking, and kissing.

With Kyle, I always gave him the best head I could. It made him loathe himself so much that he'd curse me out, hit me, hurt me, and then shoot hard down my throat. And Luke loved it too.

All men did. Even my…

Fuck…

I shuddered.

My room in the trailer. My knees on the floor. His cock in my mouth—

I closed my eyes and redoubled my efforts. Why now? Why was I thinking of it now? Was it from being called Mitchell? Was it because I wasn't hurting enough yet?

Why hadn't Luke dished out more pain?

With a greedy sneer, Luke gripped my hair roughly in one hand and tweaked his own nipples with the other. His cock stiffened, and I knew he was close, but he pulled my head off his dick, not letting me finish him.

I kept my mouth open, hoping he'd shove back in and fuck my throat hard. I didn't want to kneel here with that god-awful memory at the back of my mind. I needed Luke's cock as a distraction. *Please.*

"Do you know what else being HIV positive means between us?" Luke asked.

I had a good idea, and I hoped I was right as I rasped, "No, Sir."

"It means I can also do this."

He forced me around to face the wall. I cried out, the pain from his grip in my hair arcing down my right side. Another memory broke free.

A rough shove to the couch. His grunt of satisfaction as he—

Luke knelt behind me, lifting my hips up and aimed his cock at my hole.

I broke into a sudden sweat, goose pimples prickling me all over as he pushed into me roughly. He wasn't as thick as Kyle, not as slender as my—

I winced, trying desperately to get my head out of that memory once and for all.

I'd had a lot of men. Been fucked by a *ton* of guys since—

I just wouldn't think about it. *Why* was I thinking about it?

Luke's cock was good-sized and hit the right spot. I pushed myself back to take it in all the way. Clenching my hands into fists, I was determined to get fucked to orgasm with a clear mind. I wasn't going to come with my father's—

Luke slapped my hip hard, blessedly stopping that thought in its tracks.

"Be still," he ordered. "I'll decide how fast I get into my nasty little cum dumpster. Because that's what you are, isn't it, Mitchell? Daddy's dirty cum dumpster."

I froze. Memory flowed over me, unstoppable as a river. The fear, the pain, the grief, the horror, the alchemy, the power, the trauma, the pleasure, the worst moment of my life, and again, and *again*, stuck on repeat.

I couldn't breathe. Luke fucked me, but it wasn't him.

It wasn't him.

"Poodle." I got the word out from somewhere deep inside, a place that had stayed sane as the rest of me fell apart. "Poodle."

Luke pulled out too fast and too slow at once. I felt sick.

Pressing my head to the floor, I said the only thing I knew to say.

Luke bent low, his face near mine, and I squeezed my eyes shut, whispering, "Poodle, poodle."

Chapter Six

Luke

"MINTY," I SAID, rubbing my hand into his hair, and then down his back soothingly. "Are you all right? It's over. The scene's over. How can I help you?"

It took him a long time to finally roll over onto his side, but even so he brought his legs up to his chest in a fetal position, heaving with suppressed tears.

"Is it okay to touch you?" I had been already, but I needed to know what I was doing wasn't continuing to distress him.

He nodded, so I ran my hands into his hair soothingly, and I hummed a soft song.

"It's all right," I reassured him. "You did great. I'm not angry. This is perfectly okay. Do you want some water?"

He nodded, and I went to pour some from the bathroom sink and brought him the huge, fluffy robe that I kept in the closet at the end of the room for aftercare time. It was comfortable, and he let me put it on him as I led him toward the bed. He took the water from me, sipped it, and then sank down on the mattress, a vacant, sad expression on his face. I said nothing more, rubbing his back and letting him process whatever he needed, while still making sure he knew I was there for him.

"Don't use the word Daddy," he finally whispered. "I want to play like this with you, but you can't—" Minty broke off, his throat seemingly closing on him.

"I understand," I said, and I thought I did. There was *something*, a suspicion growing inside me, based on his reactions, based on his needs... I didn't want to assume. But still, I was fairly certain. "That word is a hard limit for you. I won't call myself that, and I won't ask you to call me by it either."

Minty nodded. We sat in silence for a few more minutes and then he turned to me. "Can we still play? Do I have to go home? I didn't want to stop, Sir. I really do want you to hurt me."

I pulled him against me, breathing in his sweaty scent. "Are you sure? It's all right if you want to end this now. We can just rest here, and—"

"No! I want to forget," he said roughly, jerking free of my hold. "I *have* to forget. Don't you understand? If I can't, then I'll just... Sir, please help. Make it go away."

I set my shoulders. Emotional pain wasn't my favorite kind to play with, and I wasn't sure I was still in the right place to do this tonight. But I couldn't let him leave now. "What do you need? We could call for a pizza or—"

"Fuck no." He flushed, his hands on mine clinging a little desperately. "Sir. Would pizza make you forget anything?"

I huffed. "No."

"It'd have to be laced with shrooms or something. Which I could go for too..."

I shook my head. "No drugs during playtime."

"Pizza won't make me forget. And I have to forget. Understand?"

"If I don't help you, you'll go back to that guy, despite our contract, won't you?"

He shivered. "I don't know, Sir. I just know I'm here for one thing, and you haven't given it to me yet." His blue eyes burned into mine. "Hurt me. Make me forget. Make nothing else exist but pain and you. Can you do that, Sir? You promised you could do that for me."

I wanted to kiss his forehead, but I held back. My stomach twisted. I could sense this was a do-or-die moment with Minty. If I couldn't hurt him when he needed it most, then he'd never trust me again.

"All right," I said. "I can do that."

He nodded, his blond hair sliding into his eyes. "How do we start?"

"It's easy. I'll count us in." I rubbed a finger across his cheekbone where I'd slapped him, feeling the slight puffiness indicating future bruising. He was so tender. If I could put this hiccup aside, I'd get to play with that soft skin even more. "One...two...three..." I stood up. "Ready?"

"Yes, Sir."

"Kneel on the floor, slut."

Minty complied with a relief I felt in my own gut. We were in the scene again.

Minty

FACE DOWN, STRETCHED over Sir's naked legs, my hard cock trapped between his muscled, hairy thighs, I took the most vicious spanking I'd ever had in my life. I hadn't even known a hand could hurt like that. I'd been hit with switches as a kid, and those had stung so bad that when I'd gotten just a palm to my ass, I considered myself lucky. But, I realized now, that'd been because no one had ever spanked me the way Sir was spanking me now.

The pain was dizzying, a deep burn that settled far into my muscle and skin. I struggled for a full breath between the tears. Though I was past fighting it now, at first I'd arched and kicked and even wrestled him, trying to escape the next strike. But Sir was much bigger and stronger than me, and while that brought back unwanted memories too, they were diluted by the better memories of so many bigger boys I'd sought out to rough-fuck me and beat me up.

After I fought Sir for a while, he'd trapped me solidly, holding my dick between his strong legs and my upper body still beneath his free palm. He'd wailed on me for what felt like an hour, going hard like he had endless stamina and a steel palm.

I was glad he didn't ask me to count the smacks the way my mom had when I was a kid, because I would have lost track almost immediately. The stinging pain had spread in a deep heat through my skin, into my muscle, and out over the entirety of my body. I swore I even felt the steady swats in my eyeballs and toenails.

I hated it.

I loved it.

I reveled in it.

I screamed out against it.

I heard the sound of rushing water in my ears as I submitted to Sir's hand. Sweat slipped down my face, and as I gripped the bedsheets, I flew. Higher than I'd ever flown on coke or X or pot. Higher than the time I'd tripped balls on acid and believed that everything in the world was made of moonbeams.

The shimmering high grew more powerful and stronger with every searing smack over my ass cheeks. Groaning, I put my head down, breathing in the fresh laundry scent of the bedsheets. Another smack. Another. I thought I might come, but I just couldn't reach that peak.

I whimpered and pleaded for him to make me come, but I knew that a spanking wasn't ever going to be enough. I needed more. Sir's hand slowed and then stilled, rubbing and massaging my ass.

"Mitchell," Sir said in that commanding voice that raked over my nipples and cock, making me feel tingly and alive all over. "I'm going to fuck you again now."

"Yes," I gasped. "Please, Sir."

I was so out of it, I didn't fully follow how he repositioned my body, but when I felt him pushing inside, I realized I had my feet on the floor by the bed, and my torso bent over the mattress. Sir stood behind me with his hands on my hips, shoving into my hole with only a little fresh lube to slick the way.

It stung—no, it fucking *hurt* the way he forced past my sphincter muscle, not bothering to be sweet or kind about it, taking his pleasure with no regard for mine—just the way I liked it and needed it. I surrendered to that pain as well, letting my body go limp as he rocked into me. My cock, though, was at full attention.

He slid in and out, hitting my prostate perfectly, but it wasn't enough. I needed him to hit me. Punch my back or sides, pinch me, claw me, or bite me. Anything. Something. I needed pain. More pain.

"More," I bit out.

"I've got you," he muttered as I moaned desperately. "Fuck, you're a tight cum-dumpster. Thought a slut like you'd be loose and useless."

He hawked up a mouthful of spit, and I jerked as it hit my back all hot and slimy.

I groaned. "Please, Sir. Choke me."

"You want me to own your life?"

I grunted, my balls hitching up, orgasm coming for me with just the suggestion. "Yes. Own me."

With a hard thrust into my ass, Luke put his hands around my throat, squeezing hard enough to make me see spots. I nearly ascended to heaven.

As he began to shove into me with rough, slamming thrusts, I struggled and fought. It wasn't just for show either. The pain of his pubic hair and hipbones slamming into my burning ass cheeks was breathtaking, and the stretch in my anus from the thick base of his cock stung. The squeeze of his strong hands around my throat was more than enough to keep me on the razor's edge of coming.

My cock rubbed against the edge of the mattress, and I moved my hips, trying to get myself off. With a cruel laugh, he jerked me up so that I couldn't get purchase.

"Sluts don't come except for Sir's cock. Got it, bitch?"

I grunted an affirmative noise, and he didn't make me repeat it. I was grateful since I was high and floating on pain and exquisite fear. He squeezed my throat hard again, making my eyes bulge and my vision go hazy and dark, and then just before I thought I'd be choked out for real—wondering if I trusted him more than Kyle to not actually kill me—he let go again.

I sucked in air like a racehorse, and then he did it again. It became a rhythm that I rode into bliss. My balls drew up tight, and my cock quivered hard. His rough thrusts kept me dizzy with prostate stimulation and pain. The pounding and choking coalesced into a pattern that became a source of otherworldly pleasure. Sir was a god, and I was his helpless sycophant. Fuck my own power. What good was it when Sir was so strong and in charge? He had the power. I was forced to give it all to him. And *he* alchemized it into pleasure and pain and breath and death...

I'd do anything he said, anything at all to keep on feeling like this.

Fifteen thrusts without the choking pressure, and then ten with it. I clawed at the sheets, trying to either get more air, or more freedom, or less dick, or... something. I needed something. Anything. *Please, Sir.*

And then I got what I needed, and it was blindingly good.

Sir surged forward and *bit* me, right in the soft part of my back beneath my shoulder blade. It felt like he took a hunk of flesh, and the searing pain tipped me over.

With Sir's hands squeezing for his ten thrusts of choking, I couldn't even shout as I shot my load. I couldn't do anything except croak out a desperate sound, scrabbling at Sir's fingers around my throat as the world exploded in hedonistic pleasure and pulsing, earthshaking ecstasy.

Dots swam in my vision, and I felt the frenzy dying down and a honeyed stupor closing in as my world faded. The pressure continued on my throat as I surrendered and went limp. I nearly lost consciousness. As the roar of darkness threatened, the pressure lifted, and I gulped in air hungrily. I convulsed again and again, the continuing orgasm wringing me dry.

Still twitching, I collapsed against the bed, my body humming and mind swimming lazily, drunk and lost in sweet post-climax inertia. I couldn't think or string together a sentence as my cells sang with release.

Sir pushed in deep and lingered a moment. I had time to wonder if he'd come inside me before he pulled out, and a splash of hot, thick semen hit my back, and another spurt landed in my hair.

Drained and shaking, I couldn't move, but Sir did that for me. He shoved me onto my back, hand moving fast on his cock, squeezing the last of his orgasm out with a gravelly cry. He straddled my face, shooting his final burst into my open, eager mouth. I swallowed it down, blissed out and riding an endorphin rush that overrode all my fears and worries.

Sir had taken me flying with his hands, his teeth, his cock, and his words. I could only imagine where he might take me if given a chance to use restraints and his cane or flogger.

I still wasn't sure if this was going to be enough for me. I loved the power I had over men like Kyle far too much, but I'd loved the power Sir had over me too.

I wanted to know.

I needed to find out.

How far could he take me? I wanted to go as far as we could get.

Luke

WHEN OUR NIGHT was over, and I'd washed Minty in the basement bathroom, pampered his bruised ass, cuddled him, fed him, and hydrated him, I'd then put him into the soft bed still naked. He'd let me do it all without protest. Lost in a daze from the scene, he seemed to be having a hard time coming back to himself. I was exhausted. I'd forgotten that the hard work went on after the orgasms and sadistic pleasure were long over.

Afterward, I put my jeans back on, pulled on a t-shirt, and left him sleeping in the bed while I took the lounge chair next to it. I wasn't ready to sleep next to him yet. That was something I'd done often with Benji, and it still brought me pain to think of how I'd ended things with him. We hadn't been in love, but we were good together.

Benji had been Jerome's last gift to me, in a way. He'd called me up a few months before he got sick, telling me that he'd found the perfect boy for me—freshly graduated with a business degree and a brand new, stressful job in finance, not to mention pretty and occasionally bratty.

We met for coffee and a compatibility chat, and for two years, the rest had been history. We'd never been monogamous, or even boyfriends, but we'd had fun together in ways we generally didn't with other people. We sometimes partied together with other guys too, and he was with me that fateful night with the guy from Atlanta. They hadn't fucked, though. Thank God.

As for the breakup... I hadn't been graceful about it. I hadn't even been mature. I'd been a good Sir to Benji up until the end, and then I'd botched the whole thing, probably ruining the entirety of our relationship in his memory. It was a shame.

At least when Benji and I started, I'd known that I could be the Dom he needed. I wasn't at all sure I could be the Dom that *Mitchell* needed. I could see there was potential for us to grow into something special. There was something about him, a delicious, angry *hurt* that I longed to unearth.

Mitchell was a resilient boy. I knew that based on what he'd taken from the self-loathing fucks at his college. But it was more than that.

It was the fearlessness in him—the way he wore women's clothes and makeup, drove a truck, and flipped the bird to convention. I knew there was even more to discover about him, more layers of his persona to peel back and examine. I was curious to meet the real Mitchell.

The Mitchell who existed when all his armor was gone.

I considered his resistance to my use of that name. One day I hoped he'd trust me enough to tell me his truth. But for now, I dozed through the night in the lounge chair beside the bed, watching over him, getting up to adjust the covers when they slipped from his shoulders and smoothing his hair back from his face. He slept deeply, which made sense after the intensity of our scene together.

He'd sung like a songbird, calling out beautiful noises of pain and pleasure, and when I got my next chance to torture him, I'd make it last even longer.

Eventually, I fell asleep in the chair, dreaming of nothing at all.

Chapter Seven

Minty

"SO WHAT WAS it like?" Windy asked, resting on the opposite bed in my dorm room. He still lived at home with his folks, though he spent many nights here on campus with me. My assigned roommate had jumped ship after he'd gotten a good look at the homo he'd be living with, AKA my pink princess ass. I'd have gotten my feelings hurt over it, but his absence meant I got a room to myself and an extra bed for my friends to sleep on whenever they stayed over, so it was a win for me.

"What was it like?" I repeated slowly, lolling on my stomach, keeping my sweats-covered ass toward the ceiling hoping the bruises healed before my classes in the morning. "Or what was *he* like?" I grinned at him.

"Both." Windy toyed with the pink chenille on the twin bed's coverlet and smiled a little shyly.

"Why? Do you want to try it?" A possessive irritation rose in me. I didn't want Windy—or anyone else for that matter—suffering under Luke's hand. It was a silly reaction to have. He was a professional Dom after all, but I didn't want to share him. "I didn't think you enjoyed pain."

"I don't." He flashed a pretty smile. "But maybe I like the thought of giving it."

I sat up, wincing as my sore ass cheeks made contact with the mattress. "Really? You want to hurt people?"

Windy shrugged, picking at the shag on the blanket again. "I don't know. I wouldn't mind hurting someone, I guess, but it's more the idea of someone kneeling at my feet, doing what I say—no matter what I ask them to do—and obeying me without question. I like that idea a lot."

"Huh, well, I guess I can see why you'd like that. Living in my shadow all the time must be hard. You'd probably like someone who worshipped you instead of me."

He tossed the pillow my way, hitting me in the face with it. "Asshole."

"See? You're already punishing me. That's half the job of a Dom right there," I teased.

He rolled his eyes. "So, seriously, what was it like?"

"Well, he was pretty dreamy," I said, sighing and falling back to my stomach again, keeping my ass skyward. "I think I'm in love."

Windy huffed a laugh.

"No, really. I think I am."

"You say that about every guy you meet."

It was true, I did, and everyone knew it. But Luke… What we'd done? What I'd felt? If I wasn't HIV positive and careening toward death, I'd already be head over heels for him. Now, for just a few hours, I wanted to pretend to be that pre-diagnosis Minty again, let myself swoon with the possibility of a real romance, and entertain the idea that I loved him.

"Maybe I do say I love everyone," I said, crossing my arms over my chest. "But this time is different."

"They're all different."

I narrowed my eyes. "They don't all make me come like a bomb went off in my balls and then hold me while I cry."

Windy's eyes twinkled. "Wait, I thought you didn't want to be held anymore? I thought that was *bête romantique merde*? I thought you wanted to be hurt. Beaten up and spit on. Stuff like that."

"I don't want to be held if I'm crying from the *pain*," I tried to explain. "I only want to be held if I'm crying because I'm *upset*."

"He upset you?" Windy went from curious to protective in a heartbeat. It was sweet.

"No," I denied, not wanting to explain what I'd been upset about. "I mean, yes."

"How?"

"It wasn't *him*. It's being positive that upset me," I said, blaming the most convenient thing. Windy had seen me cry about my diagnosis more than once already, and he'd held me through the first few days after I'd finally confessed the truth to him.

He came to sit next to me, putting his arm around my shoulder. "I'm glad he's understanding about it."

"He's positive too," I said, turning to hug him. "We fucked raw," I admitted with a silly grin. "It was amazing."

"You…he's…" Windy's dark eyes went hard.

"What's wrong with that?" I shoved him back so there was distance between us. "We're both positive. We can't catch it twice."

"You can catch other things," he pointed out. "Like herpes, or syphilis, or—"

"I know, I know." I rolled my eyes. Of *course*, Windy was harshing my buzz. He'd taken over for Daniel after Peter and the demands of Daniel's fucked-up life had stolen my usual lecturing best friend away from me. "But we both had clean STD tests."

"Please. You've been letting that monster fuck you in the ass without a condom. He could have anything."

"Luke isn't a monster."

"Not Luke. Kyle."

"Oh, him." For the last few hours, I'd forgotten Kyle existed. After leaving Luke's house floating on clouds, I'd thought of almost nothing but Luke and his muscled arms, his comfortable chest, his strong hands, and his thick cock. "Yeah, I guess so."

"You guess so?"

"Look, if Luke wants to take the risk of getting something from me, that's his business."

"He's HIV positive too. If you gave him something, he could get really sick, really fast. It could be—"

"Stop!" I covered my ears and buried my head under my pillow. "You're ruining it."

"I'm being reasonable."

"If I wanted that, I'd have called Daniel."

Windy sighed. "I love you, and I'm looking out for you. I'm just surprised he'd go through with raw sex like that."

I tossed my pillow aside, sitting up. "He said he's okay with the risks. He's got clear tests, and I've got clear tests, and aside from Kyle, I haven't been fucking anyone."

"It's not safe."

"I don't fucking want *safe*," I spit out. "And maybe neither does he."

Windy raised his hands in surrender. "Got it. Sorry I asked."

"Me too." I tugged my hand through my hair and sighed. "Last night with him… He spanked me so hard. Fuck. I want to do it again. Be with him. Tonight. Now. I want to be in his basement right now getting slapped silly."

"His basement?"

"Yeah, it's like his dungeon. There's a big bed set up with really nice sheets and pillows. And there are other things too. Like a bench to restrain me on, and a table. There's a Saint Andrew's on the wall. So many toys. I didn't even know what all of them were! There are some chairs too. A bathroom. And some cages."

"Cages…"

"Yeah." I sighed happily. "I wonder what it's like to be fucked through the bars of a cage. He's going to put me in one. I'll get to find out. Holy shit, I can't wait."

Windy scrubbed a hand over his face. His half-moon eyes squinted skeptically at me. "When will you see him again?"

My smile slid away. "Not until tomorrow night. He usually works Fridays but, for me, he's taking the time off."

That wasn't true. He'd told me that most of the time we'd need to meet on Sunday morning and end our sessions by Monday afternoon at the latest for him. Since I had class, it'd have to be over by Monday morning for me.

Though I was reconsidering continuing school at all. What was even the point of it when I was going to die in a few months or a year? The idea of dropping out had been creeping into my mind ever since the diagnosis.

But then I'd have to move back home, and my mom would know, and…

No. It made it all too real.

But, yeah, the only reason we were meeting on Friday was because Cherise had talked their manager into giving *her* the Friday shift so she could make a little extra for her grandson's soccer team's equipment fees. The manager had agreed.

Still, I *liked* pretending Luke had taken that time off just for me, and it wasn't as if Windy would know the difference.

"He enjoyed hurting me," I whispered. "I could tell."

At least, I was pretty sure Luke had enjoyed himself. He'd come after all, but I still felt guilty about having used my safe word during the night. And humiliated.

I couldn't believe I'd been forced back in time that way. I understood why, of course. The word "Daddy" had pushed buttons in my brain, and the rough fuck, with that word ringing in my ears, had felt far too similar to when…

I squeezed my eyes shut. No.

Windy knew about the rape, of course. All my close friends did, but I didn't like talking about what happened to me back then. That was why I hadn't told Luke about it last night. Still, I wondered, given enough time strapped to a torture device in his basement, would I confess everything to him—the actual whole, *real* truth—if he took me apart enough, if he examined my insides?

Yeah. I would if he could...

Even with as scary as that was, maybe I wanted it to happen.

"Minty?" Windy asked, scooting closer to me again. I realized he'd asked me something, but I'd been zoned out. He rubbed my back carefully, clearly not sure where all the bruises might be. "Are you really okay?"

"Yeah, I'm great."

He eyed me warily, his disbelief evident. But I didn't need him to believe in my fantasies. I knew I was still a mess, but I'd be fine if I could just get back to Luke's dungeon. Pain was a time-stopping sensation that held me in place, and Luke was the magician who knew just the right amount of it to dole out to scare me.

"You hungry?" I asked.

"I could eat."

"Well, if you'll stop worrying about me, I'll buy you a hot dog with chili from the cafeteria."

Windy lifted his nose in the air. "Thanks, I'll pass."

"A package of taffy?"

He hesitated. "Saltwater?"

"Of course."

He frowned. "I still think doing it raw with him is a bad idea, but I guess you're both grown men—"

"With a terminal disease, and we know what we're doing." I rose from my bed and grabbed his hand. "C'mon. This will all go down easier with a spoonful of sugar... or taffy."

Windy followed me out of my room and into the elevator that would deposit us in the lobby. We were alone as the numbers flashed by. When the car came to rest at the ground floor, he whispered, "I'm scared for you."

"I'm scared for me too."

"Just please be careful."

I said nothing as I led the way from the elevator to the dorm cafeteria.

I'd already told him a dozen times or more. I didn't want to be careful. Careful was for people with a future.

Danger was for me.

Luke

"Hey." Minty's voice was sleepy and sweet from his end of the line.

I glanced around Knox Supplies & News. The only customer was our regular, Terry Jackson, and he wasn't going to buy anything. He never did. He'd just look through the latest porn mags that had "mysteriously" worked their way out of their black, plastic wrapping.

"Good job keeping our phone appointment."

Minty's hesitation made me wonder if I'd already misstepped in praising him. Still, this wasn't a scene, it was a check-in.

"It's not like sitting around in my dorm room doing my homework and listening to my neighbor play Rush's 'Tom Sawyer' on repeat for the last five hours is so much fun that I'd forget about it. Did you know his mind is not for rent?"

"What?"

"Nothing. Hi."

"Hi." I cleared my throat and shifted on my stool by the cash register. The scent of plastic, rubber, and berries filtered up from the trash can at my feet. Earlier, while restocking, I'd found a two-pack of strawberry-flavored condoms had been ripped open and the sickly-sweet contents dropped onto the floor. Between the torn wrapping on the porn mags and now this, I was starting to think the morning-shift employees were sleeping on the job.

"I've missed you," Minty confessed.

I couldn't say I'd missed him, even though I'd done nothing but think about him all day. Missing, for me, required more familiarity, a spot in my life that had been filled but no longer was. I missed Jerome, I missed Benji, I missed my father, and sometimes I missed Betsy, even though she was just a phone call and an hour and forty-five-minute drive away.

"What's that mean to you? Missing someone."

"It means I think I'd be a lot happier if I were with you. Especially if I were naked with you, and you had me tied down to one of those contraptions in your basement. Speaking of,"—his tone changed from seductive to curious—"how did you afford all that stuff? Isn't it expensive?"

"It is," I agreed. "But, for the most part, I inherited it."

"From who?" He laughed, and it brought a smile to my face too. "A kinky grandfather?"

"Yeah, in a way. But not a blood relative. My first Dom, the guy who taught me everything I know about the work… Jerome."

"You had a Dom?"

"I did."

"So, you took Dom lessons from him?"

"Kind of. I was his sub at first, but it didn't work out for me. But he was a great master to learn from."

"Is there a school to be a Dom?"

"Not really. Jerome lived in Chicago for a while. Learned everything he knew about the scene there, and then moved back down here to help support his parents. He was a teacher by day at a local high school, and a dungeon master by night." I cleared my throat. "Anyway, he died a couple years ago. Left the house and everything in it to his sister. That included his personal dungeon. She freaked out when she saw the stuff he owned, and I offered to take it all off her hands. She gave it to me for free so long as I got it out of his house before their parents saw it."

"Wow."

"Yeah."

"Did he die of AIDS?"

I picked up a small bouncy ball I kept in the give-a-penny-take-a-penny and bounced it hard on the floor. It flew up, and I caught it easily. "Yeah."

"How'd he get it?"

"Same way you and I got it."

We were silent a moment, and I tried to remember what I'd intended to review with him when I called. Talking about Jerome's death hadn't been on the list.

"But what about your house?" Minty asked. "It's pretty great. I mean, better than my mom's place, by far. I know you don't make that much at the porn store you work at. Can you really make so much money being a professional Dom?"

Something in his voice told me he had another question he wanted to ask too, but I couldn't figure out what it might be without clearing this one up first. "Yes and no. Yes, I made enough money Domming to buy my house, but no, I'm not making that kind of money right now."

"Why not?" His voice hitched up. I tuned into it with the intensity of a sadist looking for vulnerabilities to exploit.

"Because I'm not doing it professionally right now."

"You're doing it with me," he reminded me.

"For free," I reminded him in return.

"Oh. Is that…a problem?"

"What? Dominating you or not charging you for it?"

"Both," he whispered.

"I could dominate you day and night and never get sick of it. As for the money, you can't afford it, and I'm not asking you to pay anyway." I flicked a glance toward Terry, who had his hand down his pants as he looked through an older copy of *Hustler*. "You're helping me as much as I'm helping you."

"How?"

"Let's just say I needed a distraction from my diagnosis too."

The bell rang on the door, and I glanced up to see a crowd of college-age girls come in, all giggling and blushing. I watched as they started their rounds of the store. With any luck, a few would be brave enough to get a dildo or vibrator, but often those kinds of girls just came in to look and titter. "But back to the topic at hand... How are you feeling?"

"Distracted." Minty chuckled, and it was a deeper sound than his usual voice and laugh. "I'm supposed to be writing a paper on the dinoflagellates of Vieques's Bioluminescent Bay, but all I can think about is that spanking you gave me, and whether or not you're ever going to actually hurt me, or if you'll just keep on claiming that you're going to and then..." He chuckled again. "Not."

I scoffed. I couldn't believe this brat. I'd sent him flying with just a spanking, I'd made him shout from a few clothespins, and now he was pushing me, saying I'd failed to hurt him yet? "You want more pain?"

"It's the only reason I'm meeting up with you." Minty laughed again. There was a bitter tinge to it. "I mean, you're really hot, and I think I could probably fall in love with the way your smile is kinda crooked on your face, and how you laugh, and how pretty your eyes are. All of you, really. But, like I said, those aren't the reasons I'm seeing you. If you aren't going to actually make me suffer, I can always get other hot guys to do the job."

I clucked my tongue, watching the girls gasp over the newest shelf of vibrators. "You're really tempting fate here, you realize."

"And you're fate?"

"I am."

Minty whispered, "Good.

Tension rushed through the line, thick and hot, making my cock grow half-hard and my face flush. I glanced at the posse of girls, who were now holding up an enormous dildo. I whispered, "We're still on for tomorrow night?"

"Yeah."

"Is there anything at all on that list of kinks you signed off on that you'd like to rescind consent to now? Aside from the hard boundary you already expressed last time?"

Minty breath came more quickly over the line. "No."

"So…anything's fair game?"

"Anything at all, Sir."

My cock throbbed to full hardness at his throaty use of my title. "You'll keep your hands to yourself tonight and tomorrow, got it? No jerking off, no playing with that hole of yours, and no one else touches them either."

"Of course not. I promised. No one fucks me but you. I signed the contracts."

"Who does your dick belong to?" I gritted out, my own cock thudding with blood.

His breath came over the line, heavy and hard. "You, Sir."

"And that sweet hole?"

"You, Sir."

I grinned and licked my lips. "You're already in love with this game, aren't you?"

"I'm in love with a lot of things," Minty murmured. "My friends all say I fall in love every day." He paused. "Or I did. Before."

I closed my eyes, imagining him on the ground at my feet, his sweet mouth open and his tongue out. "I'm going to teach you to love pain so much you can't tell the difference between it and pleasure."

"Or the difference between pain and love?" He said it with a sarcastic slide that made me smile. He was such a masochist, and the sadist in me was roused by that.

At the same time, best to nip this in the bud.

"Love comes in a lot of forms; some of those are painful. But there's a difference between abuse and the fun kind of pain."

"Oh, no. Is this a lecture? I've already had one of those today from my friend."

"Well, you're a very naughty boy, so I bet you need a lecture several times a day." I watched as Terry put the copy of *Hustler* down on the rack, and then moseyed on out the door, leaving me alone in the shop with the college girls.

"Lectures don't do it for me, Sir. Spankings? Yes. Those clothespins you hurt me with? Yes. But they aren't enough. So, what's next? What are you going to do now to keep me in line?"

"Do you really want to know? Or do you want it to be a surprise?"

"This one!" a girl said, holding up an enormous, purple dinosaur-dong novelty dildo. "Let's buy this one. She'll love it."

"She'll choke on it!" another cried.

"It doesn't go in her mouth, dummy. It goes in her pussy."

They all cracked up at that, while the girl who'd uttered the p-word covered her mouth like she'd said something unforgivable.

"You're doing all right?" I asked again, trying to remember what my responsibilities were to him as a Dom. "You're in a good place? Mentally?"

"I'm in a very bad place, Sir," he whispered. "In my head, I'm on my knees with your cock in my mouth, and—"

"Mister, we'd like to buy this." The girl's voice was sharp and impatient as she plopped the dino-dong on the counter. She flipped her long red hair over her leather-coated shoulder and stared at me like I was going to deny her the right to her novelty gift.

"Mitchell, I have to go."

"Yes, Sir."

"I'll see you at my house tomorrow night at 6 p.m. Eat dinner first. I won't be feeding you until we're done."

"Yes, Sir."

The redhead popped a faint brow, a sneer on her lips. "Mister, are you on a personal call at work? Because we'd like to buy this *now*, please."

I rolled my eyes, turned my back to her, and whispered, "Be clean, inside and out."

"Yes, fucking Sir, aye-aye, Cap'n. Clean as a whistle."

My heart softened, thinking of him in his dorm room, sitting on his bed, the phone pressed to his ear, saluting me from afar. "Don't forget, I'm the only who gets to hurt you."

"I remember."

"Mister!"

Minty giggled. "Sounds like someone is in dire need of a vibrator."

"A dino-dong actually, but yes. Later, Mitchell."

"Later, Sir."

After taking the cash off the redhead and her friends and sending them away with the novelty dildo wrapped up in a discreet bag, I sat back on the stool and considered putting another call through to Minty. But I shouldn't seem overeager. I was the Dom after all.

He was the one who should come begging.

Chapter Eight

Minty

"CLOTHES OFF," LUKE said to me as soon as I entered his house again.

No sweet greetings then. No "how was your day, honey?" or a kiss on the lips or a hug. Nothing that could be construed as a relationship.

That was the way I'd wanted it, though, right? If he asked me how I'd been, or tried to be tender with me, then I'd forget the real reason I was here and, in the end, I wouldn't be satisfied. I'd go back to Kyle. Though, I was beginning, more and more, to wonder if my need for Kyle's pain and my need for Luke's pain were entirely different things, and if they might be able to exist side by side.

Not that they *should.*

But I hadn't been able to stop thinking of Kyle after I got off the phone with Luke the night before. It hadn't made sense. By all rights, I should have been thinking only of what Luke might do to me once he had me naked and restrained in his basement, but instead my mind had run to Kyle—wondering what *he* was doing, whether he'd noticed I hadn't come back around, and whether or not he cared.

I wanted him to care.

Which was sick. Messed up.

I wanted Kyle to give a shit about me, and not just because I was the hottest hole he'd ever gotten his rocks off inside. I wanted him to care that I wasn't coming over to offer myself up to him any longer. Because if he cared about me? If he not only blew his load like a volcano in my ass, despite hating himself, but if he also started wondering if I was okay, wanting to protect me? Then what kind of all-powerful god was I? *Any* small god can make a guy come, but it takes an omnipotent one to turn a straight guy gay and harness his sexual desire into affection as well.

But Kyle hadn't called, hadn't come by, hadn't sought me out since he'd choked me into unconsciousness and left me for dead.

And now I was here with Luke in his dungeon, and he was going to torment me until I lost my mind. *He* was going to be the god, and I was going to be the plaything.

Fuck.

How was I supposed to get my power needs met when I was the one giving up control? When I was letting myself be used, and hurt, and brought to the brink of sanity by a guy who loved doing it?

Not that I wasn't excited about our night ahead. I'd had to fight the urge to jerk off all day just thinking about what Luke might do to me. But there were different kinds of needs in this world. I loved being punished for being a bad person, but I also loved being so almighty and formidable that I was elevated to a status beyond good and bad, beyond morality.

That I became pure, blinding power.

"Did you hear me?"

I snapped back to the present. "No, Sir. I'm sorry, Sir."

Luke tilted his head. "Are you with me now?"

"Yes, Sir."

He pondered me, his brow furrowed. "Are you in this with me?"

"Yes, Sir."

He nodded. "All right. The scene begins now. Our safe word is poodle."

"Yes, Sir."

Luke snarled, grabbing hold of my hair and tugging hard enough that stars burst in my vision. "Clothes off."

I undid the snap front of my short blue jean skirt, kicked away the material where it fell, and then started on the buttons of my loose, lacy blouse. I looked like a whore in this outfit, the kind that literally walked the streets, but it worked because I *felt* like a whore turning up at Luke's house to get beaten up and fucked. I didn't know what he thought of the outfit, but I knew Kyle would have lost his mind over it. He'd have beaten the shit out of me and then fucked me into oblivion.

"Pick it all up," Luke said, releasing my hair and motioning at the clothes. "Go down the stairs. Put them on the chair. Wait on your knees."

I smirked. "And if I don't?"

Luke's smirk outdid my own. Slowly, he reached out and took hold of my balls, squeezing them until I broke into a sweat. I held onto his arms for balance. Panting, nausea rolled in my gut. "Yes, Sir. I understand, Sir."

Luke released me, made sure I could stand on my own, and then opened the basement door. He stood aside, waiting with his arms crossed over his t-shirt, his bare feet wide apart and his jeans hugging his already hard package.

The basement was the same as when I last saw it, except he'd changed the sheets on the bed. They were now a royal red, and the white comforter lay folded on one corner.

I set the clothes on the chair just as I had last time and carefully knelt, my knees digging into the coarse concrete, and my balls still twinging from the rough handling upstairs. The sweat that had burst out on my skin was drying now, leaving me shaky and a little cold.

The lights went out.

I held very still.

A flashlight beam came down the stairs, and then Luke descended after it, his jeans still on, but bare-chested. His swooping blond hair danced around his face and the shadows bounced off the walls. He crossed to a lamp and turned it on, put the flashlight down next to it, and then faced me. The low glow made the room shadowy and soft, mysterious in a way.

"Slut, open your mouth."

I did. My cock, which had been half-hard, grew fully erect.

Luke crossed to me. The lamp backlit him so I couldn't see his face well in the low light of the room. When he reached me, he shoved his fingers into my throat. I gagged and tears sprang to my eyes. Wrenching my head back, I jerked away from his probing.

"What the fuck?" I spit out, the back of my throat aching from his touch there.

The slap on my cheek rocked my head to the side and the tears that had gathered from the gagging spilled over. Holy shit, he wasn't being gentle or pussyfooting around tonight. He was going for cruelty, and suddenly I wasn't sure I could handle it.

With Kyle, I knew what to expect—senseless brutality—and in that way I had the control. Now, here with Luke, with all the options spread out around us—whips, clips, chains, restraints—I abruptly realized just how much I didn't understand about what I'd signed up for when I'd checked all those boxes. My heart raced, my hands started to shake, and when I got my head back center, chin up and gaze focused on the shadow where his eyes must be, I gritted my teeth against the temptation to poodle out of this.

"You'll accept whatever I put in your mouth, or ass, or ear, or bellybutton, or any other hole or crevice in your body. Understood, slut?"

"Yes, Sir," I whispered.

"Open your fucking mouth."

I did, shocked that my jaw was trembling, and he put his hand on the back of my head to hold me steady. He shoved his fingers back into my throat and explored the soft tissue there. I gagged, making horrific sounds, but I hadn't eaten much all day, and I'd cleaned my ass out thoroughly in the dorm bathrooms before coming. I was as empty as I could get.

"Look at you," he whispered.

I gagged again as he wriggled his fingers around.

"Now hold still." He shoved his fingers deeper. My eyes rolled back. I convulsed as I retched hard, and a rush of stomach acid filled my mouth. He released my head and withdrew his fingers. "Swallow."

I did. I had no choice. Spit and mess were all over my chin and some of it burned into my nostrils. My eyes stung.

"Open again."

Reluctantly, I did, and this time he unzipped his pants, pulled out his cock, and pressed it into my mouth. I opened wide, tilted my head back as he stepped forward into my space, and let him go deep into my throat. I held myself still, letting him feel my throat work him as tears ran from my eyes. My chest ached. I needed to breathe, but I couldn't pull oxygen in around his girth.

"All I'd have to do is put my hands here," he whispered, sliding his fingers into my hair and holding my head steady. "And I could choke you out just like that."

I groaned. I'd been choked out from a dick only one other time. Of course the guy to do it had been Kyle. He loved making me go unconscious for him.

Luke pulled free, and I gasped for air. He didn't put himself away again entirely, leaving his pants unzipped and unbuttoned, but he tucked his dick inside, taking a step back.

His gaze was too soft. He almost looked pleased with me, and I didn't want that. Not now.

"Are you ever going to hurt me? You keep saying you will, but then you don't. Sir." I purposely tacked on the honorific in the most disrespectful way possible.

His eyes shone with merciless excitement and arousal. "Oh, you fucking brat. You don't even know what you're asking me to do to you."

I squeezed my fists tightly. The fear of what I'd brought on myself rushed through me like a drug. I was instantly higher than I'd ever been from a bump of coke. "Show me then," I bit out. "I want to find out."

"Oh, you will," he whispered, grabbing me by the hair again and hauling me to my feet. "When I'm done with you, you'll be wishing you could eat those words."

"I doubt it, Sir. I doubt it very much," I panted as he tugged me across the room by my hair.

He spun me around, pushed me to a wall, and only hesitated for a moment when he saw the lingering bruises from his spanking on my bare ass.

"Holy shit," he whispered, before lambasting me with a harsh smack of his hand. "Still covered in my marks. Jesus Christ, boy, I'm going to maul you up good."

"Fuck yes, Sir," I said on a whine, as the pain of pummeled bruises gripped me. "Hurt me. I need it."

The swats escalated, and once I was shouting, clawing at the wall with my fingers and dancing from foot to foot in agony, he suddenly stopped. As I tried to catch my breath, he was there behind me, pushing himself against my back.

"Mitchell?"

"Yes, Sir."

"You're going to feel that for a week."

"I hope so, Sir." I felt dizzy, endorphins tracing through my veins. I wanted to go flying again like I had last time.

"But first you're going to scream for me."

Luke

I KNEW THE easiest way to take his breath away, to transport him to another place, would be to hurt the most sensitive part of him. Plus, I always had fun doing that to a submissive, especially if they'd never had it done before—and I knew Minty hadn't—because invariably, at some point, there was utter terror in their eyes, and my inner sadist got off super hard on that.

I considered his poor bruised ass, glancing between the bed and the bench, and finally decided on strapping him to the bench. He was a pain slut. He'd like the additional discomfort of his bruised butt on a harder surface than a mattress.

"C'mere," I said, pulling him forward into a cuddle against my chest. I cupped his head and pressed his tear-wet face against my pecs. "Lick my tits."

He didn't hesitate, licking and sucking my nipples with his greedy mouth. I stroked his hair, letting him work, getting hard again as he did. I decided to quickly, succinctly take him apart so that he'd shortly be a screaming, begging mess.

"Stand up straight, slut," I said, tugging him off my nipple with a quick jerk to his hair. He must have had bruises on his scalp from all the hair pulling the other night and earlier because he winced harder than before, and enough tears came to his eyes that a few drops slipped down his cheeks. Fuck, that was beautiful. I wondered what it would take to make him truly cry. Those were tears of pain, not the sobs of a cracked-open boy laying his soul bare for the man who'd mastered him.

"Over here," I said, dragging him by the hair again to the bench and shoving him down toward it. He was aroused, his cock pearling at the tip with pre-cum. I wished part of this scene could involve me sucking him off, but I also knew that wasn't what Mitchell needed. If any part of my mouth was going to touch his cock or balls, it'd be my teeth. No sweetness. Not for Mitchell. Not today.

Positioning him on the bench, I got the restraints ready. I showed them to him. "What's your safe word again, slut?"

"Poodle, Sir."

"Say it if you need to," I said, though I was sure he would. Our prior scene experience had proven that, though I was still sorry he'd had to use it at all due to a hard boundary being hit mistakenly.

"Yes, Sir."

I strapped him up the way I wanted—head to the bench, hips to the bench, ankles to a short spreader bar, and wrists to ankles which kept him open and exposed. He was shivering, his nipples hard and his cock harder. When I had him locked down, I reached for his nipples and pinched them both, hard and long, until he whimpered and squirmed from the pain.

"Look at this nasty hole," I said, leaning close to get a good look at his anus, checking for any tears from where I'd fucked him last time. I knew he was at increased risk for infection, but if I went too easy on him, he'd hurt himself worse with someone else. "Your hole's hungry for my cum isn't it, bitch?"

"Yes, Sir."

I slapped the knot of muscle hard, accidentally grazing his bruised ass cheeks too.

He jolted. "Sir!"

"You don't get my cum in your ass until you've earned it."

"How can I earn it?" he begged. "I'll do anything, Sir. I want your cum."

I spit on him, aiming for his face but hitting his chest, and then I gave in to my own lusts and knelt to dive between his cheeks. I stuck my tongue up his hole, licking and sucking as he squirmed against the restraints and panted, whining with pleasure. When his asshole started fluttering around my tongue eagerly, I pulled back and bit the flaring rim. He screamed, more in shock than pain.

"That's just the start," I whispered, standing up and wiping my mouth with the back of my hand. "You're going to beg me to stop before we're through."

He shook his head, his eyes dilated and his breath coming fast. "No, Sir. I won't. I want it. Hurt me. Hurt me so bad I won't forget it for the rest of my life." He laughed bitterly. "My short fucking life."

I didn't think he knew what he was granting me permission to do, though I'd made sure the checklists and forms were very clear, and he'd understood exactly what he was offering up at the time. But new subs never really understood. Not until they'd experienced it.

I wondered if he'd use his safe word again. I was all right with that. That's what it was for…

"Get ready," I told him, touching his cock with one finger, sliding it to the tip. He tried to lift his hips, but the restraints held him steady. "This is going to hurt."

Minty

I HADN'T KNOWN.

I hadn't realized the possibilities.

All the excruciating, tormenting, awful, glorious possibilities.

At least not when I'd checked off Cock & Ball Torture on the checklist of kinks I agreed were on the table for our scenes, but *now* I knew.

My dick and nuts were trussed up with leather ties so tight that they were aching with constricted blood. My nipples were hurting in the teeth of some very wicked clamps that Sir had put on me just before he'd taken my breath away with the first flick of his fingers to my tight balls.

He'd started out just flicking them with his fingers, shockingly hurtful with them tied to bursting. Then he'd moved on to swatting them with his palm—which was gaggingly painful. Then he'd taken a riding crop down from the wall of implements, and now I had no idea where I ended and where pain began. I was riding on an endless loop of it, shocked I could still breathe. But I did, the breaths coming out dressed in screeches and screams, and all the while Sir kept on tapping my balls with that crop until I thought I'd throw up or die, or both.

Eventually, like hitting a wall, I felt that dizzying drop from my usual consciousness followed by wild, soaring flight. Up, up, up. High as I could possibly go. Pain wracked me, but my mind was elsewhere, dripping with honey and bliss. Pain transformed into pleasure, and the pleasure back to pain in an infinite pattern that I could feel, but barely understand.

"That's it," Sir said gruffly. "Been waiting for this. Look at you. Just look at you."

He sounded happy about it, like he was praising me, but I didn't dwell on that. I focused on the pain. I wanted him to spit on me again, call me names, hit me, and demean me. I needed it. I begged.

Sir, like a god on high, answered my prayers. "Filthy slut. Nasty cum-dumpster. Begging like a pig for more. You want more, bitch? I'll give you more."

I moaned as he tugged on my ankle restraints, and then knelt on the short platform of leather padding I'd used to climb onto the bench. The position put his cock level with my hole. After a quick spit and a swipe of my pre-cum gathered in a pool on my belly, he nudged his cockhead inside my hole. I grunted as he pushed harder against my tender rim, still aching from his earlier bite.

"Sir," I whimpered. "It hurts."

He slapped my bruised ass, and I yelped. "It's gonna hurt more," he said, shoving in harder, and I shuddered all over.

I loved being rough-fucked. I loved it so much, possibly more than most anything else in life. I'd gone to hideous lengths to get boys to put their dicks in me like this, and yet none of them had ever had the creativity to tie my balls up while doing it. It took the pain to a whole other level.

Sir got fully seated inside me, and then he smirked. I'd already learned that was a dangerous expression on him, and I wanted to cover my genitals, prevent whatever was ahead now. But I couldn't.

He didn't go for them at first. Instead, he removed the clamps from my nipples, tossing them aside as I shouted at the sting of blood rushing back into my tender tissues. I jerked at the restraints, wanting to rub my nipples and grab my cock, torn between needing to soothe the pain and jerk off to the pleasure.

But Sir chose for me.

He took hold of my dick, stroking at the same tempo as his thrusts into me. With his other hand, he flicked my sore balls at random. I screamed, gagged again, and heaved. I almost threw up, but the sensations were far too entrancing for me to even consider saying poodle. I wanted this pain. I wanted to hurt.

I wanted Sir to own me body and soul, to make me his plaything, and for my body to be at his service. I stared up at him, seeing him as a god, as the god *I'd* been to Kyle—and found myself fascinated by his manly form. He was my master. I was his boy. I was going to suffer as long as he found it entertaining to make me scream and cry.

I loved it.

Here, split on his dick and enduring his pain, I was free. Just me, agony, and his thick cock in my ass rubbing against my prostate and making my insides sing in opposition to the breathtaking pain. It was stunning, and I was *stunned.*

"Filthy slut," Sir bit out between thrusts. "Look at your cum-hungry hole. You're just taking my cock like you were made for it. *Fuck.* You're a greedy whore."

"Spit on me," I pleaded. "Please, Sir. Please."

"You think you deserve my spit?" Sir snorted. "No, you only deserve this." He pulled out of my ass, stood up, and while I panted desperately, horny and empty and aching from head to toe, he pinched the head of his dick until his hard-on eased, and then he pissed on me.

Tied down like I was, I couldn't move, couldn't resist. The word poodle came to mind, but I didn't say it. Warm piss flowed over my hard cock, my throbbing balls, my heaving stomach, and filled my belly button. It was thicker than water, denser, and I was shocked to be so degraded, so used. He'd told me he would do it—and I'd checked the box on the list—but I hadn't known how it'd make me feel. Like trash. Like a dirty, used boy for Sir to humiliate. As I struggled through the feelings, he pissed up over my chest, and then into my gaping, shocked mouth. I sputtered, spitting it out.

"Swallow it," he ordered, gripping my jaw, re-aiming his dick and pissing the last of his stream inside. It tasted salty-sour, tangy and overwhelming, and I gagged again, but I managed to get it down.

"Mitchell," he said with a sneer. "You're going to regret spitting my piss out."

I gasped as he twisted my nipples brutally and then moved back down between my legs. I thought he'd fuck into me again, but instead I screamed as he ran something sharp over my balls. A knife? A fucking knife on my balls? I'd ticked off knife play, but hadn't he crossed it off again? When? How? I hadn't seen him get a knife.

I stared at the ceiling, my breath hitching in and out. Terror pooled in my gut. I felt like I was going to die or levitate from my body.

Looming over me, the bastard smiled—no, he fucking *grinned* like he was a demented monster, and I felt the stinging sensation across my balls again. Was he cutting them? Cutting *me*?

"*There* it is," he said with a sadistic tone. "There's the true fear I love to see. Been waiting for it to show up."

"Sir," I gasped. "Please…"

"You don't need your balls, do you, boy?"

I sobbed, fear wrenching through me so hard I rattled the bench with my shaking.

"Got a word you want to use?" he asked.

The sensation of splitting and cutting raked over my tight balls again. I screamed, pleaded, *begged*, but I wasn't going to say the word. I wasn't. I refused. If he cut me, severed my balls, then…I deserved it.

Sir looked like he might say more for a moment, but then he held up a blue, plastic ruler, demonstrating the sharp edge. "Not a knife, but it felt like one, huh?"

"Sir," I whimpered. "Sir…"

His eyes softened slightly, but I didn't want that.

"Don't, Sir," I grunted. "No."

His smirk returned. "You're shaking like a leaf. I love it."

He ran his hands over my body, and then pinched my tender nipples again, making me howl.

"Please, Sir," I whispered. "Please." I didn't even know what I was begging for, but he did.

"Think you deserve to come?" He asked, as he pushed two fingers into me and searched for my prostate. When he found it, I jolted. "Let's see if you can earn it."

He milked my prostate and watched my face with one of those grins that I'd now learned meant he had another painful, sadistic idea to throw at me.

He bent low and started biting my tight scrotum. Small nips that hurt like hell, but didn't break the skin. I clenched and released my toes, my prostate sparking pleasure through me, my cock throbbing, my nipples still screaming and my balls in an agony of sharp bites.

"Oh, fuck," I groaned, not sure how to get out of this, or how long it was going to last, but needing it over. I'd been scared witless, I'd been hurt, and now I wanted to come and be done with this endless torment. Being with Kyle was nothing like this. It was brutal and usually fast. This was long, drawn out, and I wasn't sure I could mentally take another moment of it.

I could say poodle, I could, but the darkest part of me wanted to break. I needed to see where this went next, what he'd do to me next. And I wanted to come. I *really* fucking wanted to come, to let the obliteration of orgasm wipe out all the rest. If I said poodle, I wouldn't get to come.

When Sir finally rose up over me and fucked into my ass again, this time lubed from whatever mystery access he had to accessories that I wasn't aware of, I groaned and closed my eyes. His cock was thick. His hands on my hips were steadying but rough. It was perfect.

"What do you say, bitch?"

"Huh?" I was dazed, not quite sure where I was in the world, but I knew I had to answer Sir, or he'd hurt me more. I'd been hurt enough for now. Probably. Maybe.

"What do you say, bitch? What do you tell me when you want this to be done?"

"Please," I whimpered. "Please, Sir. I need to come."

"Ah, you need to come?" He laughed softly and chill bumps rose on my skin. "Will this help then?"

He slapped my cock back and forth on my stomach in time to

his thrusts. My eyes rolled back, pain and pleasure twisting together in my mind.

With a nasty grin, Sir leaned over me and said, "Come on, Mitchell, show me what your cum-hungry hole wants from me. Or can't you get off like this?"

He slapped my cock again harder, harder, *harder*.

I shouted and cum spurted from my dick, ecstasy ripping through my gut in hard, pulsing clenches. I *screamed* as Sir grabbed my dick and worked it hard, jerking me past the point of endurance. Struggling against the restraints, shaking and panting, I begged, "Please stop, Sir. Stop, stop, Sir, please! Oh, Sir, I can't, I can't, Sir, please!"

"No," he said, laughing. "No fucking way."

"Sir!"

"No, you cunt. Take it."

His hand kept moving on me, and the thickness of his dick in my ass grew more and more uncomfortable. Pain wrenched me inside and out.

"No," I warbled. "Oh, *fuck* no."

He laughed.

A horrible, undeniable memory rose to the surface of my mind. It was too much. Too real. The pain was too familiar.

I meant to say poodle. I did. I really did.

"Stop, Daddy! Please, *please* stop! You're hurting me, Daddy, stop."

I was sobbing, crying with the words "Daddy" and "stop" on my lips yet again when I heard Sir declare, "Poodle."

Chapter Nine

Luke

I GOT MINTY out of his restraints and CBT bindings quickly. Pulling him to my chest, I cuddled him close, and he started gagging softly.

"You're all right, baby," I whispered. "I've got you. It's over. All that...now and *then*...it's all over."

He clutched me like a lifeline, and when I picked him up to carry him to the bed, he slung his arms around my neck, his smaller body heaving against mine. I couldn't believe that twice in our short time knowing each other, we'd both already called out of scenes.

I wondered if it was even emotionally safe for him to play these games. But then I reminded myself what he'd been doing to himself instead, and with whom, and I didn't think this could be much worse for him, and hopefully could still be better.

"I'm sorry," he whispered eventually, still clutching me as I held him on the bed now. "I ruined it."

"No, you're all right. It was an intense scene for your second time. I went too hard."

"No," he said, voice trembling. "If you went softer, I wouldn't ever come back. It *has* to be this. I need it like this. I need to hurt."

"Mitchell," I murmured, struggling not to kiss his temple.

He'd said no kissing. He'd been explicit about that, and I would respect every wish of his that was reasonable to entertain without letting him know I was doing it. And no kissing was one of them. "You don't have to talk to me now or ever, but I think you need to talk to someone."

He huffed. "Like who? A therapist? What are they going to do? Tell me it wasn't my fault that my father raped me?"

He said it with so much bitterness that I could taste it in my own throat. "Is that what happened?"

He nodded.

"And what we did just now? It triggered that memory?"

"The end, yeah. The part where all I felt was how thick your cock was and how much it hurt after I'd come..." He swallowed audibly and went on, "He raped me, and it hurt a lot, and I begged him to stop. I *begged* him."

"I'm so sorry," I soothed. "I know you did."

He went very still, and I waited. There was more. I didn't know what, but I knew it was big. Bigger even than the truth that his father had raped him. "I came," he whispered.

For a moment, I thought he meant earlier with me, but then I realized. "It's normal," I said. "People come from all kinds of things."

I should know. I regularly made people—even Mitchell himself—come from agony. "It doesn't mean anything."

"Doesn't it mean that deep down I enjoyed it?"

"Oh, baby, no."

"But I did, though. I came really hard, and he..." Minty went *very* still and then burrowed tighter against me. I held him fast. "He saw that I came, and I thought he'd kill me. He nearly did."

"I'm sorry. That should never have happened to you. It shouldn't happen to anyone."

"I hate him."

"I hate him for you," I said.

"I didn't *mean* to come," he whispered.

"Our bodies respond to stimuli," I reassured him. "That's all. Just like you came earlier for me despite how much pain I had put you through."

"But I liked what you did," he admitted. "It felt horrible." He shivered and whimpered. "I loved it."

"I loved hurting you," I said. "It felt good to me too."

I felt dizzy with anxiety. I'd never dealt with something like this, with someone in the grip of this kind of trauma.

We rested a moment in each other's arms, and he didn't pull away or get angry. I breathed in his scent, tried to let the smell of sweat and sex fill me up. I breathed through my fear, trying to talk myself down. He was whole, here with me, cognizant, and this was going to be fine. So what if I'd never dealt with anything like it before? I was here now. I had him. We'd get through this together.

But what if we couldn't? What if I didn't have what it took? Being with Minty was already more than I'd bargained for, and this? This was too much. It was terrifying to think at any second I could push him into a memory like this. I already *had* more than once. I didn't think playing with him was safe at all—not for him, and not for me.

"But wait," Minty said suddenly. "You never got to come."

He sat up, his eyelashes fluttering guiltily. "I could blow you. I'm really good at it."

"I know you are." I remembered just how good his throat felt. "But this has been a lot."

I felt a little sick, and the last thing I wanted right now was an orgasm. I just wanted to grab onto a flotation device and swim us both to a safe shore where we could find help because I sure as hell didn't know what to do with this. "We need to rest right now. We should cuddle, drink water, shower, and come down from all that."

He didn't argue with me. I guided him to the bathroom in the basement and turned on the rudimentary shower. As I washed us both, he leaned against me, trembling. Facing the showerhead with him beneath the spray, I soaped up his hair with relaxing, lavender-scented shampoo. He was nearly purring as he rubbed his face into my chest while I worked my fingers over his scalp. I tilted his chin back and rinsed the suds from his hair, and then took my turn under the warm stream. Afterward, I toweled him off and helped him sit on the small bench I kept in there while I dried myself too.

Back in the basement bed, he snuggled up against me. I stroked his back and arms, and he sighed. "This is nice," he whispered. "A year ago, I'd have wanted just this and not the other."

"Yeah?"

"Yeah."

"And that changed because…" I knew the answer.

"The diagnosis."

"So, if you weren't positive, you wouldn't want me to hurt you?"

He squirmed. "I don't know. I think maybe yes, but I'd want this part more than the pain." He indicated where my arms were latched around his waist. "I used to be a romantic, you know. In love with love."

"You're still a romantic."

He snorted. "You just put me through hell, and you think I'm a romantic?"

"I know you are. No one takes pain like that without being a romantic at their core. You want flowers, kisses, anniversary trips to romantic hotels, and you also want to give up your whole self to someone and trust they'll know what you need."

"I did want all those things," he agreed. "Now I don't know what I want. I think I just want to feel something other than dread."

"Is this working, though?" I whispered. Maybe he'd say what I was afraid to say right now, but what I suspected I might have to say later. This wasn't a good fit. *We* weren't. "This is the second time what we're doing together has brought up—" I stopped.

"I know," he admitted with a shrug. "I didn't expect that. You'd think what I do with Kyle—" He patted my arm. "I mean did. What I *did* with Kyle. I'm not doing it anymore, I promise. Anyway, you'd think it was more like what my father did to me."

He sighed. "And it *is* more like it. In every way. It's why I'm drawn to it."

My stomach twisted. "What do you mean?"

He shook his head. "I don't want to explain it. Not now."

I let his rejection of my request sink in for a moment. He'd sounded final. A firm boundary. I wasn't going to poke at it. Not tonight. Maybe I didn't even want to know. If I wasn't going to be his Dom going forward, he didn't owe me anything at all.

"All right," I agreed.

He wound his arms around my arms, helping me to hold him. We were silent for a long time, letting our breaths sync up, letting our skin cool down.

"It probably sounds stupid to you, but I want to stay here in this room forever," he said eventually.

I ran my eyes over the implements, the bench, the table, and the cross on the wall.

"It's not stupid. This room is a safe place." Or it had been, until tonight. Now I felt like this room wasn't the place of control it'd always been for me. Minty's past made it a dangerous room with dangerous play.

Minty laughed. "Oh, God. No, it's not. This room is terrifying. But here…"

"Here, you're not in reality."

"Yeah."

"It's an addictive feeling. I know." Had I gotten him hooked on something that now I didn't know if I could continue to deliver?

The nausea ramped up, and I hoped I was hiding my discomfort. "Unfortunately, I have to go to work, and you have school, so…neither of us can stay here forever."

He chuckled, that same dark noise I'd heard over the phone. "I'd be willing to drop out. Live here with you. Clean your house. Suck your cock. It'd be a great job. And I could love you," he said softly, turning in my arms and clinging to me a little shyly. "I think I already do."

I remembered what Barry had said, warning me the kid fell in love with someone new every day and would probably fall for me too. He'd confessed to it himself, hadn't he? I rubbed Mitchell's back some more and said, "That's a pretty dream. Why don't you think about that while you fall asleep right now? When you wake up in a few hours, we'll need to go our separate ways."

"Or I could just stay here," he said again, his fingers digging into my skin. "Wait for you to come back from work…"

Despite my doubts, I was tempted. Minty was such a gorgeous sub. When he was in pain, he shone with it, and it did all kinds of wonderful things to my libido. Hell, spending more time with him might even be the *right* thing to do, given the kid's upset earlier.

But I also knew if I said yes now, it'd just lead to Minty thinking this relationship was going to be more than it was. More than I was thinking it would ever be possible to give him. I wasn't going to be enough for him, not with all the baggage he was carrying around.

I was scared, and that was no place to Dom from. I needed time to think.

"You'll go back to your dorm," I said firmly. "There'll be no more talk about staying."

He went still at my side, his breathing halting for a long moment. He sat up and gazed down at my face, but after a few moments he murmured, "Yes, Sir. I promise."

"Good." I tugged him to my side and cuddled him close, wondering if this would be the last time I held him.

Minty

"WHAT DO YOU think love is?" I asked, sipping the beer my best friend Daniel had brought with him along with the takeout pizza he'd picked up from Stefano's on the Strip. I figured if anyone knew the answer to my question, it'd be Daniel. He was newly in love, and he had a good idea of how to be a boyfriend, how to treat someone the way they deserved to be treated.

Ha. The way I "deserved" to be treated? What even was that anyway?

"It's desiring the other person's happiness above your own," Daniel said. He made it sound so simple and obvious that for a moment I felt dumb. "Why do you ask?"

"I'm considering falling in love for real." I bit into the pizza, the cheese sticking to the roof of my mouth and burning it. Another injury to go with the bruises Luke had left on me.

Daniel took a swig from his own beer bottle, and I could tell he was calculating a response. This was one of the reasons I'd been avoiding him lately—not returning his calls, not answering the door when he knocked, and never going out to his house in Kingston. Not even when I was in the area visiting my mother. Daniel was just too *good*. It was annoying.

"Is this about the guy Barry has you seeing?"

I bristled. "I'm not a child. I'm not being sent off to sex therapy by my daddy."

Daniel raised a hand. "I didn't say you were."

"I just wanted to know about love. Don't make this about *that*."

"About what?"

I couldn't answer because *I* didn't even know what I meant. There was just something about Daniel and his perfect face, his gorgeous body, his wealthy background, and his wholesome life and brand-new perfect love that kept getting under my skin ever since my diagnosis.

Daniel would never turn up HIV positive. *Daniel* used condoms every time he fucked. Even with his precious Peter, probably.

Not that I hadn't also used condoms every time I'd had sex. At least for the last few years until I got my HIV diagnosis. It's just that one broke. The wrong one.

Daniel's condoms would never break. Not that I wanted one to break. I adored him.

God, I was a mess of contradictions these days.

The phone in my room started ringing. I stared at it. Daniel stared at me.

"Aren't you going to get that?" he asked.

I shrugged.

My answering machine picked up.

You've reached the pony-est, golden-est, most sparkling boy in the whole wide world. Me! Leave your name and number, and I'll think about calling you back. If you're my type. Ha!

I remembered recording the message. I'd been in a great mood. The first day of the school year. That was before I'd decided to go get myself a horrible diagnosis for my mother's birthday.

"You haven't come around."

It was Kyle. His voice sounded stilted and rough, but beneath it was a vulnerability I was certain only I could pick up.

"I know I was rough last time. Maybe too rough. But you usually like that…"

Daniel's eyes were glued to my face. I held completely still, going for impassive and unbothered.

"Listen. I'll go less hard. Not soft. You don't fucking deserve soft. Besides, I'm no fag…" His breath hitched. *"But you are."* The sound of his swallow came through. *"Come over. I'll be around."*

Daniel's jaw worked.

"But don't you dare fucking call me and leave any of those god-damn queer messages on my machine like you used to do. It gives people the wrong idea."

I sighed. Kyle was never going to be happy caught up like he was in what other people thought of him. He liked boy-pussy better than girl-pussy—if he even liked girl-pussy at all—and he needed to accept it.

The way I saw it, in my own way, I'd been *helping* him to accept it. I'd been *forcing* him to. Making him admit to himself again and again that *I* made him come his brains out, that *I* made his knees tremble and his muscles spasm as he shot his load. *Me.*

Daniel twisted his fingers into the hem of his t-shirt, his knuckles going white as the message went on.

"But get your ass back over here. Or the next time I see you, I'll remind you why you shouldn't ignore me."

Another beat, a strange huff of vulnerable breath, and then a threat: *"You have one day."*

The dial tone rang through the room for a long moment after the disconnecting click. My machine switched off.

The tension between me and Daniel, already high, ratcheted up even more. It felt like air was water, and I was pulling it in through my nose by sheer force alone. Daniel gazed at me, full of judgment.

"Minty..." He reached for my hand, and I didn't let him take it.

I shouldn't have let him come to my dorm room today. I should have continued to avoid him. I knew my irritation made no sense. Not even two months ago, I'd have beaten up anyone who told me I'd ever feel this way about Daniel.

Despite how grating he was nowadays, I still loved him. I'd once been *in* love with him, back in high school, in another life. He'd been my first love, actually, but he never saw me that way. He'd dated a dreamboat named Kevin back then, and by the time *that* ended, he'd put me firmly into the box labeled "Friends." Maybe I never had a chance with him, but now I didn't *want* a chance with him, because who could stand all that sheer goodness lying in bed next to them every day?

Peter, apparently. And Peter could have him.

I wanted someone who'd say horrible things to me, spit on me, and fuck me like I was scum beneath their shoes like Kyle did. But I wanted all that and then to be tucked up in bed and held tight. The way Luke had held me after my breakdown.

God only knew if Luke would *ever* be willing to meet with me again. I'd told him too much. He had to be wondering what he'd gotten himself into…

New anger bubbled up beneath the old. I'd probably fucked things up with Luke too. Maybe I should go back to Kyle after all. He didn't ask questions… He didn't bring up the bad memories of being helpless, just the good ones of being powerful. Of being a god.

"Why are you angry with me?" Daniel asked, tilting his head like a golden retriever. I wanted to punch him. "I just want to help you."

I bit into my pizza slice and chewed furiously. He sat cross-legged across the rainbow rug I'd bought for the floor of my dorm room. It was soft beneath our butts. When I swallowed, I dropped my slice back in the cardboard. "You think it's wrong, don't you? What I'm doing."

"What *are* you doing?" Daniel asked. "I don't even know." He let his slice glide back into the box, and fuck me if it didn't slot right back into the place he'd picked it up from. Aside from the missing bites, it looked like he'd never touched it to begin with. He was magic.

"You won't even talk to me."

"I was *trying* to talk to you. I asked about love. You belittled my feelings."

His mouth dropped open, and his eyes went wide. "I answered you seriously, and I just wanted to know who the question was about."

"It's about my Dom, my lover, my sadistic fuck-machine."

Daniel blinked. "Does he have a name?"

"Not that you need to know."

"Minty… What's happening? Why are you being like this?"

Guilt tugged at my gut. Daniel had taken care of me in high school, protected my femme ass from all the bullies and used his rich boy clout to keep me safe.

After the rape, he'd taken me to therapy appointments and went to every court date and even gave damning testimony about my father's character. In college, he'd protected me while I went on acid trips, and shroom trips, and pot-laced country drives trying to outrun my demons.

Why was I doing this to him? The hurt in his eyes said he didn't know either.

"You just try too hard," I said. "You act like you're okay with what I'm doing, but you're not. You think it's gross. You think *I'm* gross."

"I've never thought that."

"You think it was inevitable that I'd turn up positive. Because I'm trash, and you know I'm trash, and you think I *like* being treated like trash."

"For fuck's sake, I've never said or thought *anything* like that."

"You wouldn't," I shot back, hot with anger that boiled incessantly in my gut. "Because you're too fucking nice to think it."

"I love you, and you're angry and scared, and"—he took hold of my hand—"a few weeks ago, you came to me and asked me to pray with you, and I did. Peter and I both did. We all cried, and I thought we'd made some kind of headway together. That you were going to let me help you, and—"

"I don't want your help," I said, tears stinging my eyes at the reminder of the Kumbaya moment I'd shared with them a few weeks before. I'd gone to him because he'd always been my safe harbor in any storm, and even with Peter being there, less of a stranger than before, but still new in my life, I'd felt safe. Just long enough to let myself feel hopeful for half a minute. The crash of despair afterward had been something awful.

Mitigated later by Kyle's violence, of course.

God, just sitting here with Daniel's perfect face was making me itch to run to Kyle. I scrubbed a hand over my hair. What was wrong with me? I was ruining everything. I wished I was back in Luke's basement. Nothing could be ruined there. Even if I used my safe word, things weren't ruined. They were just… changed.

I could be as ugly, angry, furious, hateful, spiteful, and un-sparkly as I wanted, and Luke didn't walk away. He just made me feel something else instead. He made me hurt.

"What are you thinking about?" Daniel said. "Your face is…" He waved at his own. "All over the place."

"I'm thinking that I'm a fuck-up, and you're amazing, and I shouldn't be such a dick to you."

Daniel's eyes flashed with agreement—at least with the part where I shouldn't be treating him like this. "You're angry, and you're taking it out on me. I have experience with that. Hell, I've lived that recently."

Right. While I was busy breaking down over my impending doom, Daniel was busy trying to wrangle a little brother and sister while his mom weathered yet another alcoholic storm and her subsequent stay in rehab. His life wasn't all sunshine and puppies and roses. He had a dead dad, for crying out loud. And yet…

Compared to me?

He had everything.

"I know you want to help, and honestly, you haven't done anything wrong," I said, standing up and kicking the pizza box aside. "But you have to go. I need you to back off from me for a while. I need to figure my life out on my own now. I don't need you here trying to fix me."

"I don't want you to feel alone," Daniel said, rising too. He towered over me. "I never want you to be alone, Minty."

"There you go. Thanks, but no thanks, *Dad*," I let the full weight of sarcasm fall on the last word. "Just stop. Please. Save all that fatherly support for your sister and brother. Save it for your mother. Hell, save it for Peter if that's your kink, but get it away from me. I don't want that paternalistic bullshit right now."

"What do you want then? I'll do my best to give it to you."

I opened my dorm room door. "Right now, I want to be left the fuck alone. Go home. Take some pizza with you—" I said, moving to shove a piece into his hand as I grabbed the beer from his other. "Leave the beer behind, though."

I took a swig from it. A six-pack would go a long way to quieting the simmering rage beneath my skin. "Just go."

"Don't forget I love you," Daniel said, dragging his feet toward the open door. He still carried the piece of pizza. "Please don't do anything crazy. Should I call Barry? He can get his friend to—"

"I don't need Barry or his 'friend' or you. Please get out."

Daniel's eyes filled with tears, and because I was in full dickhead mode, satisfaction welled up in me seeing them.

"I just want to help," Daniel said, gruffly. "We've been best friends for a long time, and we'll get through this, but you need to—"

"But *you* need to go," I said, shoving him out of the room. "I'll call you when I'm ready to talk. Don't call me."

I shut the door in his startled face and leaned back against it. I felt like I should cry, but I wasn't even close to tears anymore. I was humming, buzzing with anger and anxiety. I downed the rest of Daniel's beer, picked up mine and downed it too.

After peeking out my peephole to make sure he was gone, I grabbed my keys from my desk and decided on a course of action. I had a few places I could go to get out of my body, out of my head, and into another world—

Kyle's dorm room.

Or Luke's basement.

And a third option that I hadn't taken advantage of in a few months.

I strode down the hallway of my dorm, down the stairs, and out into the autumn light. Daniel's figure was visible heading toward the library where Peter worked—no doubt going to cry on his shoulder. I turned the opposite direction.

It was the opposite direction from Kyle's dorm too.

I tracked down my truck where it was parked on Neyland Drive and jammed my keys in the ignition. Two beers didn't make for an entirely sober Minty, but I was far from drunk either. My liver was good at filtering all sorts of alcohol and drugs. I'd tested it plenty of times.

Pulling out into traffic, I pointed my car west. We'd see if I could handle this in a different way. With a different kind of pain. In another space.

Chapter Ten

Luke

"I THINK I'M in over my head," I said, sipping a beer and watching Barry wipe down the bar. His bald head glinted in the low light, and he moved slower than usual. He'd been at the library earlier working a shift, and I could see he was exhausted.

He and Robert were building a house on land he'd inherited out in Strawberry Plains, but scraping together the necessary funds was taking a toll. Between Robert in the guise of Renée doing her drag act in Nashville the last few weekends, and the expense associated with trying to get her documentary film about the art of drag into the festival circuit, the financial stress was coming down hard on Barry. I could tell.

I'd recommended professional domination to him a few times as a much more lucrative side gig. With Barry's background and his easy but firm manner, he could make some good cash. But Barry had shaken his head when I suggested it. He and Robert had an open relationship, he said, but that kind of thing would feel like cheating.

"I'm not just in the deep end of the pool," I went on. "I might be in the deep end of the ocean."

"With Minty?" Barry asked, looking up from working out a stain on the bar, his eyebrows furrowing.

I nodded and took another sip.

That got his attention. He tossed the rag aside, and came to lean his elbows on the counter, studying me. "The deep end of the ocean, huh?"

"I thought I was well-versed in all this. I've read the pamphlets out of Chicago's Hellfire Club, and the stuff from New York about trauma and consent. I've discussed the psychology of S&M with Jerome and his friends at length, and I've seen a lot of wild stuff go down with subs over the years…"

"You've been in the trenches." Barry agreed. "That's why I chose you."

"I know. But Minty's got some big fucking issues." I paused, examining Barry's face, not sure if he knew or not. "Things that might get in the way of us being a good fit. With *any* of this being a good fit, really."

"Ah," Barry said, straightening up and starting to clean the counter again. "The situation with his father."

"You know about it?"

Barry nodded. "Violent toward him and his mom his whole life, and then when he was …" He glanced up at me, his expression grim. "You know the rest?"

We eyed each other until we both felt sure we both knew, and then began talking around it anyway. "I think so," I said.

"He didn't tell you about it?" Barry asked. "I thought you had an intake process for that kind of thing."

"I asked the usual questions, yes, but he didn't give the full picture."

"Meaning?"

"I asked about a history of assault. He put down yes, but then went on to write that he'd deliberately sought it out and even asked for it, and I assumed—"

"Ah," Barry said, shaking his finger at me. "That's where you went wrong, isn't it? Assuming anything. I'm surprised you made a mistake like that. I never knew you were human enough to screw up that bad, Luke."

I rolled my eyes and swallowed more beer, pushing down the guilt. It was true. I'd wanted to blame Minty at first, put it on him for 'withholding' relevant information. But the truth was I hadn't followed up. I'd been...

What?

Too arrogant? Too worried about my own history? Too convinced that I knew what this kid needed and why? I'd assumed he carried around plenty of self-loathing—check—and a need to be humiliated—check—and had a taste for pain of all kinds—check.

But I hadn't dug deeper than his answers on the form. I'd let myself assume his issues were the usual—being bullied, being queer, being positive, being powerless when he needed to be powerful.

And that was all true, especially the last, but the *way* it was true was...

Christ.

I didn't quite know how to handle something like that.

"You know how subs come in a few flavors?" I asked.

"Go on." Barry waited for me to explain.

"Like some subs come into a scene because they're wanting to experience a certain kind of stimulus—pain, bondage, whatever. That's it. That's *all* they want. They trust me to give it to them, and I get off on that."

"Uh-huh."

"But other subs come into the scene seeking *relationship*—that really beautiful interaction that can only happen between a Dom and a sub who are both feeding into each other's needs and wants."

Barry gazed steadily at me.

I scrubbed a hand over my face. "I assumed—no, I *know* that Minty thinks he's the first kind of sub. Here for the pain and nothing else. But..." I shook my head. "Given his circumstances, I don't know if that's even safe for him—"

"Safe for you either."

"Right. Should *I* take on the emotional risk of applying the stimulus he wants when the fallout is so great and so unpredictable? Especially when we don't have, and he doesn't seem to want, the safety of an in-the-scene and out-of-the-scene relationship to balance it out."

"So, you're going to bail?" Barry asked, reading my mind like the asshole he was. "He's too much for you?"

I sighed. "You make me feel like a shit when you put it like that."

"I'm not *making* you feel anything," he said.

Goddamn, he really would make a good Dom.

"Right," I agreed. "I'm worried I'll fuck it up. Fuck *him* up."

"Minty's already fucked up."

"Yeah, but this is a fine line I'm walking. So fine, it's nearly invisible. I tip over one way, and I damage him. I tip over the other, and I lose him. He goes back to truly dangerous shit. I don't know where the bombs are. I hit two of them in our first few scenes together. I've never had to call a safe word so soon with anyone— not even when I was the sub—but during our last scene, I did it. I called it myself."

"Wow." Barry's brow wrinkled in concern. "Are you okay?"

I thought about that, really thought about it, as I took another long draw from my beer. "I don't know. There are things I can relate to with this kid. The fear of our mortality, the need to hurt someone—or in his case, the need to be hurt—and the yearning to say 'fuck the risks' to get what we need."

I paused and pressed my lips together. I didn't know what Barry would say about this, since he could be a stickler for safety. But what would "being safe" do for me now? Nothing whatsoever. The deal was done.

"I fucked him raw," I admitted, and waited for the backlash.

"And Minty agreed to that?" Barry laughed, low and rumbly, though not with any sort of amusement. "Why am I asking? Of course he did."

He let out a long *hmmph* sound, and then gazed at me knowingly. "There are other STDs, you know."

"Not from me," I said. "I've been tested and haven't fucked anyone since Benji months ago. If that changes, I'll suit up."

Barry blinked in surprise at that, but didn't question me. "And Minty? He's definitely not been celibate."

"It's my risk to take."

Barry shook his head. "With your diagnosis? That's foolish. You're willing to risk getting sick for raw sex with a sub?"

"Not a sub," I corrected. "*This* sub."

"Because he's positive too."

"Yes, but also…" I felt my face heating.

I was embarrassed to admit it, but I'd never gone bare as a top with anyone else before him. My HIV infection came from a rare, reckless adventure into bottoming with an untrustworthy top, and goddamn my fucking bad luck. "Look, we're getting off track now, talking about one kind of risk, when I'm worried about another."

He motioned at me to get on with it.

I sighed. "I thought *I* was going into it for the stimulus too. You know? Go in, hurt him, get off on his pain, get out. But…I don't think that's what I'm there for anymore."

"You realized you want the Dom/sub relationship."

I blinked, admitting, "I don't want to die without having had that again with someone in my life. And, messed up or not, fucking him raw brings me closer to what I'm looking for in the dynamic."

"Christ," Barry said, a hint of fed-up-ness in his tone, but also a note of understanding. He had to understand and relate to wanting more out of his sexual interactions. He loved Robert, after all. But I also knew they always used condoms because Robert slept around a lot, and was, so far, negative, and they wanted to keep it that way.

"I get it," he said, putting his hands up to ward off my defensiveness. "It's worth it to you because you're so sure you're going to get sick and die anyway. So, you're going to wring every drop of pleasure out of life now. If that's what you want, why aren't you shooting up heroin then? Sucking up a line of coke?"

"Because those aren't my drugs of choice," I said, calmly. "Believe me, if they were, I would."

"Your drug of choice is sadism."

"Yeah. I enjoy hurting people, and then loving them whole. The things they let me do to them make me dizzy. Minty? He'd let me do almost *anything*."

"Did he list any boundaries at all?"

"Not at first." I shook my head. "But, like I said, we stumbled on one. I didn't even see it coming."

I ran a hand over my neck. "He safe-worded almost immediately. I was proud of him for doing it, but also confused, and when he explained why..." I trailed off. "I should have called it all off then. I should have ended it at that moment because I'm not equipped for this, Barry. I don't know how to handle this safely for him."

"But you *haven't* called it off."

I shook my head. "No. Being his Dom is... heady. But this last time, we were in an intense scene, I was fucking him, and it was *so good*, but suddenly he—"

The contract between me and Minty didn't specify that what happened in our scenes was private, mainly because I wanted him to be able to talk about what we did together if he needed to seek out counsel for it. But this was the first time in my experience as a Dom that *I* needed to seek out counsel.

"What'd he do?" Barry asked.

"He started pleading for me to stop."

"Normal," Barry said. "I'm sure you were hurting him a lot by then."

"I was. But… he begged for *Daddy* to stop, and it wasn't me he was talking to."

Barry whistled low. "Oh, shit."

"I called the safe word, and he was…" I shook my head. "He was a mess. Still wanted to make me come, though." I chuckled. "Fuck. That was more than I knew to expect. I handled it as best as I could. Aftercare for hours until I had to leave for work, and when he left my place, he seemed a little light on his feet, woozy and high still, but all right enough. But now I can't stop thinking that I should have ended things completely the first time he used his safe word. I'm not equipped for this."

"You keep saying that, but really who would be?" Barry asked, and I sensed he meant it both ways—that of course I wasn't, but also, sincerely, who out there was a better option than me for this? "He's self-destructive and near suicidal in his risk-taking lately. If not you? Then who? Are you just going to leave him to it?"

I scrubbed a hand over my face. "He's not my responsibility."

Barry tilted his head, observing me.

"In a scene, he is, yes. But this…"

"I get it. If it's too much, it's too much."

I squeezed my eyes shut, a sense of failure dropping over me, reminding me of every other time in my life I'd let myself or someone else down, starting with my father and ending with Benji. Or would it be ending with Minty?

"I'm not sure I have what he needs…"

"Then you have your answer," Barry said.

Okay, maybe it'd end with Barry then. There was no keeping the disappointment out of his tone.

"What if I don't like that answer?"

He slapped the bar and turned away. "Talk to him then. Ask if you're enough." He walked around the bar and over to the tables across from the stage, taking down the chairs and wiping the tops.

Ask him? Ask *Minty* what he needed?

I laughed to myself. Christ, what a concept. A basic one at that.

If I was going to keep dominating Minty, then I needed to get my head in the game and keep it there.

Minty

SENSEI KATO WAS already teaching a class when I arrived. It was just after four, and schools had let out half an hour before, giving students just enough time to choke down a snack and get into uniform.

I was one of his cherub-faced students not too long ago. In Sensei's dojo, I'd been safe and sound, and very fucking good at what I did. A star pupil.

But the thing about Aikido was that it was all about nonviolence, about shifting the energy so that an attack failed or bounced back on the attacker. It wasn't a martial art that was good for getting rage out.

For me, that was kickboxing. And *that* was taught by Sensei's son, Sensei Junior. Who was currently standing at the reception desk, frowning at the new computer his father had reluctantly installed a few months before, his dark brown hair sticking up everywhere, like always.

"It's still giving you trouble, huh?" I asked, sauntering up like I was wearing a skirt and lipstick instead of the sweatpants and t-shirt I'd pulled on earlier when Daniel arrived.

"Fucking piece of shit," Sensei Junior muttered, glancing up to make sure his dad was still teaching and out of earshot. "I'm tempted to just dump it in the trash."

I grinned. "Let me see. What are you trying to do?"

Sensei Junior let me around the desk and, within a few minutes, I fixed the enrollment error his thick fingers had caused. "There."

"Thanks," he said, eyeing me from head to toe. "What's your damage? You look like hell."

Sensei Junior was tall, thick, and muscled. He was like his father in every way except for the light streaks in his hair—which he either got from bleach or from his white mother—and also his priorities. He loved the martial arts, but he liked to kick ass. He'd opened a side business of the dojo a few years back to teach kickboxing to the less peace-inclined students.

"Just having a fucking horrible year," I said with a cute smile. I always flirted with Sensei Junior, even though he was straight as a ruler. Mainly because, while I had no doubt he would *never* fuck me, he seemed to like the attention. It softened him up, and that made it more likely he'd do what I asked. Of course I'd crushed horribly on him back in high school. Thought I was in love. Declared him my one and only. The usual for me.

My declaration of *une année horrible* had him frowning with concern. "Yeah? Why's that?"

"Personal and private shit," I said with another glimmer of cuteness.

Sensei Junior rolled his eyes. "Forget I asked." But then his gaze sharpened on me. "You're all right, though? You're not in trouble?"

I could tell he was ready to crack his knuckles and offer to help kick someone's ass, and I wanted to take him up on it. But there was no way he could kick the ass of a virus.

"I just need to get some tension out." I inclined my head toward his side of the dojo where a fully outfitted kickboxing studio was set up. "You'd be the perfect target." I twinkled at him again. "If you're game."

"Ha." He glanced at the computer, squinting at the screen. "This says I've got nothing scheduled, right?"

He tapped the green blinking calendar. "Fuck this. It makes no sense."

I glanced over the schedule. "I don't see anything." I elbowed him with a laugh. "Just someone named Colleen Sinclair at ten o'clock tonight. Kind of late for a private class, isn't it?"

Junior blushed. "Yeah. That's a girl I'm seeing. A total babe. Might marry her."

He walked to the main door and locked it. "Come on. We've got forty minutes before Dad will be done with the munchkins and their parents start to show up. Plenty of time to mop the floor with your butt."

We started with hard punches against the bag, kicks that sent it flying, and later a couple of hand-to-hand matches that were rough enough to get my blood pumping—and to sting my already existing bruises, as well as add a few more. Especially when he landed a kick that sent me flying across the mat. It felt good. Almost great.

But it was all just a little too safe.

Junior never really went after me. Not like he was *actually* going to mug me, or kill me, or rape me. It was all just pretend, just practice.

Still, when the alarm on his watch went off indicating it was time for us to stop fucking around and for him to get back to his job, I was feeling better. I was also satisfyingly sore in a deep, muscular way that only a scene with Luke or an encounter with Kyle achieved.

Blood pumped through my body, I was sweaty and breathing hard, and I felt alive. Very much alive.

How was it possible that inside me, swimming in my blood, there was a disease that was going to take me down?

"Minty," Sensei Kato called out as he walked away from a young mom who was cooing over her daughter's latest martial accomplishments. "It's been a long time."

He struck me on the shoulder like the straight man he was and then pulled me into a hug. I let him hold me, feeling small in his arms.

Sensei had never held back in affection for me, not even when I verified that I was as gay as a nest of birds. He'd simply said, "Yeah, we don't really give a shit in this dojo about things like that. If anyone here gives you trouble, let me know. I'll handle it."

Today, he thumped my back one last time before releasing me. I wondered if there was something about me that attracted protective types: Daniel, Barry, Sensei…

But not Luke. I couldn't honestly call him "protective," could I? Not when he purposely caused me pain and pushed me to the edges of what I could handle.

I liked that.

While it felt good to be protected and safe, I needed to be trusted to know my own limits too. I *wanted* Luke to trust me, and I was afraid that after our last scene, he didn't anymore. I didn't want to be treated with kid gloves—not physically, not emotionally. At least Luke didn't try to "help me" or fix things the way Daniel did. I needed Luke to believe in my ability to cope, to take pain, to deal with it.

And I wanted him to get off on that too.

I wanted my pain to feed his pleasure and his pleasure to feed into my pain. I didn't want Luke to only hurt me and get nothing back. I wanted that feedback loop, the call and response of something more…

"You're a million miles away," Sensei Kato said, clapping his hands in front of my face. "I asked what brought you here, but I see from your sweat-stained pits "—he gestured at my t-shirt—"that you were getting some aggression out with Joey."

Joey was Sensei Junior, but only his father called him by his real name.

"I kicked his ass," Sensei Junior said, punching at the computer with just his index fingers, scowling like it was currently kicking his. "He's gotten weak."

I shrugged. "I didn't come here to win. I just came to fight."

Sensei grunted. "You were gifted in Aikido. You transferred kinetic energy so well. You could easily topple men twice your size. But now you're all about the violence. Where did I go wrong with you and Joey?"

"It's the testosterone, Dad," Sensei Junior said. "Minty and I have too much of it."

"That fairy? Too much testosterone?" The whisper reached us from the clot of parents still helping their kids into their shoes and coats.

Sensei turned.

All the parents went quiet, and their darted glances let us all know just which man had made the nasty remark.

"That's not acceptable here. I never want to hear anything like it again," Sensei barked. Then he turned back to me, put his hand on my shoulder and squeezed. "Ignore that piss ant."

"Ignore him?" I asked loudly, putting my hand over my heart. "After he called me a *fairy?* What a compliment! He must think I'm beautiful." I batted my lashes at the dad in question.

Gritting his teeth, the man rushed out with his embarrassed son following at his heels.

I laughed.

It felt good to laugh. I hadn't done enough of it lately. Here with the fluorescent dojo lights and Sensei protecting my honor and Sensei Junior about to toss the computer in the trash can, I felt a glimmer of what my post-rape-but-pre-diagnosis life had been. This evening at the dojo hadn't been as mind-silencing as one spent in Luke's basement, but it had been enticingly, seductively normal.

Could I *have* normal again? Was I allowed?

And what about the symbiotic relationship I wanted with Luke? The give and take of lust and pain… but also something more than that. Something personal and real. Was that something I could have before I died? Would Luke want to give it?

Probably not. After my confession, I'd be lucky to get one more scene in the basement before Luke called it quits. I'd seen the discomfort in his eyes. He'd tried to hide it, but it was all over him like perfume.

My gut twisted. Renewed anxiety snaked in. The old temptation to go to Kyle's dorm wormed into my mind…

No.

I shook my head, determined to stick to the conditions of my contract until Luke gave up on me. Which would undoubtedly be sooner rather than later.

Hell, it'd probably be tomorrow.

Chapter Eleven

Luke

"HAVE A SEAT," I said, pointing to the sofa in my living room. "Before we go downstairs, I want to talk."

"But we *are* going downstairs?" Minty asked, his expression growing tight and wary. I thought he might walk right back out the door if I said no.

"Of course. We agreed to a scene today."

"Then why do we need to talk?"

"I think you know why," I said firmly, indicating the sofa again. "Now let's get this done so we can play."

"I don't want to 'play'," Minty bit out, anxiety straining his voice. "I want to hurt."

"You'll hurt, but first we'll talk. I'm sure talking will hurt too."

Minty's nostrils flared. I thought he might protest again, but he took a seat at the edge of the sofa, legs together primly beneath his short, lacy skirt, and the end of the matching lace tie in his hair trailed down over an exposed shoulder. The sleeveless t-shirt was a rather butch addition to his otherwise very feminine outfit, but it worked with his general androgyny and the hyper-masculine cowboy boots on his feet.

He clasped his hands together on his knees, reminding me of church and fervent prayers. I didn't know if he was sending some up or not, but he certainly looked the part. The anxious expression.

The tension in his shoulders.

"Your father raped you," I stated. There was no room for beating around the bush. "That makes some of what we're doing here together emotionally fraught."

"Don't get academic on me now. I don't want that."

"Well, it doesn't matter what you want, does it? I'm the Dom here, and you'll listen and talk to me about what I want or—"

"Or I can go? What if I do go?" Minty stood then, challenging me. "What then?"

"Then you'll go, and you'll find some other way to hurt yourself that won't be nearly as good as what I can give you, and you'll probably get yourself killed in the process." I crossed my arms over my chest and sat down in the chair opposite the sofa. "Go on, then. Go."

Minty wavered. I could see his brain turning it over and over. "Kyle wants me back. He's begging for me."

"Go to him then," I said. "I'm sure what he gives you is better than the whips I had planned for you today."

His jaw clenched and released. He contemplated my words. I could see the temptation to leave in a fit of bratty defiance warring with the temptation of the promised whips. "You swear you'll use them? You won't back out of it if I stay?"

"I promise to use them, and I promise to make you scream."

"Until I cry? And beg?"

I felt the sadistic smile creep across my face. "Until you break."

His eyelashes fluttered, red rose in his neck and cheeks, and he sat down again with a soft, breathless, "Okay."

That was what I thought.

"Your father raped you," I said again.

"Yes."

"How often?"

"Isn't once enough?"

"It's certainly one time too many."

His eyes clouded, and he looked away. "I'm sorry about what happened last time I was here. I really didn't expect that I'd say *that* during…" Minty looked up with a fragile expression in his eyes. "I don't know why I'm like this."

"Like what? A masochist?"

"I guess. I don't know why I like to get fucked like I'm being raped." He said that last so quietly it was almost as if he hoped I wouldn't hear him. "I shouldn't want that."

"Why the hell not?"

"Because I *was* raped and… and…" He shivered. "That was horrible."

"Of course it was." I paused, waiting to see if he was going to say more. When he didn't, I said, "You know, it's not unusual for people who have experienced sexual violence to be drawn to BDSM. Some even want to recreate their rape in the safety of a scene. It's a way to take control, make strength out of something that once left them feeling powerless."

Minty chewed on his bottom lip. "I don't know. Maybe."

"I'm not offering to do that. I'm simply saying that you're not alone in being drawn to BDSM scenarios and pain after a sexual assault. The voluntary release of control to a trusted Dom and choosing to experience pain in a sexual context can be healing. It's the choice that matters."

Minty turned that over in his head. "Like how when I'm with Kyle, I'm choosing to let him do those things to me. He thinks he's in control, but the truth is *I have the power*, even though he's beating me down, hurting me, and forcing me."

"Exactly. Before, when your father hurt you, there was no power because there was no choice."

"But…"

"But what?"

His eyes darted down to the floor and stayed there. His voice was nearly a whisper as he filled in the blank he'd left in his speech. "That's not true. I had power."

"Tell me what you mean by that."

He shifted uncomfortably, but didn't argue. A part of me suspected he *wanted* to talk about the rape in more detail, probably had wanted to for a long time.

"I was thirteen when my dad—" he broke off and swallowed the next words.

"Go on."

"I've never told anyone this. Not my old therapist, not my case worker, not anyone."

"Tell me."

"I don't think I can."

"I know you can," I said forcefully. It was partly encouragement, but more of an order. The Dom voice did a lot to subs, and Minty was no different.

He swallowed hard, his eyes fluttering. Finally, he spoke again, "I was thirteen when he did *that*. To me."

My heart cracked open with pain for him, but I stayed quiet, letting him talk.

"During it, part of me just checked out, went to another place."

I nodded.

"But another part of me was very present. I felt…" He stopped again, his breath coming in short and fast. He glanced up at me, terror in his eyes. His pulse thudded visibly in his throat.

"Whatever you say, I'm not going to be surprised," I said as calmly as I could.

"You will be. It's…" He shook his head. "It's very bad."

My own heart rate was up. I was wading into deeply murky waters. I was taking a very big fucking risk.

"Would it help you if I said the words?" His gaze caught on

mine, and he looked so frightened that it took all my courage to push on and not back out. "All right. You felt powerful, despite not having a choice. Because he wanted you. Is that right?"

Minty pushed a loose strand of the longer part of his hair back off his face, before tightening the lacy tie with shaking hands. "My dad ignored me most of my life. Later on, he hit me whenever he noticed me. I hated being hit, but I hated being ignored more."

"He didn't ignore you that day."

"No. He didn't. I was wearing a dress. My mom's dress, and I'd put on a touch of eyeshadow—" He squeezed his eyes shut, grimacing as he remembered. "He went crazy when he saw me. Shouted that he'd show me what it was like to be a girl if that's what I wanted to be so badly." He looked at me with his blue eyes shimmering. "I already told you one of the worst parts."

"Which was?"

"I came," he whispered, looking up at me.

"You did tell me that. And I told you that was just physiological."

He huffed. "I *didn't* tell you that I egged him on while he did it." His voice gave out and tears glossed his eyes. "I've never told anyone the truth."

I took a slow breath before saying, "There's nothing you can say that will make me feel differently about you."

He stared at me. "Are you sure about that?"

"Try me."

He sounded strangled as he pushed on, "Okay. Um… At first, I begged, like what I said to you last time…"

He looked at me, willing me to understand.

"'Daddy, you're hurting me, please stop'?"

"Yeah." He wiped at his face. He was sweating now, and if I was reading him right, he was dizzy too. "I *begged* him. It hurt so much. But when he didn't, when he was inside me, and it was done, and it wasn't going to stop…" His voice grew stronger, and his eyes flashed. "I got so fucking angry. Like I could murder him, like I could move *mountains* with my rage. I felt powerful. Strong. In control. And I told him…" He hesitated.

"Go on."

"I told him that he'd always remember—" He broke off again, shame crossing his face.

"Go on, baby," I whispered, leaning forward, ready to catch him if this confession was too much. My hands shook too, and I hoped he didn't notice. "It's okay to tell me."

Mitchell licked his lips. "I told him he'd always remember how he'd made his *own son* come with his big, fat dick. I told him he was *good* at fucking me, that I loved it, and that *he* loved it too. I told him his cock fit in me just right, like it was made for my hole, like *I* was made just for him to use." His voice went even lower. "I told him that he was the best fuck of my life."

"Was that true?"

Minty's eyes fell to the carpet. His shoulders shook. "At that point, he was the *only* fuck of my life."

My throat felt tight as I asked, "Those things you said to him…you were only thirteen. Where did you learn to talk like that?"

"I don't know." He shrugged, looking small. "It just came out of my mouth, like the words had always been there just waiting for me to say them."

He shivered. "I don't know how else to explain it. The more I talked, the more I felt like I was breaking *him* instead of him breaking me. The power"—he ran his hands over his body, like he could feel it coursing through him even now—"was intense." He swallowed thickly. "When he was done, panting and shaking on my back, I told him he'd always remember how his little boy had made him come like a goddamn freight train."

His pulse pounded in his throat. "I don't know where I got that either. But I'll never forget saying it."

I breathed in shakily. "And then?"

"He spat on me. He hit me, kicked me, beat me up. I felt proud, though. I hated him so much, and I *wanted* to make him hate himself for what he'd done, what he'd enjoyed."

"And did he? Hate himself?"

"I don't know." He pressed his lips together. "I hope so."

"Is there more? Anything else you've never told anyone?"

"Yeah."

"Go on. Tell me now. It's okay."

He took a stuttering breath. "The last time I saw him, he cornered me in my bedroom at my mom's place and asked me to blow him. He didn't even seem ashamed. Just said, 'If you're still the whore you used to be, get on your knees for Daddy.'"

"Did you?"

His breathing hitched. "If I said I did, would you hate me?"

"No, baby. No, never."

His face contorted, and I didn't know if I believed him when he whispered, "I didn't. I spit in his face, and then I got in my car, drove to campus, and taunted a frat boy into beating me up."

"What did that accomplish?" Though I already knew the answer, I wanted to hear him say it.

"It was what I deserved."

"For what?"

He glared at me. "You know for what."

"For making your daddy want you?"

"Yes, and for before."

"For making him come and for coming yourself?"

"Yes," he whispered.

My heart was going wild, but we were in this deep. I had to come out the other side with him. I had to get us both there safely.

"And how long do you need to be punished for that?"

He shrugged, and his eyelashes were wet with tears.

"The HIV," I went on. "Was that another way to get punished, or was it the accident you claim it was?"

"It was an accident," Minty said, softly. "A broken condom. But I knew the guy was positive when I let him fuck me. Part of me…"

"Don't stop now. You're so close," I said, softly. "Tell me."

"Part of me thought, 'if the worst happens, I deserve it.'"

"Oh, baby."

"I don't want to die, but I don't know how to live with this… this thing in me," he said, rubbing at his chest over his heart, sobs building in his throat. "I want it gone. I want to put it down and walk away from it."

He pounded his chest. "But it won't go away. I've tried getting high, and having sex, and pretending everything's fine, and getting hurt, but it keeps on being there inside me."

"Have you considered loving that part of yourself instead?"

He stared at me.

"If it won't go away, maybe the thing to do is to hold it closer and love it with all your might."

He laughed bitterly. "Love the part of me that, what? Egged my father on? Told him I loved it? Said it was the best fuck of my life?"

"Yeah. Love that past version of you. He saved you."

Minty shook his head. "I hate him. He's disgusting—and he's ruined my life. He's cocaine, and heroin, and every other thing people wreck themselves with. Please. Can't you just beat him out of me? Please?"

Carefully, I pulled him into my arms. He trembled against me. I whispered, "All right. Why don't we try doing both?"

He broke down into sobs.

✦   ✦   ✦

Minty

LUKE HELD ME with my head to his chest, letting me hear his heartbeat. I quivered at the warmth and tenderness of his comfort. I wanted to thank him for it, beg him for more, and I also wanted to beg him to *never* comfort me like this when we were in a scene. I shivered in his arms. Was it greedy and impossible to want both?

Luke murmured, "That day, when you could have let him break you, but you didn't?"

I nodded, tears leaking down my cheeks and wetting his shirt.

"You were the strongest you've ever been. You took charge in the only way you could. You wrestled the control of the experience out of his hands and into your own."

I squeezed my eyes tight, the memory of that surge of power making my cock hard. Luke's scent held me fast in the present, though, and I snuggled closer to him.

Luke went on, "And you did that by doing something so outside the bounds of what's traditionally acceptable that you've become deeply ashamed of your proudest moment, baby."

"How can I be proud of it?" I whispered. "It's sick."

"No, it was survival. You protected your psyche by rewriting the scenario giving yourself power and control. You did what you had to do."

"I could have—"

"You could have what?"

I whispered, "I could have gone limp. I could have fought harder."

"You chose to be stronger than either of those things. You chose to redefine the experience. I want to help you hold that strength close and love yourself for what you did in that moment."

I tried to imagine feeling proud of what I'd done that day, and all I could think of was going to Kyle, making him come, owning him the way I'd owned my father. I shuddered. Nothing was healthy about that. No matter how good it felt, no matter how much of a god I became.

Luke stroked my hair. "The next thing I'm going to say is challenging. Are you ready?"

I nodded, clinging to him, listening to his heartbeat speed up.

"I think one way you could try to love the Minty you were back then—the *Mitchell* you were—is to challenge your fear of Daddy play. Do you want to push against your shame today?"

"How?"

"Play in a way that lets you embrace that you egged him on, that you reached orgasm, and that he did too, at your urging."

"Stop," I moaned. "Don't say it like that."

"It's true."

"Sir, I want it to *not* be true."

"That's not how life works, baby." He stroked my hair again. "You don't have to agree. This isn't a deal killer for us. We'll carry on today even if you decide not to call me Daddy. But I want you to really think about it. Think about the Mitchell of that day, how much love he wanted and needed and *deserved*, how proud you should be of him for surviving what he did, and then honor his survival by refusing to be ashamed of his choices. Just consider it."

I shook my head, pulling back to look at his face. But part of me wanted to test it, to croak out "please, Daddy" as I stared into his hot eyes.

It wouldn't be so scary. He looked nothing like my father.

But I didn't.

Instead, I let him lead downstairs, strip me down, and take me over to a stainless-steel rod suspended from the ceiling near the wall of implements. He gagged me with a soft rope and strung me up to it with leather-covered chains. My arms were held extended, and my legs were spread by a bar, too, leaving me exposed and helpless, but with plenty of room to twist and move.

He pressed a hard, red ball into my hand, telling me to drop it if I wanted to use my safe word.

Then he went to the wall of implements and took down his flogger first. I started shaking before he even landed the first of the warm-up strikes. Eventually, he returned to the wall for a wooden paddle, and the heavy pain that echoed through me with each strike made me sweat.

By the time he'd escalated to a short, red whip—which viciously bit into the skin of my upper back, my ass, and the backs of my thighs—I was dancing from toe to toe, dripping with sweat and tears, drooling everywhere, and hard as hell. A pool of pre-cum grew between my legs where my cock was steadily weeping.

"Gorgeous pain slut," he muttered, and I shivered at the words. He came close behind me, pressing his hairy chest and stomach to my stinging back. "I can feel the heat just pouring off you, baby."

I stiffened, loving the praise for the first time ever, adoring the way he called me baby, but also wanting him to call me names, to spit on me, to tear the pain out of my mind and memories.

"You hate it when I'm sweet, don't you?" he whispered. "At least when we're down in this room."

I tried to shrug, but couldn't in my restraints. I squeezed the ball tightly so I wouldn't drop it by accident as he scratched his hairy chest against my whipped back again, making me hurt in a way I'd never imagined.

He gripped my throat from behind, squeezing with one hand as he reached around and slapped my balls with his palm. I struggled, relieved that there was no escape. I could fight all I wanted, but I was going to *hurt*, and he was going to make me feel it.

"That's right, you little slut," he gritted out. "You're horny for humiliation, yeah?"

He released my throat, knelt, tugged my sore cheeks roughly

apart and spit on my hole. "Fucking whore. Craving cum. Living for it."

When he shoved the head of his cock into me with just the spit from his mouth, I groaned and bore down, aching for the rest of him to slide in. But he withheld the satisfaction, just fucking the crown in and out, uncomfortably popping past the rim.

I tried to trick him into going deeper by leaning back as he shoved in, but I had no real leverage and not much room to maneuver, chained up like I was.

Sir pulled all the way out, leaned in and whispered in my ear, "Do you deserve my cock?"

I groaned, shaking my head. I didn't. But *fuck* I wanted it so bad.

"I didn't think so. I'll let you have this instead."

He moved away, and shortly I heard something being dragged toward me. Something heavy.

I squirmed and twisted my head around, finally seeing that he'd brought over the machine I'd spotted the first day. It looked handcrafted out of wood with a pump of some kind, and it held a metal arm with a dildo attached.

A hell of a dildo too. Thicker than Sir's cock, and longer.

I'd heard of this sort of thing, even seen some instructions for building one in the back of one of the porn magazines at Chelsea Station, but until I saw Sir's dungeon, I'd never known anyone who actually had one.

"You have your ball," Sir told me. "You can reject this now and end the scene before we start, or if we get going and this is too much for you, then you can end the scene at any time. Just drop the ball."

I squeezed it even more tightly. When I felt the thing move into position between my legs, I sucked in a long, anxious breath, and tried to let it out slowly.

"This is going to feel so good," he said, as he shoved it closer to my hole, lined it up and then carefully extended the arm a little longer so that the dildo's lubed head rubbed against my entrance. "Don't worry."

I wasn't worried. I was excited. But I was here for *pain*. I needed it. Where was it?

But that thought went out of my head as soon as the dildo breached me solidly. After fitting the head inside me, Luke stepped away to turn on the machine. The first thrust in was slow and steady, but then he increased the rate, and I stood immobilized by the chains as the dildo opened me and worked my hole until I was shaking in pleasure, groaning in need, and dripping a puddle onto the floor from the tip of my dick.

"That's good," Luke said calmly. "Look at you squirm. Not as nice as when you squirm on my cock, but it's a pretty sight."

I'd reached the place again where I really didn't want his praise during the scene, but if he was going to let me come on this big dildo, then I wasn't going to drop my safe word ball just to argue with him about it.

I felt him approach. He had the mean, red whip in hand. "Feels good, just like I said, yeah?"

I nodded in agreement, my eyes on the whip, a sharp worry penetrating my pleasure-fogged brain.

"This, though," he said, showing me the whip with that sadistic grin that both made me harder and scared the shit out of me. "Won't feel good at all."

I groaned behind the gag, shaking my head. He waited to see if I'd drop the ball, but I held tight.

"Let me show you what I mean," he whispered, and then with a quick snap, he flashed that whip across the back of my thighs just below where my balls were drawn up tight to the base of my cock.

I screamed, the sound muffled by the gag.

"Nice, right?" Then he laughed, and I felt tears slip down my cheek.

"That's what I like to see," he said, wiping them away with his thumb and a fake sympathetic pout. "Is the poor little boy crying? Because of a little slap?"

He let the whip draw back and then snap against my chest, right over my nipples. I struggled, the machine still plunging into me, and when I fought, it rammed against my prostate, making me shout for another reason.

"Mm," he murmured, rubbing his stubble against my cheek and then down my neck, kissing my collarbones and sucking on my now sore nipples. "So fucking pretty when you hurt."

He stood. "Don't fight, though. Don't want the toy to come out now, do you? It's the only part of this that's going to feel good. You'll want that."

I was shaking like a leaf. Fear and lust roared inside me. He stepped back and began snapping the short whip against my thighs and my upper arms. He moved on to my chest with a focus on hitting my nipples, and then around to my upper back. He didn't spare my trembling ass cheeks. The worst came when he knelt behind me and carefully lifted one of my feet, causing me to shift my weight and the angle of the dildo. He kissed each toe which tickled and made me laugh through my sobs, and then he whipped the bottom of my foot once. It was like a firecracker going off against my skin, and I howled as he released my foot and went back to targeting my hips for a few more strikes.

"There now," he said, like he was gentling a horse. He came around to my front again. "Look." He indicated my cock. "You're almost ready."

I moaned. The machine had fucked me into a haze as the whip made my skin burn. I moaned again as he wrapped his arms around me, rubbing his hairy chest and the front of his jeans against my angry skin. He grabbed an ass cheek in each palm and spread me so that the dildo fucked in and out with more friction.

"Mm, you are just so fun to hurt," he said, rubbing his cock, still sticking up out of his open jeans, against my body. He was dripping too. "Do you think you deserve Sir's cum?"

I shook my head. I'd never deserve it. He had to know that. But I *wanted* it. I wanted it so bad.

"Hungry cum slut," he murmured like it was an endearment. But then he switched tone. Harder. Meaner.

"He wants it, but doesn't think he's good enough for it," he said as if I wasn't in the room. It was depersonalizing, like I was a thing for his entertainment.

"Let's see if the nasty slut will come from this."

He knelt in front of me, and before I even realized what he planned to do, he grabbed my scrotum in one hand and started whacking my balls with the flats of his other fingers. I struggled. The ball was there in my hand, and I could drop it, but I also felt that sudden—

Hard…

Terrifying…

Beautiful…

Rush.

I was falling and then flying. So high. So scarily high, with no end in sight to how good, bad, and beautiful it felt. I sobbed, cried, begged through the gag for more, more, *more*, though he couldn't know what I was saying.

He didn't stop.

I started to choke from the pain, and he rose to release the gag from my mouth. Then, as I gulped in harsh breaths, he fell back to his knees and, with a wicked grin, started banging on my balls again. I went out of my head, out of my body, and yet felt every single swat.

Flying, flying, high on pain, high on the thrust of the dildo in my ass, I crested into a vibrant explosion, screaming as I came like a pulsing, jetting firework of pleasure. I shot all over Sir's face and hands, and in his hair as he knelt there slapping my balls. He didn't stop. He went on and on, even after the orgasm was well over, and I shook, convulsed, gagged, and almost vomited from pain, from pleasure, from both combined.

When I gained lucidity again, Sir was behind me, inside me, fucking into my body instead of the machine. With tears, I welcomed him and praised him, thanking him with sobs still echoing in my chest and throat.

"Thank you, Sir. So good, you're so good, Sir. So good to me. Please, *please*, thank you, Sir, thank you. Please, you're amazing… this is amazing…"

I babbled, and he bit my shoulder again, grunting hard as he shot into me. I loved the sensation of him filling me, especially the hot, slick slide as he pulled out and the cum leaked down my legs. I wasn't supposed to be allowed that, but with Sir, I could have it. He wanted to give it to me.

I hadn't earned it.

But he'd given it.

I shook with gratitude and expended lust. Pain from the ball torture still wracked me, even as Sir took me down and carried me to the soft bed. I was limp in his arms. Drained and purified by his work on my body. There wasn't a dark spot of thought in my head. Only peace, and yes…

Love.

I loved him for giving me this. And for the first time in my life, I loved someone who wasn't a figment of my imagination.

In the afterglow of a scene that had cleared out all my despair, at least for the moment, I recognized that Sir was someone I couldn't live without.

Someone I didn't *want* to live without.

Chapter Twelve

Luke

I SAT ON the chair by the bed again, watching Mitchell sleep soundly on the bed, all the fight and tension drained from him after another intense scene.

He'd loved it. I'd seen the shine and gratitude in his eyes before, but nothing like what I saw tonight. He'd clearly never felt anything like subspace or flying before he met me, and he was hooked, probably as in love with that feeling as he'd ever been in love with anything or anyone in his life.

He thought he was in love with me, though.

I recognized *that* look too. The one that gobbled me up as the source of this new gift of sensation, pain and pleasure, and the ecstasy that floated a sub higher than he'd ever been before.

Mitchell had looked *stunning* sporting that expression. I wished in some deep little pocket of my soul, the part that craved a relationship with my subs, that it *was* about me.

But I knew better.

He barely knew me—in fact the only things he knew about me involved who I was when we were in this room, or when we were talking about being in this room. He didn't know the me that shat on a toilet like everyone else, or the me who watched terrible nighttime soaps and taped every episode I missed. And he had no idea about the me whose father was a stroke-victim-turned-homophobic-asshole, and whose mother was barely holding it together. He didn't know the me that visited my sister with Down Syndrome at her boarding facility every single month.

He also didn't know the me that had dropped out of college so my parents could afford that facility, or the dream I'd once had of being way more than an employee at a sex shop, an occasional phone sex worker, and a professional Dom. I still had the textbooks from the only semester of college I'd been able to attend before Betsy was sent away from home. I didn't resent her for it. She was the best thing in my life. Loving, cheerful, a bright spot in a lot of darkness, but even she didn't fully know me. She had no idea that her older brother was a sadist through and through.

Mitchell *only* knew that about me.

It was like I was two different Lukes sometimes. The one Betsy and my family knew, and the one that everyone else met—Dom, sex shop worker. The third Luke—the aspiring student—wasn't known to anyone now. He'd barely been known to me.

And, likewise, I knew almost nothing about Mitchell except his most raw and carefully hidden parts. I didn't know his major in college, his taste in music, if he spelled the tomato product as ketchup or catsup, or if he liked horror films more than rom-coms.

I knew what he looked like when he was asleep, though. He was beautiful. Probably just as beautiful as when he was strung up and almost hyperventilating from pain. Or as beautiful as when I hurt him so badly that his eyes lit up with fear. Only in sleep, his cheeks were pale instead of flushed, his lips were softly open instead of stretched around a gag or my cock, and his breath came in easy, flowing sighs that were quieter than the whimpers that escaped him as we played.

I wondered what he was dreaming about. I wondered why I cared.

Despite my yearning for a relationship with my sub—with

Minty—I knew he was here for pain and bondage only. I was doing a job for him. A free job as a favor, one I felt unequipped for emotionally, but a job all the same.

And, God, the job had been rewarding tonight. The way Minty had flown was a sight to behold. The expression of rapture on his face when he came was unlike any I'd ever witnessed on another sub. It was angelic, and if someone informed me I'd been torturing a seraphim, I'd have believed them. Because he looked like wings might sprout from his back, and a halo might appear over his blond head. He was so gorgeous when he was flying that I had to be careful to rein myself in because it made me start to fly too.

And the noises he let out when I hurt him! Those were incredible. Maddening.

I couldn't remember the last sub I'd had this kind of reaction to. Not even Benji, and I was with him for two years. He'd always gotten me off, satisfied me and let me play with his pain harder than any of my former subs, and I'd loved that. But the way that Minty just dove into the agony? The way he rode that terror I brought out in him? And how my inner sadist gloried in the gorgeous glisten of tears in his eyes? Unparalleled.

Tomorrow was Saturday, and we had all day to play and do aftercare before I had to leave for Knox Supplies & News. We hadn't agreed on a new scene yet, and as I faced all these unknowns about him, my mind turned over an idea. I was tempted to ask him to strip naked for me and play a game of twenty questions where every answer was rewarded with a slap across the face or a belt to the ass.

But I shouldn't get too curious about him. Not now. I didn't have any idea how long he and I could last, but I didn't want to count on anything beyond a few days in advance. He could decide to leave because it wasn't enough. I could decide I didn't have the skills to handle his emotional damage.

Or he could get sick and die.

Or I could.

We had to embrace right now, today, these moments, because we didn't know how many more we'd have, and getting to know each other on any other level? What did that matter when what we were doing was so much bigger? So much stronger and epic. Full of cum, spit, pleasure, screams, and fear.

But as I drifted off, a thought crossed through my mind like a cloud over the moon, obscured, not entirely fully formed, but it was still there when I woke up to find him sleeping curled up on the floor at my feet.

You can't let him die without knowing him.

Chapter Thirteen

Minty

"PURPLE, SIR!" I said, breathlessly, bracing myself for the slap. It landed on the opposite side of my face and my head spun. My dick was hard, of course, and his was too, but he didn't seem intent on moving past this game anytime soon.

"Your favorite candy."

"Twizzlers, Sir!" This time he used the crop that he kept twitching against his jean-clad thigh. It landed on my upper arm, and I jumped.

His cock was visible through the open crotch of his unzipped jeans, and I wanted to ask him to pull them down, let me suck the wet head that shone with each step he took.

"Any siblings?"

"No, Sir." The crop landed on my other arm.

"Best friends?"

"Yes, Sir. Daniel and Windy."

The reward was a clamp with sharp teeth placed on my left nipple. I shifted from knee to knee, the concrete making bruises from all my kneeling over the last day. Still, I couldn't remember thinking about my diagnosis or impending death in the last sixteen hours. Just Sir and pain. My new favorite things. And I'd tell him that if he asked.

I could love him. I could truly love him in a way that was real, because he'd seen the worst of me, and he hadn't run away. Instead, he'd held me, hurt me, and made me fly.

I wanted to swoon from the crushing weight of my feelings.

"Do you suck their cocks?"

"No, Sir?" I said it like a question, and his lips quirked up in a kind of amused smile I hadn't seen before. It made my heart skip. He was hot. I'd always known that. But he was cute too.

"I asked," he said, as he readied the other clamp for my right nipple, "because some people are friends, and some people are sex friends, and some people are both."

"I don't fuck Windy or Daniel, Sir, or let them fuck me. They wouldn't even want to, and I…" I bit back a cry as he fixed the clamp on, breathing harshly as I finished my thought, "I wouldn't want to either. If I thought they wanted me like that, that'd kind of break me, Sir."

He glanced up at that, his expression as intense as ever, but a softness, like candlelight, flickered in his eyes. He touched my cheek, more gently than I usually wanted, but this time it sent a flare of warmth to my belly, pooling there and making me feel soft too. "And what about me?"

"You, Sir?"

"If we became friends, but I still wanted to fuck you—"

A smile broke over my face despite knowing I should probably act like I didn't care at all. Was I dreaming? Did Sir really want to hurt me the way I needed *and* be with me outside of this room? After what I'd told him? Champagne joy popped all through my veins.

Sir kept his hand on my cheek and asked quietly, "Would that break you?"

Panting, I teased, "I thought you *wanted* to break me, Sir? Isn't that what I'm doing here?"

Sir's eyes closed a moment, and he let his hand grow rough on my cheek, pulling down hard to clench my jaw and force my mouth open. "Breaking you is a goal of mine, yes."

"I don't fuck my friends," I said. It sounded distorted around his pull on my jaw. "But I'd make an exception for you, Sir."

He reached down, took hold of my balls, and I held very still. I knew he had no qualms about causing me pain there. He squeezed, but not enough to really hurt, just enough that I broke out into a cold sweat of anticipation. "What if I wanted to see you outside of these sessions? Take you to lunch? To dinner?"

"A date, Sir?" My heart was about to beat out of my chest, both in fear for my balls and in hope. Was it possible he wanted more from me than my tears and cum?

Sir swallowed, conflict warring on his face, and then he said in a voice that would have made my dick flex and my nipples zing with arousal if they weren't being actively hurt. "Yes. A date."

He clutched my balls a little tighter, and his eyes moved down to my lips. "What happens on a date, Mitchell?"

"We'd go out, Sir, to a movie or dinner, or something like that." His eyes stayed on my mouth, and with a bolt of clarity I knew what he wanted to hear. "We'd kiss. Then I'd let you do whatever you wanted to me, however you wanted. You wouldn't have to hurt me, unless you wanted to, Sir. I'd let you… just fuck me, if you wanted that."

His eyes fluttered closed again, and then the pressure on my balls grew until I squealed. His lips twisted into that sadistic smirk, and he let go of me, leaving me alone on my knees. He whipped out his cock, squeezed the head, and said, "Open your mouth."

I winced. I didn't love piss play, but he knew that already, and now he used it most times we got together. I held still as he aimed, and the pungent flavor filled my mouth. I swallowed as some spilled over my throat, and then Sir shoved me to the floor, pissing in my hair and down my back. The heat of it was simultaneously gross and soothing, and when he was done, he used a hand in my wet hair to pull me up to kneeling.

"You look pretty all wet and ripe."

"Thank you, Sir?" Again with the question. I didn't know if I wanted to be told I was pretty in the middle of a scene right now. But then again, the idea that he wanted to go on a date with me, that he truly wanted to kiss me and treat me as a person instead of a thing to hurt and fuck was intoxicating. For that reason, I was glad I was pretty.

"My nasty little fuck toy," he said. "Get on your hands and knees."

I did as he ordered, my hands gripping the rough concrete as he came around behind me, whistled under his breath, and checked the plug he'd stuck in my ass as my "reward" for one of my first questions. I thought it'd been whether I liked cats or dogs better. I wasn't sure what he'd have done if I'd said cats. Maybe a prostate massager instead. He had one of those sitting out too.

"Do you think this hole deserves Sir's cum?"

"No, Sir," I whispered, yearning to put my head down into the wet pool of piss beneath me and stick my ass up in the air to make it easier for him. Instead, I stayed still, wondering what he planned to do next.

"I have a surprise for you," he said with so much sadism in his tone that my heart thumped hard, and a new rush of adrenaline hit my bloodstream. I started to shake, and I knew he saw because he laughed. "Let's get this out."

He pulled the plug out with no real care, and I yelped as it exited me, leaving me feeling empty and raw.

"Now," he said, and even without looking around I could hear that he was working something out of his back jeans pocket and then unwrapping it from plastic. He dropped a ball of plastic wrap by my head. "Let's see what you think about this."

I moaned as something cold and tingly slid into my hole, a flared base catching the edge of my clenching rim.

"What is it, Sir?" I gasped.

"That's for me to know and you to find out."

I felt the tingling grow, and when Sir walked around to the front of me again, using his hand on my chin to pull me back up to kneeling, I began to understand. The prickling grew to stinging, and the more I clenched down on whatever was in my ass, the more it burned.

"Do you feel it?" Sir asked.

I nodded.

"Is it good or bad?"

"Both, Sir."

He brushed a hand through my piss-wet hair, peered into my eyes, and then, with that same self-satisfied smirk, he undid the clamp on my right nipple. I grunted, my entire body clenching at the pain and the burning in my ass intensified, adding to the burn in my chest, going deep into the muscle. I felt like I was on fire from chest to hole and back again. Tears came to my eyes, and Sir's smile grew more delighted.

"That's good, baby," he whispered.

I gulped and blinked at him, a reply coming to mind that I was shy about using. He saw it, though.

"Tell me," he ordered. "Do you need to use your safe word?"

He sounded genuinely concerned, so I shook my head, and whispered, "No, Daddy."

He paused. "Mitchell, I'm going to stop for a moment, but I promise we can come back to the scene. Ready? We're stopped now."

I blinked at him, tears coming to my eyes again with the burn from the thing in my ass. "Yes, Luke?" I tried out his name. I'd never said it to his face, though I was saying it all the time in my mind these days. Luke this, Luke that. Luke, Luke, Luke. He was all I thought about anymore. I was failing at school and going to die, but at least there was Luke and his basement, and this look in his eyes that meant he cared.

"Do you want to call me Daddy during today's play?"

I gulped. "Yes."

"And can I call myself Daddy? Or is this just something for you? Either answer is okay."

"You can too," I said, my voice shaking. "I've been thinking it over, and I'm ready to try it."

He touched my hair, stroking through it gently. "In the future, let's talk about these possibilities before we're in the scene. I don't mind stopping whenever to clarify like I did just now. I'm not angry or upset. But if you've been thinking about it, then in the future, let's talk about that kind of thing in advance."

"Okay, Luke."

His lips quirked. "Good boy, Minty."

I quivered.

"Are you ready to go back to the scene?"

Since the burning in my ass hadn't stopped, I wasn't sure that I'd ever left, but I nodded and said, "Yes, please."

Luke narrowed his gaze on me. "Yes, please, what?"

"Yes, please, Daddy."

He brought his fingers down to my lips and touched them, a softness in his eyes I'd never seen before. "I wish I could kiss you."

"You can, Daddy."

He shook his head then. "No, not now." Then his voice changed. It was firm and in control and fierce, and I shook all over at the sound of it. "Suck Daddy's dick," he said, rising and pushing his jeans down. "Make your daddy come."

The words rang a bell in me that ignited the shame in my heart so that it burned as much as whatever he'd put in my ass. But I did as Luke said, taking his cock into my hand, and then swallowing him down.

"Fuck," he cursed, hands curling into my hair to tug and pull as I did my best to drive him out of his mind. "Holy shit, Mitchell. Fuck. *Fuck!*"

I would have smiled if my mouth weren't full, so I kept on working. His knees began to shake, making me feel delirious, and when he pulled out of my throat, gripping my jaw open and then plunged back in, taking control, I went limp and let him.

The burning in my ass and the way he took my breath away by shoving deep into my throat ramped up my arousal. He pulled free, slapped my face again, and whispered, "Filthy slut, you want to make Daddy come, don't you?"

"Yes," I got out around the saliva and hoarseness from the throat fuck. "Come for me, Daddy."

The words were both like and unlike what I'd said that awful day years ago. They echoed it, but they didn't send me hurtling back there. Probably because I could see Luke, his pupils dilated with arousal, his wet mouth where he'd chewed on his lip to hold back his orgasm, and his angry expression—like he was furious at how much he wanted me.

It was *that* that sent me flying straight into a wall of intense orgasm.

I shot like a fountain all over the concrete, onto Luke's legs, and over his feet. As I did, my asshole reached a state of fire that left me shouting even as I came down from the high of climax.

Luke's mouth twisted in that way that let me know he was enjoying my pain and pleasure, but mostly my pain. My body sang with it, and he drank up the song.

"That's right," he whispered. "Come for Daddy. You filthy whore."

"Yes," I said with a shaking voice. "Yes, I'm your whore."

"Always my whore. Keep your eyes open; look at Daddy," he said, taking himself in hand and jerking until he shot onto my face, aiming for my eyes.

The stinging pain of the semen hitting my eyeballs matched that in my ass, and I shouted again, rubbing at them until Daddy caught my hands in his and clutched them to his chest, kneeling in front of me to whisper in my ear, "Daddy's cocksucker did a good fucking job. Too bad I'm gonna have to punish you for enjoying that."

And then he did.

He jerked my cock hard and ruthlessly even though I'd just shot off. He gripped me close, so I couldn't push him away, and he didn't let me squirm. My eyes burned horribly from his semen. My cock screamed with agony as he worked it. The pain made me clench my ass, and that burning sensation grew unbearable. I was on fire, and I was hurting, and—

"There," he said, like he knew the moment the memory swamped me. "Feel that. Go with it."

I struggled and it did no good, the pain in my ass was unbearable. *Shoved flat on my belly on the sofa. My father's weight on my back.* "Daddy, stop, please, please," I gasped. "Daddy, Daddy, it hurts, stop."

"You know your safe word," Luke's voice vibrated through me.

I did know it, but the memory had me, and as much as I hated it, I wanted to see it through. The pain, the rage, the words I'd screamed. "I made you come, Daddy. Your son made you come."

"Yes," Luke whispered. "Tell me what you did."

"I came for you, Daddy, and you came inside me. Me! Your son! Mitchell!"

"Such a sweet boy," Luke cooed. "So strong and proud. So powerful. You made Daddy come so hard. Powerful, strong boy."

He dropped my cock, and I shook in his arms, the pain still

burning through my ass. I didn't know what to make of what I'd said. It was strange because I knew he wasn't my father, but the words, the praise, and the way he was carefully touching me now, reaching down to pull whatever it was from my asshole, and nuzzling my neck felt so paternal. In the right way.

I wanted more from him, more affection. More, more, *more*.

"You did so good, Mitchell," he said, and then he showed me the thing that'd been inside me. "Raw ginger. It's called figging."

I breathed in and out, feeling dizzy as he tossed it aside now.

"Let's let you rest," he said, helping me up, and then lifting and carrying me to the shower the way he always did. I clung to him as he turned the hot water on. He didn't resist, pulling me tight against him as the spray rained down on us both. I wanted him to kiss me. I needed it.

"Please, Sir," I murmured. "Kiss me."

"I'm sorry, baby, but we'll have to talk about that when you're sober. Right now, you're somewhere else. I don't want to violate your rules when we're not in our right minds."

"Were we in our right minds earlier when I called you Daddy and you let me?" I asked, sounding dreamy and far away, barely audible over the rush of the water.

"We'd talked about the Daddy thing before. We've never discussed kissing."

"Take me on a date, please," I said, hope rising in my heart as I closed my eyes, and he started washing my hair tenderly. "Take me on a date and kiss me."

"Sweet baby," he murmured. "If that's what you need, then I will."

Chapter Fourteen

Mid-October 1991
Luke

I'D PROMISED THE kid a date while still drowning in overwhelming sex pheromones, satisfied lust, and sadistic glee. I should never have brought it up to start with, but more than that, I shouldn't have agreed.

Now I was standing in the lobby of a university dorm building waiting for Minty to come downstairs. I had a bouquet of roses I'd grabbed from the supermarket, and a vague plan for our date that didn't involve dinner or a movie, but did involve getting to know each other better.

And this was a mistake.

A dumb, horny, emotional mistake.

Okay, more emotional than horny since I always blew my load like a volcano whenever I was with him, so I couldn't really blame my dick. It was my betraying heart. The stupid thing wanted to be witnessed and cared for, wanted to love and be loved, and for some unknowable reason, it'd gone and set its sights on Minty.

Minty! Of all subs! Of all people!

The kid had a truckload of issues, and I wasn't the guy to work through them with him. Not outside the dungeon. Maybe not even there.

But tell that to my mouth that had asked him on this date, and to my hands that had bought these flowers, and to my stupid heart that flipped when he walked out of the double doors, and to my eyes that widened when I saw him.

Pink barrettes in his hair, a silvery skirt that went down to his ankles, cowboy boots—of course—and a white, spaghetti strap shirt beneath a soft-looking, pink cardigan. He was gorgeous, and sexy, and sweet like a vanilla ice cream cone. I had to admit that because of the way he liked to dress, I was confused when he expressed adamancy that he wasn't transsexual, but I figured he knew better than I did.

It didn't matter to me anyway.

Right now, outside of the dungeon, he was so brazen, so defiantly himself. His outfit, his style, even the sway in his walk did it for me. I couldn't stop from admitting that truth to myself as he finally stood in front of me with an amazed, sweet grin, hands out for the flowers.

"You got these for me, Sir?"

"Luke," I told him, pressing the flowers into his hands. "We're not playing right now."

He grinned even wider, his blue eyes sparkling. I wasn't sure I'd ever seen him truly happy before this moment. It looked good on him.

"These are for me, Luke?"

"Obviously."

"Let's, um…" He glanced over his shoulder. "Do we have time to take them up to my room? I don't want them to get wilted."

A sudden keen interest in seeing his room came over me. "Sure."

He took hold of my hand, and I realized I'd never held it before. Not like this anyway. I'd clenched it in passion or in emotional support, but this was just simple, common touch. His fingers slid easily between mine, and I nearly brought them up to kiss the back of them.

I didn't, though, and not just because there were already plenty of people staring at us with less than friendly expressions. But because I knew if I did, then it meant I was a goner. That hadn't been what this between us was going to be about. I'd thought it was going to be about BDSM, about keeping him from hurting himself in other ways, about comfort and cum—

Fuck it.

As we stepped onto the elevator, I did pull his hand up to my mouth, and I kissed the soft back twice.

Minty stared at me like I was someone he'd just met. I guess, in a way, I was.

The hallway down to his room was empty of people, but still quite loud. Dorm room doors were open and music, television sounds, and chatter poured out from most. Several guys had girls in their rooms, in their laps, or in their beds. No one said anything to Minty until he was keying into his room.

That was when a big guy stepped out from the bathroom across from his door, halted his steps as soon as he saw Minty, and then cut murder-eyes toward me.

Minty, for his part, hadn't noticed him yet, but when I raised a brow at the big guy pointedly, the fellow sneered.

I figured he was just another homophobe, an asshole for sure and bigger than me, but probably too frightened to take me—a grown adult—on. I was right in a way, but in another way, I was wrong.

As Minty's key finally engaged, Jerkface stepped up between us and used his meaty arm to block the entry. Minty froze, his body going tight and coiled, his expression passing through an odd mix of fear, worry, and bittersweet sadness.

"So, this guy's the reason you aren't coming to my room for your usual beating?" Jerkface asked so quietly that no one but us could hear his words.

Minty cleared his throat, lifted his chin, and put on the tough guy persona I'd glimpsed so many times since we'd met—and had the pleasure of breaking apart. He said sweetly, "If you want to suck his cock, Kyle, I'm sure all you have to do is ask."

Dickhead sneered. "As if I'd ever—"

Minty's expression faltered, and then he said quietly. "I'm sorry." His head inclined toward me. "You're right. He doesn't want me to see you—and so I can't. I know what we did together meant a lot to you, but—"

"It meant nothing to me," the guy spat out, jaw tensing and releasing as he glared at Minty. "Say that to anyone, say *anything* to anyone, and I'll kick your ass."

"Don't threaten me with a good time," Minty said with a wink, flirting with the bastard.

My stomach went acidy.

"But I'm not the one stalking you in your dorm, now am I?" Minty murmured. "People will talk if they see you with me, and we know you don't want that."

For some fucked-up reason, it sounded like Minty genuinely cared about this Kyle guy's boundaries. This had to be the asshole he'd been letting use him, the violent prick who'd choked him and hurt him recklessly.

My hands balled into fists.

Kyle swiveled his head around looking to see if anyone was watching. Only one other guy was out in the hallway now, but he had his nose in a book and wasn't paying any attention.

"I wasn't stalking you. I was visiting Stanley," Kyle hissed, motioning at the room next to Minty. "He's a frat brother."

"Stanley went home for the weekend."

"I didn't know that, or I wouldn't have come over." Too defensive. Full of shit.

"Mm-hmm." Minty patted his arm. "Does *he* know about your love of my hot boy-pussy?"

"I will kill you."

"Hey," I interceded, putting my arm out between the two of them. I didn't like how he was leaning in, getting in Minty's face, teeth bared like he might fucking bite. "My guy here doesn't want you around anymore, got it?"

"Your guy? You a fag or—" Kyle growled, turning to Minty. "This guy's the boss of you?"

"He's my Dom, so yes. Luke tells me what to do, and I do it." Minty straightened his shoulders, peering up into Kyle's face. "So, I can't be your punching bag and slutty cum-hole anymore. I'm sorry. Truly."

I was baffled at the sincerity in his voice. Had he actually *liked* this guy? Did he have *feelings* for him? Was I *jealous?* Jesus Christ.

Kyle seemed confused too, staring between me and Minty. I didn't know if it was the Dom/sub thing that had his slow little mind spinning, or if it was the way Minty touched his arm with sincere care and spoke to him tenderly.

"What we had was important to you," Minty said. "You needed it as much as I did, and I'm sorry I can't let you have it anymore. It meant a lot to me too, for what it's worth. You understood me, and I thank you for that."

"*Understood* you? I hate you," Kyle whispered, glancing around again. His Adam's apple bobbed nervously.

"I know," Minty said, stroking his arm again. "And that's what I needed. I hope you can find someone else to make you come like I can make you come, but I doubt it. There aren't many guys like me out there. Most aren't willing to take a beating like that. I'm so sorry, Kyle, but I can't help you anymore."

"*Help* me?" Kyle shook his head. "You're insane."

"Of course I am. What did you think it meant that I let you do what you did to me and actually liked it?" Minty withdrew his hand from Kyle's arm and pushed on into his room. "I really can't talk anymore right now. My Dom and I are going on a date. Good luck to you. I really hope you get what you're looking for. You're really good at it."

"Good at it..." Kyle trailed off, and then glanced up at me. "Good luck, dude. He's a fucking maniac."

I wanted to defend Minty, tell Kyle not to speak that way about my...my what? Not my sub, but *yes* my sub. Minty wasn't my boyfriend, but the way I wanted to wring this monster's abusive, nasty neck told me that I was in deep emotionally. Yes, the desire to murder this asshole told me I'd entirely lost my footing and was absolutely drowning.

Shit.

I really shouldn't be doing this. I was thirty-four years old. I had HIV and would probably start getting sick sooner rather than later. In the meantime, I had a sister to take care of and parents who needed help. By all rights, I had no room in my life right now for love. I'd told Benji that, and I meant it.

But what was this feeling in my chest—this protective, urgent feeling—for this unreasonable blond twink I had every intention of fucking in a vanilla and sweet way tonight?

I wasn't dumb. I knew what it was.

Fuck.

Kyle had already stalked away by the time I'd sorted through my feelings and thoughts and come up with what I'd wanted to say—*touch him again and you'll answer to me*—so I swallowed the threat down and followed Minty into his dorm room.

The walls were covered in posters, like most dorm rooms were from what I recalled during my brief time in college. There were two beds, both made neatly, and a set of colored twinkle lights wrapped around an exposed pipe running across the ceiling of the room. They were on, but so were the overheads, so they didn't add much to the ambience.

"I'm sorry about him. He's missing me is all," Minty said, putting the roses in a vase on his desk next to a hand-drawn poster of various colored blobs and arrows. At the top, it was labeled "Photosynthesis," and above it was a giant poster of assorted salamanders of the world.

Next to it was another, smaller print of different kinds of butterflies, and across the room there was a fourth poster, this one of animals on the endangered species list, and beside it a large photo of a young Jane Goodall with a chimpanzee friend, and beside *that* a plastic placard urging recycling.

I blinked. I hadn't imagined Minty—lacy, pretty Minty of the makeup and the skirts—being this into nature and biology.

On the back of the door was a long white, red, and black poster of a meditating Asian man and the words *True victory is victory over oneself.* Above it on the space between the door and ceiling was a photo of Minty with a trophy in hand, standing next to a tall man. Both were wearing martial arts garb.

There were a few music-related posters too. The B-52s and the classic "Faith" shot of George Michael's ass. Next to the bed, there was a collage of fashion models sporting wild clothes and makeup, all of which I could see Minty aspiring to wear.

"He really needed to fuck me," Minty said softly, as he stood in front me, worry creasing his brow. "You're not angry, are you? I promise I haven't let him touch me since I signed our contract. Not even once."

I cleared my throat, my brain spinning between the new information about Minty's interests, martial arts history, and musical taste, and this absolutely unhinged take he had on his situation with that Kyle asshole.

I sucked in a slow breath and started with the most important thing right now. "I'm not angry with you, and I believe you. Don't worry about that."

I touched his hair, brushing back a soft piece that had come loose from the barrettes. "But Mitchell—"

"We're not playing now. It's Minty."

"Fair enough. Minty, he doesn't *love* you. You know that, right?"

Minty sighed, leaning against me.

I wrapped my arms around him. I'd never really held him like this—clothed and not covered in sweat and cum—but it felt right to hold him now. I wanted to keep him here in my arms, protected from the assholes of the world who would want to hurt him in ways I couldn't control or, worse, who'd just want to hurt him until he bled or broke or died.

"He hated me," Minty agreed. "He hated how much he wanted me. I liked how that felt, loved it even. But, no, I guess he didn't love *me*." He pulled back and gazed up at me. "But you don't love me either, do you? So, what's the difference? He needed to fuck me and hurt me, just like you need to—"

"No." I cut him off, and my jaw clenched before I spoke my next words. "He's nothing like me."

"Isn't he? He just doesn't have a fancy contract for me to sign. All he had was my word that I'd show up, and we'd take what we needed from each other. I broke my word without even a goodbye fuck. I'm sure he's hurt by that."

"Hurt by that!" I wanted to shake *him,* but shaking my head would have to suffice. "Baby, he didn't care about you."

"Do you?"

"Why else would I be here trying to take you on a date? Why else would I want to hunt that asshole down right now and put my boot on his neck? Make him promise to never talk to you again? I care too much. *Fuck.*"

Minty's eyes danced. "You're jealous."

I rolled my eyes.

"No, you are! I see it in your face. That, and how much you want to kill him for fucking me." He chuckled gleefully.

"Not for fucking you, for hurting you!"

"For hurting me in a way you don't approve of, in a way that you never would."

"I *would* hurt you like that," I gritted out. The need to squash that asshole Kyle like a bug overwhelmed me. "Say the word, and I'll structure a scene where I hurt you just like he did."

Minty licked his lips. "I like the sound of that, but there was no scene with Kyle. He just…hurt me. And you'd never do that. You'd always insist on—"

I didn't understand what came over me, but I shoved him down on one of the beds. Surprise lit in his eyes, but he didn't say no or struggle against me. I had to stop myself from tossing his skirt up, ripping off the pretty panties I knew I'd find there, and shoving myself into his ass without lube, without care, just to prove to him that I could hurt him the way he needed, the way that fucking asshole had.

But as I stared down into his gleaming eyes, I held myself back. This wasn't what I'd wanted for tonight. I'd wanted to be sweet. Romantic. Go on a date and afterward indulge in some tender, vanilla sex.

Because *hell yeah* I cared.

Too fucking much.

My breath came in and out, hot and hard, my dick pressing against my jeans, my heart thudding. Minty stared up at me, his own chest heaving and his eyes on mine warily, watching my every move. If I didn't do this now, what would he think? He'd think I couldn't give him what Kyle did, and he might go back to him.

I had no choice.

If I wanted him to believe I was enough for him—and *when* had that become my goal? I was just supposed to be keeping him alive, Jesus Christ! But if I wanted him to believe he didn't need Kyle, then I had to hurt him, wail on him, and fuck him brutally.

Gazing down at Minty, the makeup on his face, the lip gloss on his mouth, and his gorgeous, slim body tight and ready to be beaten, I couldn't do it. I knew I needed to, but I didn't *want* to. Not like this. He was right. I needed it to be a scene, something with a defined beginning and end, and clear limits. I didn't *want* to be Kyle, even if that was what Minty needed from me.

I sat down by him on the bed, my shoulders shaking, my throat tight. I didn't want to hurt him like that. Down in my basement it was different. There, pain was fun, hot, intense. Here, hitting him, making him cry, would make me feel like I was a monster, a jealous, abusive dick as bad as Kyle.

"I don't want to hurt you tonight," I whispered as Minty ran his hands up and down my back comfortingly, sensing my distress. "I want to take good care of you tonight. I want to—"

I stopped short of admitting that I wanted to be sweet with him, maybe even make love to him—something I'd only attempted a few times as a young, dumb kid who hadn't lost his idealism yet. But for him, *with* him, I wanted to try.

Kyle thought Minty was insane? No, *I* was crazy. Wanting this with him was madness. I barely recognized myself, and why? It wasn't like Minty was special. He was like so many other kids, so many other subs.

Except he wasn't.

He was empathetic to a fault, powerful and strong, and he gave himself up to me like a dream. He *wanted* me to crack him open, and I would. One day soon, I'd find the right place to press or whip and he'd come apart like a bag of beans and spill his insides everywhere.

But that would be different. That wasn't tonight. Tonight I wanted—

This.

I wanted *this*.

Minty had shifted his head so that our lips were nearly touching, his breath against my mouth, and his hand twining up into my hair. My heart thundered madly, and I felt poised on the precipice of something beyond my understanding. "Kiss me," he whispered. "We're sober. We're not playing. I want it…"

I did too. No need to fight my desire for his lips now.

I touched our noses together, breathed in his scent, and gave in. The kiss started soft, sweet, and reassuring, but then I lost all sense of what vanilla might mean, pressing him down against his mattress, losing myself in the scent of his skin, the taste of his lips, and the sounds he made as I made out with him like a horny teenager, exploring his mouth with mine.

"Luke," he whispered when he pulled free to gasp for breath. "I think you like me."

I chuckled. "I guess I do."

"And I think that I lo—"

I put my fingers over his mouth. "Don't say it."

He pulled my hand away. "But it's true."

"Is it? You barely know me."

"I know enough." He smiled, kissed my lower lip, then my nose. "I know that just being near you makes my heart sing. Like that dumb Carpenters song my mom always used to listen to when I was a kid. She played it while she cleaned. She loved it."

I couldn't help but laugh.

"I think there's nothing you could tell me that would make me hate you," Minty said slowly. "You could even say that you wanted to end this, and I know I'd still love you."

"Minty—"

"I *do* love you," he interrupted, putting his hand over my mouth this time. "I love you, and I won't take it back."

I pulled his hand off. "You're not allowed to love me until you know who I am."

"Is that a challenge?"

"If it needs to be."

"Then let's go," he said, standing up, straightening his skirt and shirt, and turning to the mirror to re-apply lip gloss and smooth down his hair. "Let's go on our date so I can know everything about you."

My dick protested, but Minty was right. Making out and humping in his dorm room wasn't the plan for the evening. Suddenly, I was anxious. What if this wasn't enough? What if he needed what Kyle gave him more than he needed—

I broke off my thoughts and focused on what *I* wanted to give him tonight. A taste of the other me. But there was more to who I was than I'd be able to show in one evening. "You can't learn everything in one night."

"We have to start somewhere." Minty reached out for my hand. "I started on my knees with you, but what it's like to *stand* with you? Or am I not allowed to do that, Sir?" he teased.

I stood and wrapped my arms around him, teasing back, "But you're so pretty on your knees for me."

Minty grinned, went up on his tiptoes to kiss my lips quickly, and then took my hand again. "Come on then. Let's go on a date. I've never been on a real one. I hope it's magical."

I snorted at his fantastical bent, so absurd but so charming. "Let's just settle for it being real."

Minty

LUKE HAD ALMOST beaten me up and fucked me back there in a fit of jealousy, or the desire to prove something to me—to Kyle too, even though he'd already gone. I knew it in my soul. Like I also knew that he hadn't been able to because, as unlikely as it seemed, he *cared* about me. He didn't want to hurt me tonight. He wanted *this* instead.

I glanced over at him, watching him lick his ice cream cone, the light of the Bruster's neon sign reflecting in his hair. We sat on the bench next to the open window, licking and talking about nothing much at all.

It was amazing. I'd never had anyone want this with me before. Well, not anyone who also wanted to have sex with me. I had friends—great friends—who cared about me and enjoyed spending time with me. But no guy I'd had sex with cared about me like Luke did, and no guy I'd ever crushed on had wanted to actually date me either. They'd been content with a few sucks or fucks at most. The others had never even been interested at all.

"I had the pistachio here once, and it wasn't the best," Luke said, ducking his head to lick a drip from his cone. "But there's no beating the chocolate."

I opened my mouth to say I preferred Baskin Robbins's chocolate for flavor, but then shut it. I didn't want to wreck this moment of easiness between us.

"What?" he asked, pressing his leg against mine. "You were thinking something. I saw it flash over your face."

I shrugged. "It doesn't matter."

"If your thoughts didn't matter to me, we wouldn't be on this date. We'd be back in my basement."

I smiled at that. He was right, of course. He wanted to know me, the everyday me, not just the me that was submissive and compliant, or fighting back so that it felt good. Then why did it feel like I was risking everything just to admit a taste difference?

"Go on," he said. "Whatever you say is fine. I can handle it."

"All right." I took a slow breath and let it out as I gusted, "I like Baskin Robbins's chocolate better."

He lifted his brows. "And *that* was what you were thinking?"

"Yeah."

"Okay, and why didn't you want to tell me? I'm a big boy. I don't need someone to agree with everything I say." He paused then, turning to me fully after glancing around to make sure that no one had come up behind us while we sat with our ice creams. "You don't think that's what I want, do you? A sycophantic submissive has never been my type. I want to hear your thoughts—here, now, like this, and back in the basement too. I like that you don't agree with me, or that you fight me from time to time. It makes you real. Not some doll."

"I didn't want to ruin our date."

"I'm not an asshole like that. I like that you're different from me."

I considered that and nodded. I had to trust that he meant what he said. If I didn't, then I couldn't trust him in the dungeon anymore either, and I trusted him implicitly there. "No dolls here, just a fairy prince at your service."

Luke smiled, and then pointed out a drip on my cone. I hurried to suck it up before it fell from the end. I laughed, remembering a stunt I'd pulled earlier in the semester, in the Before Times. "Hey, do you want to hear about a performance art piece I did?"

"Performance art?" His eyes twinkled.

"Yeah. I'm an artist sometimes, you know."

"I didn't, actually. But I can see it. You're creative in other ways." He gestured at my clothes.

"Why, thank you." I gave him a glimmer of my sweetest sparkle. "I do take pride in my clothes. This was a genius piece of art, though. It was great. I wish Peter had filmed it—"

"Peter?"

"A friend. He's a photographer, and he just took pictures. I wonder if he's developed them yet. Anyway, like I said, it was fantastic. I got an ice cream cone from the university canteen—vanilla, like this one, only without the chocolate sprinkles, and I took it outside."

Luke bit into his cone, crunching and listening to me. I was tempted to lean over and lick a drop of chocolate off his chin, but who knew if someone might see us and give us crap about being queer. I was obvious enough with just the way I was dressed. I didn't want to push my luck, so I indicated his napkin and then waved at my own chin. He took the hint and wiped the chocolate drop away.

"And then what?" he asked.

"I laid down on the sidewalk, kind of out of the way of the main path, but not where everyone passing by couldn't see me. Being seen was important."

"Mm-hmm?"

"Yeah, and, oh! I have to tell you about my outfit because it was key to the performance! Absolutely key. A skin-tight sleeveless T-shirt, and a pink tutu skirt over my best blue jeans."

"Sounds cute, baby."

"I was very cute!" I licked some more ice cream, the sweetness coating my tongue and sliding down my throat. "So, just picture it. Me, lying there with the cone above my head." I lifted my cone up briefly to demonstrate. "Can you imagine it?"

"Absolutely."

"And then I let it melt, dripping onto my face. It went every-where, all over my neck and hair too. Next to me on the ground was a sign reading 'Cream My Face', which was the name of the art piece I was doing."

He chuckled then, taking another bite of his cone.

"I waited until the entire ice cream had melted, and then I

yelled, 'Cream my face!' and turned the cone upside down and dumped the rest onto myself. It was great! A real crowd pleaser."

"I bet," he said, laughing. "That's…amazing." He peered at me with a look of discovery in his eyes. "I had no idea."

"No idea that I'm an artist as well as the sexiest femme-boy scientist in the world?"

"Yeah, exactly that. I've been clueless. Not about the sexy part, but the rest."

I preened a little before devoting attention to finishing my ice cream cone.

"So, you're interested in science, nature, trucks, martial arts, cowboy boots, performance art, tutus, makeup, women's clothes…" He ticked the things off. "What else will I find out about you tonight?"

"Whatever you want to know."

He glanced around quickly and then combed his fingers through my hair, pushing a strand behind my ear, and then leaning close to brush a kiss on my cheekbone. "I'd like to know everything. But, like I said earlier, that'll take some time."

"We don't have a lot of that, do we? So we better fast-track it." I ignored his grimace at the reminder of our HIV positive state. "What about you? What are your hobbies? What do you love to do?"

Luke popped the last of his cone in his mouth, chewed, and dusted off his hands. I had a feeling he was stalling for time. Eventually, he said, "Well, my biggest hobby used to be the Dom stuff. I started out in it just for fun. Eventually some problems came up in my life that made me need to do it for money. After that, it was still fun, but it was also a job. That changes things."

"Yeah, if I got paid to do 'Cream My Face,' that'd sure change it. I mean, I *did* get paid. I left a tip jar out for the second performance and pulled a nice wad of cash. But if I had to do it like I depended on that to live? It would feel different."

"It would, but I don't know if it would have the same problems associated with it as turning my Dom hobby into my Dom job. There's a lot of responsibility to being a Dom. It doesn't end when a sub walks out the door. I have to be careful that what we do in a scene doesn't impact them in a negative way in the outside world."

"Yeah, of course." I knew from experience that what he did to me in his dungeon affected me for hours and days after it was over.

"Given all that, I had to take a break from it after my diagnosis. I wasn't in the right space mentally for a very long time. I'm getting by with my income from the shop right now, so long as I watch my expenses and only take my subs on cheap dates for ice cream." He winked.

I smiled. "I love this date."

"I'm glad." He paused. "That responsibility, though...that's part of why I was worried about us at first. What we do is on the edge. I worry sometimes that it'll make things harder for you, instead of better."

"Don't worry," I said, putting a hand on his arm. "I'm fine. I'm doing better than I have in a long time."

My stomach twisted oddly, and I couldn't put my finger on why. "You're giving me what I need."

For now.

The thought was unwanted, but there all the same. I wondered if it flashed over my face because Luke's expression also shifted.

I hurried on. "But that's what you do for a job. What do you do for fun?"

"Fun..." He trailed off, a distant look coming into his eyes. "I don't know."

"What do you do on your days off? When you're not at the shop, and you're not doing the Dom stuff—" and hadn't he said during one of our intake conversations that he hadn't been with anyone, much less as a Dom in months? "—what do you like to do with your time?"

"Hmm."

I could see that he had an answer, but was reluctant to share it with me. Pressure tightened my chest. I rubbed it, not sure why I felt hurt. "You don't have to tell me," I said, trying to fake like I didn't care. "It's not my business. We're not dating. We're just *on* a date. It's not the same thing."

"Baby," he sighed. "It's something I don't talk a lot about. Not that I'm ashamed of it, but it's private and I've never really talked much about it with a sub."

"Do you do something creepy?" I asked, suddenly worried.

"What?" He chuckled. "No."

"Then what?" I'd just told him he didn't need to tell me, but now I had to press. I needed the worry in my chest to resolve.

Luke sighed, thought another moment, and then confessed, "I have a sister I take care of."

I frowned. Did she live upstairs while we did whatever it was we were doing in the basement? Did she *know*? Gross. This too must have also reflected on my face because he laughed and took hold of my hand.

"No, no, she doesn't live with me. She lives at Riverwoods, a facility for disabled adults over on the Cumberland Plateau. She has Down Syndrome, and my folks are older now, and they can't take care of her any longer."

"Oh." Immediately, some puzzle pieces clicked into place. I could picture him with a sister who needed care. I imagined he'd be good at it. "What's her name?"

"Betsy."

"Is she older than you or younger?"

"Younger, by six and a half years. She's great," he said, a smile spreading involuntarily over his lips. For an instant, I was jealous of

Betsy that he was so uncomplicatedly happy at just the thought of her.

But that jealousy faded as his smile drained away. "I helped take care of her until I left for college. I was only there a year when my dad had a stroke that left him… changed. I went back home and took care of Betsy for a long time while Mom cared for Dad, but…" He shook his head.

"It sounds like a hard situation. My friend Daniel has to take care of his younger brother and sister because his mom's an alcoholic, and it's rough for him too. I don't know a lot about Down Syndrome, but it seems like maybe Betsy is, in some ways, a kind of permanent little sister?"

"She's her own person," Luke said a little defensively. "But, yeah, she'll need someone to look after her to some degree for the rest of her life. In the end, as Dad's health and mind deteriorated and took more and more of my mom's focus, my folks decided the place for her was in Riverwoods."

"How did you feel about it?" I sensed tension in him.

"I felt selfish."

"Why?"

"Because part of me was glad to be able to get back to my own life, go back to being a Dom and working a real job that paid money. Being with Betsy is always fun and rewarding, but I missed having my own life."

I scoffed. "It's not selfish to need to be your own person. I'd go insane if I couldn't be myself and live the way I need to live."

Another flicker passed over Luke's face, and I knew what he was thinking. The way I was living lately was insane enough.

Well, he had no idea how much I'd lose it if I also had to go live with my mom in the trailer, in that room where my father had asked me…

I shook the thought away.

"So, do you have a picture?" I asked, swinging my feet under the bench.

He dug his wallet out of his back pocket and unfolded a photo he kept there. He turned it toward me, showing me his sister. She was laughing with a wide mouth and broad-set eyes that were scrunched up too much to see the color, and dark, almost black hair that was cut into a messy, loose bob. "That's Betsy."

"She's pretty."

"Yeah." He put the photo away and went quiet again. "I go to see her once a month. Riverwoods isn't some awful institution. It's a nice place that takes her out on field trips and gives her an appropriate amount of freedom. She's even got a part-time job and has started dating someone. She says she's in love."

"That sounds good for her. See? If she'd stayed home, she wouldn't be in love now. And being in love is great." I took hold of his hand again. I enjoyed the way his fingers fit between mine.

Luke smiled wryly. "I hear you're a fan of it."

I froze, caught out and wondering what else Barry had told him about me. Obviously not enough since Luke had discovered my trauma on the fly in the middle of a scene. But if Barry had told him about my weakness for love, Luke might have the wrong idea of me.

"In the past, I've always loved the idea of love," I got out, trying to phrase things carefully. "But I'm not delusional. I've always known I was just pretending. I knew none of them loved me back."

Luke was quiet a moment, examining me. "You're worth being loved back."

"Am I?" I released his hand. "I don't know if that's true. But I'd like to be." I rubbed my arms, a chill gripping me. "I don't want to die alone."

Another silence, and then Luke asked, "Your mother wouldn't be there for you?"

"I won't give her the chance."

He frowned. "What do you mean?"

"At the first sign of my T-cells tanking, or at my first real illness." I slashed my hand across my throat. "Fin. Over. Dead. I won't give anyone a chance to sit with me while I go. It'll be fast, and it'll be permanent."

"Minty…" he breathed, his brows dropping low.

"Don't tell me you haven't thought about it. You've got the diagnosis too. You know where this ends up." Fuck, I'd gone down the worst possible path now. The one that acknowledged all the horrible shit he and I both wanted to forget tonight. But it was too late. It was out there.

"I've…" He cleared his throat, his head dropping slightly. "I've thought about it. Of course, I have. But—"

"We could make a pact, then. When it's time for either of us, we'll have a final scene together, and then we'll let the other go do what they need to do."

"Do what, exactly?"

"End our lives and be out of everyone else's hair."

He stared at me, and I could see the beginning of silver mixed into the blond near his ears. He was young to be graying, but it seemed saddest that he'd never live long enough to see it through.

"For God's sake," he gritted out. "You can't say shit like that and smile through it. You can't…"

"Why not?"

"Because it's…I…I'm not ready to give up on my life yet."

"Of course not," I huffed. "But when the time comes? I'm out of here. It's not like I'll be missing anything. I can't have *forever*. You know that, and I know that."

"Christ…"

I tore at the napkin on the table between us. "Sorry. I'm ruining it." I stood, straightening the silver skirt I'd been so eager to put on for the kind of date I'd longed for my entire life. "I don't need a date. I've never really had one before, and this one hasn't ended on the best note, but that's my fault, I know."

I wasn't eager to go back to my dorm room to be confronted by the flowers Luke had brought me, but it was better than being confronted by his wrecked eyes.

"We should go. I should…" I stopped before I said "study," because there was no way in hell I was going to do that.

If this evening was going to end like this, then maybe the stuff we did in the basement wasn't enough for me after all. Maybe I simply didn't deserve the attention of someone like Luke, someone good and loving who adored his sister and would never beat me up and fuck me without prior consent. But I knew someone who would.

"Sit down," Luke said, using *that* voice. It made my body obey like I was an automaton. Once I was back on the bench, he turned to me. "Okay, I'll agree to your pact. You'll come to me when you're going to do it, and I'll give you what you need. If that's a scene, okay. If that's for me to hold you, make love to you, then that's what I'll do too. If it's just to pretend you're not about to off yourself, all right. All I ask is that however you do it, no one else gets hurt."

I shuddered. I hadn't expected that. "And you? What will I give you if you come to me first?"

He shook his head. "I won't. I have Betsy, and I've gotta do everything I can to stick around for her. I owe my mom that. She needs me."

"No one needs me, so…" I shrugged. "It won't hurt many people when I'm gone. They'll keep going just fine."

Luke shook his head, took hold of my hand, and kissed the back again. "I don't believe that, but I also don't think it's right to pretend that a day won't come when I might share your thoughts.

It's true that eventually I'll be better off leaving my family in a hurry instead of draining their bank accounts and hearts with a prolonged sickness."

"See? I knew you were smart and would come around," I murmured, though my heart ached to see him give up like that. I wanted him to be more optimistic for both our sakes, but I could see he knew the truth. We were doomed. It was only a matter of time and how we chose to go out.

"Sorry. I made this date kind of suck," I said. "I think I was channeling my friend Daniel for a minute."

"Yeah? What's he like?"

"A party-pooper."

He laughed. "Oh, yeah?"

"Always. But he's still one of the best guys in the world." I stood up. "Come on. Was this it? You were just going to take me out to ice cream and be done with it?"

"No, I had more planned."

"Onward then."

He glanced around before sliding his arm around me, tugging me close, and hugging me tight. I sank into his arms. "You're a terrifying surprise," Luke whispered. "I want to use a whip to get to the heart of you."

"You can do that. I'll let you."

"I know you will. But not tonight. Tonight, we're going to keep things light from now on. Only things that make us smile."

I drew back and gazed up at him. As he released me, I murmured, "Deal. For the rest of tonight, only things that make us smile."

Chapter Fifteen

Luke

A s I pulled into the lot outside of Minty's dorm, I was pleased with how the rest of the evening had gone. I'd considered taking him home to fuck him, but the sexual energy of the night had turned dark after our conversation at Bruster's.

If we went back to my house, I figured we'd end up in the basement, and I didn't want to do that. I was sincere when I said I only wanted things that made us smile for this evening, and while fun times in the dungeon would eventually lead to smiles, in the short term they'd lead to crying, shouts, and pain.

"Want to come up?" Minty asked, turning to me in the darkness of the car. I could see the blond of his hair backlit and glowing, but his eyes were little more than glistening sparks in the night.

I hesitated, thinking of how awkward it felt to be a man in my early thirties going up to a college boy's dorm room with the full intent of fucking him.

"It's okay if you don't," he said, opening the door. "I was only—"

"Hey," I said, grabbing his arm before he could get out. "Do you put out on the first date?"

Minty halted, his brain turning over my question, looking for the accusation or judgment before he responded.

"Because I do." I gave him a half-smile I wasn't sure he could see. "I promise I'll make it good for you."

Minty shut the door again and turned to me, his hands on my face, and his mouth on mine. His lips were soft and warm, slick with lip-gloss, and he tasted of cherries as he kissed me.

I pulled away, whispering, "Stop, or you're going to make it even more awkward to walk through the lobby. Not only will I be the old guy in the dorm, but I'll have a hard-on that makes it clear I'm the old guy with bad intentions toward the pretty college kid I'm with."

"Seems like good intentions to me."

I grinned, but we didn't talk more.

The walk through the dorm wasn't as awkward as it could have been, but only because all eyes were on Minty. Did he deal with this every day? Whenever he came in or went out? Did the straight assholes gawp at him like he was an alien or a monster all the time? Christ. He was a strong man. So much stronger than he gave himself credit for.

I was still haunted by the proclamation of his suicidal intentions. Mainly because I couldn't decide if he was brave or selfish, strong or weak. I wasn't sure I could judge properly because Minty was a rare breed. The kind of man who'd done something completely taboo in his most helpless moment, and in doing so had wrestled power from the man raping him. If he could turn that vulnerability into strength and rageful power, then who knew what he was capable of?

So maybe planning a suicide was bravery, or maybe it was just the coward's way out. I didn't know. I wasn't the right man to answer that question.

When we reached Minty's door, I was half expecting the bathroom door across the way to pop open and for Kyle to reappear, but he didn't.

Inside, with the door locked behind us, lit up by the colored twinkle lights twisted around the pipe, Minty didn't waste time.

He pulled his spaghetti-strapped shirt off and slid his skirt down and, yes, he had on lacy panties, just as I suspected he would. He had a hard-on too, making those panties look uncomfortably small. The head of his cock poked out above the waistband as he stood in front of me, all pale limbs, and pink lips, nipples, and shiny cockhead. Fucking gorgeous.

I reached out to him, and he walked toward me with his head tilted back and his eyes shining with heat. I kissed him, pressing against him, feeling him rut his hard cock against my jean-clad thigh. Breathless with the taste and scent of him, I asked, "Do you have supplies?"

"Are we using condoms tonight?" he asked, confusion creasing his brow.

"No, but we'll want lube."

"No rough fuck?" He sounded almost sad about it.

"Only things that make us smile, remember?" I murmured, kissing his cheekbone, and then sighing into his ear to make him shiver.

"If you're sure…" he sounded nervous, almost as nervous as the first time he'd knelt for me.

I didn't know if that was because he needed some pain tonight, or if he simply hadn't ever been handled like this before. I decided not to ask because getting rough was off the menu. I wasn't in the mood, and he wasn't going to get it.

Part of being a man's sub sometimes meant *not* being hurt. He'd learn that too.

"I've never done this before," he whispered, as he lay back on his small dorm bed, watching me shed my clothes. "Most of the time I'm just fucking hookups. They're not cruel, but they're not tender either. So, yeah, I've never done it all gentle or whatever."

"Not even your first time?"

His breath hitched, and his eyes slid away from me.

Oh right, fuck.

"Um, *no*, and my second time was just like this horrible sort of train situation? I was drunk, and there was a pool table, and three…no, four guys. That was before I got vigilant about condoms. Before Daniel convinced me to be." He huffed and added, "Some good that did in the end, yeah?"

Silence fell between us as I pulled my pants off and tossed them aside.

"Sorry," he whispered. "Only things that make us smile. I forgot."

I shook my head, crawling onto the single mattress, holding my body over him. "When it comes to sex, I want to know it all, every feeling, happy or sad or bad." I lowered myself against him, our skin touching everywhere except where his pretty panties blocked our cocks. "It's important. I don't want to think we're having a sweet, loving moment when internally you're reliving trauma."

"Loving?" His voice hitched. "A *loving* moment?"

I could practically hear his hope that I was saying I loved him. And it wasn't as though I didn't, but it also wasn't as though I did. Yet.

I nuzzled his neck. "Love can be an action, not just a feeling."

"An action?"

"Mm, yeah." I kissed his throat, feeling him shiver against my body. "This is loving, right now. This kiss." I gave another. "And this." I moved to kiss his mouth, and we were lost together. The thumping sound of music drifting in from all the other rooms above, below, and beside us melded with the beating of our hearts. We kissed like we were innocent again. Like we'd never been hurt.

"Baby," I whispered when we came up for air. "You've got me so confused."

"About what?"

"About what we're doing," I murmured, smelling his hair and the heated skin of his neck. "You. Me. I didn't plan on us."

"There's an us?"

"There's been an us since you barged into the back office at Knox Supplies & News and tried to hand back that contract."

Minty ran his hand into my hair, feathering his fingers through it gently, a smile drifting onto his lips. "You liked me that day?"

I laughed. "You were like a present wrapped up in my favorite things—ballsy, determined, beautiful." I slid a finger down his throat, over his Adam's apple, and over his pale chest. "Bratty."

He grinned, wrapping his arms around my neck, and tugging me closer. "Sir—I mean, Luke, you don't normally open up so much."

"No, I guess I don't."

"I like it."

"Do you?"

"Yeah, I like knowing you. The real you."

"The Dom is the real me as much as everything else. It's a piece of me that I can't deny."

"Good thing I don't want you to deny it then." He fluttered his lashes at me, and then pressed his arms up and back, crossing them at the wrists, and lifting his chin provocatively. "This 'love is an action' thing? What else does love do?"

I kissed him again then, holding his arms down at the wrists, giving him a hint of dominance, but not enough to take over and turn this into a scene. I released him only to take off his panties and reach for the lube to slick my fingers. As I investigated his hole, I was surprised to find a small butt plug already inserted.

Minty giggled. "Your face. You look so surprised!"

I blinked rapidly, feeling the size of it—small, flared base, indicating a slender plug; probably a model I was familiar with from the store—and I tugged lightly. It pulled right out. Yes, it was a model I knew. I wasn't sure what to do with it, but Minty took it from me and tossed it onto the floor. "I'll clean it later," he murmured. "I took care of things down there before you came to pick me up, just in case. So, yeah, surprise."

I slid two fingers in easily, laughter choking me as I said, "Aren't you always?"

Minty twisted his hips, taking me to the base of my fingers, and nodded. "Minty Surprise. I should, um, that's good. Right there. Fuck." His eyes rolled back, and then he panted out, "I should figure out a performance art piece with that title. It can involve Peppermint Patties or, ah, fuck, that's so *good.*"

"Or?" I encouraged, both amused and curious to see what he'd say—but also the sadist in me had awoken, and the game of making him talk while I fingered him, working his prostate and his rim, was too much fun to resist. "Go on."

"Peppermint Patties, or, um, candy canes? Oh, God, that could be dirty, yeah? A Christmas performance piece."

"Who'd see it, baby?" I whispered. "I don't think the campus police are gonna let you fuck yourself with a candy cane on the sidewalk outside the UC."

"No, probably not." He gasped in pleasure, his hips jolting up. "But can you imagine the tips I'd make?"

I laughed again, twisting my fingers before pulling out and adding a third. I didn't really need to prep him so well. Minty was accustomed to taking a cock without lube, but I wanted this to be a smooth ride for both of us. I worked him open more, asking him questions, helping him design a concept for his candy cane Minty Surprise performance—which, in the end, sounded more like a porn scene than anything else.

When his thighs were shaking and his hands were clenching and releasing where he'd left them crossed at the wrist above his head, I grinned at the power I felt rising inside. I loved giving this kind of sweet torment too.

"I want to call you something," Minty whispered, his hips shuddering with restrained lust, and his hard cock slick at the crown with pre-cum. "I *need* to call you something."

"Luke's not good enough?"

He shook his head. "It's okay for a date, but now, like this…ah, this is…you're killing me."

"What do you want to call me?"

I could tell he had a pet name in mind, but was shy to say it. I didn't know how I felt about that either as it'd been ages since I was involved with someone who wanted to give me a pet name. With Benji, it'd only ever been Luke when I wasn't Sir.

I worked a fourth finger into him as he hesitated to answer. "Want to take a fist?" I whispered, kissing his inner thighs, and then his balls.

"Fist?" he panted. "Tonight?"

"No, not tonight."

"Mm, I could take it tonight," he said, reaching down to stop my hand from withdrawing, touching my wrist, and peering at me with wide, hot, needy eyes. "I could. I'd be so good at it. I'd open up for you."

"I know you would," I said, pulling his hand free of my wrist and kissing the fingers. "Put your hands back above your head." It wasn't an order, I didn't use my Dom voice, but he obeyed anyway.

"When?"

"When *I* want to," I said. "And only if you tell me the name you want to call me. It can't be Sir. Not when we're like this. Times like these are separate, different."

Minty's breathing came so fast, his chest so flushed, I was worried he'd pass out before he told me, and if he had, I wouldn't have been sure if it was from pleasure or the worry that I'd reject his chosen name.

"It's not Sir," he whispered. "But we've used it in play, and—" his hips jolted again, and he gasped. "That's, that's a lot," he moaned. "That's going to make me come."

"Mm, no, you won't," I said it easily, but I was dominating him without meaning to. It'd been a long time since I had a sub who brought that out in me so effortlessly. "Tell me."

"I…I'm embarrassed to say."

An inkling began to grow in my mind. "Even better then," I whispered. "Then it's something you really want. Give me your truth, baby."

"Okay, Daddy," he whispered. "That's my truth. I want to call you Daddy."

I kissed both his inner thighs, and nuzzled his balls, my mind sliding through the various implications of this, wondering if it was healthy, hoping it was because I was going to agree. No doubt about it.

I liked the word in his mouth, the sweetness of it now that it didn't scare him, now that it was his idea. And the near-devotion it held when he called me by that formerly-forbidden title definitely appealed to the Dom in me.

"You can call me Daddy. You can call me anything you want, but especially that."

I rose back over his body, kissing him sweetly as he groaned and gripped my hair with one hand, holding me in the kiss. For my part, I held his other wrist down, shifted between his legs, and when he lifted his hips, I aimed toward his open asshole, thrusting the head of my cock inside with little effort.

Minty's head went back, eyes fluttering. But when I stroked deeper, he brought his chin down, eyes on mine. He breathed, "You feel good, Daddy," very softly, and with a honeyed sweetness that made me ache all over, like I'd rubbed sugar over my gums. "So good."

He gazed up at me solemnly, pupils dilated, pink lips open, and his wet tongue peeking out. I was torn between watching him watch me and kissing him again. In the end, I settled for releasing my hold on his wrist and twining both hands into his hair, holding his head in place, demanding without words that his gaze stay on me.

Overcome with emotion and lust, I whispered a question that I hoped he knew how to answer. "Who's fucking you, baby?"

"You are, Daddy," he answered back, his cock leaping between us. "Daddy's fucking me."

"Mm, and who's loving you?"

"Daddy is."

I kissed his nose. "You feel so good, so hot and tight. Squeeze me. That's it. Oh, baby, you're so sexy, so incredibly hot."

"You are too," he said, keeping his eyes on mine, the blue rim of his irises nearly swallowed by his pupils. "Luke?"

"Mm?"

"Will you stay with me?"

My brain was too focused on the sweet tug of his rim along my shaft as I withdrew halfway, enjoying the squeeze, to process his meaning. "Here? I can stay here."

"Okay," he said, with a sigh that let me know I'd missed something, but I couldn't figure out what right now. His hands gripped my shoulders, and his hips flexed up to meet my thrusts. "Daddy, please make me come."

I kissed him again then. He sounded so desperate, so needy, and I sensed it wasn't just because he wanted to shoot his load, but something else inside him too. I wanted to show him how it felt to have a man make love to him, to be a precious person in someone's arms, gifted only with sweet pleasure and avoiding all pain. But when he nipped my lower lip, I pulled away, shocked, and stopped mid-thrust to grip his jaw hard.

"What was that?"

"I don't know, Daddy," he said, his hot, lust filled eyes glinting with mischief. "You tell me."

I held still in him, letting my body weight immobilize him, forcing him to feel my cock halfway in his body. I enjoyed how he squirmed, trying to get more and failing. "This isn't a scene."

"I know."

"We're being loving."

"Can't you love me a little harder?"

I pondered his question and then moved my hand from his jaw down to his throat. He shook beneath me, as if that alone almost sent him over the edge. "My love isn't good enough for you?"

"No, Daddy," he whispered, his eyes gleaming as I gripped his throat harder. "I need more."

I gritted my teeth, not liking my sub telling me what to do, of him thwarting my plans for our lovemaking. I'd imagined the scene—

Wait.

Scene.

This wasn't lovemaking if it was on my terms. Then it was just another scene I'd designed, only coupled with the lie of me telling him it wasn't.

"This the way you want me to love you?" I asked, tightening my hand on his throat and thrusting hard.

"Yes… It's an action, not a feeling, right? So, love me harder."

I tried to give us both what we wanted. A hand on his throat, and harder, sharper thrusts, while still kissing his mouth and cheeks with a soft fondness I'd never given him in a scene.

Minty groaned and clutched me close, his legs trembling with lust. "Daddy, I want to come," he got out around the pressure I kept on his neck. His face was flushed, and his pulse throbbed against my palm. "Make me come. Please, Daddy."

His cock jumped between us with each iteration of the word,

and I shifted to make sure I was pegging his prostate with each thrust.

He gazed at me, his eyes glassy with need, and then he groaned. "Fuck, Daddy, you feel so good."

He shook against me, cum spurting between our bodies, his legs hitching against my sides and his hands coming up to claw at where I clenched his throat slightly harder.

I didn't let up.

When he dropped his hands and his asshole stopped convulsing on my cock, I let go. He sucked in a breath, his body shuddering with the need for air, and I plunged into him, held his gaze, and came too.

The orgasm was rolling and sweet, not the harsh, brutal pumps that overtook me in the dungeon scenes, but a drawn-out, quivering pleasure that emptied my balls into his ass. He moaned, taking it, his lips darting out to lick his lips as he held eye contact, watching me come for him.

"Luke," he whispered when I collapsed on him. He stroked my back. "Was that okay? I'm sorry. Did I mess it up?"

I shook my head. "That was real, wasn't it? That was how you wanted me to love you?"

"Yes." His voice quivered. "But is that all right?"

I kissed his shoulder. "We're learning each other now. This is part of it."

He held me tighter, squeezing his asshole on my softening cock, and I buried my face in his neck, breathing him in. He was right. This wasn't what I planned or wanted with him tonight, but I'd been honest too. This was real. This was how he made love.

It wasn't the scene I'd planned.

But it didn't matter.

I still wanted him.

Part II

November 1991

Chapter Sixteen

Minty

"**H**AVE YOU EVER been fucked by someone who liked you?"

Peter glanced past me to where Windy was huddled beneath the blanket we'd grabbed from my dorm room. The three of us sat underneath the big oak tree on the Hill in the lowering autumn sun, ignoring our responsibilities to enjoy the newly cool weather. "Yes?" he replied.

"Who?"

"Daniel? And Adam? Both the guys I've been with liked me—still like me, I guess."

"Hmm." I'd already known that, of course, but I was still trying to put my finger on why things with Luke had gone the way they had.

When we first met, he'd seemed to agree with me that everything needed to be business-like between us for this to work. But as we'd met for scenes, and I was forced to show him more of my fucked-up damage, he changed. I changed too, of course, and we kept on changing until he made that request to take me on a date.

Then there was the date itself… Such a weird mix of give and take, sad and happy, sweet and sexy. It'd been like I gorged on a fruit basket of new emotions and sensations, and now I couldn't stop turning over the apple of how it felt to be fucked by a guy who liked me. All of me. Even the me that I was when I wasn't seducing or being seduced, when I wasn't kneeling or fighting, or getting brutally or cheerfully screwed by a stranger.

"It's weird, isn't it?"

"Uh, no?" Peter said, predictably.

"What about you?" I asked, nudging Windy. "You ever been fucked by a guy who actually liked you?"

"Sure." He shivered beneath the blanket. My Army surplus jacket kept me warm, but Windy hadn't gone home to pick up his winter clothes yet. Hence the blanket. "Stephen, my first boy-friend."

"Right. High school sweetheart who didn't tell anyone about you and later got some girl pregnant at ETSU."

"Yeah." Windy sighed. "You can't have everything, I guess."

"No, you can't." Or I couldn't anyway. I had a guy who liked me, who had fucked me like I was special, and could take me apart in his basement. Yet we were both going to die soon. So *everything* wasn't in the stars for us.

"What's this all about?" Peter asked.

"His Dom, clearly," Windy said, shading his eyes. The sky was wide, blue, and dotted with fluffy clouds, and the stark tree limbs above looked gothic against it.

"Yeah," I agreed. "He likes me."

Peter's brows drew down. "Do you like him?"

"Yeah. I'm in love with him. Obviously." I caught myself doing what I always did, tossing out the word love just because it made me feel good, optimistic. But the weight of my diagnosis jerked me back down, and I reconsidered my statement. "I mean, I think I might really be in love with him this time. For real."

I must have sounded serious in some way that Peter and Windy weren't familiar with because Windy sat up, and Peter scooted forward. Both of them took one of my hands in theirs.

"What happened?" Windy asked.

"He took me on a date. He told me stuff about his life. Like how he went to college, but had to drop out, and other personal stuff too."

"Like?" Windy prompted.

"He has a sister, Betsy. She has Down Syndrome, and he really cares about her and considers it his duty to be there for her to make sure she's okay."

"That's good," Peter said.

"At the end of the date, we fucked, and it was different. It wasn't like when I go to his basement to get hurt. He did choke me some in the end, but the actual fuck was…" I squirmed. Heat rushed into my cheeks.

Normally, I had no problem talking to my friends about all the random sex I had, but this was special. Different.

"It was…" Peter urged me on.

"He wasn't trying to hurt me or dominate me. He just *liked* me and wanted to make me feel good. He wanted to be inside me because he feels, I don't know, tender or something towards me." I plucked a piece of brown, dying grass and threw it in the air. It fluttered to the ground again. "It was weird."

"You sound like you're not sure if you liked it," Peter said.

"I'm not sure I did," I admitted. "I mean, I came pretty hard. He was good at regular sex. Not like some assholes I've had. I felt like he was really into me, and into knowing me. But after he left? It all felt like a lie."

"A lie?"

"Yeah, like he hadn't really fucked *me*, he'd fucked some idea he had of me. But I can't think of any untrue thing from the entire night. I was myself, and I let him see me, the real me. He seemed to like that. For real."

"Of course he did," Windy reassured me.

"But after he'd gone home, I tossed around all night feeling sort of—" I flailed my hands around. "Scared?"

"Yeah?"

"Yeah. I felt scared, and alone, and like there must be a sick twist in this somewhere."

It wasn't like I didn't know what the sick twist was. Finally finding someone who got me and who gave me what I needed in every way, only for there to be an expiration date. Worse, there was no way to know for sure when that date was, or how long it might take to reach it.

"Have you told him this?" Windy asked.

"No, I don't want him to think I didn't enjoy it."

Peter squeezed my hand. "But you didn't?"

"I did a little." I tugged my hands back, twisting them in my lap. "I think I should have enjoyed it a lot, but it was like he was telling me he loved me in a language I didn't understand."

Peter hummed softly, and Windy muttered, "*Je t'aime.*"

"Right. Like that. Then… it was only when he started speaking some of the words I *do* know that I felt right about it."

And by "words," I meant actions, and by actions I meant choking me.

"But then it was over, and he left." I grimaced. "He didn't insult me, or smack me, or make me feel like a whore even once." I grabbed another piece of grass, twirling it between thumb and forefinger. "I don't know how I feel about that."

"*Mon ami,*" Windy said, slinging his arm around my shoulder. "That's intense stuff."

Peter's brows furrowed again. "This girl I went to high school with? Her parents were psychologists. Maybe you could benefit from talking to someone like them? They were good people."

"Like I have the money for that."

"There's free counseling on campus through the Student Psych Center."

I rolled my eyes. "You think some twenty-one-year-old grad student is going to know what to say when I tell them about my history, about what my father did to me, and that I'm a total fucked-up mess now because of it?"

"Would you have preferred your Dom had hit you on the date? Called you a slut?" Windy asked, ignoring my last comments.

I sat up straighter. "Yeah. It would have felt normal and expected between us. This felt like…" I struggled to come up with an example. "You know how church choirs usually sing their hymns backed by organs or piano? But now they've started having these early services for young people with religious rock bands singing praises and stuff?"

"No," Peter said, of course, because he didn't ever go to church despite his father being the head of the religious studies department at the university. Also, he was a Jewish atheist.

"My family's Catholic," Windy reminded me. "No rock bands."

"Okay, well, just believe me. In white, Appalachian churches, this is happening. I know because my mom still makes me go with her sometimes. Anyway, the first few times she took me to the rock band worship, I was like, 'Yeah, okay, this is a service, I guess, but is it worship? I like it, but it is *church*?'"

"Okay, I'm following you," Peter said.

"So that's how I felt. I liked it, but was it sex?"

"Maybe it was lovemaking," Windy offered.

"That's what he said."

Peter and Windy shared a long look, and then Peter cleared his throat. "He really said that? Or is that some of your wishful thinking?"

"He said that. I swear. He said love can be an action and not a feeling. So, it's not like he said he was *in love* with me. He just wanted to fuck…lovingly, I guess. And I came, and it was good. Different. But weird. Was it sex, though? Or was it something other guys who aren't me get to have with people who truly like them?"

Windy blinked at me. "Wow, you're all up in your head about this. I think you have to tell him."

"What if he—"

Windy put a hand over my mouth. "Shh. No what ifs. Just talk to him."

"I agree with Windy," Peter said, getting his stuff together as the bell in Ayers tolled. "Sorry. I've got to get to class, but Windy's got your back on this."

"Actually, I gotta go too," Windy said, dropping the blanket as he stood and stretched, his green shirt riding up and showing a slice of his nearly hairless stomach and his deep belly button.

"I thought you were skipping class with me?"

He shook his head. "Sorry. Big test at the end of the week. I can't miss this lecture."

Windy and Peter said their goodbyes, but Windy lingered a moment after Peter had walked off. "By the way," he said, squatting down next to me. "Next time you talk to your Dom, can you ask him how a person gets trained to do what he does? I'm interested."

I scoffed. "For real?"

"Yeah." His eyes darkened. "Got a problem with that?"

"No?"

"Good."

I gathered up my blanket, pondering so many things—whether what Luke and I had done felt right, trying to picture Windy as a Dom, and wondering why he wanted to try it. I thought about Luke's sister Betsy and whether I wanted to meet her, and what it meant about me and Luke if I did. I wondered if I could convince him to fuck me the way he had the other day and then, afterward, take me into his basement and beat me for it. A punishment for letting him love me.

My brain was in complete overload by the time I arrived at my dorm room with my arms full of the big blanket.

I keyed open my room, and as I did, someone pushed me hard from behind. I let out an *oomph* as I tripped over the trailing end of the blanket and fell inside to the floor. Rolling over, heart pumping from adrenaline, I saw Kyle step over the threshold. He shut and locked my door behind him. His mouth was tight, and his eyes were wild as he shoved down his sweatpants and whipped out his hard cock.

"Suck it."

I blinked, my mouth filling with saliva. My dick rose hard and fast against my jean skirt. I was already crawling toward him in a dazed, overcome instant, moving automatically.

With shaking hands, I reached for Kyle's dick, and my mouth dropped open like I was a dog and Pavlov had conditioned me. Instantly, Luke's face flashed into my mind. I saw him in his basement, shirtless, with his scary red whip, ready to beat me with it. Then I flashed back to the intimate fuck we'd shared in this very room the other night, and the fact that I hadn't heard from him since his call the following day to check on me. It all sped through my brain faster than light as I took hold of Kyle's dick.

With a satisfied grunt, Kyle grabbed my hair and shoved into my mouth.

Then he was using me.

I could have fought in any number of ways, but I felt paralyzed. He gripped my hair so hard that tears came to my eyes. When, after a few moments of gagging on his dick, I began to struggle, pushing against his thighs with both hands, he held me fast. One hand gripped the back of my neck, and the other alternated between holding my jaw to keep it open and slapping my face hard enough to sting. The tears that had already sprung to my eyes slipped down my cheeks.

"That's right. Cocksucking bitch."

I struggled against his thighs, trying to pull off his cock, but he gripped my head and pulled me forward until he was down in my throat, cutting off my air as he held me fast, my nose in his sweaty pubes.

"Die eating it," he grunted, hunching so that his cock moved incrementally as I struggled for breath. "I fucking hate you, you piece of shit, faggot, whore."

He pulled out then and hit me so hard I fell on my back against the blanket. I was disoriented by the strike—in the past he'd mainly kept to my body when landing punches—and as I tried to get my bearings, he pushed my jean skirt up and my tights and underwear down. He flipped me over. I barely had time to register the shift in position before his weight was on me.

I fought hard then, the memory of my father flashing in my mind—a similar weight and build as Kyle—and as he fit the head of his cock against my asshole and breached me painfully, I twisted and fought. He lurched forward, burying himself in my ass with a searing pain that made me feel sick. Covering my mouth with his hand, he started to thrust. Rage surged through me. I opened my mouth and bit the fleshy palm of his hand, clamping down hard.

Shouting, he punched the back of my head, and I almost blacked out, seeing stars. But when he pulled out of me, sitting back on his heels to inspect the damage to his hand, I rolled onto my back and spit in his face, another echo of my past. As he reached up to wipe the saliva from beneath his eye, I barked out, "I've got HIV, motherfucker. Hear me? I've got HIV."

Kyle's face paled before growing even more purple with rage. My gut dropped through the floor. He was going to kill me.

He grabbed my shirt and punched my face. Rising to his feet, he kicked me in the side twice before backing away in terror. He barely got his cock back in his sweatpants before he'd flung the door open and raced out of my room.

I panted on the floor, crying and trembling. Had I been raped? Had he *raped* me?

I didn't know for sure. I thought so. But it wasn't as if what he'd done to me was any different, or our interactions before I bit him at all dissimilar to what they'd been every other time before. It was just that this time, *this* time I hadn't wanted it.

But I hadn't said no either. And every other time I hadn't said no or yes.

There'd been plenty of interactions with Kyle that went down just like this, only they'd ended with me greedily sucking down his cum or taking it up the ass until I'd spunked too.

And if I didn't want it, why hadn't I fought back from the start? I knew Aikido. I'd won tournaments. I had that damn trophy. But I'd gotten up to my knees…I'd reached for his cock…I'd opened my mouth…

I shakily kicked my tights all the way off, straightened my skirt, padded barefoot to lock the door, and threw off my coat. I curled up on my bed, staring across the room. Just a few nights ago, I was in this bed with Luke, and I'd spent the last few days wondering if what we did was good, if it had even been sex to me.

This, though…

What just happened had recently been my baseline idea of a hot hook-up. I'd always considered what Kyle and I did consensual, even when maybe it wasn't. I didn't know anymore. I just knew I hadn't come back to my dorm room expecting Kyle to be here, and yet…

Had this happened before I'd met Luke, I would have considered it a lucky encounter.

Fuck.

I squeezed my eyes tight and my asshole too, still feeling the burn where Kyle had roughly shoved inside.

Luke's rules spun through my head. If I told him about this? If I said what'd happened, that Kyle had gotten into my throat and my ass, would he believe me if I said I hadn't wanted it? That it wasn't me breaking our contract? Or would he leave me behind? Good riddance to stinking trash. Adios to the difficult little liar?

And what good was being *liked* really if that kind of abandonment was still possible?

Being liked was stupid.

Being raped was more my speed.

I pulled the pillow over my head, that final thought sinking in like a tattoo on my brain. Permanent, indelible.

My heart and head were lost in a haze of feelings, disjointed thoughts, imagined accusations, and horrible memories—and none of it gave way to anything except scattered sleep.

I stayed in bed for the next two days. I didn't eat. I got up only to pee and grab a sip from the hallway water fountain. I didn't go to class.

And I sure as fuck didn't answer any phone calls.

Chapter Seventeen

Luke

"H AVE YOU EVER put yourself out there, Bets, and then had the person reject you?"

"Rodney didn't reject me," she said, giving me a silly wink.

"No, I guess he didn't." I tweaked her hair, and she rolled her eyes, batting at my hand.

"Why?" She tilted her head, looking me up and down. "Do you have a boyfriend, Lukey?"

I smiled, taking hold of her hand and squeezing it. We sat by the big fountain out in front of Riverwoods. It was another beautiful fall day, and we'd assembled a picnic from food our mother had provided.

"Do you?" she prodded, poking me with her finger and giving me her big, wide grin that never failed to make my heart feel a little lighter.

"I thought I might," I admitted. "Believe it or not."

"Does Mom know?" she asked, giggling.

"No. It never got serious enough to tell Mom about him." Not serious enough, huh? Then why was my heart aching like Minty had stepped all over it in red high-heeled shoes. I was sure he had a pair in a closet somewhere.

"She said she doesn't care now, remember? About you liking boys?"

I nodded. Mom hadn't handled my initial coming out as well as she could have, but she'd come around in the end. Dad had struggled even more, but this post-stroke father of mine couldn't accept me at all. The last time I'd had dinner at their place, he'd lamented again that they'd passed their genes on to two dead ends. Which was a fucked-up thing to say, but that's how he was now. Dad was fucked up.

Even though Mom was accepting, and I tried not to care what this version of my father thought of me, I couldn't imagine going home with Minty on my arm. He was gorgeous, sexy, and stunning in so many ways. But those same ways would leave my parents' jaws hanging open. I hadn't even begun to think about how I'd introduce him to them before he stopped answering my calls.

Now I wished I'd never taken him out on that date, never tried to 'make love' to him. I kept thinking back to how I'd sensed the next morning on my way out the door that something was bugging him, that I'd gone wrong somehow. Now I knew I'd definitely gone wrong by not staying and asking him about it then and there.

But I'd decided to let it go. And now what? Was he letting that asshole Kyle tear him apart again? With no class or caution, no caring or skill?

I wiped a hand over my face.

"What's wrong?" Betsy asked. "Did you love him a lot? Like how I love Rodney?"

"No," I said, but my gut twisted in a way that called me a liar.

I didn't love Minty or Mitchell, or whatever he needed or wanted to be called. I'd Dommed him, and he'd been a dream sub in a lot of ways. I'd felt things for him, stuff I didn't like feeling, and I'd let myself open up to the *idea* of loving him because—

Because I was going to die.

And I didn't want to go out without having shared that kind of thing—love—with another person. Did that mean Minty was just in the right place at the right time? That my feelings weren't even about him? Were they about *me?*

Why didn't that make me feel better?

"Lukey, you don't seem okay." Betsy said this with quiet empathy, her hand resting in mine and squeezing. "I know I'm not as smart as some of your other friends, but you can talk to me."

My heart wrenched. "You're plenty smart, Bets. It's not that."

"What is it then?"

"I guess I don't know what I feel or what I want."

"Oh. Like when Rodney told me he was going to get his mom to buy me a ring, and I was confused because I didn't want him to?"

"Rodney's buying you a ring?" I frowned. They were both legally old enough, but how would it work? Would they stay at Riverwoods together? Or would they—

"Don't worry, Lukey. I said no."

"Why? I thought you loved Rodney."

"I want to date a few more years." She smiled again, her eyes twinkling. "I like dating. I didn't get to do it when I was a teenager. Now it's more fun. We can have sex, and no one can stop us."

I blinked. "Um…"

She giggled. "Are you going to give me a safe sex talk too?"

I huffed. "No, I'll leave it up to Mom to do that."

Betsy laughed again.

"I do feel like that, though," I said. "Like what you said about the ring. I didn't go into this, uh, *situation* with this guy to fall in love. I didn't mean to develop feelings for him. But when I started to feel them anyway, I wanted to see if—"

Was that what I'd wanted? What *had* I been doing with Minty?

"Hell if I know what I wanted to see, Bets. But what I do know is I scared him off."

"Because you liked him too much?"

"Yeah. I don't think he wants to be liked by the men he's sleeping with."

Betsy's brow creased, and I realized I'd said too much, but then she said, "Julianne's like that. Across the hall from me? She sleeps with guys and when they like her for it, she tells them to go away."

"Julianne has Down?" I asked.

Betsy shrugged. "Yes."

"And the guys she sleeps with also…?" I didn't know how to ask.

Betsy frowned then. "She's a grown-up. She's twenty-nine. She can choose for herself."

I nodded, though some part of me worried all the same. I was glad Betsy seemed content with Rodney. "I guess you're right, Bets."

"I am."

We ate in silence for a few minutes, Mom's chili going down easy. Then, as I unwrapped the homemade lemon cookies, Betsy's favorite, she asked me, "Did the boy you like *tell* you he doesn't like to be liked? Before you started dating?"

"Sort of."

"But you liked him anyway?"

"Yes."

"Maybe call him and tell him you're sorry."

"Sorry for liking him?" I laughed.

"Sorry for breaking his rules," she said. "You taught me that, remember? People have rules, and if you break them, then you need to say sorry."

I nodded. I had a lot of rules, especially when I was in Dom mode. Minty had held up his end of the bargain until I messed things up. I supposed it *was* time to call again, and if he didn't answer, I'd have to stop by.

Even if he didn't want to continue with me, I still wanted to make things right. I needed to admit it'd been me who screwed up and ask for his forgiveness.

"You're right. I'm going to do that."

"When?"

"Tomorrow."

"I'm glad. Now, will you come inside and meet Rodney's little turtle? His name is Toots, and we have a toy racetrack he walks around."

"Sure," I said, crumpling up all the trash and shoving it into the bag I'd brought. "I'd love to meet Toots."

Minty

I SQUEEZED MY eyes shut harder against the knocking on my dorm room door, hoping that whoever it was—was it Kyle again? Back to finish the job?—would just go away.

"Minty! It's me!"

Oh, fuck. It was the other horrible alternative. Luke. He was here, and now I'd have to tell him, and he'll know, not just suspect… And I'll have to explain why I didn't answer the phone and instead let him leave twelve worried messages on my answering machine.

"Mitchell? Are you in there? Open the door."

That voice. Using that name.

As always, I was helpless to resist it, and I stood on shaky legs to shuffle to the door. I unlocked but didn't open it, calling weakly, "Come on in," as I headed back to my bed and mostly covered myself in the blankets.

I wore just a pair of briefs and the stench of sweat caused by anxiety and fear and lack of showering. I was disgusting. This was the last way I wanted Luke to see me for the last time. I'd really been hoping he'd just drop me altogether, and I'd never have to worry about seeing him again. I didn't want to face him.

"Minty?" Luke's voice was low and tender as he shut the door behind him and stepped cautiously through the shaded and shadowed room and over to my bed. "Are you all right? Are you sick?"

The fear in his tone reminded me that of *course* he might come to that conclusion, given our shared status.

"I've been worried about you," he said, grabbing a chair and dragging it over to the bed, sitting on it and peering at where my head poked through the sheets. "At first I thought you'd just bailed on me because I—"

He cleared his throat. "And maybe you did, because maybe—"

"Luke," I said. I hadn't really spoken in several days, and my voice was all grated and horrible sounding. "I'm fine."

"You're not sick?"

I shook my head.

"So, I did drive you off?"

I squeezed my eyes shut. For a smart guy, a good Dom, he'd just stupidly given me an easy out. I could say yes, and that would be… that. I didn't think Luke was the kind of guy to beg for me to give him another chance.

But I couldn't lie. I shook my head.

"I didn't?"

"No."

"Then why haven't you been answering your phone?"

When I didn't reply, he got up and flipped on the light, sucked in a breath, and a nightmarish expression distorted his features.

I winced. I'd managed to keep anyone in my dorm from noticing my face, though I'd looked at it in the mirror enough times to wonder if this bruise was bad enough to leave some kind of permanent mark.

"Holy shit," Luke whistled. "You're hurt." He touched my swollen cheek gently, sliding down to my split lower lip. "Who did this? That asshole? It was, wasn't it?"

I froze. I didn't know how to answer. If I said yes, then he'd assume I'd been going behind his back, against our agreement, but if I said no… Then he'd assume I was lying. After all, why else would I be in bed, ignoring his calls?

"He did," Luke said. "He hurt you."

Gently, he urged me to sit up, and when he got a look at the contusion on the side of my naked torso, his mouth went flat and his eyes grim. "Mitchell, did you go to him?"

My lips trembled, my chin quivered, and tears welled behind my lids. I kept them shut, not wanting to see his disbelief when I shook my head no.

"You didn't go to him?"

I shook my head again.

"He did this to you without your consent?"

I nodded. I thought so, at least. Maybe. It was confusing.

Luke sat on the bed beside me, pulling me into his arms, and I fell against him, sobs breaking free for the first time since it happened. He stroked my hair, murmured quiet words, and when I finally calmed down, he said he'd be right back. He was going to get some water and coffee for me.

He must have just gone down to the canteen in the lobby because he was back before I had time to stop panicking about what he was doing here and what was going to happen now. He came back in with a cold bottle of water, a hot cup of coffee, and a hot dog with chili on top. The scent of it made my mouth water.

"Here," he said, using the wooden desk chair he'd pulled over as a makeshift table for the things he'd brought. "When did you eat last? It's been a while, hasn't it?"

I wasn't sure, actually. But I still couldn't bring myself to talk to him. Silently, I took a sip of the water, and a sip of coffee, and the difference in temperature felt like a wake-up call to my stomach.

When I picked up the hot dog and stuffed it in my mouth, I suddenly remembered how eagerly my hands had gone for Kyle's dick, how I'd had him between my lips before I'd had the sense to try to stop it. I gagged before I could swallow the bite.

"Is your mouth okay?" Luke asked.

I nodded.

"Do you want me to cut the hot dog up?"

I agreed, and he used the plastic knife and fork from the canteen to dismantle the phallic dog and turn it into chili covered bites of meat and bread. I closed my eyes and dove in. From past experience, I knew the flavor was good, but in my misery, it tasted like ash.

"Baby," Luke whispered when I'd finished the food, the coffee, and half the water. "Did he... I mean, can I look at you?" He motioned downward, indicating my ass. "Is everything okay there? No tears? No infection setting in?"

"He didn't tear me," I whispered. "I've had worse fucks than this." I choked on the words. Memories of the first time I'd had a man on my back and not wanted him there filled my mind. What I'd said to my father had been oh-so-different from what I'd said to Kyle. But somehow, I'd done it again. I'd flipped the power dynamic. I'd spoken words that, like magic, had stolen his power and made him afraid.

"Then what?" Luke said, stroking my hair sweetly.

"I bit his hand hard enough to draw blood." I could still remember the metal taste of it on my tongue. My stomach threatened to revoke the tenancy of the coffee and hot dog. "Then I told him I had HIV. That stopped him. He freaked out."

I motioned to my lividly purple side. "Kicked me. Ran."

"Baby..."

I couldn't believe he was holding me, kissing my hair, assuring me that I was all right, that everything was going to be all right now.

I whispered, "Why are you being so nice? I thought…"

"What? What'd you think?"

"That you'd be angry."

Luke shook his head. "No way. I'm not angry. I'd never be angry."

"But our contract—"

"Said that if you went to him on your own, our Dom/sub relationship would be over. It said nothing about our friendship. Nothing about…us."

"Us?"

"Yeah. Us." He kissed my head again. "And even if you did go to him—"

"I didn't!"

"Even if you had—"

"But I swear—"

He shushed me. "I believe you. Just listen to me. Even if you had, I can't walk away from you."

Tears pricked my eyes. "Why?"

"Because I've messed up too."

"How?" Had he slept with someone else? Dommed another person? My stomach twisted anxiously.

"It's complicated, but I talked with my sister yesterday, and she helped me realize something."

That stilled me. I dislodged myself enough from his arms to be able to see his face as he spoke.

"When this started between us, you didn't want me to…" He swallowed. "Let me rephrase it. You said you wanted me to hate on you. To treat you like I hated you."

I nodded.

"You made it clear you didn't want sweetness from me. Or kindness. Or love."

My heart jolted.

"But I violated your boundaries. I started to feel things for you. Good things. Warm, wonderful things. Kind and loving things. I'm sorry."

"Don't be," I whispered, touching his arm.

"I crossed your boundaries," he stated again.

"I needed you to cross them."

"Still…I'm sorry. If that's why you…" He waved his hand around.

I shook my head. "It's not."

"You're sure?"

"Yes."

"There's more I need to say. I've never wanted to—" he shuddered, a vulnerability passing over him like a storm cloud over the sun. "I've never wanted to fall in love. With Betsy and my parents, I always knew I'd have a lot of responsibility for the rest of my life. Adding a romantic partner into the mix seemed messy. What if they didn't like Betsy? What if—"

I whispered, "I'd like her."

He smiled and kissed my forehead. "Rumor has it, you like most everyone."

I shrugged. "Not that it's served me well, but yeah."

"Okay, so you'd like Betsy," Luke said, slowly. "But say Betsy didn't like *you*—"

"You think Betsy wouldn't like me?" Offense straightened my back and dulled the shot of pain in my side from the rapid movement. "Why?"

"Betsy would love you," Luke said, his lips twisting in a fond, amused smile. "Let me finish."

I let out a sharp sigh, but covered my mouth with my hand to keep myself from interrupting again.

"All I'm saying is that Betsy is non-negotiable, and if she didn't like the person I loved, then I'd have to reconsider having them in my life. One day, she may need to come live with me and whoever I'm with. And, so in the past, that'd never been something I wanted to deal with."

I released my mouth as he paused to take in a breath and said, "I don't think that's true. You can't blame Betsy for you thinking life is easier without romantic love."

Luke blinked at me a moment. "No, no, you're right. I can't. Not entirely. I used to see romantic attachments as a problem. Being a professional Dom meant I couldn't get involved in situations where jealousy might come into play, or expectations of monogamy could be formed, or—"

"But now things have changed?" I hoped it was because of me, but I knew it was more likely because of his diagnosis. And when Luke spoke, I was disappointed to find I was right.

"Now, with the risks of being HIV positive, I don't know how long I have before..." He cleared his throat. "I can't in good conscious Dom the way I did in the past, moreover I don't want to. I want to Dom selfishly, and not necessarily for money. I want to do it because it makes me happy, because the sub in question arouses me, fits my life, and..." He paused, clearly struggling to admit whatever needed to say next. "And I only want to Dom someone I like, maybe more than like."

He touched my hair gently. "Someone I want to be with outside of my basement. I guess it comes down to one, very selfish thing: I don't want to be alone. I want to be loved by someone before I die."

Leaning in, Luke nuzzled my neck, breathing in my scent, and I let him. "Minty, I want to experience whatever it is that we could be together—friendship, love, Dom/sub scenes, all of it. Because you're right, fair or not, we don't have a lot of time, and I'm not going to waste whatever amount I do have on self-imposed rules about who I'm allowed to be with and when or how. But I recognize that goes against everything we agreed to at the start. It's important that you're honest with me now. Do you want what I want?"

I touched his lips with mine, gently since my lip was so busted and sore. "I do. I want all that too."

"Do you?"

"Yes."

"To do that, though, to have that, we have to trust each other."

My stomach churned. Anxious sweat broke over me. "In that case, I need to tell you something."

He tensed. "I'm ready to hear it."

"About Kyle. I didn't invite him in. I didn't *want* him."

"I believe you."

"But…" I started shaking, the memory of what happened still scary and bright in my mind, and the fear that Luke would stand up and leave me here after hearing the whole truth made me feel nauseous. He held me tighter, trying to steady me. "When Kyle shoved his way into my room, I reacted all wrong."

Luke pushed my hair off my forehead, his eyes going soft and worried. "Whatever you did to still be alive is right."

"Wait." I sucked in a shuddery breath. "I was coming back to my room, opening my door, just like last time." I shivered again, fear slipping through my veins. "Kyle pushed me from behind. I fell inside. I was on the floor. He came in. Locked the door. Got his dick out and I—" Shaking my head, I fought shallow breaths I couldn't quite control, making me shake and hyperventilate. "It was just instinct, I swear."

"I know," he murmured, though he didn't know. Not yet.

"I got hard. And I went to him on my knees. I opened my mouth. But…" I shook my head, my mind going to that moment, those seconds when everything had changed, like I was living it again. My voice went low and quiet, and my words came out in present tense. "I don't want it. I've changed my mind. But he forces me. And I let him. I let him throat-fuck me." I winced. "And he hits me so hard across the face… And then he's on me, pushing in me, and I just…bite him. I bite him so hard."

"Baby, that's good. That was so good."

I was back with Luke now, shaking and scared as hell. The memory had me almost gagging in terror again. "I'm scared, Luke."

I wanted so desperately to call him Daddy right then, but I didn't know if I was allowed to anymore. "I thought he might kill me."

"Shh. It's okay. I'm with you." He brushed his fingers through my hair, soothing me, and I wanted to feel soothed, but it was too chaotic in my head.

"Why? Why are you with me? I don't understand." My voice shook. "Don't you get it? I didn't tell him no. I went to him on my knees with my mouth open. I got hard. You can forgive me for that?"

Luke carefully took hold of my bruised chin, angling my face so that I was looking him in the eye. "There's nothing to forgive."

"I should have fought! I know Aikido. I should have—"

"Stop. There are no 'shoulds' when you're surviving an attack. Remember what I've said about that? About your father?"

"But this wasn't like that." Only it *was*… My gorge rose, but I swallowed it down.

"It was violence. It was an attack. You did what you did because that's how you've learned to cope with sexual trauma."

"But what if I wanted it?" I whispered. "What if some part of me wanted it?"

"Baby, shh, maybe some part of you did, the part of Mitchell who's learned to loathe himself. But that's not *you*. You're not defined by that. The real you, the Mitchell deep inside is powerful and strong, and he loves himself enough to do incredibly hard things. He knows how to save himself. And he does. Every time."

I leaned my head against his chest and breathed in and out. I wanted to believe him, and for a few minutes, I let myself.

Those few minutes stretched into hours.

Then days.

Chapter Eighteen

Luke

A WEEK AFTER the attack, Minty was still scared of Kyle, worried that if he left his room to shower or take a piss that Kyle would be there waiting for him. I wanted him to press charges or report Kyle to the university, but he wouldn't even consider it.

"I encouraged him to be that way with me," he'd said, stroking fingers through my hair as I rested my head on his naked chest, listening to his heartbeat to reassure myself that it was strong. "I can't accuse him of something *now*. He couldn't read my mind. He didn't know things had changed."

I tried to convince him that Kyle absolutely knew things had changed, that Minty had told him straight to his face that he couldn't have sex with him anymore, that I was his Dom, and I'd forbidden it. But he wouldn't listen. Some twisted part of him was still softhearted toward Kyle, and I couldn't get him to budge on his opinion of the rapist piece of shit.

Eventually, I let it go, but I shared his worry that Kyle might approach him again somewhere on campus. So, I started picking him up after his last lecture of the day. I'd either bring him with me to Knox Supplies & News to hang out and study while I worked, or I'd take him back to my place to watch movies on the sofa while stuffing our faces with popcorn and pizza, or whatever trash I had around.

Until today.

When I picked him up after his last class—Biology Senior Seminar, his favorite—he said, "Let's go to the grocery store."

"Why?"

"I'm tired of eating crap."

I didn't argue with him, though I did confess that I was a lousy cook. He'd reached to cover my hand on the gear shift, squeezing it gently before he said, "Don't worry. I'm a great cook."

As I watched him chop onions, season pork, and prepare side dishes, he seemed so pleased and fond, like he was happy to be doing something for me, as if he took pride in it. It was a good thing my mother had forced various cooking implements on me, as well as a full set of pots and pans, when I'd moved into my own place. Minty was using what seemed like all of them.

"All right," Minty said, putting the various dishes in the oven and setting the timer. "We have forty minutes. Do we have time for a fast visit to the basement?"

I pulled him close, nuzzling his neck and untying the apron from around his waist. "Forty minutes isn't enough time to play," I said. "Let's start the movie."

"No," he said, pushing away from me. "You haven't fucked me since"—he waved his hand around—"it happened." His lips went tight. "Do you not want me anymore? Do I gross you out now? Or—"

I pulled back. "Gross me out? That's what you think?"

How had that been his takeaway from me cuddling him endlessly, checking his bruises, asking about his day, taking him to work with me because I couldn't stand to be away from him, and tucking him into bed with me most nights? I just didn't know.

He shrugged. "You're so gentle with me. Like I'm a child. You don't, you know…" He huffed, "Toss me around or choke me or kiss me like you're dying to get inside me."

I blinked at him. That was all true, but it was because I wanted *more* than all that. I wanted more with him than I'd wanted from anyone ever before, and my inner sadist had been shocked silent at all these other feelings I had running through me. Like fondness, protectiveness, and so much tenderness that I sometimes felt nauseous from it, like I'd eaten too much sweet food too quickly.

"Do you not want me anymore?" Minty's voice shook.

"Baby, I want you," I whispered, tugging him into my arms again. "I want you safe, healed, and healthy when I take you downstairs."

"Fine, but what about just taking me at all? I'm okay, you know. My asshole, my body…I can take being fucked and choked a little. I want it."

"Choked a little," I repeated. Some part of me I didn't recognize murmured in my head, *He's too fragile now, just love him, make love to him. Be gentle and sweet.*

But that wasn't who Minty was, and it wasn't what he wanted. Of course it wasn't. It wasn't what *I'd* ever wanted from anyone before either. And yet, here I was dreaming of stripping him slowly, kneeling, and sucking him off like he was the most precious angel sent from God, and it was my honor, my *duty,* to make him come and keep him safe.

Christ, was this what being in love did? Did it make a person soft?

Staring into Minty's confused eyes, though, I knew I had to push away that urge in myself or rework it entirely. Minty couldn't take soft love any more than I used to be able to take giving it. For him, gentleness was like torture.

Like torture…

My inner sadist woke with a well-rested smile, and it spread all over my face.

Minty

I SHIVERED. "OH…THAT look. I've missed it."

"I think you're going to regret seeing it," Luke said, his eyes gleaming.

"No," I countered, shaking my head. "Never, Daddy."

"Oh, Mitchell. Now I just want to prove it to you." He clicked his tongue, calling to me. "C'mon then. Let's go."

He led me upstairs to his bedroom, a place where my pretty clothes lay strewn about mixed in with his much less dainty ones.

"Here?" I asked. "Why not in the basement?"

"Because here's where I want you to be." He pushed me back onto the bed gently.

I frowned. "I thought you were going to hurt me again finally."

"I'm going to *torture* you," Luke said, that sadistic smile crossing his face again.

My pulse picked up speed and my cock stiffened. He pointed at the bed. "Get on your back. Spread-eagle. Now."

Heart thrumming with anticipation, I centered myself on the mattress and star-fished my arms and legs.

"That's right," he murmured, reaching under the bed and withdrawing a box of toys. He opened it, displaying nothing truly hardcore. All of it was rather vanilla in the scheme of things, but still exciting. "So gorgeous, baby."

"Don't be too nice to me."

"I get to decide how I am with you. This is a scene, isn't it? Playtime is my time."

I opened my mouth to argue, but then just nodded once, clenching my jaw tight.

"What do you say?"

"Yes, Daddy."

"That's right. Daddy decides."

My cock grew rock hard with his words, and I squirmed. Luke grabbed one wrist, tugging it toward the bed's poster and tied it with a soft, black rope. He took hold of my opposite ankle and pulled my body taut. I let out a soft squeak; the healing bruise on my torso ached when pulled like that.

"Your safe word is poodle," Luke said. He moved to tie my other wrist to the bed post, and then crossed to my opposite ankle to tie me there too. I was immobile.

Luke sat on the mattress near my chest, and pushed my hair off my face, trailed his hot fingers over my cheek, and then brought out a blindfold from his box of tricks.

I licked my lips as he secured it so I couldn't shake it free.

"Nice," he praised. "You look so pretty."

I frowned again. That wasn't what I wanted to hear during a scene. I wanted rough treatment and name-calling.

"You hate that, don't you?" Luke said gleefully.

Oh, God. I suddenly knew exactly what he meant by torture and what he planned to do.

"No, don't." I tensed all over. "I won't like it. Please."

"Your safe word is always there for you."

Fuck him. I'd wanted to go to the basement and get hurt. I didn't want this, but I mashed my lips together to keep from saying the word. Part of me wanted to peace-out of this right now, but another part wanted to see it through. Could I *let* Luke love me?

I turned my head away from him in protest, but otherwise stayed silent. If I weren't blindfolded, I knew I'd be staring at a blank wall by the window.

"Good boy."

I huffed.

"Mitchell, prepare to be tortured." He laughed at my sharp inhale. "Now."

As the minutes raced by, I was praised more than I'd ever been praised in my entire life, and I hated it. Each word out of Daddy's mouth felt like a lie, like a papercut on my heart. I wanted him to slap me, to choke me, to bite the skin of my scrotum, to *hurt* me, goddammit. I *needed* it.

But he didn't do any of that.

He kissed every inch of my skin; he told me I was beautiful, smart, strong, powerful, sexy, and so many other compliments I thought I might barf. He took my dick into his throat and lovingly brought me so close to orgasm I had tears running down my face. When he'd moved away at the last moment, shutting down the ecstasy that would wash away all this agony, I screamed in rage.

He licked my nipples and pinched them gently with warm fingers, and then nursed them with a thoroughness that felt like worship. He sucked my toes and my balls, he kissed the shell of my ear and sucked the lobe until I was hyperventilating, angry that it felt so good, scared that I liked it, hating it, loving it, *hating* that I loved it.

Right now, *I* was Kyle.

I wanted to punch Luke, kick him, spit in his face, but I was tied. When I tried to spit, Daddy just dodged it or wiped it from where it landed—sometimes on me, sometimes on him—and then noisily licked it from his fingers. All the while telling me my saliva was delicious and sweet, his favorite spit in the world, and praising me for my brattiness, my "beautiful" struggles, and whatever else he could say that would hurt me. He knew just where to aim those love arrows.

Eventually, my tight anger turned hot. I tried to bite him when he kissed me, but he managed to get away with only a small nip. I cursed him out, I told him I hated him, I spit out anything cruel that came to mind.

But never poodle.

He couldn't rim me in my current position, but he lubed his fingers and slipped two into me, moving so gently and delicately that I screamed—long and loud—raging as he fingered my prostate like it was something fragile.

"I swear to God, I'll make you sorry," I muttered. "You'll pay for this."

He chuckled. "Mm, sure I will."

I thought of what I might do. I thought of what I could say that would make him stop—not poodle, but something that would make him want to quit on his own. Make *him* safe word.

The answer came to me. I opened my mouth to say the words, but he'd gone back to sucking me off, and I wondered if this time he might let me come. I breathed in and out as me ramped me up again, my hips lifting as I struggled to reach the bliss that would make this torture pay off.

When he released my dick before I could, I spit the words out. "I'll go back to him. I'll let *him* hurt me if you won't."

Luke froze.

After a long, terrifying moment, he ripped my blindfold off, and the look on his face wasn't what I expected, or even what I wanted. My chest rose and fell with quick breaths and my blood went cold as I took in his expression.

Devastated. Wrecked. I'd hurt him more than I'd ever hurt anyone before.

I waited for him to say poodle. I knew he would.

But he didn't.

Instead, he untied me, took my hand, and pulled me up from the bed. "Come on. Dinner will be done in nine minutes."

"Luke—"

"This scene isn't over," he said sharply.

"Daddy, please. I'm sorry."

"Dinner," he said, pointing toward the door to his room. "Finish making it."

"Yes, Daddy."

"It's Sir tonight."

I gulped. That felt like a punishment in and of itself. "Yes, Sir."

He adjusted his dick, and then went into the en suite, closing the door behind him. I walked downstairs and into the kitchen just as he'd asked and stood staring at the timer on the oven as it counted down.

Why had I done that? I'd destroyed the night. Sure, I hated what he was doing to me, but wasn't that the point of it? Worse, I'd targeted where I knew it would hurt Luke the most. Was it worth it?

Tears slipped down my cheeks as the timer clicked over another minute.

Fuck. *Why* couldn't I let someone love me? Especially when I really wanted them to?

Chapter Nineteen

Luke

I TURNED ON the water spigot and splashed my face. My hard-on had evaporated when Minty's hurtful arrow had lodged in my chest, leaving me feeling unfulfilled and frustrated. No, more than that, I felt hollow, like I was bleeding out from the wound.

Which was ridiculous. Subs said cruel things to their Doms all the time. My past boys had made all sorts of threats, and I'd never responded so emotionally before.

I had to shake this off.

Why couldn't I shake it off?

I checked myself in the mirror again, hoping I looked steady enough to join Mitchell in the kitchen. But no, I still couldn't go out there. My bewildered expression wasn't going to help anything.

If I went to him looking like he killed my puppy, I'd mess up everything. I'd show him that he *could* hurt me, that he had that kind of control over my heart and my head, and then he'd leave. He'd see that I was weak, and he'd hate that as much he hated being loved.

I splashed my face again.

I needed to get back in control. Suck up my feelings. Stamp out whatever affection was growing relentlessly in me, and just be mean to him again. Give him what he'd wanted from the start—pain— and give up on what I'd come to want.

Love.

I sneered at myself. Could I sound more pathetic and pitiful?

Eventually, the intensity of my pain died down and a cold, numbness settled in behind it. Ready to face Mitchell finally, I left the bathroom and walked on rubbery legs down to the kitchen.

As I entered, Mitchell switched off the oven and the timer. He dropped to his knees, still naked, head down and tears running off the end of his nose, dripping to the linoleum floor.

"Sir, I'm sorry." He glanced up at my face, and then dropped his eyes again, his chin against his chest. "I only said it to hurt you. I didn't mean it."

A sob wrangled its way out of his throat. "I was angry. I didn't mean it."

"Don't lie to me." I was shocked at the iron in my quiet voice.

Sadness flowed in me, like the cold, still waters at the bottom of the river. I didn't have the emotional intelligence for this. I'd always known I was in over my head with him, but this…this breakdown on my part proved it. I had no business playing with him. I had no business loving him. He didn't even want that from me.

I remembered what Betsy said to me about rules. No matter what Mitchell had said when we talked, I was violating the boundaries he'd made clear from the start. He was allowed to love *me*, whatever that meant to him, but I wasn't supposed to love *him*. He didn't want it. Not the way I wanted to give it now. He wanted…

Shut up. I stopped my escalating thoughts.

That wasn't true. He *did* want my love. He'd wanted it from the beginning. I knew that now. He'd eagerly agreed to dating me. He told me he wanted the things I wanted too. The problem was I kept insisting on having my way. Wanting him to let me love him the *way* I wanted it, not the way he needed it.

Fuck. What am I doing? I'm all turned around.

"Sir," he whispered, keeping his head down. "I'm sorry I lied. I just wanted to hurt you, Sir, and I knew if I said I'd go to Kyle, it would hurt you because—" He dared a glance up again, and this time whatever he saw on my face, he didn't look away. "Because I know you love me. I know you haven't told me that you do, but I just know it. And I abused that love. I'm sorry."

I blinked at him, taking an involuntary step back.

I love him.

I did and he knew, and I knew, and it was horrible. Love was fucking things up between us more than it was helping him or me. This new feeling kept me from being what I was *good* at being. It was making me a terrible Dom.

"Sir?"

I swallowed. "Yes?"

"I love you too. I can't promise that I'll never say something like that again, Sir. When I panic, I get vicious. Like with my dad and Kyle. Earlier, what you were doing to me, Sir? Loving me like that? It did something to me, something to my insides, and it was torture. Just like you said it would be. I hated it."

"You have a safe word," I reminded him. "You remembered you could use it, right?"

"Yes." Mitchell walked on his knees to me, reaching out with his hands to grip the outer seams of my jeans. "I remembered. But I didn't want to use it. I hated how I felt, but..." He closed his eyes and swallowed, like he didn't want to admit to the truth and felt sickened by it. "But I knew I needed it. Sir, I *need* to be okay with being loved like that. I want to find a way to *like it* before I die. I don't want to be alone. I don't want to die before I can feel in my heart—" He touched his chest, looking up at me so earnestly that I felt my throat tighten again. "Until I can *feel* safe being loved and enjoy it."

I took hold of his chin, keeping his gaze. "I think you may have to learn to love yourself first."

He closed his eyes, remaining silent.

"Think you can do that?"

He shook his head, reconsidered, and then shrugged. "I don't know, Sir. Can you teach me?"

I let out a self-deprecating laugh. "I don't know. I'm starting to wonder if I really love myself either. I think we both have a lot to learn."

"And not a lot of time to learn it in." He buried his head against my legs, his shoulders shaking. "I love you so much, Sir. I know you don't believe me—no one ever does—but I do. So, please don't give up on me."

I bent over, rubbing my hands up and down his naked back. "Don't give up on me either."

I didn't think it was right to demand that, not when we were still technically in a scene, and maybe not ever. But I wanted him with me, safe by my side, for me to love and hurt and protect. Even if I was a mess and swinging from emotion to emotion, thought to thought, fear to fear.

"Never. I promise." Mitchell rubbed his face against my jeans, his tears starting to soak through, and I suspected he was rubbing snot on me too. I didn't mind. I hauled him up to standing and hugged him close, still careful of his lingering bruise. "The scene's over."

"Okay." He choked on another sob. "I'm sorry. I fucked it up."

"No," I murmured. "I did."

"How?" he pulled back and gazed up at me with teary eyes and, yes, a runny, red nose.

I sucked in a breath, my thoughts warring in my head. Be honest and risk him feeling like I was too weak to be depended on? Or keep it to myself, and be less brave than he was being right now?

"Please, Luke." He stroked my neck with his hand, going up on tiptoe to tangle his fingers into my hair. "I can take it."

"Take what? This isn't your fault. I have no criticisms of you."

"I can take your hurt. I can support you too, you know. Let me."

I couldn't help it; tears rose in my eyes again and my throat ached. My voice sounded gritty with effort when I spoke. "I don't want you to have to deal with my hurt. I'm the Dom, and—"

"And you're *mine*," he murmured, kissing my neck and jaw. "I love you. Be honest with me. Please."

"Christ." I closed my eyes against his sweet, pleading eyes.

"Tell me."

I sucked in a quivery breath. "All right. I'm afraid if I'm vulnerable with you…"

My knees felt wobbly. When was the last time I'd been this exposed to anyone? I couldn't remember. Maybe not ever. "I'm scared you'll think I don't have what it takes. I won't be strong enough to keep you."

Mitchell cringed. "I'm sorry. It's my fault you feel that way. But, if it helps, I'm in love with you. That's not something Kyle can ever give me."

I sighed, my pulse hammering in my throat. I took hold of his hand. "All right, I'll try to be less insecure. As your Dom, as your lover."

"I kind of like it that you're insecure too," Minty admitted, clinging to me even tighter. "It makes me feel like we're equals. And even though I need you to hurt me, I also want to feel like I have power over you too. And when you show your hand like this, I see I do."

"Minty…"

"Is that very bad of me?" He added a spin of seduction to his question.

"Yes."

"And are you going to punish me for it?"

I huffed a dark laugh. "You have no fucking idea."

"I can't wait."

"Well, you'll just have to because I don't have it in me tonight."

"See? There you go. Expressing weakness isn't so hard, is it?"

I rolled my eyes, but tugged him closer to me, nuzzling his hair.

"It's like Aikido. Being vulnerable on the mat doesn't mean you open yourself up to get knocked out. It's more about staying open so you can push and pull, give and take." Minty drew back and looked up to me. "It's like…you and your training partner have to move together until you can resolve the conflict—the training fight—in a mutually beneficial way."

I frowned, confused. "I'm sorry, baby. I don't get it."

"I'm saying you can trust me," Mitchell went on. "You can be vulnerable with me, Luke. I want you to be, and I can handle it. Please give me a chance to prove it to you."

I couldn't bring myself to promise anything. Not just yet. There was still so much anxiety roiling inside me. Was I truly enough? Could I *ever* be enough for him?

I closed my eyes and bent to rest my head against Mitchell's shoulder. He rubbed my back, and I took in his comfort willingly. We held each other for a few minutes, and then Mitchell said, "We should get dressed and eat before the meal is ruined."

"Yes," I agreed. "Let's."

Minty

THAT NIGHT, AFTER dinner, we curled up on the sofa together, watching the premiere of CBS' new crime drama, *Silk Stalkings*. He held me in front of him, arm tossed over me and his chin resting on top of my head. I felt secure and safe, and I liked it.

I pondered the new equality I felt with Luke now. Messed up or not, fair or not, using Luke's love for me to hurt him had shown his weakness so plainly that, for a moment, I'd felt powerful. Sick, but true.

Before, I'd always felt like Luke had the upper hand in whatever it was we were building. He was the Dom. He was the older and stronger of us. He took care of me in so many ways. He protected me. He hurt me and made me sing with pleasure and pain.

And over the last week, I'd started to wonder what did I give him? I allowed him to exercise his sadistic needs. I helped him to feel strong and powerful in the face of impending death. I let him fall for me, an emotion he'd never felt before. But what did all that amount to really, if overall I was a liability, a dead weight around his feet?

In the end, that wasn't true after all. I had a power he needed and craved. After I'd wielded the magical, weaponized words and seen the terrible outcome, heard the insecurity fall from his lips, and held him afterward, I realized I had strength to let him be what no one else in his life ever had—weak.

After Chris and Rita successfully investigated and solved a model's murder, and the station had gone to commercial, Luke picked up the remote and muted the sound. "Baby, I was thinking…"

"Mm?" I rolled around so that I was facing him, nearly sliding off the sofa in the process. But Luke's strong grip kept me from going over the edge.

In this position, I had a good view of his chin and nostrils, and each gust of breath hit me in the face. I breathed in on purpose, taking in the air that had just been in his body, feeling dreamy and calm now that our crisis had passed.

"The other day, I got an invitation to a local event, and I wondered if you might want to check it out?"

"Sure," I agreed easily, nosing his t-shirt collar aside and kissing the soft skin at the base of his neck.

He stroked my back. "You should hear more about the nature of the event before you agree. No more checking all the boxes before you've read and considered them all, remember?"

"Ooh, is this a kinky event?"

"Yes."

My heart pumped harder, and I grinned with excitement, squirming until I was sitting up and better see his face. I patted one of his cheeks and took in the hint of anxiety in his eyes. "Tell me about it then."

"It's an invitation to a party at Knoxville's only operating dungeon."

My mouth dropped open. "What? For real?"

"Yeah. Want to go?"

I choked slightly, my eyes flying wide. "Do I?"

"We don't have to."

"Of course I want to go." I gripped his shoulders and moved him onto his back, and I climbed on top of him, straddling his thighs. "What are we going to do there?"

"Talk. Watch," Luke whispered. "Learn."

"Play?"

"If you want to."

My heart pumped hard. "Wow. I don't know."

"You don't have to decide now. In fact, you shouldn't. See what's on offer first, and then make up your mind."

I licked my lips. "All right. Yeah. This could be fun. When is it?"

"This weekend."

"Don't you see Betsy this weekend?"

"We could go after. It starts late. There'll be plenty of time to drive back, get ready, head over."

I shivered, the idea of going to a real, live sex dungeon making me feel a little dizzy. The evening had been so full of emotion already. I felt like I was on overload.

Luke seemed to sense it. He rubbed a hand over my chest, and then whispered, "It's been a long night. You don't have to decide now."

"I know. But I do want to go. I want to see what it's like."

Luke's arms tightened around me, and his voice grew tense as he asked, "Okay. We can talk about it more tomorrow. But, tonight, I want to…"

I stroked over his forearms comfortingly. "What do you want?" I encouraged.

"I want to try making love to you again. This time, no scene. This time, just us. Can you try? Do you want to?"

I thought about it, a fist in my gut. I suddenly understood the "why" of something I'd never been able to explain it before. To let someone love me? I'd need to let myself be truly weak. The protective power I'd learned to wield was strength made of pain— both the infliction and the endurance of it. Sex without pain was, to me, sex without power, without agency.

But now that we were more equal, maybe I didn't need power if we were both going to be stripped of it. If we were both going to be vulnerable and bare.

"It's all right," Luke went on. "We don't have to."

"No," I said, breaking out of his arms and sitting up so I could see his face, and he could see mine. "I want to try it. I can't promise anything. But I want to try."

His eyes went soft and a little timid. So different from the man who'd choked me against the wall of his office at the sex shop. So different from the man who'd made me cry with his whips on more than one occasion and laughed at my tears. God, I loved that guy too.

But this one? He was a jewel.

"All right, are there any rules? Boundaries?"

My heart beat hard. "Yes."

"What are they?"

"Don't be mean to me, don't be rough, no matter what I say or do. I want to be loved, Luke. I really do."

"All right, baby. I'll try if you'll try."

We stood and headed toward his bedroom again, and this time I *was* going to surrender. I was going to *love* being loved.

Chapter Twenty

Minty

SLIPPING THE BORROWED clothes off, leaving them pooled on the floor next to the bed, I slid beneath the covers, feeling timid and hoping to hide that I wasn't hard—not yet.

Luke tossed his clothes onto the chair across the room and headed toward the bed with his hard cock swinging. My mouth watered at the sight of it, and I wanted him to straddle my chest, hold my head down, and fuck into my throat—

But no.

That *wasn't* what I wanted. He was going to love me. I was going to let myself be loved, and I was going to love him back. With none of the violence that kept me from feeling out of control and vulnerable.

Instead, I was going to be scared—truly scared—raw, at the edge of what I could manage to endure, and then I'd just…let go. My heart pounded, my pulse rushed, and the terror that poured through me woke up my cock. Could I do this? I was beginning to think I could.

Peeling the covers off me, Luke gazed down with soft, loving eyes. He straddled my hips, letting his balls graze my hardening cock where it lay flexing against my stomach. I reached up and ran my hands over his tight stomach and pecs, tweaking his nipples experimentally.

Leaning over to the bedside table, he grabbed the lube and positioned it on the pillow beside us before settling on top of me. His legs cradled my hips, and his hairy chest skimmed over my nearly hairless one. I rubbed his nipples, pinching and rolling them between the pads of my thumb and index finger. Staring into my eyes, his breath came in shorter and shorter until he kissed the tip of my nose, my eyebrows, and my temples, before kissing my mouth.

Our tongues moved together, familiar and sweet. Our breath tangled and our bodies crushed against each other, seeking friction and pleasure. I flashed to times when I'd had similar encounters with men in the past—all fun and games, all of them hungry for me, and not a single one of them had loved me. They'd been using me to get off.

This man loved me. He loved me with his tongue, his lips, his cock and hips, and with his hot, adoring gaze as he rose over me, reached for the lube, and shocked the hell out of me by reaching around to use it on himself.

"Ever done this?" he asked, knowing from the forms I'd filled out that I considered myself an exclusive bottom. "Do you want to?"

I nodded.

Of course I'd fucked someone before—that was *how* I'd decided to be an exclusive bottom. But I'd never fucked a man I loved, just a stupid boy who'd complained the entire time that I wasn't doing it hard enough. Maybe it would be different if I did it with love. If I moved inside Luke with this gooey, warm affection powering every thrust.

"You do?"

"Yeah, I want to," I murmured. "Please let me."

His lips tilted up at the ends, his eyes still gentle as he peered down at me. "I'll let you," he agreed. "But let me handle the penetration. I don't do this often."

A flower bloomed in my chest at those words. I'd known it of course. He told me when he'd explained his HIV status that it'd been a one-time mistake.

"Let me just—" He reached between his legs, using a lot of lube and his own rough fingering to open himself up. I shivered watching, my mind scrambling at the implications.

After far too long, and also what seemed like way too soon to be physically truly comfortable yet, Luke gripped my dick and positioned me at his asshole.

"You can take your time," I whispered.

"No," he gritted out. "I want it like this. I don't want to wait." His head tipped back, exposing his long neck. His mouth fell open, sweat broke out on his forehead, and he groaned loudly as he sat back and took me in.

My lashes fluttered at the tight, hot grip of him, but I managed to keep my eyes open, watching as a flush rose up his chest and into his throat, watching as his stomach muscles quivered while he sank deeper onto me. I saw the moment when my cock became a challenge for him to take in—the shifting of his weight on his knees, the subtle shock of in-taken breath…

God, he was gorgeous. I loved everything about him.

I didn't know what had gone wrong with the one time I fucked a guy before—maybe it was just that he'd been so negative about it—but the heat and friction, the slickness of Luke's interior walls, and the way he trembled as he took me all the way in felt amazing.

"Baby," he said, voice shaking. "Are you okay?"

"Yeah," I said, putting my hands on his haunches, holding him down on me. "You?"

"Good. Fantastic. You feel nice. You fill me up."

I murmured, "I can't believe I'm in your body. Raw."

Why this felt different than when he was inside *me* this way, I didn't know, but it felt holy. If rock-and-roll service wasn't church, this definitely was. Even if most Christians I knew would denounce it, call us sinners, and hate us. But they were wrong because this was what true love felt like. This hot mess in my chest, this ache in my balls, and the need to please that filled me from my toes to my crown. I wanted so much to make Luke feel good, to make him come for me. To love him with my body.

"I wanted to do it this way," he murmured. "Because you don't have habits or memories that might trigger your resistance. I thought we might have more success."

His voice remained thready and higher pitched than I'd ever heard it, but he sounded hopeful that I'd agree his idea was working.

I said, "It's good. It's helping."—because it was.

He bent low, some of my cock sliding out of him as he moved and brushed my hair off my face with both hands. Peering into my eyes, he murmured, "Fuck me, baby? Please fuck me."

I didn't look away as I took hold of his hips and squared my feet on the bed so I could lift my hips and penetrate him again. His expression shifted, eyes rolled up, lashes fluttering, mouth opening in a dazed little O, and I was lost. It was glorious, the sensation, his reactions, the way he let me pound him like I was trying to drive my heart's adoration right up into his ass.

I wasn't on the edge of sanity like how I got when we played rough, when he topped me, and choked me, and spit on me, and said horrible things to me. But this was just as good in its own way. It was peaceful, intense, and beautiful. I felt like my skin was electrified with love and kindness, with pleasure and sweet desire.

Tears filled my eyes more than once at just how pure my feelings for him were, like my love was pouring out of me in my sweat, and *his* love came gushing out of him in small sounds. Our love being made so beautifully together.

Luke's eyes were like the sky, blue and glowing, and when he started talking, after what seemed like a lifetime of delicious fucking, I hung on his every word, filling every hole in my heart and mind, stuffing them with this delirious, dripping sugar, forgetting to hate it.

"You're the best thing that's ever happened, baby. The most beautiful boy I've ever been with. I love the way you smell. The way you breathe. I want to make you part of me forever, press against you until we're one. I need your cum, baby. I need it in me. Fill me up." He whimpered. "Make me yours. I want to be yours."

"Oh," I groaned. "You're mine. All mine."

He kissed me again, and we lost ourselves in the push and pull, the ebb and flow of our bodies, of the pleasure. Cresting and then pulling back again before the climax could sweep us away felt as easy as breathing. When Luke broke our kiss and lifted off me, I cried out, wanting him back on my suddenly cold cock.

"Baby," he whispered, reaching for the lube again. Was he going to reapply? He seemed plenty slick to me. But instead, he shifted us both until he knelt between my legs, pushing them apart. Gazing at me, he asked, "Can we still love each other like this if I'm inside you?"

I whispered. "I don't know. I wanted to come in you."

"I'll let you come in me," he agreed. "But let me feel you from the inside again? Like this? With love?"

I groaned, my cock twitching and my hole gripping lightly. I wanted it. He hadn't fucked me in way too many days, and I needed him inside. But what if I ruined it? What if it triggered that asshole in me who demanded things had to get ugly?

"Let me try," he whispered. "If you don't like it, I'll stop."

"Okay. Try it."

The slick of lube was cold, and I hissed. He kissed my nipples as he fingered me slowly. Flashes from earlier in the night and the torture of this kind of fingering rose up, along with the urge to fight, to resist.

"Breathe, baby," Luke whispered. "Don't close your eyes. Look at me."

I pried my lids open, letting my legs splay out, freeing up space for him to move inside me. He was so gorgeous—red lips, flushed skin, and hot devotion in his eyes.

Surrender. Let go. Let him love you.

I imagined my heart was trapped inside a giant locket and with every press of his fingers he turned the lock, again and again until it burst open. *There.* My heart was beating, beating, *beating* with love and need and fear. So much fear.

I sucked in air shallowly. I was too exposed. Too vulnerable. It felt like Luke could kill me with a single glance, cut me open with a word. I resisted the urge to protect my heart again. Fighting it was enough to make me sweat—or maybe that was the way he perfectly targeted my prostate and made me beg for cock.

"Please, Luke. Fuck me. I need you. I love you. Love me back."

Lurching up, he kissed me, and withdrew his fingers. With practiced ease, he hooked my knees over his elbows and bent me back, pressing his cock against my loosened asshole and pushing inside with one, long, firm stroke.

"Look at me," he said as my eyes drifted shut in satisfaction. "Eyes on me."

I obeyed, but that fear sliced through me again. All that love. Aimed at me. His expression of adoration, his sweet smile, his infinite tenderness. I wanted it, but I didn't deserve it.

Shut up. You do. You deserve it.

"I'm getting scared," I murmured.

He turned his head to kiss one of my knees, and whispered, "Me too. Can you take it? Do I need to stop?"

I shook my head. His admission softened the panic that had started to rise. We were doing this together. Afraid together.

Risking it together.

The fuck stayed gentle, rolling, and slow. I fought against the need to have it harder, faster, crueler, and tried to stay focused on the here and now.

I concentrated on the scent of Luke's sweat, on the heat building between our bodies, on his treasure trail brushing against my hard cock with every thrust. The sound of our flesh slapping together, the hunger in his eyes. The heat of his kiss. The tagging of my prostate and the slowly mounting pleasure that never seemed to break.

Yet, I wrestled myself. Fear and love grabbed each other by the throat, and the violence I craved exploded in my mind instead. Moment by moment, I wasn't sure who was winning. I fought the urge to scream, to spit in Luke's face, to bite him.

I tried to hold on to the affection that glowed in my heart. I fought to keep my heart open, to let him see me—really see me—as a person and not a sub, as a lover and not a project. I tried to be equal to him, to not let the rage that frothed in me boil up and over.

I tried so hard. Fought and wrestled. Fought and fought.

And lost.

"I hate you," I bit out. "I hate you for this."

My throat squeezed and a scream built inside me. I didn't hate him. I hated myself for ruining everything again. Luke's rhythm stuttered, but then he gripped my jaw and stared into my eyes, his thrusts fluid. "I love you," he murmured.

I loved him too, but I needed to be punished. No amount of trying to get ahold of myself was working. "I don't want you to love me. Not like this. I can't take it."

"I know, baby." He nuzzled my cheek and kissed my open mouth. "I'm going to help you."

He thrust into me again and again, releasing my jaw. My head tossed back and forth on the pillow. I wanted to come, to obliterate this urgent frustration, this fear and self-loathing that tossed around inside me like water in a half-filled pitcher, spilling out as tears.

Just as I was on the edge of orgasm, furious that his body could still make me come, Luke withdrew in a smooth motion. A new flame of rage licked inside me, denial of climax *again*, after I'd let him love me like that—or at least tried—after I'd held back my instincts to bite and spit? That was just sadism.

My sadist didn't seem to see it that way, though. He gazed at me softly as he positioned himself again over my hard cock. "Ready, baby?"

I bit my lip hard, as he held himself still, the tip of my cock at his entrance. Angry, I reached out, took hold of his hips, and shoved up into him. The heat of his ass engulfed me like water quenching the flames of my rage. Just like that, I wasn't furious anymore. I was possessed by him. Held in his body. He felt so slick and soft inside, so beautiful.

I loved him again.

The seesaw of my emotions left me unbalanced as I surged up, trying to flip him over. He let me, and as I plunged into him, his legs hitched up by my sides. His bigger form supported my weight, and his slick cock rose up to meet my thrusts. I rode the change.

"That better?" he asked, rubbing up and down my back, letting me fuck into him harder than he'd fucked into me. "Need to control me? Have my ass to express your love?"

I bowed my head, pressing my forehead to his upper chest, feeling the beat of his heart through where our skin was connected—above and below. He stroked my hair, my back, and my ass, and released sounds he never made while topping me. Soft noises, breathy grunts. When he clenched around me, my head spun.

So sexy, so hot and all mine now. I owned this man's ass, his heart, and possibly the rest of his time on earth—so long as I didn't let my fucked-up-ness ruin it.

"I'm gonna come."

I wrenched my eyes open to watch. I needed to see his face as I fucked him to orgasm. He wormed a hand between our bodies to jerk his own dick while he stared down at me. I watched as his eyes grew unbearably heated, sweat broke over him again, and his lips pulled into a sensual grimace.

"Come," I ordered. "Come for me."

He groaned, lunging to grab me for a kiss, but I held back, needing to see his face splinter with pleasure. His legs twitched against my sides, his breath stalled for a moment, and then he jerked hard, his cock spurting hot, thick wads of jizz between us as his asshole convulsed around my cock. But his face—

God, his face!

His eyes rolled back, his lashes fluttered, and his mouth fell open in a cry that filled the bedroom. It filled my mouth too when I pulled out and surged up his body to kiss him. His stomach shuddered as his orgasm crested so hard that he couldn't break free.

Finally, he collapsed, ending our kiss to pant desperately and stare up at the ceiling, dazed and shaking all over.

"Gorgeous," I said, kissing his chin, and then moving to shove back inside his asshole to feel his heat again. That got his attention, and he blinked back to reality, shifting his gaze back to mine.

I saw his plea that I understand he was too sensitive for a hard fuck now, or even a mild one. "Don't worry," I said. "I just want to feel you still."

His lids slipped closed again, and I kissed his chin, affection welling inside me, making me feel a hot and sticky mess in every way. "I made you come," I said, kissing his collarbones, and then slowly pulling out of him again. "I fucked you and made you jizz everywhere."

"You did." He eyed my still-hard dick. "But you didn't get off."

"Not yet."

"I wanted to feel it," he whispered. "Your spunk in my ass. You in my ass."

"Yeah?"

He nodded.

So, I knelt between his legs, and stared at his face as I jerked my dick. I soaked in the red of his cheeks, the blistering, intense adoration in his gaze, and when my climax came closer, I pushed back inside him and thrust twice before clutching his hips and shooting deep.

Cum erupted from me in hard pumps, and I kept my gaze on Luke as I filled him up. When I pulled out, I pushed some stray spunk back inside his reddened hole, and then crawled up to lie on my side next to him. He rolled onto his side too, and we peered into each other's eyes.

"How does it feel?" I asked.

"Knowing I have your cum in me?"

I nodded.

"Fucking hot."

I smiled. "Yeah. I love it too."

He rubbed his nose against mine and smiled back. "I love you."

I kissed him, and we held each other, naked and making out for a long time.

Part III

Late-November 1991

Chapter Twenty-One

Luke

BETSY WASN'T SURE about Minty. I could see it in her eyes as we sat down at the outdoor picnic bench and Minty started unloading the basket.

"I made most of this," he said, pushing his floral headband back more on his head and squinting into the sun as he glanced up to see her reaction. "I know Luke usually brings you stuff from your mom, and I hope you're not disappointed, but I think he's not ready to introduce me to your parents yet."

He gave a hopeful grin. "So, I did my best. I hope it's okay."

Betsy tilted her head, considering him.

Minty babbled on, "This is chocolate pudding—not the powdered kind, though! It's my mom's recipe. I loved it when I was little. Um, and this is a beef chili-cheese casserole. Luke said you like chili and that you aren't a vegetarian, and so I thought this would be a good choice. This one was my grandmother's recipe. She's dead now. It makes me remember her. And this is—"

I touched his wrist. "It's okay, baby. Betsy's not that picky, are you, Bets?"

Her gaze shifted from my hand on him over to the food he'd brought, and my heart hung suspended, afraid that this was about to go very badly.

"I like chocolate pudding. Why do you wear girls' clothes?" she said without segue.

"They make me look pretty," Minty said, shrugging. "Does it embarrass you? I can go change." He flushed. "I have some boy drag in the car."

"You *do* look pretty. And *I* like how he dresses," I said, the warning and defensiveness evident in my tone, but Betsy didn't take her eyes off him.

"I've never seen a boy like you," she said. "You look like the elf in my fairy tale book. He has white-blond hair too. And he wears a crown." She indicated Minty's headband. "Do you have pointed ears?"

Minty turned his head from side to side, letting her see both ears. "Sadly, no. But how great would it be if I did?"

"Really great," she confirmed, reaching out for a plate, and indicating the chocolate pudding. "Let's have that first."

"Okay!" Minty agreed, excitement and relief pouring off him.

There was no way I was going to be the voice of reason and insist we all eat something healthy before sucking down a vat of chocolate pudding. Not with a crisis so narrowly averted. I put my plate out. "Me too."

"How did you meet Lukey?" Betsy asked, digging into the pudding and leaving a smear of it behind on her face. I fought the urge to wipe it off. She was grown now and got irritated with me if I tried to take care of her in that parental kind of way.

Minty shot me a panicked glance.

"He came into my work," I said.

"At the sex shop?" She said it so easily that Minty choked.

"She knows where you work?" he asked, trying to catch his breath after I banged his back.

"I'm not a baby just because I have Down Syndrome," she said, defensively.

I caught Minty's eye reassuringly as I said, "Yeah, Betsy knows where I work."

She nodded firmly. "I want Riverwoods to take us on a field trip to a sex shop. I don't see why they won't. We're grown-ups, and I want a vibrator. I saw an article about them in a magazine of Rodney's."

I bit my lip. Betsy could be so open that sometimes I forgot other people weren't used to how carefree she was in expressing herself.

"If you can't convince them to take you, I could buy you one and mail it to you, or bring it here," Minty said.

I couldn't stop my brows from quirking every which direction as I imagined Minty in the shop, looking around for a vibrator for my sister. Horrifying.

"We've scandalized Luke," Minty whispered to her. "Look at him blush."

Betsy laughed. "He's a prude."

"I work in a sex shop," I muttered. "How can I be a prude?"

"You are, though."

I wasn't about to mention my BDSM work to prove a point, and I hoped Minty wouldn't either. Betsy knowing about the shop was one thing, knowing about the rest was not okay with me.

But my worry was unnecessary. Minty just shrugged. "I don't know about that, but the offer stands on the vibrator."

"I can pay you back," she agreed. "Up to ninety whole dollars. That's how much the vibrator cost in the magazine, and I've been saving."

"How about we talk about less sexual things?" I suggested. "Surely you have something else you could chat with Minty about. You don't even know him. Aren't you curious about who he is? Ask him anything. Anything at all."

"Okay," Betsy agreed. She pondered. "Did you buy anything?"

Minty frowned. "When?"

"At the shop. When you met my brother."

Minty darted a glance my way. "Um, I bought a class package."

"They sell classes there?"

"It was a special kind of class."

"A *sex* class?"

"Yes?" Minty answered, uncertainly.

"Oh, I want a sex class!"

"Betsy!" I said sharply. "No more talking about sex."

It was on her mind a lot now that she and Rodney were doing it, but I really didn't want to share any more about my or Minty's personal life, or hear much more about hers.

Minty went back to the pudding. Betsy did too. We sat in silence for some time, until Betsy asked, "Have you two done it? Like up the butt? Rodney saw it in a magazine and wants to try that."

"Jesus Christ, Bets."

I stood up and walked away from the picnic table as Minty said, "Yes, we do. You'll need some pointers before you just jump into things there. Anal sex isn't like vaginal sex. First, you need condoms for sure. And second, you'll need lubrication."

I scrubbed a hand over my face. "I'm just going to—" I motioned toward the long, drawn-out walk on the flower path that went around the building. They did all they could around here to make the grounds pleasant for the residents, having gone so far as to put in a manmade lake and stocking it with koi.

"So long, prude!" Betsy called as I headed down the path.

I was glad Riverwoods allowed for their residents to explore more mature things as they got older, offered sex education classes, and were liberal with condoms to offset the STD risks, but sometimes I wondered if they shouldn't be more conservative than they were about it all. Especially in light of HIV. It was far too easy for something to go wrong in the heat of the moment...

I knew all too well.

I turned over the memory of the night I'd let the wrong guy top me. I remembered the cold chill that had fallen on me when he called four weeks later to tell me the news. The sudden knowledge, deep in my gut, of what was to come.

I wondered what it'd been like for Minty. Did he know intuitively the moment it happened? Or had he been blindsided that day in the health center when he got his results? I rubbed my chest imagining him there alone and afraid, hearing that diagnosis from someone who didn't love him. I hoped they'd been kind.

As I passed by a bench with another visiting family, I waved and tilted my head back. The trees were really starting to turn gorgeous colors up in the mountains. The magnificent red of the sugar maples were breathtaking.

I paused to throw some rocks in the pond, watching the ripples expand over the water. Cause and effect. HIV and Minty had been like that in my life. They'd both dropped into the water of me, and I was still feeling the aftereffects. Ever expanding and irreversible.

I stuffed my hands in my pockets, watching bright leaves twirl to the ground. The scent of earthy autumn was all around, and I took it in with deep breaths.

It was good to be alive. To see the color slide down the mountain slopes. To glance across the pond to see my lover and my sister happily interacting. The light shone in Minty's hair. His hands moved like birds, fluttering as he spoke.

I saw him make a filthy gesture to illustrate something he was saying and snorted. Great. Betsy and Rodney would be getting up to anal sex in their facility beds, and there was nothing I could do to stop it. I supposed it was good Minty was educating her on it. Especially given that HIV didn't discriminate.

Speaking of, I wondered how the dungeon scene had changed in the months since I was diagnosed. I supposed we'd find out tonight. I'd been unsure about attending when I first got the invitation. I normally ignored them, even before my six-month break from the lifestyle. But, somehow, I thought Minty would enjoy the experience. Or at least be intrigued by it. That's what I hoped anyway.

Even knowing all of that, anxiety around taking Minty to the dungeon had lingered in my gut from the moment after I mentioned it, when his eyes had lighted with interest. With his trauma, and my persistent insecurity about being enough for him, I wondered if I'd done the right thing even bringing it up. It felt like a damned-if-I-do/damned-if-I-don't situation, because if I didn't offer the dungeon experience to Minty, despite my gut feeling it wasn't a good fit, then he might try to escalate his kink elsewhere…

I shook my head at the stubborn darkness of my thoughts, wanting to embrace the little time we had left with my sister. We needed to get back on the road soon if we were going to have time to prepare for the party. Minty would want to do an enema, just in case.

I swallowed down the strange jealousy that descended at the thought of what "just in case" might mean at a dungeon.

I sighed. I was the Dom. I could wrangle myself and these emotions. Everything would be fine.

When I returned to where they sat, Minty was animatedly telling Betsy about various kinds of salamanders. She sat with her chin in her hands, staring at him like he was an angel come to earth, and listening with all her might.

"So that's why when I graduate—" Darkness passed over his face. "I mean, if I get to graduate, I want to go into working with river habitats and protections. To save more species of salamander."

"I want to be a singer in a band," Betsy said, oblivious to the shadow that had glanced across his features. "But I don't know if I can. Now I live here, and only Lori knows how to play an instrument. Bassoon."

"Betsy and the Bassoon would be a cool band name."

She giggled.

"Hey," I said, dropping down next to them. "Sorry to interrupt, but Minty and I need to go."

"Already?" Betsy pouted.

"Sorry. It can't be helped."

Her shoulders sagged.

"I'll be back in a few weeks. And I'll be able to stay longer then," I reassured her.

"With Minty?"

I glanced to him. "Maybe."

She sighed.

"I can come," Minty said, with a smile. "I don't have anything better to do right now."

"What about school?" she asked, tilting her head.

"Eh, who needs it?" He shrugged.

"You do. To become a salamander scientist."

He blinked rapidly and then nodded. "You're right. But I don't think that's actually gonna happen for me."

"Why?" Betsy demanded.

Not sure what Minty might say, and not wanting to worry my sister with the specter of AIDS, I interrupted with, "Let's go ahead and put the leftovers in the fridge in your room, and you can share it all with Rodney when he gets back from his day out with his folks."

That made her brighten and by the time we left her alone in her room, she was cheerful again. Though she didn't forget to say, "See you soon, Minty!" before she shut the door behind us.

"She was fun," Minty said, as he buckled his seat belt in the passenger seat. "I was enjoying hanging out with her. But I'm also excited to get on with our night. What all do I need to do? Clean myself inside, obviously, but what else? Do a little X to get into the mood?"

"Rule number one of going to a dungeon—never show up high or drunk. Sober play is the only safe play."

Minty saluted. "Aye, aye, Sir."

"But as for what I want from you tonight, how I want you to be—I just want you to be authentic. No fake reactions. I want you to feel sure of everything you do there. Anything makes you uncomfortable? We can leave. No questions asked."

"Yes, Sir."

The first gurgle of excitement regarding our plans for the night stirred in my gut. Because this next part was something I'd planned especially for him. "When we get to the house, I have a surprise for you."

"A surprise?" His voice lifted eagerly.

"Yeah. A gift."

A grin broke over his sweet face. "What kind of gift?"

"A filthy one."

He sat up straight, eyes going wide. "What *kind* of filthy gift?"

"Just wait. It's a *surprise*, remember?"

Minty sat back, looking straight ahead as we pulled out of the lot. His face was blank, but I could tell his mind was humming with thoughts of the surprise I'd promised him.

Chapter Twenty-Two

Minty

"I S THIS WHERE it is?" I asked, shifting around on the brand new, pink butt plug Luke had inserted before we'd left the house again.

It'd been his filthy surprise for me, and while it was a very pretty shade of pink—similar to my toenail polish—my favorite part of it had been the post-douche insertion. He'd teased me for ages before finally putting it in.

"This is it," Luke said, navigating into some dodgy street parking in a warehouse district near the Old City.

As I peered anxiously into the dicey, dark street, he came around the car and opened my door like a gentleman. Helping me out, he put my arm around me, indicating the gloomy building in front of us. "He we are. Knoxville's only operating dungeon."

"It looks scary."

"We don't have to go in."

"No, I still want to…" Though my excitement was waning at the sight of the dingy, unattractive building. We took a few more steps before I pulled him to another stop. "I don't want anyone else to touch me."

Until that moment, I hadn't been sure. But as my heartrate skyrocketed, and my palms went wet with sweat, I knew that tonight I wanted to be Luke's and Luke's alone.

Maybe I'd always wanted that? It seemed more and more likely.

Luke squeezed my hand. "Of course. You're mine to hurt, re-member?"

"Yours," I agreed. With a shaky breath, I adjusted my floral headband, squeezed my ass around the reassuring solidity of the plug, and put my shoulders back. "Do I look okay?"

"You look beautiful, baby."

"Then let's go."

The dungeon, as Luke had called it, was really a divided-up warehouse with painted-over windows so that it looked abandoned from the outside.

The inside, though, was another story altogether.

The main room wasn't that large and there weren't *that* many people inside, but there were still more than I'd have imagined. Almost as many as a busy night at Lord Lindsey, the most popular dance club in town. In the center of the room, the otherwise wooden floors glowed with red lights set beneath squares of clear tiles, lighting up the bare legs and bodies I could see in the gloom, turning them a lurid pink.

The walls were painted red with black crown molding, and the ceiling was draped with silky red fabric. Two enormous fans circulated the air, causing the material to move in undulating waves. The effect was very dark, making it hard for me to see, even though we'd walked in from the early autumn night outside.

Music thrummed. It struck me that it wasn't that different from what was played at my favorite gay club, Tilt-a-Whirl. The room felt dark and animalistic, the atmosphere highly sexual. The BDSM-flavored song "Master and Servant" by Depeche Mode took over from "Head Like a Hole" by Nine Inch Nails as we moved deeper into the room.

I clung to Luke's hand, and he kept me close by his side. We definitely weren't dressed for the occasion. Some men and women—in all sorts of pairings and groups—wore leather thongs, pants, and straps. Others wore nothing at all. One woman wore only a set of fake dog ears, and another wore just a swirl of gold paint on her nipples.

There were queer people there too. No one seemed to bat an eye over them. In fact, on the stage set up to the right of the main room, there was a man with an erection tied to a cross similar to the one in Luke's basement letting another man snap a flogger against his thighs and chest.

"What do you think?" Luke yelled in my ear.

"It's always been here? And I just never knew?"

"No. The police will shut this exact location down any day now. But the dungeon will just go to another warehouse, or to an old farmhouse in the countryside, or a house in the suburbs. The community finds a way to thrive."

"Hey there, Luke," a shirtless, wiry-haired older man greeted in a booming voice as we finally made it to the bar. "Long time, no see, buddy." A small, thin man knelt at his feet, a bald spot gracing the back of his head. He kept his eyes on the floor.

"Baron, good to see you." Luke nudged the kneeling man with the toe of his tennis shoe. "Willy, you good down there?"

The man didn't look up, but he nodded.

"Willy's getting too turned on watching all the fun tonight." Baron laughed, flicking the side of the man's head with his middle finger. Willy winced. "He knows better than to get hard for anyone but me."

"Willy," Luke scolded with a laugh.

"And who's this?" the man asked, eyeing me up and down with a glint in his eye. "Pretty. Young. Fresh."

"He's mine," Luke said, tugging me closer. "Name's Mitchell."

I snuggled in tighter, worried that this man might touch me. There was something about the way he smiled that I didn't like.

"Well, you're going to be popular around here, Mitchell," Baron said with a snort.

"No, I'm not," I said, lifting my chin. "I'm Luke's. Just Luke's."

"Pity." The man nudged Willy with his boot. "Right, Willy? You'd like to see me wank him, wouldn't you?"

Willy's dick, which had been half-hard, now pushed up to full mast. He nodded.

"Not happening," Luke said, rolling his eyes. "We're just here to see what the scene's like these days."

"Different than before," Baron said with a sigh. "All kinds of rules now. You can spank, jerk off, fist, and torture—but no more sucking or fucking. They'll kick you out. AIDS, you know." He moved his hands around. "I mean we've probably all got it already, so I don't see the point, but the club says it's a liability."

Luke and Baron chatted a little longer, and I scoped out the room. It was all so much *more* than I'd anticipated. I wondered why I'd expected anything less.

"Hey, sorry, but have you seen Ryan?" Luke asked, interrupting Baron's talk of HIV's impact on the community.

I frowned, wondering who that might be. Why had Luke never mentioned this guy before? Was he someone Luke played with sometimes? I realized that while I'd said I didn't want anyone to touch me, we hadn't made any rules about people touching *him.*

"Room six, if that's what you're here to see."

It was too loud to talk effectively, though, so I kept quiet and held on to Luke's hand as he pulled me toward a hallway lined with closed doors. He came to the sixth one and knocked, waiting only a few seconds before opening it and gesturing inside. "What do you think?" he asked.

Inside, there was a slim, dark-haired man on his elbows and knees on top of a big plastic-wrapped rug, with another man directly behind him, elbow deep in his ass. I stopped in the doorway, shock jolting me still. Loud music bounced off the walls of the room, and yet the sound of grunts and heavy breathing rattled from the same speakers.

Luke gripped my arm and pulled me back, speaking directly into my ear so I could hear him over the noise from the main area of the club and Room Six, too. "Have you ever seen someone get fisted?"

I shook my head.

"That's Curtis," he said pointing out the heavier, brunet guy with his hand buried in his partner's ass. "And that's Ryan."

"Oh."

Luke shut the door on the scene. "We don't have to watch," he reassured me, squeezing my hand. "It's up to you what we do. I'd wanted to ask Ryan to help us out with a favor, but I didn't know he'd be deep in a scene so early in the night."

My heart pounded, and I felt a little dizzy. I wasn't sure if it was with fear or lust, or confusion. I only knew I was overloaded. Stupidly, I asked, "What'd you want to talk to him about?"

Luke pushed some stray hair off my forehead and trailed his fingers down my cheek, gazing into my eyes, trying to read me. It was shadowy in the hall, and I wasn't sure how much of my expression he could see. His face was a dark blob haloed in shiny blond. "Last week at Knox Supplies & News, you mentioned a friend of yours wanted to learn to Dom."

Right. I'd told him about Windy's desire. I'd almost forgotten, but Luke hadn't.

"Ryan's an experienced sub. He could teach him the ropes."

"But aren't they…" I didn't know if I should ask. It wasn't my business.

"Are you asking if Curtis and Ryan are a monogamous couple?" he asked.

"Yes."

"Not at all. Ryan's between Doms right now. He's looking for someone regular and steady. Curtis's a stopgap, from what I've heard. They play hardcore, as you saw, but they aren't committed."

I turned from Luke, opened the door to the room again, and stared inside to where Ryan was groaning, face red and slick with sweat, and I imagined Windy where Curtis was now. Hand shoved in Ryan's ass, a satisfied smirk on his face.

"Let's go find another room," Luke urged. "Or we can dance, or head home. Whatever you want."

"No, let's stay." Bald curiosity had me in its grip. "I want to watch."

Luke's brows did a small dance, and in the shadows of the club, I couldn't be sure if he was happy with my response or not. Whatever the case, Luke tugged me through and shut the door behind us. He led me to a front row seat and guided me down beside him.

The music pounded through the room's speakers—some sort of heavy metal—but microphones were set up next to the play space. Curtis and Ryan's words, grunts, and slick sex noises broke through the hard guitar and drums.

"There you go, sweets," Curtis said. "Just ride that for a minute. Feel that stretch."

Ryan gently moved forward and back on his hands and knees, screwing himself on the man's forearm. He groaned, trembling all over, and his soft cock drooled fluid onto the plastic-covered rug.

There were a few other occupied seats holding a couple of lone men with their dicks out, slowly jerking and watching. They seemed almost sleepy about it, like they'd been there a long time and hadn't seen what they'd come to see, but hoped it'd show up any second. They weren't even keeping rhythm with the music.

I gaped at the scene in front of me, a tumble of feelings rolling around inside. Horror, fascination, lust, and fear. Would Luke want me to take his fist in public like this Ryan guy? I suddenly knew with certainty that I didn't want that.

In fact, I didn't think I wanted to take a fist at all.

I'd been open to the idea when Luke mentioned it because it sounded painful and hot, but now, watching it happen right in front of my face, I didn't want anything to do with it. Fisting seemed impossible even though I could plainly see it was not. The plug in my ass was plenty big enough.

"Sir," I whispered, feeling that the two of us were also in a scene so long as we were in this place. "Do you want us to play like that?"

Luke said, "Only if you get off on that idea."

I chewed my bottom lip, watching as Curtis scooped a bunch more Crisco oil from a can and applied it to his arm and fist. Ryan's waiting ass was gaping immensely, open and hungry, and more than a little terrifying.

"No, Sir. I like what we do alone."

"Me too." Luke stroked my hair.

I loved the intimacy of our interactions, and the way pain was so much more special when it was just between me and the man giving it to me. What I'd done with *Kyle* even seemed more intimate to me than *this…*

Suddenly, it was all too much. All of it. Everything. I'd wanted to watch, but now I was done. I turned to him. "Actually, Sir, can we go?"

"Absolutely." Luke stood and took hold of my arm, pulling me up.

As we passed through the main room, Luke shouted in my ear, "Should I leave a message for Ryan with the bartender? Do you think your friend would be interested?"

I nodded, clarifying, "Yes, but hurry. I want to go home."

Luke frowned. "We can just head out."

"No, leave the message," I yelled over the music.

While he talked to a guy with pitch-black hair and a dog collar behind the bar, I glanced around the dance floor. The sexual shenanigans that went down at Tilt-a-Whirl were nothing compared to this. Off to the side there was a woman being fucked in both of her lower holes by two men who were thrusting in and out to the beat of "Personal Jesus."

Message delivered, Luke threaded his fingers through mine and led me toward the door we'd entered just a short time before. We dodged a short woman walking with a chubby man on a leash at her feet.

Once we were back outside in the alley between warehouses, the moon shining down on the buildings, Luke pulled me to face him, smoothing his hot hands over my even hotter cheeks. "You okay?"

I hiccupped a weird-sounding laugh. "I don't think this is the place for a romantic like me."

"I'm sorry, baby. I shouldn't have—"

"It's okay," I cut him off. "I wanted to come. I had no idea I wouldn't like it."

Luke searched my eyes and then glanced around. "Come on. Let's get back in the car. This isn't the best neighborhood to stand around in the street at night."

Driving down Magnolia Avenue, headed toward Luke's house, he squeezed my knee. "I'm sorry."

"Why?"

"I suspected it might be a mistake taking you. I should have gone with my gut."

"No, I wanted to see it for myself. It was just…" I shook my head.

"It was what?"

I sighed. "When we're in your basement, do I look like that?"

"Like what?"

"All—" I waved my hands around. "You know."

"I have no idea what you mean, baby."

"Do I look crass? Like, I know I'm trash, I've always known that—"

"*No.* And no you're not."

"I try really hard to look pretty all the time, but those men and women? They looked sweaty, and like they were *trying* very hard, and…" I groaned. "I don't know what I'm saying."

"You look gorgeous in my basement."

I nodded. "I thought so. I mean, I hoped so."

"Tell me what bothered you the most. The exhibitionism? The activities? The fisting?"

"All of that," I said. "It's not anyone's business what I look like when I'm hurting. Just yours."

Luke's lips tweaked into a small smile. "Or when you're coming for me?"

"Loads of guys have seen me come," I said, crossing my arms over my chest. "I'm very pretty when I'm orgasming. I've watched myself in the mirror, so I know."

Luke laughed.

"What?"

"You are. You're the prettiest guy I've ever seen."

I was smug for a moment, but then I asked, "If you thought I wouldn't like it, why did you tell me about the invitation? Was it really to talk to Ryan?"

Luke shifted gears, and something in the beat of silence told me I was right to ask. "I wanted to show you there was more I could give you. If you needed more humiliation, or if you wanted other people to give you pain, there are ways to meet those needs. You don't have to go back to Kyle to escalate your kink."

I chewed my inner cheek for a moment, parsing through the confusing feelings bombarding me. Was that actual *hurt* in the mix? Yes. Why, though?

"I don't go to Kyle—I mean, in the past, I didn't go to him to 'escalate kink.' I went to him because in his sick way he needed me, and in my sick way I needed him, and those sick ways we needed each other came together in a satisfying way for me."

Luke shivered. "I know. That's what scares me so much."

There it was. That vulnerability I'd begged him for. Now I needed to do my part by stepping up and reassuring him. "Luke, I love what we do together. I love *you* and everything you do to me. I don't want to 'escalate our kink.'"

"I just needed you to know it was an option."

"Do you want to escalate it? Do you need more?"

Luke shook his head, and his hand trembled as he moved to shift gears again. "No, baby. I want you all for myself. I don't want to share."

"Okay. Then I thank you for taking me tonight. It taught me a lot." I start to number things on my fingers. "First, I don't want public sex. Second, I absolutely do not want to be fisted. Ever."

Luke laughed.

"Third, as my Dom, you will do anything for me, even things you don't want to do. Especially if you think I'll benefit from them in some way."

"Baby—"

"Shh, I'm not done yet. Fourth, you still think I might leave you for Kyle. I won't. I promise you. I will never, ever return to him. Say you believe me."

Luke took hold of my hand and kissed my fingers. "I want to believe you."

As much as that hurt to hear, I knew Luke was just being vulnerable and honest with me. That was what I'd asked from him, wasn't it?

Now I had to be strong enough to hold his insecurity without deepening it into a conflict. Aikido to the rescue. I breathed in and let it out slowly, nodded, and turned to face the window as I said, "I understand. I'll prove it to you. I promise."

Luke

MINTY LOOKED AMAZING locked in a cage.

Naked, his painted nails clinging to the bars near his head and his sweet ass lifted back toward the end where I'd affixed a dildo for him to ride. It was deep in his hole, and he was writhing on it greedily.

I'd spanked him when we first got back home, upstairs in the living room, sitting on the sofa. Then I'd ordered him to the cage in the basement, and he'd complied without question. I'd never locked him into it before, though I'd threatened to plenty of times.

I finished drinking a cup of water as I watched him staring at me with his glittering blue eyes, his lips slick and begging for my cock. "Please, Sir," he whimpered. "I want to drain your balls."

I laughed. "I bet you do. But not yet."

He groaned, twisting his hips so the dildo worked over his prostate. The cage was currently positioned on a sturdy coffee table so I could fuck into his mouth or ass at will. He was flushed and sweaty. The expression on his face wasn't that different from Ryan's as he'd worked himself to a frenzy on Curtis's fist. But Minty was so much prettier than Ryan. So much more mine.

"That's enough," I said, stalking to the cage and hitting the side of it, jolting him. "Don't you dare get yourself off."

Minty's lips curled up in a snarl, and he stared me right in the eye as he worked his hips again.

"You little shit," I muttered. "Open your mouth. Now."

Minty grinned like the cat who'd got the cream, but when I removed my dick from my jeans and *didn't* plunge it into his throat, his expression darkened.

"That's right. Swallow it."

"Sir, I—"

I aimed, and the stream of piss was tight. It stung lightly as it pushed through my engorged cock. Minty winced as it splashed over his lips and chin, and then he started gulping, swallowing like I'd ordered.

I smiled, changing my aim and pissing into his hair, dousing his face all over, and getting his lashes wet with it. He groaned, twisting his hips on the dildo, riding it as I soaked him.

"You're going to pay for that," I muttered, the stream not stopping. "As soon as I finish this."

Minty shoved back on the dildo, riding it as I kept coating him. "Sir," he whimpered. "I'm going to come, Sir."

I grunted, cut off what was left of my stream, and went to my wall of implements. There was one hanging up there that Jerome had created himself. He'd done wood and metalworking on the side—making weapons and axes mostly—but that skill had come in handy with sex toys too. And *this* was a torture device that I'd only endured once and had safe-worded out of almost immediately.

I opened the cage door, which pulled the dildo from his ass in a rush.

"Fuck!" he cried, wincing at the rough way the head of the dildo snapped from his anus. "Fuck, Sir. That was mean."

I laughed. "Yeah? This is meaner."

The humbler Jerome had made was a wooden device that fit around the testicles and cupped the back of the thighs, leather ropes and cuffs attached it to the ankles. It was a matter of minutes before Minty was trussed up and stuck in a predicament between where I had latched his wrists to the front of the cage, and the place where his balls were tied to his ankles. If he moved back and forth, or any other way for that matter, the humbler would tug his balls painfully.

"Now," I said, closing the cage door again so that the attached dildo slid back into his slicked-up anus. He groaned with pleasure at being filled. "Fuck yourself on it."

Minty tried to obey and quickly stilled, his back breaking out in a shiny sweat. "Sir?" he asked in a small voice. "Please take it off, Sir."

"Got a safe word?"

"I do, but I don't want to use it."

"Then hold completely still or fuck yourself. Those are your options."

Minty shifted back and forth, but the nauseating pain of having his balls jerked in the humbler stilled him completely. He breathed heavily, sweat slicking his back and forehead. His eyes were hot and angry as he glared at me through the bars.

Back at the wall of implements, I chose a traditional crop and headed back to the cage. Kneeling in front of him, I kissed his nose through the bars. He growled at me, and I laughed. "You look really good like this. Maybe I'll keep you down here for a few days. Think you can sleep this way?"

A flash of fear in his eyes told me I still had the power to scare him the way he needed. I'd never leave him down here like that, but that he believed I might—for even a few hours, much less days—was heady.

I showed him the crop. "Now, let's see how well you take your punishment."

He gulped.

"Safe word?"

He shook his head.

I aimed the crop carefully, not wanting the leather to land on the bars instead of his skin. The slaps weren't as forceful as they could have been, but they were enough to get him dancing inside the cage. Shifting from knee to knee, panting and whimpering, he groaned with every movement beyond a few centimeters as the humbler jerked his balls.

"Sir," he panted. "It's too much."

"Sir doesn't care."

"Sir, please."

"Open up."

He hesitated but then opened his mouth and this time I fed him my dick. I held onto the bars across the top of the cage, sliding in and out of his throat, rocking him back and forth on the dildo and forcing the humbler to tug his balls. He shivered and sweated. Lines of it slipped down his shoulders and over his back. His haunches tightened and released, and belatedly I realized he couldn't use his safe word with my dick in his throat.

"Snap your fingers for me," I said.

He grunted as I pushed deep, but he snapped his fingers with both hands.

"Good. Now, that's your safe word. Snap—even once—and we'll end it."

He groaned acknowledgment, but I pulled out to be sure. "I'll snap," he said, his voice hoarse from use already. "I promise."

I fucked his mouth gleefully then. His muffled cries of pain from the humbler vibrated through my cock and balls, and I slid my hands past the bars to hold his hair as I took his throat.

His eyes rolled back. His body moved with mine, absolutely no resistance.

"That's right, baby," I whispered. "Take it like a bitch."

Tears slipped down his cheeks, but I didn't stop fucking his mouth. He heaved breaths in around my cock, gasping when I pulled out of his throat, and then gargling like a drowning man when I plunged in again.

"I love you," I said. "You're my princess, my boy, my dirty fucking whore. I love you covered in my piss, and I love you clean and sweet in my bed, and cuddled up with me on the couch. I love your sweet goddamn holes so much. Love to fill you with my dick."

He groaned around me.

"And I love the way you swallow my jizz like it's fucking delicious. I love your face when you come. I love how you laugh, and the way you think, and all your jokes." I couldn't believe I was making any sense at all. I was lifting out of my body, my orgasm building roughly as I choked him on my dick.

"I love you, Mitchell. I love you. Fuck, *fuck,* I love you." I threw my head back and came. His throat worked around me, and I pulled out enough to let him nurse the head of my dick through the final volleys of cum.

"I love you too," he whispered when I finally removed myself from his mouth. "I love you too, Sir. Luke. I love you."

I bent down to kiss his mouth and saw that he'd come inside his cage. There was a pool of it, and his dick was still twitching from the orgasm. I licked his lips. "You shot your load. Knew you'd love the pain." I kissed his tongue when he stuck it out at me.

"Fuck, baby," I said, breathing hard and feeling dizzy. "That was good."

"Can we do it again?"

I laughed, shaking all over and utterly exhausted, but my boy was begging for a second round.

"Give me a minute," I said, going around to check that the humbler wasn't too tight or damaging his scrotum and balls. "I'm going to need a breather."

"Can I wait in the cage for you?" Minty asked, his question ending with a groan as I opened the door and the dildo slid out of his gaping ass.

"You like the cage?"

"I'm safe here. Yours." He sounded breathless as I checked the humbler, and then he shifted, whimpering, as I un-trussed him and removed it. His balls looked a little swollen after the rough pulling.

I'd need to ice them later. Another way to hurt my boy.

"Nothing to do in there but be my fuck toy, yeah?" I said, tossing the humbler aside. "No responsibilities. No stress."

"Thank you, Sir," he said, as I closed the cage again, the dildo sliding right back into place. "I love being your fuck toy."

"And I love to hear you scream. You haven't screamed yet tonight."

His eyes brightened, anticipation laced with fear. "I'd like to scream, Sir."

I laughed. "Oh, yeah? Well, why don't you beg for it then?"

"Please make me scream, Sir. *Please.*"

"So fucking gorgeous."

Fifteen minutes later, Minty was screaming his head off, and joy flowed inside me like a river. Happiness, love, lust… As unexpected and even unwanted as this relationship might have started out, there was no denying all my needs were satisfied in the person of Mitchell.

My sweet, dirty, horny boy.

Chapter Twenty-Three

Luke

"**I** HAVE TO go see my mom," Minty said over breakfast two days later, his lips twisting up miserably. He'd spent the night again, this time in my bed, where we'd practiced lovemaking. He'd still needed to be the one on top to get all the way through without fighting me, but it was hot, and we both enjoyed it.

I paused in eating my cereal to glance his way. "You don't want to?"

Minty shrugged, his brows low, his eyes directed out the window into the scrubby back yard full of gray-brown bushes and faded out grass. I should make it nicer back there. Plant some winter flowers and evergreen shrubs, but I didn't have the time, money, or inclination. I'd rather invest what time I had left—

I broke off that thought. I refused to become like Minty, so certain I'd die soon that I was nearly banking on it.

As he continued to fret over whatever was going on in his head, I took a final few bites of cereal before taking the bowl to the sink to rinse. When I came back, he was winding his fingers together restlessly and gnawing on his lip.

Taking hold of his hands, I stilled his fingers and joined our hands instead. "Hey, look at me."

He lifted his eyes from where he was now frowning at our fingers. His blue eyes shimmered with a dark emotion.

"What has you so upset?"

He shrugged and chewed his lip some more, gaze darting back toward the window. "It's not a big deal."

"Tell me anyway."

He let out a heavy sigh, his shoulder slumping. "I haven't told her. About the diagnosis."

"Do you want her to know?"

He shook his head.

"But you think you should tell her?"

Another big sigh. "There's nothing she can do about it. Why make her suffer for a longer time? If things go the way I plan, then she'll never need to know until I'm gone."

"Baby…"

"I don't want to hurt her."

"You need her support, though."

Sharply, his gaze swiveled back to me. "How? Financial? She's broke."

"Emotional."

"At what price? Her peace of mind? Her happiness?"

"How about at the cost of your own? You need your mother right now."

"Does *your* mom know?" he challenged me.

I flinched, caught out. "She's in her seventies now. It's possible I'll outlive her, and she'll never need to know. But your mom is young. You said she had you just out of high school."

"She's been through so much," Minty murmured.

"So have you."

He shrugged. "I can take it."

"Baby, you shouldn't have to 'take it', not without her help. She's your mother."

Minty shook his head. "She doesn't need this."

"No one needs this," I reminded him.

"My mom…" He trailed off. "She was abused as a kid. Then she married my dad after she got pregnant with me. He was abusive too. And then he—" Minty wrenched one of his hands free of my grasp to wipe over his face. "He did what he did to me. She had to endure the entire fallout from that—"

"Baby, you were the one he raped."

"Yeah, but she was broken by it, and they almost took me away from her. After he was convicted, he spent five years in prison, and—"

"Just five years?"

Minty nodded. "Good behavior reduced his sentence."

"Christ."

"I know."

"Baby…"

He pulled his other hand from mine, crossed his arms over his chest, and leaned back, diverting his attention to my lawn once more. "After he got out, he came to see us twice. The last time, he tried to get me to—You know. I told you before." Minty's jaw clenched tight, and his breath came in panicked huffs. "I lunged at him. Tried to bite his face. He kicked me to the floor. I was scared he'd hurt her too. He spit on me, and then he left. I haven't seen him since."

That wasn't the same story he'd told me before about what had happened the last time he saw his father. In that one, he'd been the one to fight off his father, spit in *his* face and go. This time…

Well, it wasn't the same, and it still didn't seem like the whole truth, but whatever had happened, he was traumatized by it.

Minty spoke from somewhere far away, still half-entrenched in the memory. "Mom hasn't forgiven herself for letting him in the house that day."

"She was there?"

Minty nodded, fading out again. "Yeah. She was in the chair

next to the sofa. He said, 'Nadine, your son's a whore. He wanted it then, and he wants it now.'"

Minty went pale as the white paint on my walls, the few freckles on his face looking dark against his skin. "I was already in my room. I heard him say it. That's when he—" He closed his eyes, swallowing hard. "You know. I already said."

"Yes." I didn't mention that every time he recounted that day, the story changed a little. I had a glimmer of an idea dancing around in my head, but clearly Minty wasn't interested in sharing the full story yet.

"Mom was devastated."

His *mom* was devastated? I wanted to find the woman and shake her. How had she ever let that monster back in their house?

"She believed him, you know?" Minty was so quiet, I had to lean closer to hear. "He'd been through rehabilitation and therapy at the prison, claimed he'd found God there too. She wanted to believe he was 'healed.'"

"Jesus Christ."

"Exactly. Jesus Christ was the problem. Her faith told her to believe that Christ's redemption is for everyone, you know?" His voice grew louder, defensive. "But Mom never did anything wrong. She didn't deserve any of it."

"Baby…"

Minty rubbed his hands over his face. "I don't want to tell her about the diagnosis. Knowing I'm dying will just bring her pain. And it was so hard for her to accept me being—" He gestured at himself. "I mean, the problem wasn't with her. Never with her. She loved me just the way I am from the very start. But she took so much crap from her church and from her old friends, and my dad, all because of me, and—" Tears started down his cheeks, which had gone from white as a sheet to flushed pink. "She always says that my future is so bright now. That all our pain is in the past. The only cloud hanging over her head was not knowing my HIV status. She wanted me to get tested. And I… so for her birthday, I thought I'd give her that." He swallowed convulsively, looking sick. "I can't give her this news instead."

"It's her birthday today?"

He nodded. "Yeah. She made cake. I got her a card. Inside I told her I'm going to take her to Biltmore House for their Christmas celebration." He glanced toward the clock on the wall. "I need to leave soon. I'm supposed to be there by twelve."

I studied his face, his shaking hands. "I'll drive you."

He snapped back from wherever he'd gone, his gaze piercing. "No."

"Yes. You can't drive like this. Look at you, baby, you're shaking."

He sighed. "I just can't tell her the truth if you're there."

"So, you *are* going to tell her?"

He covered his face and curled in on himself. "I don't know. Maybe. No? I think no. Not on her birthday."

"Then let me come with you."

"And introduce you as what? My Dom? My Master? The guy I beg to hurt me?"

My heart twisted at his attempt to put distance between us to cover his vulnerability. "You'll introduce me as your boyfriend. That's what I am. You know that."

He sucked in a quivering breath. "Are you?"

"Of course. You practically live here with me. You've made promises to me, and I've made them to you. You're the only guy I want to be with, and the only guy I've ever loved like this."

"Love as an action or a verb?"

I smiled. "Both. I told you so while I was fucking your throat the other night, didn't I?"

He blinked. "That's…you can't keep…" He cleared his throat.

"You've only ever said it when we're fucking, or we've just finished fucking, or we're in a scene."

"So?"

"You can't just tell me that during a scene or when we're having sex. It's not fair."

"Why? You seemed to like it."

Minty tore at his hair in frustration. "I did, but now I think it wasn't enough."

"Oh?"

He met my eyes. "Because it needs to be romantic."

"Our scenes aren't romantic?"

He blushed. "I guess, it's like this: I already know I make you come so hard you lose your mind. You might say you loved me just because you shot your brains out your dick and into my ass. That's not the same thing as a sober love confession."

I laughed, my throat gritty with emotion—anger, sadness, hurt for him, and fondness all rolled into one. "That so?"

"Yes."

"Then ask me to tell you now. Nicely."

"I won't ask," he said, crossing his arms over his chest again. "I'm telling you how it's going to be. It *has to be* romantic. So don't say it again—scene or no scene, fucking or no fucking—until you've fixed the problem."

"Bossy bottom," I murmured, closing in for a kiss. He dodged me and my lips landed on his cheekbone. "Let's wash up and get out of here. I'm looking forward to meeting your mom."

Obviously still conflicted, Minty let me tug him to his feet. "All right. I just need a few minutes."

A "few minutes" turned out to be an hour and a half while Minty fidgeted with his hair and clothes, choosing the perfect number of colored barrettes, and picking out the right skirt to go with his frothy, yellow shirt, and then deciding between some ballet slippers he had and his cowboy boots.

I watched him put on his makeup and choose his clothes with a new understanding.

This wasn't just his style, his self-expression, and his bravery.

This was his armor too.

When it was time to leave, he was ready.

Chapter Twenty-Four

Minty

I'D NEVER TAKEN any of my friends to my mom's house, except for Daniel. Well, technically, Windy had come with me once, but I'd made him wait in the car while I ran inside and grabbed a few things from my old room. My mom hadn't even been home.

So, when I pulled my truck to a stop in front of the trailer, I couldn't help but see the place through Luke's eyes, and what I saw was grim. The gray-blue siding was slick with the earlier rain, and the low-hanging winter clouds were the same color as the worn, wooden steps that led up to the front door. Luke's house wasn't all that big, but it was ten times nicer than Mama's mobile home. Daniel's mom had been generous in gifting it to us, but she hadn't been extravagant in the least. There were no extras, and there was no hiding our poverty.

"This is it," I said, unbuckling my seatbelt and hopping from the cab of the truck with ease. The soggy, grassless ground squished beneath my cowboy boots. I closed my loose, green military surplus jacket around me to block out the cold. "Home, sweet home." My distaste for the place seeped into my tone.

Luke shut the door of the truck behind him, stuffed his hands in his pockets and rocked back on his heels, examining Mama's short, evergreen gardenia shrubs, strung over with blinking Christmas lights. "Looks cozy."

It had been once, back before my father had found us here. I used to feel safe in the trailer. I'd loved when it rained, especially. Being tucked up inside with a hot mug of coffee, snug in my bed while the rain came down had been its own kind of heaven.

Now...

A drop of rain hit my head. It slid cold and slow down my cheek.

"Let's do this," I said, straightening my shoulders. I checked my crossbody purse to make sure the birthday card was still tucked inside.

Luke crowded up on the step behind me as I knocked on the door and then flung it open, stepping into the warm living room. A kerosene heater sat in the corner, keeping the temperature toasty despite the chilly, wet weather.

"Sugarbaby!" Mama cried, coming around the corner from the kitchen, her eyes alight with happiness at seeing me. She wore a blue, long-sleeved housedress that brought out her eyes, and her blonde hair was loose, hanging down her back. I summoned a smile. It was her birthday, and I needed to be happy. In some ways, I *was* happy. It was just there was so much I was keeping from her...

"Happy birthday, Mama." I breathed in her scent as she folded me into her arms. When we broke our hug, her eyes strayed to Luke who stood behind me. With a delighted smile, she shot a thrilled glance my way before asking, "And who is this handsome man you've brought with you?"

"Mama, this is Luke." I gestured between them. "Luke, this is my mama."

"Mrs. Arnold, it's a pleasure," Luke said, like he was royalty and had been born with social graces running through his veins. He put out his hand, shaking Mama's delicately. "And happy birthday, ma'am. I hope you don't mind me crashing your party."

"Any friend of Mitchell's is always welcome." She gave the word *friend* a special emphasis that made me roll my eyes.

"Yes. He's my boyfriend," I said, testing out the label. It felt good, and when Luke smiled to hear it, it felt even better.

"Ahh!" She clapped her hands together and bounced on her toes. It seemed that Luke was probably gift enough.

I laughed at her antics. "Surprise!"

"You hadn't said anything about a boyfriend," she scolded, still grinning from ear to ear. I smelled her famous lasagna coming from the kitchen and noticed that her skin was broken out, the way it sometimes did when she had eaten too many of the free gut bombs from her job at HeyDey Burgers. "Are you keeping secrets from me these days?"

Yes. So many secrets, actually.

I cleared my throat. "We just became boyfriends this week."

Luke scoffed, pulling me close to his side. "I don't know about that. We've been seeing each other exclusively for a couple of months now."

Mama looked between us, her smile fading. "You kept this from me for months?"

"Look what you did," I teased Luke, slapping his chest lightly and trying to keep the mood light. "Don't be silly. We've been dating, but it hasn't been serious—"

"It was serious for me," Luke said.

My heart leapt. My smile slipped into shyness. "Yeah?"

"Of course." He turned to my mother again. "We've been dating a little while, ma'am, but I'm sure Minty wanted to make sure it was going to last before bringing me home."

"Well, I'm so glad he has." Mama beckoned us to sit down on the sofa.

I hesitated, the ever-present stain catching my eye, but I guided Luke to sit down anyway, shifting so that I perched with my ass on the edge of the seat. Even so, I could *feel* the stain behind me and slightly to the left. It radiated with shame.

Determined to block it out, I smiled at Mama as she took the La-Z-Boy chair opposite us. Cruelly, the memory ripped through my mind: *My face pressed to the sofa cushion, agonizing pain—*

"Here's your gift," I said, shoving my hand into my purse and withdrawing the card. I held it out to her, hoping I could distract myself with her joy when she saw what I'd bought her. "I hope you like it."

She took it from me, but put it aside. "That can wait." Her eyes gleamed and her smile teased. "Do you know what can't wait? Getting to know Luke here."

Stars shone from her eyes as she took him in. I turned, truly seeing him for the first time all morning. I'd been so preoccupied with my own thoughts and feelings that I hadn't really paid attention to anything else.

He was handsome, like always, but he'd scrubbed up extra nicely. His matte-blue sweater brought out the glossy highlights in his eyes, and his shaggy, dark-blond hair was artfully tousled in a way I often admired. He didn't even use product. He just put his hands through it, and somehow it came out like that.

Pride flooded me. Luke was my boyfriend. Mine. And I'd brought him home to my mama, and she was impressed. This was going better so far than I'd possibly imagined when I woke up this morning.

Mama leaned forward, elbow on her knee and chin in her palm. "How did you meet?"

On the way over, we'd agreed on a story.

"We met through a friend," Luke said. Which wasn't even untrue since Barry had arranged our introduction.

Mama tilted her head. "Oh? Which friend? Daniel?"

She adored Daniel. Who didn't? "No, Barry," I said. "He's known Luke for a while, but it just occurred to him recently that

Luke and I might get along."

Mama laughed. "Better late than never."

"Exactly. Everything in its own time," Luke said calmly, taking hold of my hand and squeezing my fingers. "If Minty had shown up any earlier, I might not have been ready for him."

Biting her lower lip and leaning back, Mama tilted her head. "You're a little older, aren't you now?"

"I am, yes."

"How old exactly?"

I hadn't counted on that question, though I should have. Would it matter? She was only six years older than Luke herself. She'd had me so young—at just eighteen.

Luke didn't hesitate or seem ashamed. "Thirty-four."

"My Mitchell's only twenty-two..." She trailed off like she wasn't sure what she thought of that and wanted us to be the ones to tell her how to feel. I was accustomed to that role, so I took charge.

"Mama," I said, leaning forward to pat her knee. "It's fine. Luke's a good influence on me." I turned to him with a smile. "Aren't you?"

"I keep him out of trouble as best as I can, ma'am."

She giggled. "All right, well, so long as you're looking after him. Keeping him safe." Her eyes tightened at the edges. "You are being safe, aren't you?"

The double meaning of the word, the specter of AIDS and everything that went with it, hung over the room like a sword.

"We're doing everything in our power to stay healthy," Luke said. "It's important to both of us."

Was that true?

In fact, I had been very much *not* doing everything in my power to stay healthy up until quite recently, and even with Luke I'd wanted to do risky things, to push the envelope of what was careful.

I drank his piss, for fuck's sake.

That wasn't exactly sanitary. Or was it? Hadn't I learned in one of my Bio classes that piss *was* the most sanitary byproduct of the body?

As I pondered that, my eyes slid toward the wall of photos my mom added to and subtracted from constantly. It covered the stretch that led to the short hallway and the bedrooms. I tilted my head. She'd changed them up again. I took in each difference from the last time I'd visited.

There was one of me as a fifth grader wearing a princess crown and holding a wand.

Another new one that showed me at my most surly—fifteen and still dressing in boy drag to save my skin.

A third new one…

My stomach plummeted.

"That's good to know," Mama said softly. "I'm glad to hear it. Keeping safe is all I ask of you both." She picked up the card, tearing into it. "All right. Let's see what you've brought your moth—"

"Stop," I said, standing up and taking the card from her hand. My heart roared as I approached the wall of photos. My mouth was dry. I felt like the breakfast I'd eaten that morning was going to come up and spray all over the green shag carpet.

"Is this—Did you…" I grabbed a framed photo from the wall and shook it at her. My voice quavered. "Why? Why would you—?"

Words failed me. The shape and sound of them couldn't hold the feeling rising in me. Hot and cold, loud and quiet, soft and rough. I was tumbled by it.

"Well, I was thinking…" she said in a small voice. Her blue eyes were wide, and her pale, blonde hair shook lightly with her head. "That was a good day, Mitchell. Remember? All of us had so much fun. Just because there was so much bad, do we have to give up the good? Marlene says her therapist told her to embrace the good parts of the past so she can move past the bad."

I gritted my teeth. "Fuck Marlene." If this was her idea, Daniel's mother could go hang herself.

I couldn't even look at the picture again, though the image on it was seared into my mind's eye anyway.

Me, age seven, sitting on my father's lap. I wore cut-off blue jean shorts and a Captain Kangaroo t-shirt. My hair was so blond it was like a halo of light on my head. Mama, looking so young and beautiful, squatted next to us on the ground. Behind us, a rushing waterfall roared, and before us, on the picnic blanket, was a half-eaten chocolate cake. It'd been a trip to Abrams Falls in the Smoky Mountains for my dad's birthday. We'd used the timer on his new fancy camera to take the family shot.

The truth was…it *had* been a good day. One of the best days our little family had ever shared. And I'd loved this picture when I was younger. It was taken before I recognized what I was, and before I started to express that side of myself, before I knew my father was drunk more often than not, and before I had any idea of the way he used his fists to convince Mama to smile or shut the hell up, and before—

Before.

I sucked in a soundless breath.

Luke rose and crossed to me, taking the frame from my hand. If he looked at it, I didn't see his reaction because my eyes were glued to Mama's.

"He's always gonna be your father, Mitchell," she whispered. "He was my husband, and—"

"He *raped* me," I gritted out, pointing toward the stain. "On that couch. And that? That mark? That's my fucking blood."

Mama's eyes darted to the dark spot, and then she rose too,

coming closer to me. "No, it's not, sugarbaby. It's just a stain."

Luke hovered, as if he didn't know how to protect me—should he keep my mama from touching me? Or let her offer the hug?

I snatched the frame from him again and when Mama reached me, I thrust it into her hands. "Burn it. I never want to see his face again. I *never* want—I never—" I swallowed a sob. "Never."

"Sugarbaby, I'm sorry," she whispered. "Please understand. I didn't mean to hurt you. I just wanted to keep a token of the good times. It wasn't always bad, remember?"

I pressed the heels of my palms to my eyelids, like by blocking out the sight of her, I could block out her words too.

She touched my arm. "He wasn't always a bad man."

I shook my head. I couldn't breathe. The walls were closing in on me, and I needed to get out. At just that moment, the skies opened up, and the clatter of rain on the metal roof of the trailer covered up every other sound. I could go out into the bluster, or I could take some kind of refuge inside.

I pulled in a shuddery breath and strode to my old room, the noise from the rain wiping out any protest Mama might have made and blanketing the sound of Luke following, though I felt him behind me keeping pace.

As soon as he had cleared the threshold, I shut the door. Leaning against it, I stared past him at the bed. The sound of the rain came down harder, though it'd been so loud before that it seemed impossible. Perhaps there was hail as well? I didn't know. I didn't care.

I was barely there.

Three years ago he'd come back. My father. The monster. The man who'd stolen the innocence from my life. The man who'd made *me* a monster too. He'd cornered me in this room.

"I sucked him off," I said, closing my eyes and banging my head back against the door. Self-loathing consumed me. I was in its belly, awash in the acidic horror of my self-hate.

"I can't hear you," Luke shouted over the noise from the hail and rain. His eyes were shadowed with dark worry, but he moved closer, pressing against me so that I felt his support physically, holding me up. I sagged against him and let myself feel his heartbeat for a steadying moment.

Then I stood on my tiptoes, pressed my lips to his ear, and I said it louder, "I sucked him off."

Luke stiffened… but didn't move away.

"When he found us here, he got me alone in this room, and he told me I'd been right. He couldn't forget fucking me. He said I'd ruined him. Said it was my fault he'd come harder than he ever had before or since. Said I was a slut and a whore. That he'd made me, and I was his hole to use."

Luke growled, but said nothing.

"He told me to suck him off. He wanted to see if it was as good as fucking my ass. If I had a talented mouth…"

"Minty…" Luke sounded devastated, the way any normal person would.

"He called out to my mom, 'Nadine, your son's a whore,' because she was there, like I said."

"Baby…"

"But she stayed in the living room. She didn't come to see. She didn't check. She pretended it wasn't happening."

Luke's jaw flexed where he grinded his teeth. His fists balled up, digging into me where he had wrapped his arms around my back, dragging me closer to him, keeping me safe.

"I got down on my knees. Right here. My back to the door like it is now, so she couldn't come in, even if she tried. So she wouldn't see…"

I gagged then, the memory filling my mind.

"It's okay," he whispered. "You're here. You're safe with me."

The hail stopped, and the rain calmed. Luke held me as I sobbed, but I wasn't done. I had to tell him everything.

"I sucked him off. Gave him the best blow job I knew how to give. He loved it. Grabbed my hair, grunted like a pig the whole time. When he came, I didn't swallow. I got up on my tiptoes and spit it in his sweaty fucking face. Then I walked out, past my mom sitting on that fucking stained sofa, reading a magazine and listening to music on Walkman headphones."

"Jesus…"

"She didn't try to stop me. I got in my truck and drove back to campus. I went straight to a frat house. Got a guy to fuck me and beat me up after. He broke my arm."

"Baby…"

"So how do I love that about myself, huh? How do I love that part of me, Luke? I wasn't in danger. He didn't hold a gun to my head. He didn't even force me. I did it for the power trip."

"That's…you…" Luke couldn't explain it any more than I could. "You're the victim, baby. You should never have been in that position. He should never have asked. This is all so fucked up."

"Yeah. It is. I am."

We stood there a bit longer. I felt sweaty and sick. Luke was trembling.

"It's her birthday," I whispered. "I guess we should go have cake."

Luke drew back. "Are you out of your fucking mind?"

I laughed. It sounded as sick as my heart. "Yeah, probably. But I love her. She's the only family I have. She didn't protect me the way she should have, but she…" I started to cry again. "She loves me. I'm her only child, and she loves me so much."

Luke didn't say anything at all. He rubbed my back, kissed my wet cheeks, and when I had calmed down again, he helped me wipe the tears away.

"Okay," I said, straightening my shoulders. "We'll go out there, and she'll say she's sorry about the picture, and I'll say it's fine, and then we'll—"

"It's not fine! Why would she want a picture of her son's rapist on the wall of her home?"

I shook my head. I couldn't defend her. I understood my mom better than anyone. I even knew the logic that had led her to make that addition to the wall—I'd indulged in that kind of thinking myself sometimes because I *did* have some fond memories of my dad. That's what was so sick about it all, wasn't it? That the man who'd taught me to swim, and who'd bandaged my cuts when I wrecked my first bike, and who'd made up a funny story about a soap-eating dolphin whenever he helped me with my bath had betrayed and hurt me in such a soul-rending way.

Would I ever recover from what he'd done? Could I? And wasn't the truth of what *I'd* done with him further evidence of how permanent the injury had been? *I* was a monster. I was sick. And now I was truly sick—with HIV—as a fitting punishment for what I'd tried to forget.

But I couldn't explain any of that to Luke. Not now.

"It's off the wall now. She won't do anything like it again."

"Won't she? She made the mistake of letting him back in this house. She put the photo on the wall in the first place. Is she seeing him again? Has she forgiven him?"

Luke's questions seared my sick heart, and I turned to pull the bedroom door open, barging out to the living room where Mama had broken open the frame and was now feeding the photo to the kerosene heater.

"It's gone," she said, as it caught fire. She dropped the flaming picture into a bowl she held in her hands. "*He's* gone. That was my last picture of him. The only one I'd kept."

"He isn't gone, Mama," I bit out before thumping my chest

with my fist. "He's in here. I can't get him out. He's never *gone*."

"Sugarbaby, I'm so sorry," she said, coming toward me with open hands. All of her attention was on me, not a glance was spared for Luke, who I knew hovered close behind me.

I took her in my arms. "Mama, you haven't seen him lately, have you?" I whispered against her soft hair. "You haven't forgiven him again?"

"No," she said with a sob. "I couldn't ever take him back. Not now. Not after the last time."

"So…you know what he did to me?"

What you did for *him*, my mind hissed at me, but I didn't say it aloud.

"He told me," she said. "I didn't want to believe him. That he'd hurt you again like that, and that you'd… That you'd…" She couldn't bring herself to say it.

"I hate him, Mama. I'm scared of him coming back and—"

"He's gone, Sugarbaby. I promise. He's *never* coming back."

I let out a shaky breath. "How do you know?"

"Because he's back in prison."

I tugged away from her. "You knew that, and you didn't tell me?"

Mama's eyes were red with tears, and she chewed on her bottom lip before confessing, "I saw it in the paper. I didn't want to upset you."

I looked at the bowl in her hands and the ash of the photo. The woman who'd put that picture up, and the woman who hadn't told me some of the best news in the world—my father was back where he should have stayed all along—was my mom, the only one I had. "How'd he get sent back?"

"He got remarried, and his new wife had a teenage daughter."

"Oh God, Mama, no."

She nodded.

I squeezed my eyes closed. "Mama…"

"I know, Sugarbaby." Her gaze shifted to Luke then. Her red cheeks went even redder. "You must think I'm a terrible mother."

I didn't take my gaze from her face, so I wasn't sure what Luke's expression said, but his words weren't gentle. "I think you didn't protect him the way you should have."

Mama's eyes welled up again.

"Now, now." I tsked, brushing away her new tears with my thumbs. I tugged her into a hug. "Don't cry, Mama. It's all over, like you said, isn't it? It's all done now."

Luke made a sound that I wasn't sure how to interpret, but I suspected it meant he didn't agree that it was all done or in the past because, like I'd already said, I was still carrying it around inside me. He hadn't been able to beat or fuck it out. Neither had Kyle, for that matter.

"Here," I said, turning to where the half-opened card was flung onto the floor. I bent to retrieve it and handed it to Mama. "Open it."

She did with trembling fingers. Luke put a hand on my shoulder and squeezed lightly, letting me know he had my back. As she read what I'd written, her lips trembled again. "Are you sure?" she whispered. "It's a lot of money."

"I'm sure. They say the Biltmore House at Christmas is stunning."

I summoned a smile, the shiny one I used to keep people from seeing how damaged I was on the inside. "You'll love the decorations, Mama. And we'll pretend we live there, won't we? We'll pretend we're rich and fabulous like the Vanderbilts."

"Sugarbaby…"

I couldn't take the agony anymore. I'd cut open the wound and let poison bleed out, but now it was time to stitch it closed again. "Let's have cake!" I said as brightly as I could muster. "And then we'll eat that lasagna you've got in the oven. I swear I could smell it as soon as we pulled up outside."

She sniffled and wiped her eyes, but she agreed. "Yes, let's have the cake. I made your favorite. White frosting on chocolate."

"But it's *your* birthday, Mama."

"And you're my favorite boy," she said tremulously. "I like to make you happy. I only *ever* want you to be happy."

I nodded. "I know you do."

Luke silently followed us into the kitchen, and when we sat at the table with the white-frosted cake between us and a few crooked candles flaming up for Mama to blow out, I caught his eye.

He looked shell-shocked, and when he gazed at me, I could see him evaluating me in a new light.

My stomach roiled, but I kept the happy smile slapped onto my face as we sang the birthday song, cut the cake, and proceeded with Mama's birthday dinner like nothing had happened. Like I hadn't just confessed to my boyfriend that I'd willingly sucked off my own father and then spit the cum in his face. Like I hadn't just proved how degenerate and unlovable I was. Like I wasn't just trash.

The rain came down in sheets again.

But the expression on Luke's face wasn't washed away.

Neither was my shame.

Chapter Twenty-Five

Luke

"YOU HATE ME now, don't you?" Minty whispered, his hands tight on the steering wheel.

The rain still came down in buckets, but the windshield wipers were doing a valiant job at slapping it off so that he could see to drive.

"Hate you?" I was deeply confused. It'd been a long, strange afternoon. The way Minty and his mother had simply moved on from the horrible "mistake" of her having hung up a family photo that'd included *his rapist*, the way they'd laughed and faked happy and pretended nothing had happened at all blew my mind. I was mystified by him and his mother both.

But hate? Where did that come into things?

Minty's shoulders were tight. "Because of what I did. You know the whole truth now." He inhaled sharply. "All of it. The absolute worst of who I am." His lip snarled up in disgust. "And you hate me now, don't you?"

I blinked rapidly, comprehending his meaning. I motioned toward the side of the interstate. "Put on your hazard lights. Pull over."

"What?"

"Do it."

Minty seemed as if he might argue for a moment, but then he

did as I commanded.

When the truck was fully stopped, the sound of the rain pounding on the roof forced me to talk louder than I wanted to. The topic was delicate, and shouting made me feel like I was angry, though I wasn't. I was heartbroken and horribly sickened by the awful crap that Minty had faced in his life—it made my own difficulties with my father pale in comparison—but I wasn't angry or full of disgust. All I knew right now was that I had to get that through to him. Make him understand that I loved him no matter what.

But the rain made that fucking hard. "I don't hate you," I yelled.

He scoffed, clearly disbelieving.

"Minty, I don't! How could I hate you? I love you."

"This isn't a romantic moment!" he protested, eyes wet with tears. "You can't say that right now."

"Fuck that," I shouted. "I'm telling you that I love you. Period. Whether you think it's romantic or not. You need to understand how I feel. Nothing you've ever said, or done, or thought, or experienced is going to change that. Nothing."

Minty whirled on me, his hands raised in fists. "I sucked my fucking father off!"

"He raped you! You're a victim! You—"

"I wanted to! For the power trip! To make him feel—to see him—ugh!" He ripped his hands through his hair, barrettes coming loose. "You don't understand! I'm a bad person. I deserve every bad thing that's ever happened to me. Even HIV, and when the time comes? When it's full-blown AIDS? I should suffer. I should go out in misery."

His shoulders wracked with his sobs, but when I reached out, he pulled away from me. I dropped my hands to my lap and tried to reason with him.

"No." I shook my head. "You don't deserve anything bad. I'm

not going to accept that, and one day, if it's the last thing I do, I'll make sure you reject that idea too."

"Stop! How can you stand to look at me? Knowing what I did?" Minty wiped at his face with his palms as the tears flowed from his eyes. "What about it don't you understand? I made it *good*, Luke! I did that thing with my tongue that you *love*. I played with his balls. I gave him the best blow job he'd *ever* had. On *purpose*. Not because I was threatened, not because I couldn't have taken him down—" He screamed in rage. "I know Aikido! I could have…I should have…Anyone else would have…"

"Baby, it doesn't matter! It doesn't matter at all! He was a bad man, and he'd hurt you, and you wanted to hurt him back, to control him, to have power over him, to ruin his life, and you did. He's in prison again."

"I *didn't*. He ruined some other kid's life first. Maybe I just made things worse for her. Maybe I made it so good that he wanted to try to find someone else to give him that feeling again."

"Minty, listen to me—"

"I don't want to listen to you."

"Fuck that! You will!"

"I won't." He opened the truck's door, and the rain doused him immediately. He stomped out into the headlights, the blinking of the hazards lighting him up in pulses as he strode into a dark, empty highway stretching out ahead.

I threw open the passenger door and chased him down. When I reached him, he crouched into a fighting stance. "What are you doing?"

"I'm going to kick your ass."

"Go for it," I yelled, the rainwater filling my mouth. I spread my arms wide. "Hit me. Kick me. I'm not going to stop you."

Minty jabbed a few times, trying to make me flinch, but then he dropped his fists and fell against me, sobs wracking him again.

The cold rain soaked us as I held him tight, rocking him back and forth, whispering in his ear, "You're a good person. I love you. Nothing you tell me is going to make me stop loving you."

"I hate myself."

"I love you."

"I hate myself so much."

"I *love* you." It became a sick call and response. He said he hated himself, and I reassured him of my love.

Eventually, he let me walk him back to the truck. I got in the driver's side after helping him into the passenger's seat.

The drive back to my house was mostly silent. Minty blew his nose into some fast food restaurant napkins he had stashed in his glove box, but said nothing more.

I didn't know what to say either. I was in so far over my head with him, but there was nothing to do now but learn how to tandem swim because I had to keep Minty from going under.

I just didn't know how.

The answer came to me when we arrived back at the house. After we took off our shoes and jackets, Minty opened the basement door. At first, I almost protested. I was wet and exhausted. He was soaked through and drained. But when he looked at me with desperation in his eyes, I knew that telling him no right then would be the wrong thing to do.

"Take your clothes off," I said. "Fold them. Kneel for me in the basement."

Minty nodded and started down the stairs.

I sat on the staircase leading up to my room and breathed in and out slowly. I had to get this right. I couldn't fuck this up.

This was the most important thing I'd ever done in my life, and I was utterly unprepared for it.

Chapter Twenty-Six

Minty

"**Y**OUR SAFE WORD is poodle," Luke said, as he slid his fingers into my hair and tightened them into a fist. "If your mouth is occupied, snap your fingers as a safe word."

"Yes, Sir," I whispered. It was the first thing I'd said since Luke put me back in the cab of my truck, soaked through from the rain.

I didn't know what he had in mind, but I'd been thinking about what I needed for the whole drive home. I had to get out of my skin, out of my mind, and I needed Luke to help me do that. The lure of Kyle, with his relentless brutality, called to me. But I knew if I left, if I went to Kyle, I'd egg him on to the point that he might actually kill me.

If it was even a little bit true that Luke still loved me, even though I was a disgusting monster, then I wanted to live. I wanted to find out what we could have together. I just needed to get out of my head right now. Some X would help. Some pot, alcohol, or GHB would take the edge of emotion off too. But, barring those aids, pain was the only thing that could satisfy my need to escape my self-loathing.

In fact, pain might be the best of all options. If I were screaming under Luke's whips, I'd be free *and* getting just what I deserved.

"Come here," Luke said, guiding me up from my knees with his hand in my hair.

His voice was calm. There was no arousal in it, no desire or heat. I didn't mind. I wasn't hard either. He pulled me in to his embrace, and I held myself tightly. His sweater brushed the front of my naked chest. The fly of his jeans rubbed roughly against my stomach and flaccid dick.

I went on my tiptoes to hook my chin on his shoulder. We breathed together. He bent to kiss the side of my neck, and then pushed me away. "Get on the horse."

That's what Luke called the wood and leather contraption that consisted of a central piece of wood that held my upper body, an open-hole face cushion like I'd seen on massage tables on TV, and four additional leather supports that held my elbows and knees. Once on the "horse," I was essentially on all-fours mid-air, with my ass on display in the perfect position for spanking or fucking. There were straps and buckles that held me in place around the middle and secured my arms and legs.

I'd "ridden" it only once before, last month after a night of teasing. He'd used a crop on me then, an intense but fun experience.

I didn't think there was any power on earth that could turn this night *fun*, but that wasn't what I needed anyway. What I needed was a way to scoop the memories from my mind, to rend the horrible, hollow, disgusting feeling from my body, to scrape me clean inside and out.

But there was no way to do that either.

The closest thing would be a scourge of mind-numbing pain.

"That's a good boy," Luke murmured as he finished buckling me onto the horse so I couldn't move. I wanted to protest his praise, but I kept my mouth closed. I was here to suffer, wasn't I? So, I'd suffer his praise too. I'd let his words of love break me apart.

My face pressed into the leather donut of the head support as I stared at the smooth, gray concrete beneath me. My mouth was clamped shut against the shame that threatened to come out in the form of vomit.

Luke gripped and released my ass cheeks, felt along my back and thighs, and then his touch was gone. The sound of his footsteps led off to where the wall of implements would provide him with a tool to hurt me.

As he lingered making a choice, I broke into a cold sweat. Dread and anticipation pooled in my gut. I tested the restraints and they held firm.

I couldn't move. I couldn't escape. I was trapped—no way to fight back, no way to run. This was what I'd wanted, what I'd needed, but now that I was stuck here, I wondered if the chaos of being beaten up by Kyle wasn't less scary. If only because I could push back, resist from time to time, suck his cock despite how much he hated it, make him come like a volcano, take control. Become a god.

Here on Luke's horse, I was Mitchell. Helpless. Out of control. Powerless. Restrained. About to take whatever Luke dished out, whether I liked it or not. Here on Luke's horse, I was the me I'd been that first time on the couch. When I'd cried and begged Daddy to stop. I was the me who'd been forced.

Until I'd taken charge.

But how could I take charge here when the man who was about to cause me intense pain couldn't be shamed or twisted around about it? When I had to choose to either find a way to enjoy it—

Did you just come, you fucking nasty slut?" Daddy bit out as I shot all over the couch.

Or I had to sink into brutal suffering and accept it.

Because there was no chink in Luke's armor for me to manipulate. He was a Dom. A sadist. He *liked* when I was in pain. That was fucked up in its own way, wasn't it? What kind of asshole got off on hurting other people? What was *his* damage anyway? And why hadn't I ever thought to ask that question before now? If I had, I could have used that information to—

Luke gripped my left ass cheek and squeezed. "Remember, Mitchell. Your safe word is poodle."

I nodded stiffly. I knew my safe word by now. Why did he insist on reviewing it every time? Christ. I wanted to curse him out for the unnecessary reminder, be the brattiest and angriest sub he'd ever faced, but my throat was too tight to speak.

"You'll call me Sir tonight." Luke's voice lowered, scraping over me with violent control. "Say it."

"Yes, Sir," I said, forcing it past the tightness in my throat. The word felt like fire in my mouth.

"Again."

"Yes, Sir." I spit on the floor, trying to get rid of the sense memory of how it'd felt to hold my father's cum on my tongue before I stood and spit it into his sweaty fucking face.

"Say it again."

"Yes, Sir."

"I'm going to take you out of your head now."

"Please."

The whooshing sound was the first warning, but even that didn't prepare me enough. A stinging spike of anguish was followed by a heavy pain, making me tense hard against the restraints. Stuck in place, I flexed my fingers and toes, trying to hold back the shocked shout. It burst free anyway. "Fuck!"

"Rubber flogger," Luke said simply. "Packs a wallop and a helluva sting."

A strike landed on my ass again with a weighty thud. The tails stung like a son-of-a-bitch. I screeched.

"That's right," Luke encouraged. "Gonna take you so far out of your pretty head, baby. Just hold tight."

Struggling hard against the restraints, panic rose in me. *Poodle,*

poodle, my mind screamed as the sound of the flogger flying through the air preceded another sunburst of vicious pain and a deep blow of heat. "Fuck!"

Without another word, Luke set up a steady rhythm. The swishing sound of the tails flying and the scent of rubber filled the space with each swing. The toy was too intense. I broke down quickly, screaming, crying, shouting, and sobbing hysterically as I struggled against the restraints.

Luke reminded me regularly, "You have your safe word."

I shook my head, and the horrible pain started again. It seemed to last forever. He didn't make me count. I tried several times to count in my head after a break, but couldn't get past three before I lost all sense of space and time.

One moment I was resisting, struggling hard, like my life depended on it, and the next I'd submitted. Given up. Collapsed on the horse, crying hysterically as Luke continued to slowly, steadily pound my ass with the flogger. My head ached from pressure of the snot in my nose and the tears falling from my eyes. The floor beneath me was wet with the fluids.

My drop into subspace came hard and suddenly. A fall, a swoop, and then I was flying through it. Endorphins breaking over my brain cells like X, lifting me higher, blissing me out. The pain was pleasure was pain was ecstasy was agony was heaven. I was in it, one with it, *riding* it. Chill bumps exploded over my skin, and I whimpered as Luke let the flogger fall again.

I lost touch with the world.

His hands on my sore ass told me it was over before his words did. "You did such a good job, Mitchell. You took that beating so well." Luke massaged my trembling, hot, and angry ass cheeks. "That's what's amazing about you, Mitchell. You're that strong."

"Sir...Luke..." I sputtered through the terms of address, my mind reeling, my ass on fire, and my heart full of an emotion I couldn't name. It was huge, vast, and threatened to kill me with its power.

He hummed a sound of acknowledgment, waited a moment to see if I was going to use my safe word, and then went on, "I'm going to unbuckle you now, and I want you to stand up. Move slowly. Your head's still somewhere else."

He wasn't kidding. I nearly fell off the horse, my muscles somehow simultaneously stiff and loose like Jell-O, as my mind raced through a sticky cloud of feeling. Was it all physical feeling? Was it also emotion? Was it mainly emotion? I couldn't tell. I was contained in it, muffled by it, lost and confused.

My head hurt. My snotty nose was gross. My knees shook.

Luke held me close and wiped away my tears and mucus. He kissed my forehead and whispered praise as he reached down to stroke my cock. It was hard. How? I hadn't even noticed it during the entire flogging.

"You need to come," Luke murmured. "Do you want to?"

From a great distance, I nodded.

"All right. You're going to get to come, but first we're gonna do something different."

I nodded again.

"There's only one rule."

I whimpered and huddled against him. The sting from my ass and haunches was still immense, and I shivered and groaned as it pulsed through me like a warning. It was so good, and so bad, but not enough. Because inside me, I was still the boy who'd come on his father's cock, the boy who'd sucked his father off, the boy who'd gotten HIV and let a bully frat boy break his arm, and—

"Whenever you feel ashamed, you have to say 'I love you, Mitchell.'" Luke kissed my hair. "'I love you, Mitchell.' You'll say that every time."

"All right," I croaked. My throat was raw from my crying and screaming.

"Do you feel ashamed now?"

I nodded.

"Say it."

"I love you, Mitchell." My voice was small, and I felt silly saying it, but somewhere, deep down, it felt like a smaller version of me took hold of my hand and clung to it. "I love you, Mitchell."

"Good boy. You're doing a great job." Luke turned me around, bent me over the horse, and checked my ass. "There's going to be significant bruising. No skin breakage. The pain will linger, though."

My skin felt like it was on fire, and every shift made it ache deeper in the muscle tissue.

He rubbed his hand over my haunches. "Who beat your ass?"

"You did, Sir."

"Every time you feel ashamed, remember how you surrendered, how you gave up and let yourself fly. Remember how you took suffering and changed it to something amazing. You're powerful. You're strong."

I moaned.

Luke landed a smack on the flank of my hip. It was like a pain bomb going off in my mind. I shouted and clenched the edge of the horse, dizzy and covered in fresh sweat.

Luke's hand went around my throat and he hauled me up, cutting off the ease of my breath. "Say it."

"I love you, Mitchell." I pushed the words through on a tiny bit of air. My cock was hard still, jutting out from me with a pearl of pre-cum on the tip. I could feel the cool air of the basement on my groin, and the rough pain of Luke's jeans against my abraded ass.

"Good." Luke released me. "This is going to get gross, Mitchell. This is going to be painful, but not physically. In your head." He touched my head. "In your heart." He touched my back. "Are you ready?"

I gritted my teeth together and nodded, bracing myself.

"Remember you have a safe word."

It was all I could do not to roll my eyes. If he reminded me one more time… Images of kicking him across the room, of pounding him with my fists, of making him see what I could do, how powerful I was, how much I held back…

Luke thrust into me, long, hard, and rough. I screeched as his hips slapped my sore ass cheeks, my fingers clenching and releasing the edge of the horse.

"Say it," Luke commanded, bottoming out in me.

"I love you, Mitchell," I croaked out. My asshole spasmed around his dick.

Luke set up a steady pace, holding my hips as he pounded into me, hard and relentless. "Again."

I shook sweat out of my eyes, but said, "I love you, Mitchell."

"Keep on. Again. Don't stop."

"I love you, Mitchell. I love you. I love you, Mitchell." My legs shook as he raked over my prostate, and the rim of my asshole burned without lube or spit to make it easier.

He leaned down and whispered in my ear, "You came for your own father, Mitchell. A huge orgasm. It felt so good. Remember?"

"Yes," I sobbed.

"You can't ever erase that. You made him come too. There will always be a part of you that remembers how hard he spunked in your ass. How good that felt."

I choked as vomit rose again. Luke's relentless fucking made my legs quake and then, impossibly, I was right on the edge of coming. "Stop."

"Say it."

"No."

"Minty," Luke whispered. "Please say it."

"I love you, Mitchell."

"Why? Why do you love Mitchell? Tell me."

"I love him because…" My mind searched for words in the haze of adrenaline, pain, and endorphins. I found some and blurted them out. "Because he tried so hard. Because he won. He fucking won."

"He showed his father who was boss, didn't he?"

"Yes. I love myself. I love Mitchell."

Luke fucked me harder. His breath coming in pants as he went on, "When you're getting fucked by Kyle, you love Mitchell."

"I love him."

"You're so strong."

"That was the strongest part of me."

"No," Luke whispered, slowing down his pounding fuck. "The strongest version of you will be the one we meet when taking praise isn't a fight. When that shame isn't living in your heart anymore."

"Get it out. I want it out." I clawed at my own chest. "I hate it. I want it gone."

"Say it, baby."

"I love you, Mitchell." I grunted out, trying to make the horrible hardness of my heart soften. "I love you."

"You're going to come now. Not for me. Not for him. You're going to come now for yourself."

"For me," I murmured. I felt dizzy. The day and night were catching up to me. The misery from that agonizing flogger mixed with the ache in my chest and throat, and I closed my eyes, focusing on the pleasure of Luke's cock moving in me. I wriggled my other hand down to stroke my dick.

I hiccupped sobs. I wanted to be clean of this. I wanted to be the old Minty. The one who'd existed before the rape, or even the one who'd existed before the HIV diagnosis…

The boy who was in love with love. Who'd believed in the future. Who'd managed to forget that he'd sucked his father off…

How had I forgotten for days and months at a time?

How?

I'm disgusting, I'm—

"I love you, Mitchell!" I shouted. My balls ached and my asshole felt tender. "I love you, Mitchell!"

"Yes," Luke groaned. "Shout it."

"I love you! I love you!" As I strove for orgasm, my heart shattered, and I wailed like a baby, and still Luke didn't give up.

"Love yourself. You're so good. You're so fucking good, baby." He slid his arm around my throat, dragging me up against his body, bending my back like a bow. The angle intensified the sensation on my prostate. My cock leaked pre-cum as I stroked it faster.

Shame mixed with the ecstasy as I grabbed Luke's arm around my neck, pressed against it to cut off my own air, and shot off hard. My eyes rolled back, I garbled incoherently, and I shuddered like I was having a seizure.

The release was gorgeous. All my shame blotted out by blinding pleasure.

We collapsed back to the horse, both of us heaving and sweating. Luke eventually pulled out, leaving cum dripping down my legs. I whimpered as he hauled me up, guided me over to the bed, and used a cloth from the bathroom to wash me off.

I was lost in a quiet place. Even as he washed away the cum and sweat, even as he hummed the whole time about how amazing I was, I was gone from the room.

Tucking me up in bed, after forcing me to drink a glass of water, Luke climbed in with me. I wished we were upstairs in his bedroom, but the bed down here would have to do. I didn't have the energy to roll over to my other side, much less walk up the stairs.

My ass was tender, but Luke applied cream. I held myself gingerly on one hip, my arm curled beneath the pillow and my head. Luke was on his side too, facing me, his gaze taking in everything.

"You doing okay?"

I nodded.

"Did I take it too far?"

I snorted a laugh.

"I'm okay," I told him.

"Did it help?" His brows twitched down, a shadow in his irises.

"I think so." It was hard to be sure. I'd come my brains out, and I'd been beaten into an endorphin release the intensity of which wasn't going to wear off for days. "I feel steadier now."

"I'm glad.

I took his hand and brought it to my lips, kissing the fingers.

"I love you," Luke said.

"I love you too."

We spooned together, breathing slowly, letting exhaustion pull us down. Luke was asleep before I was. I rolled over in his arms and gazed at the way his face looked so much younger. Every worry and wrinkle was gone.

I stayed on my side, just breathing his breath and watching his eyes move back and forth beneath his soft lids.

He'd pulled out the stops for me tonight. He'd gone darker and deeper than he'd probably ever wanted to go, and it hadn't been for him. It was for me. He might be a sadist, but he wasn't into this kind of psychological shit-show, I knew that.

I also believed that he loved me. Who except for a man in love would take this horrible journey with me? Who else would make *me* take it for my own sake?

He loved me despite how fucked up I was. And I loved him.

I loved him so much that I didn't want to admit what I'd come to realize as I lifted out of subspace tonight. There was no way to get this horror out of me. No way at all. Just like HIV, the rape was a part of me forever, lingering in my cells. I'd known it would be from the moment my father had shoved his dick into me.

The only way to truly escape the shame was to cut it out. And the only way to cut it out was to die. And I wasn't ready to die yet. Not just yet.

Part IV

December 1991

Chapter Twenty-Seven

Luke

"WE HAVEN'T SEEN you since before Thanksgiving," Mom said, patting the hunks of ground beef into the meatloaf pan. It wasn't exactly a guilt-trip, more like concern. I knew she'd heard about how I'd canceled on seeing Betsy last weekend too. The first time I'd ever done such a thing.

Bets hadn't seemed to mind, though. She'd been invited to go to camping with Rodney's family for the weekend after Thanksgiving, and with me not coming, she was free to go. She'd sounded plenty excited about it.

"Yeah. Sorry about that. Work, you know. Always asking more of us than we want to give."

She cast me a curious glance but said nothing more as she continued to stuff meat into the pan.

I leaned back in the kitchen chair and struck a casual pose, hoping that was the end of it. How was I supposed to explain that I'd been sticking close to Minty, sharing intense scenes and intimate alone time rather than visiting with my family? And I especially couldn't tell her that I'd chosen to go to Asheville and visit the decked-to-the-heavens-and-back Biltmore Estate with Minty and his mother for Thanksgiving itself rather than come home to Johnson City for the holiday.

After what had happened during our visit to Nadine's trailer, I wasn't ready to let him spend a full day alone with the woman, much less an overnight trip. Minty had somehow scrounged together enough money to pay for not only tickets to the enormous Biltmore House itself, but for a stay in a hotel room with two queen beds, room service, and an indoor pool. I had no idea how he'd done it. More performances of *Cream My Face* maybe?

When I'd told Minty I was coming along to Biltmore, he hadn't argued, which told me he didn't feel safe with his mother yet either. But no one would have ever guessed by his demeanor when we'd arrived to pick her up for the trip. He was like a sunbeam personified, all happy eyes and flashing teeth. If I didn't know the spiraling-out mess he'd been ever since he saw that picture on Nadine's wall, I'd have believed the act. But I knew better. Like his fashion, the silly, carefree, outrageous flake persona was a layer of armor over his soft, vulnerable core.

For her part, Nadine had been just like him. Cheerful, sweet, and full of gratitude for the gift of the trip, acting like nothing had ever happened. Again, if I didn't know for certain she still had that stained sofa in her trailer, or if I had somehow managed to forget that she'd framed a photo of her son's rapist, I'd think she was a joy. As it was, I saw her as a child—broken, fragile, and cruel without meaning to be.

The Biltmore House had been, as expected, a craze of pre-Christmas spirit, and the meal we ate at the Stable Restaurant was expensive, but delicious. I'd paid for it on my credit card, despite Minty's protests, because I'd had no idea how he planned to cover the bill. Maybe he'd thought he could swing into the kitchen and convince the chef to let him pay with his ass? Maybe he'd planned to dine-and-dash? I didn't know. But there was no way I was letting him spend more on his mother. If I paid, at least I could tell myself it was a gift from me to *him*. She was just along for the ride.

"Where's your mind, baby?" my mom asked in the here and

now. "You're somewhere else today."

I sighed, scrubbing a hand through my hair. "Oh, just thinking about a friend who's having some problems."

She washed her hands, put the meatloaf into the oven, set the timer, and sat down next to me at the table. She touched my cheek. "You can tell me about him, you know. In fact, I wish you would."

I tensed, but she grabbed hold of my chin, so I couldn't pull away. I met her gaze, heart in my throat.

"Please, Luke. Tell me about your boyfriend." She dropped her hand. "It's okay."

"Oh." I felt stupid when I realized. Betsy must have told her. I didn't know why I hadn't considered that she might. I'd never explicitly told her not to, and she and mom were close. Maybe some part of me had wanted Betsy to be the one to tell her.

Mom smiled, tilting her head slightly. "I'd like to hear about him from you. Betsy sings his praises. She says he looks like a fairy prince."

I swallowed against a lump in my throat, caught out like a kid. "He does." My voice sounded gritty.

Her smile crinkled the corners of her eyes. "What's his name?"

I was sure she already knew. Betsy must have told her that too, but it was right that she should hear it from me. "Minty Arnold." I paused. "Well, Mitchell, really. But he prefers to go by Minty. It suits him."

"How long have you been seeing him?"

I did the math. "Around three months now."

She took a quivery little breath. "Did you think I'd be upset?"

My heart sank. How could I explain? There was so much about Minty that was…so much. He wasn't a guy I'd met in a usual way, and he wasn't a usual man. "No, Mama." I sighed. "He's…"

"He's what?"

"He wears makeup, and he dresses in…*fashion*. He's really…"

"Gay?"

I snorted. "Flamboyant. I'd say we're equally gay, what with both of us wanting to have sex with men."

She ignored my crass poking at her. "You thought I'd judge him, or that I wouldn't like him because he's like that? My hairdresser is fey, and I like him just fine."

"It's not that I didn't think you'd like him, but I know you struggled in the past with *me* being gay. And I'm not… like that."

"I know it's asking a lot, but I'd like you to forgive me for the past."

"I have. But he's way more obvious about it all than I am, and I don't want to ask him to change. I like him the way he is. If he came over here dressed in boy-drag—"

"Boy-drag?"

"What he calls it when he has to dress to meet society's expectations. It's not that he only dresses in femme clothes. He just usually adds at least a touch of something pretty."

"Is he transsexual?"

"No. I think he's somewhere in the middle most of the time. He likes to be a pretty boy. But if he came over here dressed in jeans and a button-up shirt…" I shook my head. "That'd be wrong for him."

"I understand." She squeezed my fingers again. "It'd be like asking him to lie about himself. I wouldn't even be meeting Minty then, would I? I'd be meeting a figment."

I let out a slow breath. "Yeah."

She got it. I had underestimated her. Why? Sure, she'd reacted badly to me coming out at first, but to be fair she'd never even known gay people existed until she was in her twenties. She'd grown up so sheltered in her tiny town in Arkansas. And when she did find out about gay people, no one had told her that it wasn't a terrible thing to be.

Or at least it hadn't been. Until AIDS.

I shut that thought down. I wasn't telling her about my diagnosis. Not now, hopefully not ever.

"I really want to meet this young man. I don't care how he's dressed or how he acts."

I ducked my head. "All right."

"Tell me something about him."

"He's amazing."

She smiled. "He must be to have captured your heart. I know you dated that other man for a long time—Benji, right? You mentioned him a time or two, but it never seemed serious."

"It wasn't. Not like this anyway." I cleared my throat. "I'm in love."

Mom's lips trembled, but she said nothing, just nodded her head.

"So, you'd really like to meet him?"

"Yes. Very much."

"I don't think Dad will be able to handle it. He'll be an asshole, and Minty doesn't deserve to be treated that way. I won't stand for it either, not when he's with me."

I only ever wanted Minty to feel safe in my presence. Unless he was feeling debased and abused in a completely consensual context like we shared in my dungeon.

"I understand, of course you'd want to protect him."

I nodded.

"But you don't have to protect him from *me*. I'll love him. I promise you that."

"You've never even met him. How can you promise love?"

"Because *you* love him, Luke. What else could I feel for a young man who makes my boy's heart melt?"

I gave her a hug, which was awkward and uncomfortable with both of us seated in the wooden kitchen chairs, but when she pulled back, she whispered, "Aw, now," and wiped her fingers over my cheeks. I hadn't realized a few tears had spilled.

"My sweetheart. I'm sorry I made you think you had to keep him from me."

I had, hadn't I? I'd believed she wouldn't be able to accept Minty the way he was. Of course, she hadn't seen him yet. Hadn't witnessed his swish-swish walk, or his bubble-gum pink, lip-glossed smile, or his tutu skirt. But, deep down, I knew I'd misjudged her.

She sat back and sighed, glancing toward the timer on the oven. "Your father is another story. You're right. He won't be kind."

"He's not even kind to me."

"No." She winced, tucked a piece of graying hair behind her ear. "Nor to me."

She sighed. "When I married him, I promised for better or worse…"

I reached out for her hand again, but she didn't give it to me. Instead, she stared up at the ceiling and spoke to it instead of me. "I know this is the 'worse' I promised him, but I don't think I ever would have made that vow had I known exactly what I was going to face. He was always difficult. Demanding. Critical. But there was so much sweetness to offset all that. Now…"

"Mama…"

With a gust of breath, like she'd been holding back for a long time and couldn't contain it anymore, she said, "I want to put him in a home. I did the math: if Betsy moved back in with me, we could use the funds we pay to Riverwoods to support your father in a residential care facility instead."

"Betsy won't agree to that. She loves living away from home. And there's Rodney now."

Mom nodded. "I know, but we can't afford both."

She brought her gaze to mine. The pain I saw in her eyes made my chest ache. "Selfish as this sounds, I can't take it anymore. I can't continue to live with him. He's not the man I married, and I know that's not his fault. But does that mean *I* have to live with the abuse he hurls at me? The horrible things he says about my friends, my mother, my daughter, my son?"

I winced. "No. You shouldn't have to put up with that, Mama."

"Even if I *should*, I can't anymore. I don't have the will or the love left in me. If he was still even a little kind? But as it is, I feel guilty about putting the care of him onto the poor nurses at the home. Who knows what he'll say to them? How he'll treat them? But I'm breaking inside, Luke. I can't do it anymore." She rose and went to a built-in desk on the wall by the kitchen door. "I've already applied at this place."

I took the pamphlets from her hands when she returned to sit at the table. The first one had Shield's Senior Care stamped over the first page. I flipped it open to see photos of smiling nurses bending over elderly men and women, fixing their covers or taking their temperature. I knew the reality would be less rosy than that. "When will you tell Betsy?"

"When I go to pick her up for the Christmas holidays. I'll have to let her know that she won't be going back. We'll have to pack her things too."

My gut churned. Betsy usually spent two weeks with us at Christmastime, and she always loved returning to Riverwoods. "That'll break her heart."

"I know." Mom chewed on her bottom lip. "He's getting worse, though."

"Worse, as in violent?"

She nodded, pushing her right sleeve up to show a handprint bruise on her forearm. "This was because I was slow to bring him ketchup for his steak. I was afraid he was going to punch me. But he—"

"You talkin' 'bout me again?" Dad's ruined voice boomed into the room. "Lies. Tells all her bitch friends I hurt her. Fucking cunt."

He crept in on his walker, the right side of his face drooping like usual. The damage to his facial muscles added a slur to his words that made him sound drunk even though he wasn't. Still, he acted ugly. The stroke had stripped away all shame or fear, leaving just prejudice and spitefulness behind.

"Richard, why don't you eat in front of the TV tonight? The Bulls are playing."

"Fuck the Bulls. Where's the damn dinner?"

"Baking."

He glared at her, turned to me and grimaced. "You're here? Fuckin' queer. Should be dead by now. AIDS isn't working hard enough."

I gritted my jaw, trying to keep back the words that threatened to spill out.

Mom rose with her cheeks flushed and her fists clenched by her side. "Get the hell out of this kitchen right now."

"What are you going to do about it?" Dad sneered. "You gonna try to move me? I'd like to see you try."

Mom kicked her chair back hard enough it tipped over before grabbing hold of his walker in a way that made me wonder if she was going to rip it out of his hands and let him drop to the floor. Instead, she leaned into his face. "I'm getting rid of you. God forgive me, but I won't live with you another week."

Dad swung his head forward, head-butting her hard. Mom cried out, falling to the kitchen floor, and I leapt up, rushing to her.

"What the fuck!" I shouted at Dad. "Who the hell do you think you are?"

Dad glared at me, and then turned to creep out of the room on his walker, cursing and muttering under his breath.

"Mom," I gasped, tugging her up. "Are you okay?"

She rubbed at her forehead where I could see a good-sized goose-egg growing. Dad probably had one too, but I didn't give a shit if he did. Let him have another stroke. Maybe this one would end his and our misery.

Mom murmured, "No, I'm really not."

"Wait there. I'll call 911—"

"No, my head is fine. It's everything else. You see what's happening here." She burst into tears. "I can't handle him alone for one more day."

I stared into her wet eyes and knew it was the truth. She was going through more than she could handle, and this was her way of admitting that she was in a very desperate and fragile place. "Don't worry, Mama. I won't leave you until I've dealt with this."

She collapsed in my arms, crying. "I don't know what to do anymore."

"I know, I know. So let me do it for you."

I didn't know what the hell to do either, but I knew one thing for sure. I wasn't leaving my mother alone with that man wearing my father's face ever again. I'd stay with her until we'd secured him a place at the senior care facility. No matter how long that might take.

But what about Minty?

He couldn't come here. He wouldn't be safe.

Not until my dad was gone.

I'd have to trust him to take care of himself. My stomach turned over with anxiety, and I held my mom closer, stroking her hair.

Minty

"YOU CAN STAY at my place as long as you want," Luke had said almost a week ago.

Now I stood alone in his basement, arms wrapped around my

middle, my gaze shifting from contraption to instrument, to implement, to cage, to chair, to bed. I reviewed that first short and strained conversation again in my head. It'd started out well enough:

"Hey, baby, I'm glad you answered."

"I almost didn't, but I thought it might be you. Is everything okay? You're late."

"Actually, there's a problem. I won't be home for a while, a week or more. I need to stay here in Johnson City with my mom."

"Why?"

"It's a problem with my dad."

"Is he okay?"

"No, and he hasn't been in a long time. But don't worry. I can handle it."

I should have called him out on that. I should have demanded why he got to take care of things on his own, while I had to strip naked, gag on his cock, and scream out how much I loved myself while he fucked and humiliated me. But in my confusion, I'd found myself saying—

"Okay. Can I come up to help?"

"No." He'd said it too quickly, as if he was afraid of me getting involved.

"Why not?"

"Believe me, baby, there's nothing you can do. What I'd like is for you to be strong for me, okay? Go to your classes, take care of yourself. Do more Kickboxing or Jujitsu—"

"Aikido."

"Yeah, and just... Please, Minty. Just be good, baby. All right?"

Be good.

What had he meant by that? I knew, of course. Don't go get myself fucked and beaten by Kyle. That's what he'd meant. The fact that he was still afraid of me doing that, even after everything we'd shared was...

Well, it should be insulting, but it only showed that I still hadn't proven myself to him.

We'd talked most nights since that phone call, but it was always hurried and perfunctory, the long-distance charge forcing us to keep it short.

I walked over to the Saint Andrew's cross, touched the wood, remembered what it'd felt like to be tied to it while he wielded a wicked flogger and whip.

Christ, I could use that right now. I *needed* it. My mind kept going back to earlier in the day when I was in my dorm and pressed play on—

But no. I wouldn't think about that.

During our last call, just the night before, I was curled up on my favorite side of his sofa, cuddling with the soft blanket he often used for aftercare. As usual, he didn't have time to talk.

"Baby, I'm sorry, but things are intense here tonight. It's not a good time for a conversation. So, let me repeat, as your Dom, these are your orders—eat well, go to class, take care of yourself. Don't let me down. I'll call tomorrow."

My mind whirled with the brevity of it all. "Yes, Sir."

"Thank you. I love you."

The dial tone ran down the line when he hung up.

Smoothing my hands over the cross, I huffed. I'd responded to the dominance in his voice like a weak, spineless submissive. I hadn't been bratty at all. Which should have *told* him something, and on another day, maybe it would have.

If I'd been in a better place, I wouldn't have felt hurt that he had a life that wasn't all about coddling and caring for me. If I'd been in a worse place, maybe I would have been awful and insisted, "What about me? What about my needs?"

Because I had needs.

Big ones. Especially right now.

The basement was quiet. I could hear my own breath and the whoosh of my pulse in my ears. I stepped over to the bed and sat down, my gaze settling on the cage where it rested on the floor.

I chewed my lower lip.

On Luke's orders, I'd been attending all my classes regularly. Being on campus wasn't what it used to be. Before my diagnosis, I'd found being a student freeing and fun. It'd been a new adventure every day—who I'd see, what I'd wear, who I might fuck, and what I might learn.

But now, campus was a parade of grief or temptation. Everywhere I looked there was something to remind me of things I wanted to forget. There was the Health Center where I'd learned my life would be very short and utterly useless, and the UC bathroom where I'd once let Kyle fuck me like a rag doll while Peter waited anxiously outside. There was the Biology Lab where I'd dissociated instead of taking notes a week after the maybe-rape with Kyle, and there was the frat house where I'd had my arm broken the same day I sucked my father off.

All of those places brought back the shame that had become integral to me.

I shoved my hand into the pocket of my jeans, touching the edge of the folded-up piece of paper I'd printed off that morning in the University library's microfiche department. It was an article about Tamara Elise Allen, the teenage girl my father had raped. She was blonde with a pixie cut and looked more like me than I could stomach.

In the photo, taken outside the courthouse just after his sentencing, she appeared utterly miserable. I could relate too well. Justice wasn't ever as satisfying as you hoped it would be, and it never erased the damage done.

I knew I shouldn't have sought out information on the trial. I hadn't even intended to do it. But I'd been between classes, avoiding my old haunts, and looking for a fresh place to hang out, one free of demons. I'd gone into the library, thinking I'd find Peter or Barry on shift working. I could hang out with them for a bit.

Instead, I'd stopped dead outside the microfiche department.

My feet had led the way in, and when I asked for the films from any Tennessee newspaper concerning a recent trial involving Ronnie Arnold, my voice sounded like it came from another world.

It only took the librarian about ten minutes to find what I'd requested, and as I sat at the machine, moving the viewfinder over the various articles, my gut roiled.

The teenager testified that her step-father, forty-one year-old Ronnie Arnold, coerced her into an ongoing physical relation-ship…

Mr. Arnold insisted the relationship was consensual and mutually satisfying…

Miss Allen cried as she described the first encounter with Mr. Arnold, which she'd endured at the age of just thirteen…

I'd felt dizzy and sick, but I printed out the last article detailing the sentencing and showing Tamara leaving the courthouse. The caption beneath the photo read—"After a brutal nine hours of cross-examination from the defense, Miss Allen and her parents were rewarded with the jury's finding of Guilty after only twenty minutes of deliberation."

She didn't look rewarded. She looked devastated.

And she would be, on some level, from now on. I'd been there in her shoes, walking down courthouse steps the supposed-victor, but really the forever-loser. There was no real way to win when the man you called Dad took your innocence. Even when I'd claimed my power during the rape, I hadn't won. I had, as Luke said, survived.

And that was all I'd ever done since that day.

Every fantasy of love, every shining smile, every playful screw, every line of cocaine, every acid trip, every brutal fuck from Kyle—all of it was just survival. Nothing more.

My HIV diagnosis had revealed the truth of me—I was a façade of glitter and gloss around an empty, sucking core of despair that could only be filled with pain and glorious fucked-up power trips. Everything else was just hollow.

What if meeting Luke and being with him the last few months was the best part of my life? And what if everything went downhill from there? It was inevitable. He'd get sick, or I would, and then what? Wouldn't it be better to go out in a blaze of ecstasy while I still felt physically healthy?

I shook my head, thinking of the sweet way Luke had held me on Thanksgiving Day. We'd cuddled together in the queen bed at that expensive, fancy hotel room while my mother slept in her bed a few feet over. I'd felt so warm and safe.

I made myself remember all the fun we'd had at Biltmore House itself too. That whole day I'd pretended we weren't dying, that a place like that astounding mansion could be our future, that we could be kings and live on a fabulous estate, and we'd be happy forever.

But none of that was true.

I was a soon-to-be-dead student with no money.

I unfolded the printed microfiche page and looked at the photo next to Tamara's. My father. Hands behind his back, a guard leading him from the room, and yet he didn't look ashamed. Had he *ever* looked ashamed? No. Not when he raped me, not when he went to jail the first time, not when he showed back up and demanded that I...

I closed my eyes. Remembered the weight of him in my mouth.

I needed pain to block it out. I needed Luke.

The last few days, whenever I'd return to my dorm room to rest between classes, I found messages from Kyle on the answering machine. He had a real way with words when he wanted to. He'd spelled out in crystal clear detail how—despite my HIV status—he still wanted to choke me out and fill me with his jizz. He said exactly that in most of his messages.

I should have told Luke about them, but I didn't. I was afraid he'd want me to do something—like take the tapes to the police or press charges.

I *should* have deleted them, but I didn't. I couldn't.

Every word was dark and fucked up, and I couldn't let go of them. Kyle was the knife I kept ready to use at any time. He could slice the horrible memories of my father out of me and strip all the shame from my mind once and for all.

I just had to give myself up to him…

With Luke gone, Kyle drip-drip-dripped through my head like some kind of poisoned honey that promised me permanent release. Whenever I remembered my diagnosis, whenever I thought of my father, whenever I looked at the piece of paper with his face and hers, side by side on the page, that flame of shame licked up the side of my face again, and I'd think of what Kyle had to offer. The pain. The oblivion. The death.

Because I still believed Kyle had it in him to kill me. He was my out. If I got sick, if I started to show signs of AIDS, then going out with Kyle's hands around my neck would be—

No.

I forced myself to give up that line of thought again. It'd be so much easier if Luke were here to distract me from it. It didn't have to be with the tools in this room. It could be with something sweet and easy—like chocolate chip cookies or a Tom Cruise movie on cable. It didn't matter. In Luke's presence, in the light of his love, I could shut it all off. But alone? My pain raged.

I strolled to the cage, crouched down, climbed inside backward, and shut the door behind me. There was no way to lock it, but if I stayed here, I'd be safe from myself.

Resting with my head against the bars, I sighed. Wow, I was

one fucked-up cookie, and Luke deserved way better than me.

I wished I were more like Peter, or Daniel, or, heck, even Windy. *He* was having fun learning the D/s ropes with Luke's friend Ryan, and he had no angst about it at all. He just liked making Ryan beg, and Ryan liked begging for him. Why couldn't my life be that simple? Why couldn't *I* have quaint little sadomasochistic needs?

A fear whispered through my mind: *You stupid cunt. Luke didn't have a family emergency to deal with; he just had to get away from you and your demented, perverted demands.*

I stayed in the cage as long as my body would let me, but eventually my aching knees and the anxious gnawing in the pit of my stomach won out. I crawled free. Immediately, loneliness and bitter sorrow washed through me.

I checked my watch to see if Sensei or Sensei Junior might still have a class going, but at nearly ten at night, it was much too late for that.

With trembling hands, I talked myself into doing something I hadn't allowed myself before: I decided to call Luke. I started toward the stairs, but stopped in my tracks. What if Luke didn't want to hear from me? No. That was dumb. He loved me. I might not be able to feel it right now, but I knew he did. I knew it like I knew my name was Mitchell.

I love you, Mitchell.

My own voice in my head, and I glanced toward the horse where he'd made me scream those words as he fucked me.

"I love you, Mitchell," I said aloud, rubbing my hands up and down my arms, the chill of the basement getting to me. Usually when I was down here, everything between us was so heated, I was never cold.

"I love you, Mitchell!" I shouted, trying to make the words sink in like a brand, like they could burn the darkness out of me. I took a deep breath and let loose a scream. It filled the entire space. Then

I tried again. "I love you, Mitchell. For fuck's sake, you little shit, I love you."

I started laughing. I was pretty sure I wasn't supposed to talk to myself like that. If Luke were here, he'd scold me, maybe even whip me, and wouldn't that be great? I'd get right out of my head—

Wait…

Was I out of my head? Was I losing my actual mind?

Or had I lost it years ago? That day with my father when I'd knelt down and opened my mouth, and—

Fuck.

I wasn't going to think about it again. I wasn't.

I knelt on the floor of the basement, pressed my forehead to the cold concrete, and took a deep breath. I let out another scream. Another. And then a third. The sound died out in the room before I sat back on my heels.

"I love you, Mitchell."

There. It felt a little more real this time.

"I love you."

I also loved Luke. I loved him beyond what he did for me here in this room and out of it. I loved him for his own sake, and if I wasn't so caught up in my own feelings all the time, maybe I could be a better boyfriend to him. I was his sub and his boy, but Luke was supposed to belong to me too.

He needed me. And I needed to prove to him, and to myself, that I wasn't someone he needed to tell to "be good" while he handled grown-up problems. I could support him too.

I looked around the room again, laughing under my breath. I'd literally just put myself in a cage to try to keep myself from making an awful, terrible, bad decision. Was there *any* reason to believe I could truly be the man Luke needed me to be? The kind of man he could depend on when things got hard?

I guessed it was time to find out.

I turned the lights off before heading back upstairs. In the kitchen, I took down the magnet holding up the contact information Luke had given me during his first phone call.

I took a deep breath, got settled in on the sofa, grabbed the aftercare blanket, and gathered my courage. I could do this. I'd be strong for Luke.

I picked up the phone and dialed.

"Hello?"

The woman's voice sounded distracted but kind. I realized this must be Luke's mom. Her tone was similar to Betsy's in a way. It also suddenly hit me that she might not know about me. Luke had never said.

I cleared my throat and asked, "Hello. Is Luke around?"

"Oh! He's... Forgive me, but...is this Minty?"

So, she *did* know about me. How was I supposed to feel about that? If she knew, why wasn't I allowed to come up and help out with this crisis?

"Yes," I replied, while these thoughts tumbled through my mind. "I'm Minty."

"Oh, my. I hadn't imagined us meeting for the first time over the phone."

"Me either." Though I'd never imagined meeting her at all. Why was that? Selfishness, clearly. I hadn't even asked Luke about what his family and Betsy thought of him missing Thanksgiving when he'd come with me and Mom to Asheville. I'd been so focused on trying to pretend nothing was wrong and that everything was hunky-dory for Mom, it hadn't occurred to me that maybe he should have spent the day with his own family. What excuse had he given them?

Questions rose and rose in my mind like a bunch of bright balloons floating up to the ceiling, impossible to ignore. What wasn't he telling me? Why hadn't I asked?

Luke's mom went on, "I want to thank you for letting Luke stay here with me for a little while. I appreciate that."

"He said it was important."

"It is," she agreed.

"Yeah…" I trailed off. Awkwardness descended.

After a moment, she sighed. "He hasn't told you the details of why he's here, has he?" She sounded like she wanted to scold him for that.

"No, ma'am. Just that your husband isn't well."

"He *should* have told you a lot more than that. He's always trying to handle things on his own, have you noticed?"

I nodded. "Yes, ma'am. He's a very independent man." And, apparently, I wasn't. I was needy and desperate and—

Stop.

"Let me get him for you. But, Minty?"

"Yes?"

"Make him open up to you about this. He could use the support. I'm not able to give it right now because, well… You'll understand when he tells you."

"All right." My stomach ached. Had he needed me all this time, and I'd been too selfish to see it, and he'd been too proud to ask?

"Also, when this is all over, I'd like you to come up to Johnson City for dinner. Would you be willing?"

"Yes, of course. If Luke wants me to come, I mean. I'd like to meet you."

"Then it's a plan."

In the silence that followed while she fetched Luke, I evaluated the conversation. She thought I should make him talk to me. And why not? He made me do all kinds of things. If we really were more than just a Dom and his sub, and we were in love and boyfriends, then he owed me things too.

"Minty? Is everything okay?"

"Please talk to me and tell me what's going on up there, Luke. I deserve to know."

His silence at the other end of the line proved that my greeting wasn't unexpected, but also not particularly wanted. After a beat, I said, "Look, I'm not okay with you telling me that you've got a family emergency, being gone for a week, but I don't get to know the details about it. We're together. You don't have to handle this alone."

"You're right. I'm sorry."

"Go on." I encouraged gently. With the sound of Luke's voice in my ear and my determination to be the boyfriend he needed, the cries of all that darkness deep inside me grew quieter. I focused on Luke. *He* was what mattered right now. Not me. "I'm listening."

Luke told me everything then, and I realized that he'd wanted to tell me all along. He'd just been afraid of burdening me with his problems when he knew I was already carrying more than my fair share of my own.

When he was finished, I scolded him. "How are you supposed to be mine, belong to me, when you keep this kind of thing to yourself?"

"I couldn't—"

"Treat me like an equal?"

"Minty…" His sigh was heavy and so tired.

I softened my tone again. "I'm every bit as capable of being there for you as you are for me." Doubts about that burst in my mind, and I dared myself to fail him. I stiffened my shoulders and lifted my chin. "I can take care of you."

"I know you can. Believe me, I wish you were with me right now," Luke said. "I'd like nothing more than for you to be at my side. But my father's emotionally and verbally abusive, and he lacks any sort of filter. Baby, you don't deserve to hear anything he'd have to say about us."

"Maybe not, but don't you deserve to have a supportive boyfriend with you through all this?"

"I can't let him hurt you," Luke growled. "I don't know what I might do if he did."

I pondered, entertaining a fantasy of going to Luke's parents' house, stomping inside and giving his father a piece of my mind. I imagined leaning over his wheelchair—did he even have a wheelchair? Luke hadn't said—and whispering in his ear, "Shut the fuck up, you nasty bastard, or I'll suck you off too. Just see if I won't. And I'll make you like it." I snorted.

"What's funny?" Luke asked with a tired smile in his voice. "Share the joke, please."

"You wouldn't think it was funny."

"Why not?"

"Because you never think it's funny when I joke about, ahem, certain past traumatic events in my life." I huffed. "You and Barry have no sense of humor about them at all."

"And neither should you." He sounded as if he'd like to spank me.

I returned to the original topic. "Please let me come help you."

"No, Minty. Stay put." He gentled his voice. "I want you safe. Are you?"

"Well, I put myself in the cage earlier," I admitted, and heard the hitching intake of his breath. *Fuck.*

"You did? Why? Be honest. I'll know if you're lying."

"I just felt safer in there."

Luke drew another breath tightly. "Are you not safe right now?"

I glanced around the kitchen. "I'm at your place. I'm safe as houses."

Luke was quiet for a long moment, and then he whispered, "Listen, if you're not okay, I need you to tell me now. I'll call Barry, and he'll—"

"I don't need Barry." I needed *Luke.* I traced a knot in the wood table. "I made a mistake."

Luke's breath caught.

"It's not what you're thinking." I told him about the trip to the microfiche department, and the article I'd printed off. "I should have left well enough alone, but some part of me didn't believe her. I had to see it for myself. He's really in prison."

"Baby, I wish I were there to hold you."

"Me too." And to hurt me, but just smelling his skin and feeling his heartbeat against my cheek would be enough. "But I'm going to be okay. I'm feeling better now, talking with you."

Luke's hesitation came through the line, but I could tell he wanted to believe me when he asked, "You're sure? Because I—"

"I'm going to be fine. You can count on me. I haven't forgotten my promises to you. You can trust me."

Luke went quiet again, and I was about to spout more reassuring nonsense, but he heaved a big sigh. "I have to trust you. I can't leave my mom here alone with my dad right now. So, I need to believe in you."

"You can."

"Just keep your heart safe for me, all right? Don't go over to your mother's. Don't let yourself go down dark paths. Don't be lured into that self-hatred again, all right?"

Lured into it *again*? I'd never left it to begin with, just kept it at bay through Luke's love and devotion and sadism. But the bad in me went so deep.

I love you, Mitchell.

"Don't worry. I'll call Daniel if I get haunted again." And I would. Because I was going to take care of myself like I promised, and sometimes that meant asking for help.

"Good idea. And, speaking of, I'd really like to meet him soon. Why haven't I met him yet? Do you not want to introduce me?"

I rolled my eyes. "I've told you, Daniel's a real…"

"Party pooper. You've said."

"Exactly. He's always bringing the mood down with his logic and his earnestness and his good, *good* heart. Ugh. He's annoying actually. Not sure why I adore him so much."

"Because he's the best person in the whole world," Luke said, quoting what I always said about Daniel.

"Yeah. Except for maybe you."

"Oh, I have no doubt he's a much better person than I am," Luke said in a naughty tone. "What kind of man does the things I do to you?"

"Not a party pooper, that's for sure."

Luke laughed, and it sounded almost like normal. "No. If there's one thing I know how to do, it's to throw a party. A *pain* party."

"Ba-dum-bum." I chuckled. "But hey, that does sound like a fun New Year's Eve plan. After we ring it in at Tilt-a-Whirl, we can come home, and it can be me, you, and the basement. You could give me a New Year's spanking."

"You're on."

My heart twisted. "Will this stuff with your dad be resolved by then?"

"I hope it's done before Christmas at the latest. I really need to get back to my job at the store. I'm pushing it as it is. I hope I still have a job to return to by the time this is over." He sighed.

"You can return to *me* no matter what."

"I'm glad for that."

"I miss you so much."

"Me too." I heard a man's loud voice in the background, but I couldn't make out what he was saying. Luke sighed. "Thanks for making me talk to you, baby. I'll lean on you more in the future. I know you're there for me. And hey, if I can get away for a handful of hours, I'll come see you soon."

"I'll be waiting."

"I love you," Luke whispered. "I have to go now."

"I love you too."

And I did. With my whole heart.

Even the darkest, blackest bits of it.

Chapter Twenty-Eight

Minty

FORTUNATELY, LUKE'S FATHER was granted a place at Shield's Senior Care home that weekend. *Unfortunately*, though, Luke still needed to stay with his mother to help get him set up there, and then to deal with Betsy. Even more unfortunately, a few nights after our heart-to-heart phone call, Luke's cabinets and fridge finally ran out of food.

Without the funds to refill them—having spent all my extra cash on the Biltmore trip for my mom—I realized I'd have to go back to the dorm to stay until Luke returned. There, at least, I had access to the University cafeterias for all my meals.

But the wisdom of going back to the dorm instead of crashing with Barry and Robert, or even my mom, was still up in the air.

I tried to keep myself busy, though, to keep my mind and body occupied with other things. I attended free Aikido classes with Sensei and indulged in kickboxing sparring with Sensei Junior a few nights running. That left me exhausted and accomplished, much like how I felt after a night in the basement with Luke.

But, also unfortunately, the results were short-lived.

After a shower, I sat down at my dorm desk to study, but started feeling itchy and restless again. I gazed at the microfiche printout, staring at my father and Tamara Elise's faces, and thinking about the virus in my veins, the death that was coming for me, and

"

wondering if Tamara Elise would think I deserved it for what I'd done.

In pre-diagnosis days, when I'd felt bombarded with bad memories, I'd get up in the night and go on a walk to clear my head. But now I was afraid I'd walk right to Kyle's room. I could *feel* the pull of Kyle and the power-charged oblivion he offered. It was like a demonic string attached to my gut, tugging and tugging.

Still, I was determined to be strong, so I'd decided to try to embrace the old Minty. The guy I'd pretended to be before the diagnosis. He'd been half-free, hadn't he? Or at least he'd managed to shove all the darkness into a hole in his heart, sealed it off, and refused to look inside, running from the truth of himself. *He'd* tried to become a human incarnation of rainbows, sunshine, and fairy dust. *He'd* shined.

So, I went dancing at Tilt-a-Whirl.

Barry was the only one of my old gang there, though, and I avoided him like the plague. He'd have asked me questions that would've torn open wounds and made them bleed. What I *needed* was Luke, but since I couldn't have him, I decided alcohol, and more alcohol, and some grinding on the dance floor with strangers—who would later complain when I refused to follow them to the bathroom or back out to their car—was the answer.

At least the thrumming music and drinks dampened the burning shame that rose in me like flames. But I woke at three in the morning, sweaty and nauseous, a dream of being on my knees in front of my father lingering like vomit in my mouth.

I wished I could call Luke and beg him to please let me drive up to see him, but I knew he and his mother were headed to the Cumberland Plateau the next morning to pick up Betsy for the holidays and, worse, to break the news to her that she wouldn't be returning to Riverwoods and Rodney. It was going to be rough. Luke needed his rest, not to be woken in the middle of the night by a boyfriend whining in his ear.

Maybe if I beat off, I could escape this horrible restless feeling.

I got out some battered old gay porn magazines I'd scored from Knox Supplies & News the last time I visited Luke at work, back before all this stuff with his dad had gone down. Flipping through the ragged pages, I jerked off like my life depended on it. But the static visuals weren't enough to make me come. I needed more.

I needed filthy, dirty, bad, and wrong. I needed pain. I needed Luke.

I *refused* to call him, though. I could be the boyfriend he needed. I could give him the space to deal with his family problems. I could be the kind of man who took good care of himself, and I *would* protect my heart, just the way he'd asked. I'd...

I'd...

I'd call Daniel.

Relief poured through me when the best guy in the whole world picked up on just the fourth ring.

✧   ✧   ✧

"So, you're really moving in with Peter, huh?" I asked.

We were drinking to-go milkshakes and sitting in his car by the Fountain City duck pond. The weather had turned colder, but the ducks looked warm enough paddling around in the mossy, green water. I hadn't told him much on the phone the night before, just that I couldn't sleep, and that I had regrets about the way I'd left things the last time I talked to him.

He'd accepted that with easy grace like he always did. Then he'd told me he forgave me and loved me and asked to meet up today. Which was exactly what I'd been hoping for, so I agreed.

The heater was on high, blowing the cold away, and my face felt tight like it was sucking all the moisture from my skin. I glanced over at Daniel as he considered my question about his choice to move in with Peter. He smiled wistfully.

"Yeah, I want to spend every minute I can with him. Sleep next to him at night. See his face in the morning. He's adorable in the mornings."

"Yeah," I agreed, though I thought Peter looked rough in the mornings in my limited experience from our road trip the prior summer. His curly hair made for some gnarly bedhead. We sat in silence for a few minutes, just the slurp of our milkshakes piercing the silence of the car.

"Hey," I said after a few minutes. "I know I said it last night, but I really am sorry about how I treated you before. I'm a big drama queen, I guess." I snorted. "Not that an HIV diagnosis isn't something to get dramatic about, but I didn't make it easy for you to be there for me. I never do when I'm in a bad place. And I'm sorry. I'm trying to do better."

God, was I trying. I felt like a heroin addict battling a craving no one knew about but me. No congratulations, no cheers for all the work I was putting in. Just more struggle, more trying not to cave to my worst impulses. More trying to be strong for Luke, for myself.

I love you, Mitchell.

The declaration rose unbidden to my head. I wished I *felt* it, though. The words never fully penetrated my darkness.

"I'm just glad you called," Daniel said. "I love you, and I always will, no matter what you say or do."

"I love you too. No matter what."

Determined not to talk about my problems, I forged ahead into some of his. "So, is Peter's ex still around and ready to sweep him off his feet? Carry him right back into the closet?"

Daniel's lips twitched, and he shook his head. "I don't think there's much danger of that."

"Oh yeah? Why not?"

He shrugged, looking embarrassed. "I trust him."

"Like trust him? Or *trust* him?"

"I love him, and I trust him."

I blinked. There was something in that comment that set off warning signals in my head. "So, you're fucking him bare?"

Daniel flushed even redder.

"You are!" I screeched, putting my milkshake in the built-in cup holder. "You can't do that. You can't risk yourself that way. He's unreliable. He left you before and went back to—"

"We weren't together," Daniel reminded me.

"You seemed plenty together that night in the motel."

"It was one night. It didn't mean anything at the time."

I stabbed a finger at him, relieved to be upset about something that didn't involve me. I didn't want my best friend in the world getting the bitter diagnosis I'd received. Ever. "I've known you to be a lot of things, but never a liar."

"Okay, fine. It meant something to me. You're right. But it didn't mean he owed me anything after it."

I scoffed. "You're such a pushover."

"Good thing I am since you're such a pain in the ass." Daniel blanched, instant regret plain on his features.

A weird pleasure settled in my gut. "Go on, feel guilty," I urged. "I like how I always get to be right now. It's the only perk of my diagnosis."

I suddenly remembered one other, and my face grew hot. Daniel, of course, noticed.

"So, what's that about?" He waved a hand at my head. "That expression?"

"Nothing."

"It's about that guy Barry set you up with, right? Luke?"

"Maybe."

"What's the deal with him?"

"I know you know," I said, rolling my eyes.

"About the S&M stuff? Yeah. I heard that's what's going on."

I picked up my milkshake again, swallowing down any nasty comments about Peter being a gossip because the truth was I was a much bigger gossip than him by far.

I just got petty sometimes when it came to Peter and Daniel. Daniel deserved so much better. I didn't know *who* he deserved, but it wasn't *Peter,* for fuck's sake. Peter, who hadn't known immediately that Daniel was the best human being on earth. Ugh.

"Minty?"

I swallowed another mouthful of shake. "Yeah?"

"Tell me about this guy. Tell me what's going on with you and him. Really."

I sighed. Daniel wasn't going to let it go. I had to cough up some rough details so he'd stop worrying about me. Just like Luke, Daniel had enough bad stuff going on in his home life. The last thing he needed was to worry about me. Maybe I had a thing for do-gooders. "His name is Luke, and I love him."

Daniel's lips quirked. "Of course you do."

"No. For real this time."

"It's 'for real' every time, Minty."

I knew I'd dug my own grave on this with my past obsession with romance, but it frustrated me that my best friend couldn't see that this time was different. Truly different.

"We do more than have kinky sex. We hang out. We go on dates. We sleep over. We're a real couple." Not so much lately, with Luke in Johnson City, but…yeah.

Daniel's eyebrows lifted, surprise and interest glinting in his eyes.

"What? You don't think someone could love me?"

"Minty, of course someone could love you. *I* love you. You're very lovable. Anyone in their right mind would love you."

"Then what?"

"I'm surprised you're *letting* him love you. That's all."

I clenched my jaw. He was right, of course. I struggled with that so much. Even after practicing lovemaking several more times, each attempt was such a fight, and I could only do it if I was on top, fucking him, coming in *his* body.

"What?" Daniel nudged me with his shoulder. "What are you thinking about? You look sad."

"I do have a hard time letting him love me," I admitted. "I guess that's why for all those years I always pretended to have romances with men I had no chance with, men who didn't even know my name." I licked my lips and pressed on. "And sometimes with men who hated me."

Daniel's lips rolled in, like he was holding back words.

"So, yeah. You're right. It's hard to let Luke be with me like that, and he wants it to be sweet between us more and more often." I rattled my straw around in my cup. "What if I can't? What if I never soften up enough to really let him in?"

Daniel put his hand on my knee. "Minty, you're healing. Give yourself time."

I frowned. "What if I don't have time?"

"You've got the rest of your life."

The sentence froze in midair. Both of us sucked in a breath.

Daniel jerked his hand back to cover his face. I didn't think I had it in me to reach out and comfort him, but somehow I found myself doing just that. I squeezed his shoulder and said, "It's all right. I forget sometimes too. Honestly, those are the best times. I can breathe then."

"Minty, I—"

"Don't." I put my hand up to stop whatever he was going to say. "Let's not talk about it. The point of it all is that Luke and I are a couple now, and I'm better when I'm with him. He knows how to handle me."

"Good," Daniel said, voice gruff. "You're slippery."

He put his milkshake in his cup holder and admitted, "I don't know how to cope with you being positive. I never wanted this for you, or me, or any of us."

"I know," I said, rubbing his back.

"I love you."

"I know."

"We were supposed to grow old together," Daniel said vehemently, turning to me with wet eyes. "We were gonna be old men on a porch of some awful nursing home, drinking stale coffee, and talking about the pretty boy nurses."

"You can like the pretty ones. I want the manly ones."

Daniel huffed, and then melted with a gooey smile. "Peter's pretty."

"He is, but he's also fickle."

Daniel laughed, sitting up straight. "You're never going to forgive him for hurting me, are you?"

I folded my hands in my lap. "As your best friend, it's my duty to hold your grudges even when you can't. Until my dying day."

Another frozen moment.

My stomach ached, and Daniel looked like he might vomit. "Can we stop mentioning death?" he asked.

I patted his cheek. "Yeah, sure. What do you want to talk about instead?"

"This guy you're in love with?"

"Luke."

"Yeah. Tell me all about him. I really want to know."

I took another swallow of milkshake. "All right."

By the time I was done singing the praises of Luke, Daniel seemed a lot more relaxed about him. I got it. Just like I held Peter up for endless scrutiny, always on the lookout for any further betrayal of the best human being alive, it was Daniel's job to be skeptical about the man I was totally *incapable* of being skeptical about right now. It was a reciprocal service.

"So, you love him," Daniel said. "For real this time."

I took the last sip of my milkshake, rattling the straw in the bottom looking for even a little bit more. "I do."

"So how is it? Real love."

"It's scary as fuck."

Daniel laughed and tapped his milkshake cup against my empty one. "I know what you mean."

"You're scared too?"

"Hell, yeah. All the time. Scared of losing him. Scared of keeping him. It's all scary."

I smiled. I hadn't imagined Daniel being afraid to move forward with Peter. I'd thought him short-sighted, love-blind, and many other things, but never imagined that he might be afraid.

"So, you *do* remember what he did this summer," I concluded.

Daniel sighed. "He's human, and humans make mistakes."

"You love him."

"Yeah."

"I know. And you should. He's a good guy." *Most of the time,* my mind supplied. "He'd be smart to stick with you."

"And Luke would be smart to stick with you."

"You think so?"

"Of course."

We dropped the subject of our men and moved on to talking about the messed-up situation with his mom and siblings. When the time came for Daniel to go home, he drove me back to the dorm and dropped me off.

After he'd driven away, I stared up at the windows of the building. Music was spilling out of many open ones despite it being December. Probably the radiators were broken, and the students were trying to regulate the temperature by letting in the chilly outdoor air.

My own room was lit up by the twinkle lights I always left on. Others were decorated for Christmas with tinsel around the frame. It was a busy, active dorm dressed up for Christmas joy. I passed through the lobby, ignoring the stares I got every time, wondering how I could be so endlessly interesting to these assholes. I wasn't even wearing a skirt or dress today. *God.*

Upstairs, safe in my dorm room, I locked the door behind me and pulled off my coat. I hung it up on the hook on the inside of the closet, and then crossed the room to press play on my answering machine.

There were thirty-one new messages.

Two of them were from my mother. Twenty-nine of them were from Kyle.

I listened to them all. Then I listened to them all again. My heart pounded.

I sat down on my bed, sweating, trying to breathe through it.

I played them a third time.

Blackness rolled in.

Chapter Twenty-Nine

Minty

I WASN'T BEING smart. I knew that.

And yet hearing the increasingly frantic tone to Kyle's messages as they'd transitioned from threats of violence to pleas to rageful whimpers to disturbingly vivid fantasies had plucked at a knot inside me until it'd come undone. I needed to see him. One last time. To help him.

Fuck, Kyle *needed* help.

By the fountain outside the campus theater, I watched as Kyle loped toward me in the darkness, hands in his coat pocket and a baseball cap pulled low. I'd insisted on meeting here because it wasn't exactly high traffic, but it wasn't entirely private either. There would be people coming and going from time to time, and if I could convince myself to run, my dorm wasn't too far away.

"Hey," Kyle said, stopping in front of me. His broad shoulders and thick arms looked even bigger in all that winter clothing. He could manhandle me like no other self-loathing queer I'd ever been with. He could be brutal.

"Hey." The wind stung my cheeks as I took him in. His square jaw and thick neck. His cheap haircut. His wide lips that had never once kissed me. He wasn't half as gorgeous as Luke, and the way he looked at me was full-on predatory. Not a hint of affection or love. Just rage, lust, and hate.

To think I'd ever imagined I could make him care.

Kyle tried to morph his face into something less terrifying. It didn't work. "Thanks for coming."

I shrugged.

"I, uh…" With a tight swallow, he checked to see if anyone was around watching or listening, and after seeing that we weren't entirely alone—a couple sat on a bench a hundred yards away—he indicated the stairs leading down to a covered area next to the theater. "Can we talk down there? It's more private."

He'd never been so deferential to me before. It was like he was afraid I'd leave before he could satisfy his needs.

I understood that feeling. I'd been living it since Luke had gone away.

Still, I almost made a comment about Kyle being happy enough to shoot a load down my throat, but being too terrified to be seen with me. I held my tongue. I didn't want him to run off either. I needed to see this through. I had to…

I studied him carefully, measuring his strength and reflecting on how I was ready this time. My Aikido defensive skills were rusty, and I hadn't gone back to Sensei Junior's kickboxing class often enough, but I wasn't going to be caught off-guard. If it came to it, if I decided I didn't want to do this after all, or he came on too strong, I could always bring Kyle down and run.

"Please," he whispered, nodding to the stairwell again. "I just need to talk to you."

The pleading note made my heart hurt. He was as lost as I could be. He needed me just as much I needed him. We were sick together in the same ways. We both had a sweating, aching, horrible need for something that would ruin our lives… Why? Why did he need it? I wanted to find out.

I followed Kyle down into the darkness.

At the bottom of the stairwell, his eyes glinted in the low light, and I stood carefully with my arms loose at my sides, ready to move quickly if I wanted to. I stayed on the balls of my feet, keeping quiet and giving him a chance to talk first. Eventually, he did.

"I miss it," Kyle admitted, like he was tearing something out of his own chest to say the words. "Nothing else is good enough."

I swallowed thickly. "You miss *it?* Or you miss *me?*"

He shook his head, and then, after a long hesitation, he nodded. A few breaths later, he shook it again. "I don't know. I *liked* how you let me beat you up while I fucked you."

He came closer as he whispered, "I've never felt anything that...that fucking *primal* with anyone else. No girl. No guy."

"There were other guys?"

"In high school." He waved them away. "They were holes to use. But with you... It was"—his lashes fluttered and he groaned, adjusting his cock—"so fucking *hot.*"

Memories raced over me of how perfectly horrible he'd been to me and how hard I'd always come from his brutality. Lust rose dizzyingly, and my cock got hard. I *wanted* to be taken and used that way again. Hurt without any love or devotion. Just flat-out used like a hole and a worthless one at that. Treated the way the whore who'd sucked his own father off deserved to be treated. I wanted desperately to drop my pants, offer my ass to him, beg him hurt me.

But I held back. I wasn't the same idiot as I'd been few months ago. I had Luke. I had promises I'd made. I held Luke's heart in my hands. I held my own.

I stared at Kyle, measuring his darkness against the sweetness of Luke's love, against the pain in his basement, against the shame that covered me and ate at me and destroyed my ability to accept Luke's love the way he needed me to, the way I never felt worthy of. Never.

"You hate that it's the best sex you've ever had," I whispered. "You hate me, don't you?"

"I fucking despise you," he bit out. "But I want you. I want to fuck every hole in your body. Every fucking day. Until you're…" His nostrils flared. "Gone. Until I've fucked you gone."

I shivered. Terror struck. It didn't make me lose my hard-on, though. If anything, it made it stronger. Because I was fucked up. I was a fucked up, stunning, devastating *god* who made Kyle need to destroy me before he could ever give up wanting me.

"You want it too," he insisted.

I shrugged, struggling not to give in. Because even though the horrible tie that bound us together was stronger than ever now that we were face to face, there was another tie too. This one to my heart. This one was golden and strong. It pulsed with potential. It told me I had something to live for.

Even if that life was going to be very short.

Kyle sneered at me, coming closer again. "I *know* you liked it too. You blew your load like a screaming whore every time."

He pushed every single one of my "hurt me" buttons. He loathed me because he needed me, and I craved that. I *needed* it.

I took a step back, but stayed quiet.

His voice dropped lower. "You loved what we did."

I tried to keep my face from reacting.

"No one else will do the things to you that I will." He spit on the ground, his breath coming in faster and heavier. "No one else would ever want to."

I didn't correct him. What Luke did to me in his basement was amazing, but it wasn't what Kyle did. It could never be. Luke didn't *want* it to be. Neither did I.

"You miss it too," he insisted again. "You *miss* me."

I gritted my teeth. My darkness missed Kyle's violence. It screamed to be fucked by Kyle again. It reminded me that when Kyle fucked me, I was powerful, stronger than a line of coke. Dizzying. Intense. I wanted it so badly…

It'd make everything bad go away while it lasted. The shame would be gone. The memories. The guilt. And if Kyle killed me? Everything bad would finally be gone for good.

Kyle must have seen the break in my resolve because his eyes grew brighter. Ducking his head closer to mine, letting his breath touch my cheek in an approximation of intimacy, he whispered, "Come with me. Tonight. I know a private house we can go to, somewhere you can be as loud as you want."

I shuddered. The reckless darkness in me wanted to see where this place was, to find out what exactly Kyle wanted to do to me there.

Impatience vibrated in him. "You're not going to say anything?" he hissed. "You're usually a mouthy little cunt."

I shrugged again, trying to play it cool, though my heart was hammering.

Kyle crept even closer. I didn't step away. I could feel his breath on my skin, his hands gripping my shoulders, his lips brushing the shell of my ear. "Don't you want to know what I can do to you? Don't you want to feel it?"

"I don't know." My voice shook. "You'd have to tell me what it is first."

He laughed "What about the thrill of the surprise?"

"Not tonight."

He licked my ear, and my knees weakened. He'd never touched me with his mouth before. "Need incentive then?"

"Yeah," I whispered. "Incentivize me."

Kyle pulled back to gaze at my face, giving me a sadistic smile that wasn't nearly as beautiful as Luke's. But it still held a horror that gripped my guts and tugged me hard enough that I took a step toward him. We were chest-to-chest. If Kyle were a different man, he could lower his head and kiss me.

He whispered, "I don't want to just hit you this time."

I whimpered, and my dick throbbed. Visions spun through my mind of being alone somewhere private with Kyle, wielding my power over him, making him hate me and want me so much that he lost his mind entirely from it.

"I want to hurt you worse than I ever have before." He touched my cheek with the tip of his index finger, running it down to my jawline. "I want to tie you down. Fuck you first. Then I wanna use a knife. Cut your skin. Listen to you scream. Watch you bleed."

Dots swam in front of my eyes.

"Then I'll fuck you again until I get close, and I'll pull out and shoot on the cuts."

Fuuuuck.

He smiled with a gleaming hatred. "Don't worry, though. I'll stitch you up myself with needle and thread. No painkiller."

Christ, he'd fantasized about this in such detail. He knew exactly what he wanted. This was so much darker than even the messages he'd left for me.

"Then I'll let you sleep a little, get your strength back. Once you wake up, I'll cut on you some more. Maybe your stomach. Maybe your fucking *face.* Put a plastic bag on your head. Fuck you while you struggle to breathe."

My knees gave out a little.

His voice grew husky. He was aroused. "Yeah, I want to cut you while I fuck you. You'll beg me to stop. You'll cry. You'll say you'll do *anything* if I just stop hurting you."

His words came out in pants. He gripped his cock through his pants. "But I won't. I'll cut you for fucking *hours.* Carve my name in your skin. Make it last. Then I'll leave you tied to the bed. No gag, because no one will ever hear you where I'm taking you. Let you scream yourself to sleep." He huffed a laugh. "I'll come back tomorrow night. Do it all again."

I couldn't pull in a breath. *Fuck.* I knew I should be scared, and

I *was*. Utterly terrified. But I was also riveted. "I'm HIV positive," I reminded him. "You can't do that with me. Blood play. All that. You can't even if I wanted you to."

He shuddered. "I'll wear gloves. I'll use condoms while I fuck you if I have to. Besides, you'll be the one bleeding. Not me."

"The virus is in my blood."

"Maybe it's in my blood too."

"Is it?" Had I infected Kyle?

Kyle shrugged. "I don't know. I don't care. You've got me so fucked up inside. Are you happy, cunt? Say you want it."

I didn't know how he knew I'd entertain this horrifying and disturbing idea, but apparently he did because he smiled again, twisted and atrocious. He was so fucking sure he had me.

"How far away is the place?" I asked, my voice shaking.

"Not far. We could be there in an hour."

"How will we get there?"

"My car's in the lot down there," he nodded toward the garage beneath the Humanities Building.

What Kyle was describing was vile, and I shouldn't have a hardon, but I did. Kyle glanced down at it and his ugly smile grew even nastier. I envisioned myself getting into his car and letting him take me where he could hurt me so badly that I'd finally escape my body, my father, my past, and my shame.

I imagined Kyle cutting out the darkness my father had left inside me. I yearned for that. I yearned to see the hate he had for me burning in his eyes as he took me apart, and as he tried to stitch me back up to do it all again. And maybe, at first, it would work. Maybe he'd get a week or so of torture out of me. Eventually, though, he'd strike the vein that would set me free. He'd kill me, and I'd be saved at last.

Dizzy, and with a pounding heart, I licked my lips and nodded. "Let's go."

His expression was pure evil delight.

We headed back up to the light, and then stepped quickly toward the doors leading down into the garage beneath. As he swung open the door to the stairway, I felt the pull of that golden rope that tied me to Luke. It tugged so hard that I fell back behind Kyle, gasping, a pain in my heart.

"C'mon," Kyle said, turning to grab hold of my arm. "Don't pussy out now."

I shook my head, wrenched away, and let fly with Sensei Junior's favorite hook kick. It landed solidly on Kyle's hip, sending him tumbling down the stairs to the floor of the parking garage below. He stared up at me, shock on his face, and then rage.

I ran. And ran, and ran.

Away from him. Away from temptation.

Away from the worst part of myself.

Away from death.

Chapter Thirty

Luke

"*Y*OU CAN'T DO *this!*"

Betsy's enraged screams rang in my head as I tossed and turned in my old childhood bedroom, trying to sleep away the guilt.

Mom and I had arrived at Riverwoods with suitcases and boxes, and when Mom broke the news, Betsy had gone ballistic. I'd never seen her so hurt and angry. I understood. None of this was fair. Not to her, not to Mom, not to me or Rodney. Not even to Dad, because it wasn't his fault that he'd had a stroke which left him abusive and cruel.

But Riverwoods wasn't going to let Betsy stay without being paid to take care of her, and neither was Dad's new Senior Care Facility.

Oddly, it'd been easier to drop him off there yesterday than it'd been to pick Betsy up today. He'd been docile as a baby deer, letting the nurses lead him into his room, letting us set up his stuff. He hadn't complained, hadn't said nasty things, and when we left, he hadn't cried or asked to come with us.

He'd seemed stunned, like a child, and for the first time since the early days after the stroke, my heart broke for him.

But Betsy? She'd yelled at us all the way home.

My stomach churned. Nothing about this was easy. I missed

being in my own bed, and most of all, I missed Minty. I'd talked to him on the phone last night, but I hadn't had time to call today, what with the drive to the Cumberland Plateau and back, and then trying to settle Betsy down.

Lightning struck outside. A downpour began.

I glanced at the clock. It was late. But maybe Minty was still up.

I picked up the phone extension I'd gotten installed in my room for my sixteenth birthday and dialed my own number first. I knew he'd been staying at his dorm more often, but I liked the idea that he could be asleep right now in my bed, waiting for me, safe and sound.

No answer.

I called his dorm and the machine picked up. I left a message, hoping he'd hear my voice and grab the receiver.

But he didn't.

My stomach turned over. Where was he? Maybe he'd gone to his friend Daniel's house? Hadn't Daniel moved to a place that was closer to campus recently?

I swung my legs over the side of the bed, paced the room, and then pulled on my robe. In the hallway, I could see the glow of a nightlight coming from Betsy's open door, and I could hear my mom in there, still humming the lullaby she used to sing to us as kids.

I went to stand in the doorway. Betsy was asleep, mouth open and her cheeks still flushed from all the tears. Mom held her hand and hummed, oblivious to me watching. My heart tugged.

I tiptoed down to the kitchen, and if Mom heard the creaky stair as I passed over, she didn't leave Betsy's room to investigate.

Behind the closed kitchen door, I tugged open the fridge and looked for milk. I'd never actually tried drinking it warm to help with sleep, but tonight I felt so wound up that I was willing to try it.

Pouring a white stream of it into a pan on the stove, I turned the gas starter until it clicked and lit, then I set it on a low temperature.

While I stirred, I thought back over the car ride home. Betsy had bargained, pleaded, shouted, hit herself, hit the back of the passenger car seat...

I hadn't seen a meltdown like that from her in years. And she was entirely justified. She'd been suddenly and unceremoniously removed from a situation where she'd been very happy and taken away from the man she loved.

Another strike of lightning, and even louder thunder. The rain pelted the windows as it came down sideways.

The stress of the day took my mind to dark places, conjuring up situations where someone might take Minty away from me.

Like if he got sick, and the hospital or his mom wouldn't let me see him. Or if he got *really* sick, and death insisted on taking him away forever. Or if he found out his T-cells had dropped, and he decided to end everything on his own terms, leaving me to struggle on without him. Or if he went back to Kyle...

I'd fight tooth and claw to keep him safe, and to stay with him too. Just like Betsy had done.

No, it wasn't fair what we were doing to Betsy and Rodney. I had to find a way to fix it.

Pouring the milk into a glass, I turned and couldn't hold back a startled yelp, clutching my heart.

In the window of the kitchen door, a ghostly face stared in. Wet, blond hair hung in clumps around blue eyes.

"Minty!" I pulled open the door and held up my milk as he rushed to grasp me in a hug. "Baby, what's wrong? What are you doing here?"

"I'm sorry," he said, ear pressed to my chest. "I tried to handle it on my own, but I need you."

I pushed him away enough to see his face. "What happened?" Adrenaline pumped hard, and my blood hummed with fear. "Are you hurt?"

He shook his head, gazing up at me strangely.

"Are you sure?"

"Yeah." He collapsed against my chest again, wet through, and I rubbed his back with one hand, holding the milk in the other, shaking with shock and worry. Guiding him to the kitchen table, I seated him in a chair and then went to put on the kettle to make some hot tea. I didn't even know what kind my mom might have, but all I could think to do was to warm him up.

"Let me get you some dry clothes," I whispered, putting my finger to my lips. I didn't want my mom coming down. This was not the state of mind I wanted her to meet Minty in, and there was nothing she could do to help, no matter what was going on with him.

Minty gazed up at me strangely. "You grew a beard," he murmured.

I felt the soft, newly grown hair on my face. It'd started because I'd forgotten to buy new razors at the store, but I'd continued with it because I thought it made me look a little older. More distinguished.

"I like it," he added softly.

"Wait here."

In the laundry room, I found a basket of my clean things. I hadn't had time to fold them before it'd been time to leave to get Betsy that morning. I grabbed a pair of sweatpants even though I knew they'd be too big on him, and an even bigger sweatshirt, and brought them out.

When I peeled his puffer coat off, I was surprised to find he was wearing boy-drag—a yellow, long-sleeved, graphic t-shirt with the Mayfield Cow on it and a pair of faded jeans. He wore tennis shoes too. Scuffed up ones. I didn't ask, though, and instead helped him shuck the wet things and tug on my borrowed clothes instead.

He looked like a child in the oversized sweats, clasping a big mug of hot tea in his hands, and chewing on his bottom lip like he was about to get a scolding. As if I *could* scold him when he looked so devastated. I had a horrible fear that I knew what'd happened. I'd hoped that over the last month Kyle had moved on from his fixation on Minty. But…looking at him now, I knew I was wrong.

"Baby," I asked, kneeling at his feet. "Talk to me."

Minty blew out a hard breath, and then groaned softly. "I did something."

"Okay." My heart pounded. Had he gone to Kyle? Had he let him use him? Or had he been assaulted?

With a trembling hand, he pointed at his coat. "Can I have that back, please?"

"You're not going anywhere."

"No. But I need to show you something."

Grabbing the coat from the counter where I'd tossed it, I handed it over. His fingers trembled as he turned the coat inside out, revealing an inner pocket. He unzipped it and pulled out a small, handheld microcassette recorder. "I don't know if it worked. I haven't listened."

I smoothed his wet hair off his forehead and pulled a chair up next to his. "Talk to me. Tell me what's going on."

"I met Kyle tonight."

My stomach flipped hard, and I thought I might vomit.

"But nothing happened," he said, putting out his hand to reassure me. His voice shook. "I swear."

I nodded. "I believe you."

"I mean, nothing happened *physically*. This…this happened." He pressed rewind on the microcassette. "If it worked."

He squeezed his eyes shut and bit into his lower lip as the recorder buzzed in his hand. "God, I hope it worked." The recorder clicked off.

"Baby—"

"Shh, listen." He pressed play, and at first, I heard only muffled footsteps and the rushing noise of what sounded like Minty's own breathing. But then I heard Kyle's voice.

Hey.

Hey. That was Minty.

And then Kyle again. *Thanks for coming. Can we talk down there? It's more private.*

Minty's breath came in faster and faster, nearly hyperventilating as he listened to the tape. He took hold of my hands and held them so tightly it hurt, but I didn't pull away. As the conversation unspooled from the recorder, my nostrils flared, my eyes went wide, and I had to swallow vomit that crawled up my throat.

"Holy fucking shit," I whispered when Minty reached out with a shaking hand to cut the tape. "Baby…baby…oh, my God."

"He needs help," Minty whispered. "He's going to hurt some-one. He's going to hurt *me*."

"Fuck." I grabbed him close, breathing in his sweaty scent from his running escape, and the hour and a half long drive he'd made to my parents' house. I had so many questions, like how he'd known the way here, like why he'd risked so much for this tape, and what the fuck he meant by saying that Kyle needed help. He needed prison! But I couldn't put any of that into words. I simply clutched him tightly and breathed him in. He was here, he was safe with me. He hadn't gone to that house of horrors with that psycho. Thank God. Thank fucking God.

"What do we do?" Minty asked, once he finally broke free of my clinging grasp. "He's not okay." He tapped his head. "Up here."

"No, he's a psychopath or… worse. He's not safe. Not for you. Not for other people on campus. Not for anyone. We need to go to the police," I said, stroking Minty's hair.

"I don't want him to go to jail," Minty whispered, his eyes wide. "I want him to get help. He needs serious help."

"What he's saying on this tape here? It's a confession that he wants to murder you. That he gets off on the idea of that. That he's delusional enough to think you'd want him to."

"I know. I just…" Minty struggled with his words, and then pushed on. "I made him this way, you know?"

"Baby, no—"

"I kept going back for more. I did this to him. It's my fault he's gone this far."

"Minty, Kyle was always like this, believe me. He's probably hurt other people."

"I goaded him into hurting me! I wanted him to! Don't you get it?" Minty choked out, "I was a god, and he was helpless to resist me."

"Fucking hell, baby." Minty thought Kyle needed help? Minty needed help too. Desperately.

Minty went on, "He wanted to take me apart, and fuck me to death, and kill me over a period of days or weeks because he can't say no to me. He can't stop wanting me. I rule his thoughts, his desires. Everything. I rule his *life*. He's willing to kill me to get me out of his head. And a tiny part of me *wanted* him to kill me."

It broke my heart to hear it, but I wasn't surprised. I'd heard the horrible truth in his voice on the tape. I'd suspected it in how far he'd walked with Kyle before attacking him and running like hell. I sensed it in how fast he'd run, because he wasn't running from Kyle, but from himself.

"Baby, why did you take the recorder?"

"For proof."

"Of what?"

Minty swallowed hard. "That he needs help. That he's dangerous."

"Why did you run?"

"Because I want to live." He looked at me with wet eyes. "Because, scary as it is, I want to live out whatever time I have left with you. Even if I'm full of this dark shit that I just can't get out of my soul." He clawed at his chest. "I want it out. But it'll be here until I die."

"Baby…"

"So, I recorded it. If he can get help, then…"

"Then what?"

"Then I can be safe."

"Because he won't want to hurt you anymore?"

"Yeah. And then I can't use him to hurt myself."

"Minty, there are other men who'd take his place. Maybe not to this demented, sick extreme, but there are men you can use to hurt yourself." I didn't know why I was planting this thought in his head. I only knew that when it came to Kyle, Minty's mind was a muddle, and I needed to clear it.

"I feel guilty," Minty admitted quietly. "I made him this way. I taught him to like hurting people, I taught him how good it can be when he does."

"Baby, that's not something you learn. You either get off on hurting people or you don't."

"*You* do."

"I do," I agreed. "But no matter how much you tried to 'teach me' or goad me into it, there's a line I won't cross—that most people *can't* cross—and he stepped over it immediately. If it hadn't been you, it would've been another guy. Maybe even a girl. I don't know."

Minty chewed on his lip. "He's going to hurt someone. And it's my fault."

I dragged him into a hug, and he let me hold him. I smelled his hair, kissed the shell of his ear, and then pulled back. "He's dangerous to you and to others, but he's had this inside him the whole time, since before you met him."

Minty shook his head. "It's like with my dad. He hurt someone else too, because of me."

"No, no, that's not it at all."

"Isn't it?" His eyes were wet and full of despair.

"No." I could see I wasn't going to get anywhere with this tonight. This was a job for a therapist, not me. I kissed the side of his head. "Listen, it's the middle of the night. We need to rest. You're safe here with me now. Do you think you can sleep?"

Minty shrugged.

"Come up to my room."

He let me tug him up and followed me out of the kitchen and up the stairs. I pressed a finger to my lips to indicate that he should be quiet, and then indicated my mom's bedroom door and Betsy's. They were closed now. At some point, Mom had gone to bed.

When my bedroom door was safely locked behind us, I pulled him toward my bed. Holding him close, I tried to calm down. I could feel my heart pounding against his back, and where my hands pressed against his sweatshirt-covered chest, I could feel his heart racing too.

"Tomorrow we'll go to the campus police," I said. "We'll play them the tape."

"I don't want him to get arrested." He reached up behind his head to touch my beard. His fingers raked through it, and he burrowed back against me more.

"Sometimes a person has to be arrested to get the help they need."

Minty shifted, but didn't say anything else for several long minutes. I'd almost managed to drift off when he whispered, "Why do you love me? I'm a mess."

"I love you because you're a sweet, loving, good person."

"I was supposed to be strong for you. I wasn't."

"You were," I reminded him. "You didn't go with Kyle. You got evidence to help protect yourself from him."

"But I came here and upset you instead of handling it myself. Or going to Barry or Daniel. You've got your family troubles, and now I'm piling on."

"I'm your boyfriend and your Dom, and I love you. I wouldn't have wanted you going to anyone else. Baby?"

"Yeah?"

"Promise you'll always find me before you do something to hurt yourself. No matter what. No matter how."

"I already promised that, didn't I? On our ice cream date. I promised to tell you before I off myself so we can have one last scene."

My heart wrenched.

"But I don't *want* to off myself, Luke. That's why I ran, and why I drove here. I want to live because being with you makes my darkness worth carrying."

I dragged him even more tightly to my body. "I love you."

"I love you too," he whispered. "We can go to the campus police tomorrow, if that's what you want."

"It's not just what I want," I said. "It's what you need."

Minty shivered against me. "Yes, Sir."

The katydids called outside my bedroom window, and I stared at the tree branches swaying in the wind as Minty's body finally eased into sleep. I was awake for several more hours worrying and stressing about Minty, and pondering the question of what made me so different from Kyle. But at least I didn't see the pearly glow of dawn.

Restless sleep claimed me before that.

Minty

"Ah!"

The small cry of shock made me jump, and I almost dropped the bowl of pancake batter I'd whipped up.

"Oh, my God, you scared me," Luke's mother gasped, clutching her chest. She tilted her head. "You're Minty, aren't you?"

I set the bowl aside, dusted the flour off my hands, and put one out for her to shake. "Yes, ma'am. Sorry."

Her fingers were cold as they clasped mine. "Luke knows you're here?" She laughed, a throaty sound. "Of course he does. He's lazing in bed while you're making breakfast?"

I smiled and turned back to the bowl. "I wake up first usually. He likes pancakes. I'd hoped, maybe, you like them too?"

"I do." She took a seat at the kitchen table, wrapping her green robe more tightly around her middle. With her disheveled blonde hair and elegantly-angled features, I saw where Luke got his handsome looks. "And so does Betsy."

My heart lifted. I'd forgotten Betsy was here.

I went back to stirring pancake batter before turning to the cabinets to search out a good-sized frying pan.

"Here, let me," she said, taking over. "You're my guest. Have a seat." She gestured at the table.

"But this was my gift to you, to thank you for letting me stay the night."

"There's no need to thank me. As far as I was concerned, you were always welcome. It was Luke's father who was the problem."

I nodded my understanding and let her shoo me over to the table. I sat and watched her find an electric griddle in the pantry by the back door. "This will make things a little easier. We can make a lot more at once." She carried it over to the counter and plugged it in.

I rose to come stand beside her. She didn't tell me to sit again, and together we started making pancakes.

"I'm sorry again to have surprised you. I should have waited for an invitation to come here, but I had a terrible day yesterday, and…"

"You needed to be with Luke. I understand. It's good you can support each other." She glanced my way with worry in her blue gaze. "Anything I can help with?"

I shook my head. "No. I'm just glad to be here."

Pouring out another gob of batter, she smiled. "I'm glad too."

Heavy stomping sounded from the floor above, followed by a loud *bam-bam-bam* noise of something being dragged down the stairs.

Mrs. Montgomery sighed. "Here we go."

Betsy strode into the kitchen with a teddy bear in one hand and dragging an enormous pink roller bag with the other. "I'm going to live with Rodney," she announced. "I called him this morning, and he said I could. Let's go."

"Honey—"

Betsy saw me then. "Hi, Minty." She was still frowning, and her face was puffy from having cried a lot yesterday, but she gave me a friendly little wave.

I waved back. "Hi, Betsy. How are you?"

"Mad," she said. "How are you?"

"Stressed."

She huffed. "Me too."

We studied each other for a moment, and then she nodded once, turned toward the kitchen door and flung it open. "Drive me to Rodney's house."

"Honey, Christmas time is for family, and—"

Betsy stamped a foot. "Rodney *is* my family. We're getting married."

I blinked. Mrs. Montgomery was silent, and with that proclamation, Betsy stepped outside, her roller bag bumping along after her.

"Married?" Mrs. Montgomery murmured, and then gestured at me. "Do you mind finishing these while I…?" She nodded at the back door, which stood open, though Betsy was now nowhere in sight.

"Sure."

Tightening her robe again, Mrs. Montgomery walked outside and firmly shut the door behind her.

The kitchen filled with an anticipatory silence. I wasn't sure what was going to happen next with Betsy, with me, with Luke, with Kyle, with life itself. I was pretty sure that once Luke woke, he'd want to help handle things with Betsy, and as soon as that was resolved, he'd want to drive back to Knoxville to take the recording to the campus police.

Nerves twittering in my gut, I flipped the pancakes on the griddle, and then stacked them carefully on a plate before filling the griddle with more batter circles. The scent of sweet and fluffy cakes rose all around me, and the odd, but not unpleasant smell of an unfamiliar house filled in the air around it.

Turning toward the window over the sink, I looked out on the view of the back yard. Betsy and Mrs. Montgomery sat side by side on the swing set, both swaying gently, and Mrs. Montgomery speaking with what appeared to be a calm, even tone. Betsy reached out her hand, and Mrs. Montgomery took it.

I wondered what it would be like to have a mother who had the capability to tune into my needs and put me first. Sure, Mrs. Montgomery had made a hard choice that impacted Betsy's happiness, but it wasn't as if she wasn't trying to soothe and understand her. She didn't expect Betsy to take care of *her* and just pretend everything was okay.

Luke was attuned to my needs. Especially when we were in his basement. There, he noticed every last twitch of muscle, every last expression that passed through my eyes, much less resting on my face. I adored the way he watched me when I was at his mercy—like he couldn't look away, like he couldn't get enough.

That was part of what I was missing while he was gone. I hadn't realized how addicted I'd become to being seen and witnessed, to being loved and understood. I was like a drug fiend, and when he'd disappeared so suddenly, it felt like a post-cocaine crash that'd lasted and lasted and lasted. The urge to fill that space with something intense and all-consuming had nearly broken me.

Outside, Betsy clutched her teddy bear tighter, and Mrs. Montgomery rose to push her in the swing, still talking. The power dynamic between them was clear—mother and daughter, legal guardian and ward. Betsy was bigger and stronger than her mother. She could take her down if she were to put up a physical fight. But she didn't.

Just like I could take down Kyle or Luke. I had the skills. I was more than capable of injuring either of them. But I didn't. I held myself in check, but with different results. With Kyle, I became a glorious god; with Luke, I became gloriously human.

It had never been clearer than it was now. I had to figure out a way to live without my "god fix." Only I could solve that problem. There'd been a moment the night before when I realized the fine line I walked with Kyle, between giving him all the control while controlling every moment, was irreplicable. I couldn't get the same needs met with Luke, because the pain he gave me didn't give *me* the power.

I needed the power. *I* needed the control.

A flash of inspiration hit me, making my knees weak. Instantly, I felt sweaty. Scared. Uncertain.

Could I...? Would *he*...?

Hearing Luke's tread on the stairs in the hallway jerked me from my thoughts, and I realized the pancakes were smoking. I quickly tossed them into the garbage and started a new batch just as Luke stepped into the room wearing sweats, a Galaga t-shirt, and bedhead.

I'd pulled on my now-dry clothes from last night when I woke up, ditching Luke's oversized things in the laundry room. Suddenly, though, I wished I'd left the oversized things on—they might better disguise how anxious I was. Luke would see it in an instant. At least I had another bigger reason to be anxious—Kyle and the recording. Luke would likely assume any jumpiness was due to what was ahead for us today. He had no idea of the brand new thoughts swirling in my head.

"Hey," Luke's voice was gritty and sleepy. "What was that thunking sound a while back?"

"Um, Betsy is leaving." I waved toward the door. "She came downstairs with her luggage packed and said she's going to marry Rodney. She wants to go to his house now."

Luke's eyebrows wobbled up and down. "His parents' house? It's in South Carolina."

I shrugged and gave him a sympathetic glance. "Seems like she's pretty determined to go. Like I said, she had her things packed."

Luke sighed, scrubbing a hand through his hair. "Where is she now?"

"On the swing set, talking with your mom."

"Good. Then I don't have to go looking for her."

"She's not wheeling her luggage down the street to catch a bus to Rodney's house yet," I agreed, as he moved across the room toward me. "I wouldn't blame her one bit if she did, though."

Hell, I'd wheel my luggage down the street in a pretty pink bag if that meant *I* could escape my current situation. Instead, I was going to be dragged back to Knoxville and to the campus police station so I could implicate my ex-lover in planning my murder.

Ex-lover, ha, my mind hissed with an eye roll. *Abuser. Almost-murderer.*

I shivered, and Luke wrapped his arms around me. "You weren't there when I woke up. I was afraid you'd left."

"Not me," I whispered, flipping the pancakes. Luke's newly bearded cheek raked over my barely stubbled one. "Betsy's the one leaving."

"She isn't."

"You can't keep her here against her will," I pointed out. For some reason, I wanted Betsy to win this one. If she got free, maybe I could too. We might be in entirely different circumstances, but we both knew what it was like to have things about ourselves we couldn't control be what determined so much of our lives.

Luke sighed. "We can, actually. I mean legally we can. But no one wants that, least of all me and Mom."

He released me, leaning against the counter, watching as I made another row of fat, round pancakes.

"Is there a reason she can't marry Rodney?"

"Aside from both of them having Down?"

"Is that a *real* reason?" I asked, glancing toward him. "They love each other. They want to be together."

"Again, legally, they *can* marry." Luke scratched at his morning beard. "We'd have to talk with Rodney's parents, figure out the logistics, and see if it sounds like a reasonable future for them both. Regardless, she can't just go there today, and—"

The door burst open. "I *want* to go," Betsy said in a teary huff.

"Darling, we'll arrange for you to see Rodney after Christmas. We can talk about all this then." Mrs. Montgomery wheeled the pink luggage back into the house.

"No." Betsy tromped over to the kitchen table, arms crossed and her teddy bear still held tightly.

"Want a pancake, Bets?" Luke asked.

She chewed on her bottom lip and glared at him before answering, "Yes. With honey."

"Coming right up."

Their mother shut the door behind her, put her hands up, and said, "I promise, Betsy. I'll call his parents today. We'll discuss it. I'm not against you two marrying. Rodney's a lovely boy. But there are issues to consider, and—"

"Chocolate chips too," Betsy said, watching Luke put together her plate of pancakes.

I flipped over the next row on the griddle. They sizzled golden-brown and perfect.

Luke grabbed a bag of semi-sweet chips from the cupboard and added a handful. "Enough?"

She nodded before turning to her mother again. "I want to marry Rodney."

"I thought you *didn't* want to marry Rodney?" Luke said. "We talked about it not long ago."

"I changed my mind."

"People are allowed to change their minds," I murmured.

Luke glanced at me, a surprised smile playing on his lips. "Like Mom said, we'll have to talk with his parents first. You can't just go to his house and crash their holidays."

"His parents love me. They told me so."

Luke grinned. "Who wouldn't love you, Bets?"

She shrugged again. Luke placed the plate of pancakes and a fork next to her at the table, and she started eating, putting her bear on the seat beside her.

Silence reigned for a moment, and then Mrs. Montgomery pressed her hands together in what looked like prayer, closed her eyes and took a few breaths, and then opened them again. "All right. Well, that's settled. Let's have pancakes."

With Betsy's crisis averted temporarily, I turned the griddle off, piled the last of the pancakes onto a serving plate, and carried it, along with honey, syrup, and chocolate chips, over to the table.

Luke made coffee and tea for us, and by the time Betsy had finished her first plate, we'd just dug into ours.

"These are wonderful," Mrs. Montgomery said to me, reaching out to pat my hand. "Fluffy, sweet. Just right."

"Better than the ones at Riverwoods," Betsy agreed, adding more to her plate. "Better than the ones Grandma makes too."

I smiled, happy to have accomplished something so pleasing to everyone at the table. Pancakes wouldn't solve Betsy's problems, but for the moment, she seemed happy again. "Thank you."

Luke pressed his knee to mine under the table, and I flipped my hand over on top of it. He smiled and twined his fingers with mine. Both Betsy and his mother noticed, but neither said a word.

We chatted idly for a few minutes, and I was able to pretend that the stressful events of the day ahead didn't exist. After Betsy had finished a third helping, she started listing all the reasons why marrying Rodney would solve the Riverwoods problem. As Luke listened, his brows went up and up and *up*. It was clear that despite her learning disability, Betsy's reasoning wasn't entirely wrong. Seeing her win, I thought I might stand a chance.

Though, I wasn't going to be trying to convince people who loved me that I'd been assaulted and threatened by Kyle. I was going to be trying to convince cops. And, in my experience, cops never liked me. Not even gay ones. I was just too unsettling for them. What with my feminine clothes, delicate features, and fairy-stamped personality, it was possible I made them feel things they were compelled to punish me for. Like Kyle.

"That was all very well-reasoned," Mrs. Montgomery said to Betsy. "If we're done with breakfast, we can call Rodney's parents now to set up a time to discuss it in person."

Betsy's smile made my heart feel warm and mushy. She deserved this. I could only hope Rodney's parents would agree.

As I followed Luke up the stairs, I heard Betsy on the phone in the kitchen explaining to Rodney why she wouldn't be coming to his house today after all. "But it's all right, Rodney. They said I can marry you."

My lips lifted at her sweetness. It was good to hear a tone of optimism replacing her pain.

Speaking of pain, the rest of the day was going to hurt in more ways than I could count. Even with Luke beside me, there was no way that what I was about to face wasn't going to slash open the angriest and darkest of my wounds. I felt sick just thinking about it.

I wondered if my time in Luke's basement had steeled me to face the agony.

Like it or not, it was time to find out.

Chapter Thirty-One

Luke

"**P**ANCAKES WERE YOUR idea, I'm guessing?" I asked, as I drove up the ramp to the interstate, headed back to Knoxville. We were taking my car and leaving his truck at my mom's place until we'd dealt with things.

"Yeah. Mornings after nights where I've made questionable choices, I make panic-pancakes. Or panicakes."

"What were you panicking about? Meeting my mom or…?" I gestured at the windshield indicating the direction we were driving.

"'Or' mostly."

"We need to go to the campus police as soon as possible. We should have gone before, when he attacked you the first time."

Minty nodded, and he looked so green that I was worried the half-dozen pancakes he'd eaten might come back up. "I know." His voice was a whisper.

I put my hand on his thigh, leaving it there. His leg trembled with apprehension. It radiated off him. I tried to think of a way I could center him. If we'd been at my house this morning, I'd have taken him to the basement and worked him over with a light flogger to get him into a calmer headspace.

As it was, I could only offer something to look forward to.

"When this is over, I'll take you home and wipe it all out of your mind for a little while. All right?"

Minty shifted, licked his lips, and whispered, "What if I want something different?"

I blinked in surprise. "You want me to make love to you? I can do that."

He shook his head vehemently. "I definitely don't want that."

"Okay…" I let my uncertainty hang in the air between us.

Eventually he spoke again. "I want to switch roles."

I cleared my throat. "Excuse me?"

"I want you to submit to me. I want to do whatever I want to you, however I want to do it."

My heart started to pound. It'd been a long time since I acted the role of sub, but I still remembered the lessons Jerome had taught me. Be still. Take it like a good boy. Get rewarded with bliss.

"How—how long have you wanted this?" I asked.

"I don't know," he said in a small voice. "A long time, maybe. I didn't realize I wanted it, though, until this morning, but now I think it's been there for a while."

"You've been dissatisfied?"

"No. Yes. Not always. It's hard to explain." He picked at his shirt. I wished we could stop by the dorm so he could don one of his beautiful outfits and wear it as armor, but I understood why wearing boy-drag to see the police was important. "I want to be the god. *I* want to be the puppet master. I want to force someone— force you—*make* you feel something against your will. I need that."

I cleared my throat. "That's what Kyle did for you."

"Yeah," he whispered. "In his fucked-up way, that's what he did."

I let off the accelerator, which I realized I'd been pressing too hard. We were flying along many miles above the limit. "I don't love pain," I admitted. "I don't enjoy it like you do."

He remained quiet, and I let the words sink into the space between us. That was the point, wasn't it? He knew damn well I didn't enjoy it, that I didn't want it, and he wanted to give it to me anyway. He wanted to try to alchemize the moment into something bigger than my likes and dislikes. He wanted to make me explode with feelings—wanted and unwanted—and *he* wanted to control it.

He'd said it himself. He wanted to be the god. He needed it.

"All right," I agreed quietly. "We can play with that. I'll need to teach you a few things first. If you want, we can start tonight."

The energy from his side of the car amped up. It was part anxiety, part fear, part excitement, and part something darker, something greedy and eager to make me his bitch.

"Okay," he said softly.

The rest of the ride to campus was quiet, but eventually Minty put his trembling hand on my leg, holding it there with a steady pressure. When we parked in the lot with the small, brick, campus police building ahead of us, Minty whispered, "Thank you, and I'm sorry for needing that, and for everything else too. But thank you."

I didn't know what to say, so I pulled him into a hug, only releasing him when he moved back. Facing front, he tugged the visor mirror down and checked his face—makeup-free for a change.

"Let's do this," he said. "I'm ready."

I wasn't, but I followed him from the car and, for the first time since we met, I let him take the lead.

Chapter Thirty-Two

Minty

THE CAMPUS POLICE were skeptical until I played the recording for them. After that, there were a lot of phone calls and shouts behind closed doors, and then, hours later, a nice-looking lady wearing a slim brown skirt, a cream dress shirt with a built-in scarf, and a brown tweed jacket sat down across the table from me and gave me what had to be her kindest eyes.

"Let's start at the beginning," she said gently.

Luke took hold of my hand, and I squeezed it hard, trying to keep my soul in my body. "The beginning-beginning? Or the beginning with Kyle?"

"Whatever you think is best."

That was the first time in my life I'd ever told the whole truth to an attorney, even the worst, most shameful truth about my dad.

"After that," I concluded, having shared the way I'd sucked him off and then spit the cum in his face. "I hated myself. I still do. Hate myself, I mean."

She made notes.

"He went to prison," I told her. "So, I've done all this before, and I really don't want to do it again."

I realized how that had played a role in my reluctance to come to the police last night. "I don't want to give testimony and have a jury stare at me, knowing what I did." I shivered. "Knowing private things no one should know about me."

"I understand," the woman said quietly, and suddenly I wished I'd paid more attention when she'd given her name. I'd been too busy disassociating and trying to keep myself from breaking into a million pieces from the memories and the brutal stares and horrified expressions from the campus police. "We'll try to keep it from coming to that."

"Can you?" Luke asked.

"'Try' is the operative word."

I felt nauseous, the world tilting on its axis for the second time in my life. What had I done? Now that I'd opened this can of worms, there was no way to close it again. I was going to end up on the nightly news, everyone was going to know my business.

Before, I was a minor, protected by the justice system. This time, it would be my word against Kyle's. Who knew what he might say? The God's honest truth? That I'd *wanted* him to assault me? Or a lie? That I was making it up to get revenge on him for not wanting me? Or worse?

"I take it back," I said, standing up.

Luke shook his head, tugging on my hand. "Minty, no. He's dangerous."

"I know!"

"We'll protect you," the attorney said.

"You can't," I whispered. "I already know you can't."

"Mitchell," she started, and I balked, lifting my hands to freeze her words.

"No. I can't do this. I won't do it. I will *not* get on a stand and say out loud all the things no stranger should ever know about me."

"He'll do this to other people," Luke said quietly. "Or he'll hurt you, or he'll hurt someone else. Maybe kill them."

The attorney nodded.

My gut churned. I sat down again. "Can you really put him in jail with what I've told you? With that tape I brought?"

"I hope we can."

Tears pricked my eyes. "Will he stay there? Or will they let him out like they did my father? What then?"

"I can't guarantee anything," she said softly. "But I promise, Mitchell, I'll do what I can to support you through this."

Facing this moment, I wanted to die. I wanted the HIV inside me to get a move on, take me over, make me leave this earth before I ever had to get on a witness stand in front of my mother and God and the press, and who knew who else, and look over at Kyle as I confessed, "He was going to kill me, but some part of me wanted him to."

"No, I want to take it back," I said again.

"Is it all true?" she asked.

"Yes, but I don't want to do this anymore."

She patted my hand. "I know you don't, but you need to."

Luke put his arms around me and whispered in my ear, "Please, baby. He's dangerous. I can't lose you. I need you."

I started to cry and eventually nodded. "Okay. All right. I will."

After that, it was too late to take things back. I'd already told the police everything, and they'd heard the tape, and they'd already arranged to meet the Knoxville city cops at the dorm to arrest Kyle and take him to the city jail.

Or something like that. I had a hard time comprehending the details. My ears felt stuffed full of cotton, and my mind was swirling with humiliation and fear.

Right now, I was not in control. I was *not* a god. I was a little gay boy with no way to protect himself from what was to come.

"It's late," Luke said, glancing at the clock. "We've been here for six hours now. Can I take him home?"

The attorney consulted her watch. "You'll keep him safe?"

We both knew she wasn't talking about keeping me safe from

Kyle, but safe from myself.

"Yes."

"The police might need more from him tomorrow, depending on what they find when they arrest Mr. Aiken—"

That was Kyle's last name? I'd never even known.

"—and search his room."

"All right. Here." The woman pushed two business cards across the table. One was hers, and it listed her name as Lydia Butler. The other card was for a woman called Pamela Novik, PhD. She tapped that one. "This is the name and address of a therapist. She's fantastic at what she does. And because she's also my sister, she sees some of my clients for free from time to time."

Luke let out a grateful-sounding sigh.

Lydia went on, "She'll be expecting you tomorrow morning at seven a.m. sharp."

"It's Saturday," I murmured.

"Mental health emergencies don't take a break on Saturdays, and neither does my sister."

I frowned.

Lydia caught Luke's eye. "He'll be there?"

I took hold of her sister's card, turned it over in my palm, noted the address of the office, and then stuffed it into the pocket of my jeans. "I'll be there."

Luke squeezed my hand again, Lydia stood up, gave me another sadly-kind look, and then we were free.

As we walked out of the campus police station, a brisk winter wind tore through my hair, and I wished it would rip me out of my body and whisk me away. Take me out of this moment, off this world, all the way to heaven or whatever waited for me out there.

"It's going to be all right," Luke said as he started the car.

"No, it's not."

In silence, we drove to his house. It was good to be home

again—and since when had I started to think his house was my home? Even though cuddling on the sofa and sleeping in his soft bed sounded appealing, I knew I wouldn't be able to settle. I was so wound up, so outside of my body, that I felt as if I could disappear.

Cool relief flooded me when Luke locked the front door behind us, and then turned directly to open the one to the basement.

"Do you want to leave all this behind for a while?"

"Yes."

"Our safe word?" he asked.

"Poodle."

"C'mon."

Chapter Thirty-Three

Luke

"**K**NEEL."

I wasn't surprised that this was Minty's first command after we'd officially laid out the terms of the night—he'd be the Dom and I'd be the sub; no impact play beyond spanking since I hadn't had time to teach him how to wield the implements yet, and instead of just "poodle" to put a stop to the scene, we'd also use green and yellow to mean "go ahead" and "slow down."

Minty was shaky in every way after the ordeal of the last twenty-four hours, and I wondered if it was a good idea to let him take charge. But I also knew that he needed it. I might not be able to make him feel like a god in the same way Kyle had, but maybe I could help him feel like he had some control again.

The concrete floor dug into my knees, and I had a brief flash of respect for the fact that Minty had never once complained about that.

"Shirt off."

I unbuttoned it and tossed it aside. The corners of Minty's lips tweaked up in a smirk. "Is that any way to treat your clothes?"

"Sorry, Sir," I murmured. "Should I get it, Sir? Fold it?"

Tutting, he fetched my shirt himself and stood in front of me twisting it up in his hands. I frowned. It was one of my favorite button-up shirts. He'd destroy it like that. I opened my mouth to protest, caught his eye, and shut it again.

It wasn't that he looked threatening. It was that he looked vulnerable. If I questioned his authority now at the very start, there was no point in moving forward.

"Open up," he said, when he'd wound my shirt into a thick rope of fabric.

I felt odd hinging my mouth open for him, and I wasn't sure what to do with my arms. Jerome always had me keep them behind my back, but Minty hadn't said. Of course, he didn't know he should guide me like that—after all, I rarely gave him orders on his posture. He did it all naturally.

"I just want to see…" he murmured, as he fitted the rope of shirt into my mouth, tying the arms of it behind my head, clumsily gagging me. "Huh. Wow."

I lowered my chin, trying to give an air of submission, but Minty just laughed. It wasn't a lighthearted sound. It was heavy with the day and the weight of his life.

"Don't bother, baby," he murmured. "It doesn't suit you. And it's not what I want anyway."

I lifted my chin again and met his tired eyes. There wasn't any real lust in them, and I could see from the front of his blue jeans that he wasn't getting hard.

"Get up."

I rose, and he grabbed hold of my hands, leading me to the bed. "Pants off. Lay down."

I obeyed and collapsed in the middle of the mattress on my back, chewing on the fabric in my mouth as I waited to see what he'd do next. Gazing up at the ceiling, I noticed the white, blank expanse wasn't very sensual. I decided to get a canopy for the bed or maybe drape some dark fabric to make it less stark.

"Pay attention," Minty murmured. He hadn't raised or hardened his voice at all, but there was nothing timid about his commands either.

I turned my head toward him and saw that he'd stripped off his own clothes too. He wasn't erect, but he looked gorgeous as ever with his pale limbs, blond pubes, and rosy nipples and cock. He crawled onto the bed, soft cock bouncing, and straddled my hips, letting his balls drop onto my semi-hard dick.

"Hands up. Touch the headboard."

I complied, and he nodded. "Keep them there. Don't move your hands away. No matter what I do."

I nodded.

Minty reached up and pulled the shirt out of my mouth. "I want to hear you," he said. "Be loud."

I cleared my throat before speaking. "Any rules about what I can say, Sir?"

He shrugged. "Say whatever you want. Just don't move your hands."

"Yes, Sir."

His next move wasn't that different from when we were upstairs in my bedroom. He slid down on top of me, rubbing against my chest hair and rutting his cock next to mine until we both got hard. I wanted to reach out and take hold of him, move him to a position that would get me off better, but I kept my hands on the headboard, letting him do what he wanted.

"I really like the beard," he said quietly, leaning forward to stroke his cheek against my new growth. "It's sexy."

"Thanks."

He sat up again, pressing his ass against my cock. His dick hadn't softened, but as he stared down at me, storms brewed in his eyes.

"Is there a problem, Sir?" I asked.

He sighed, touching my face, running his fingers through my beard. "The problem is I don't want to hurt you."

"You don't have to."

Groaning, he covered his face with his hands. "I thought this would work, but…"

"It's not," I surmised.

He shook his head, flopping over onto the mattress next to me. Resting on his side, he trailed a hand through my chest hair. I kept my arms raised to the headboard because he hadn't said to take them down, and no one had called out of the scene yet.

"I think I was wrong. I don't think I'm Dom material."

"There are a lot of ways to be dominant. You don't have to hurt me or choke me, or do anything painful at all. You could tickle me, or just make me lay here with my hands up for a while. You could make me sing Ave Maria in a Scottish accent. You could ask me to suck you off or play with your nipples. As your sub, I'll do whatever you tell me to."

He nodded, his brow furrowing. "I don't know what I want." He huffed. "Isn't that the problem with me anyway? I never know what I want."

"You wanted to try this. You were sure of that earlier. So, maybe tonight just isn't the right night. It's been a long day, and maybe you just need me to give you a massage and take you up to bed."

"A massage?"

I nodded.

He pondered this, chewing on his bottom lip. "And then you'd carry me upstairs?"

"Yes."

"Like I'm a beautiful maiden in a romance novel?"

"Sure. If you tell me to, I'll do it."

Minty continued to think it over. "What if I want you to make a bubble bath for me and then wash me slowly from head to toe?"

I laughed. "Baby, I'd love nothing more. Um, I mean, Sir."

He shook his head. "That Sir business is ridiculous. Call

me…Your Majesty."

I grinned. "Yes, Your Majesty. I'll be happy to wash you."

His eyes brightened and a smile played at his lips. "All right. Let's try this again."

"All right."

"Ready?"

"Yes."

He cleared his throat and lifted his chin regally. "First, let go of the headboard. Second, suck my dick, and third, once I've come, carry me upstairs to a bubble bath. Oh, and not over your shoulder like I'm a bag of potatoes, but all romantic-ish. Like I'm a fairy-boy bride."

"Yes, Your Majesty," I said, moving to take hold of his hips and nuzzle his cock. It'd deflated during our conversation, but the sensation of my beard against the tender crown woke it up again. I nibbled gently at his scrotum as he worked his fingers into my hair.

"Then in the bath, you'll clean every inch of me."

"Mm-hmm," I agreed, my mouth full of his dick.

"And once we're in bed, you'll fuck me good and hard. And you'll bite my nipple when I come."

I popped off. "Yes, Your Majesty."

"I didn't say to stop sucking me," he scolded. "Are you being disobedient?"

"Unthinkable, Your Majesty." Soon he was moaning and tugging on my hair. His thighs quivered and his hips trembled as I worked him.

"You'll brush my hair and my teeth."

"Mm-hmm," I got out around his dick.

"And you'll eat my ass while I watch an episode of *Magnum PI*."

"Anything you want," I agreed, quickly getting back to sucking him off.

"And you'll do it all because I'm amazing," he whimpered.

"Because I'm a petty, needy, pretty god."

"Yes," I pulled off to say. Saliva strung from my lips to his cockhead. "You're my god, Your Majesty, and I worship you."

"That's right."

I went back to sucking his cock again. But it didn't escape me that, unlike when *I* was in charge or we were making love, he didn't shy away from the compliment.

"I command you to tell me how beautiful I am when I come," he said, as his balls drew up and orgasm grew closer.

I stopped working him with my mouth and used my hand to drive him even closer to the edge. "You're so beautiful, Your Majesty. You're the most beautiful boy—"

"Fairy," he inserted.

"—fairy—"

"Prince."

"—fairy prince I've ever seen. There's no one as beautiful as you."

Minty was straining toward orgasm now, his chest and cheeks pink and his eyes shiny. "I love you," I went on, spilling compliments as quickly as I could think of them. "You're so good, and sweet, and sexy. You're my favorite person in the world. And I especially love when you get all flushed and shaky when you're about to blow your—ahhh!" I laughed, diving down to swallow his jizz as it flew from his dick.

His hands clutched at my hair and he convulsed, moaning and quivering. "I'm beautiful. I'm a fairy prince," he murmured as he twitched through the aftershocks. "I'm your god."

Afterward, once he'd slumped back, boneless, I wiped my mouth with the back of my hand, adjusted my dick in my pants, and moved to scoop him up into my arms. He wasn't as light as he looked, but I could handle it.

"Tell me that I'm a good boy."

"You're such a good boy, Mitchell."

"That's right," he said imperiously, even as his eyelids drifted shut. I cradled him to my chest. "But it's Your Majesty."

"Right. You're a good boy, Your Majesty."

"I should punish you tomorrow for calling me the wrong thing." His brow furrowed as he pondered what punishment I might deserve. Then he sighed. "I have a lot to deal with in the morning actually, so maybe the next day. But don't worry, you'll be punished for sure."

"Happily, Your Majesty."

"You won't be happy when I make you clip, file, and paint my toenails."

"Your wish is my command."

"Because I'm in charge."

"Yes, you're my fairy prince, my beautiful little god."

He smiled. "I like that." Then he pressed his head to my chest, held onto me, and said as I carried him upstairs, "Thank you for taking care of me."

"Always, Your Majesty. I love you."

Lightness grew in my chest around my heart. This wasn't what I'd expected tonight, and it seemed like it wasn't what he'd envisioned either, but somehow it felt deeply right and true. As if the Minty at his core, the undamaged, beautiful, wonderful, fantastical man he was always supposed to be had surfaced in our play, ready to grow and heal.

"I love you," I panted as I reached the stairs up to the bedroom. "I'll carry you anywhere."

"You will," he agreed. "Whether you like it or not."

"Okay."

"I love you too," he said, as I put my back into getting him up the next flight. "But you'll still have to paint my toenails. I bought a new shade of pink."

"Yes, Your Majesty." I was huffing and puffing and sweating a little from the effort as I deposited him onto my bed. Hands on my knees, catching my breath, I turned toward the bathroom.

"Use the lavender scented stuff," he called out.

"Yes, Your Majesty."

When I came to collect him for the bubble bath I'd prepared, he was asleep. His blond lashes lay on his pale cheek, his pink lips were open in a small O, and every bit of worry and fear had drained out of his expression. I couldn't bear to wake him, so I tucked his naked body beneath the blankets, kissed his cheek, set the alarm for his therapist appointment in the morning, and went to bathe myself. Afterward, I climbed in beside him.

I vowed I'd protect him from this night on.

I'd never wanted a new boy, but I had one. The best boy. The boy to end all boys. I'd protect him forever, whatever it took. I'd call him Your Majesty and serve as his willing bodyguard until the end of time, until we both died—however soon that day came. No matter what, I'd make him feel loved, and I'd keep him safe.

After everything he'd been through, he deserved that. We both did.

Chapter Thirty-Four

Minty

PAMELA NOVIK'S OFFICE was in the basement of the Psychology building on campus, and this early in the morning it was just starting to bustle with the arrival of secretaries, receptionists, professors, and grad students. It was still a few more hours before the undergrads could be expected to show their faces.

The police hadn't called last night or this morning. I'd woken in the night feeling listless and scared again, half expecting the pounding of their fists on the door demanding to know why I'd lied about Kyle and arresting me in his stead. But they hadn't even called before I left for Pamela's office.

Luke had wanted to come with me, but he had to be at work. He'd already missed too much lately with the circumstances around re-homing his father, and then yesterday with me. "I'm sorry, Your Majesty," he'd said, batting his eyes above his new and fascinating beard. I kept wanting to touch it. "But I'll find someone to go with you. My little god will be protected."

I reminded him I didn't need protection; I knew Aikido. But he'd ignored me saying, "Sorry, it's protocol, Your Majesty."

I'd snorted, amused and annoyed by how eagerly he'd bought into my fairy prince style of domination, but also touched. He clearly enjoyed worshiping me and, for some reason, in this context alone, I could let him.

After I consented, he'd called Windy and asked him to escort me to the appointment. Which he had.

Now my friend waited outside in the hallway on a stiff-backed chair, while I sat on a sofa across from Pamela in her quiet, windowless office. She looked a lot like her sister—including having kind eyes—but dressed with a lot more pizzazz. I admired her layers of patterned shirt, sweater, and scarf—all different, but all complimentary.

As for me, I'd carefully chosen out a pink sweater, pink tights with red hearts on them, and a fluffy, navy lace skirt that I'd found in a costume shop downtown. I wore pink lip gloss, some glitter on my cheekbones, and loads of mascara. On my feet were my cowboy boots.

I was armored up and ready to run. Let Windy and all my fear chase me if they wanted to.

Pamela leaned back in her overstuffed loveseat, looking sleepy and sucking at an enormous mug of coffee. "Can I get you anything?" She waved at her coffeepot. The room smelled like a mixture of coffee and peppermint, and there was a small Christmas tree in the corner decorated with lights and angel ornaments.

I shook my head. I was still jumped up enough on the adrenaline of having turned Kyle in and the terror of what followed to not need any liquid sources of anxiety.

"Mitchell," Pamela began, leaning forward with those dark, kind eyes. "I'm excited to get to know you, but first, before we start, I have some interesting news."

I braced myself. Interesting news was a curse in China, wasn't it? Something like that.

"As you know, the police went to your abuser's dorm last night with an arrest and search warrant."

I nodded.

"Well, apparently, they found things there which led them to the house where he'd intended to take you. After getting an emergency warrant for that property, they found things there. Incriminating items. Unrelated to you."

"Unrelated to me?"

"Yes." She cleared her throat. "I wasn't given the details, as I'm not your attorney. You can find out more from Lydia possibly, but I'm not certain she'll be able to give you much more than what I've just told you due to confidentiality issues. But the implication is that he had materials—photographs? maybe video—of criminal behavior."

I squeezed my fists tight. "Like what?"

"Well, we could speculate based on what you know of him, but truthfully, I don't know. I wasn't told. If you should decide not to press charges, there's a chance you'll never truly know either."

"Not press charges?" Was she encouraging me not to? Lydia had seemed to want me to press charges very much.

"Lydia said to tell you she'll speak with you later today. But they have enough, Mitchell. They don't need you." She sipped her coffee again, and my stomach tumbled over and over. "They can prosecute him and get him off the streets with all they've found. To quote the police captain who called her this morning, 'his goose is cooked,' and he'll be looking at years in prison."

My mind swirled. What had they found? Child stuff? Rape tapes? Had he harmed someone before me? *Killed* someone?

"As I said, I'm not your attorney," Pamela went on, "and you really should consult with Lydia before you decide, but what I'm saying is, if you don't want to go through it again, you don't have to. You did the right thing going to the police. Your recording was enough to get the search warrant, and now they don't need your testimony to put him away and protect others from him."

I stared at her. The strangest emotions and sensations rolled through my body. First, and most startling, was hurt. I hadn't been special? I hadn't been the only person on earth to push Kyle to these sorts of extremes? I'd been one of…how many? And one of how many of *what?*

Then another emotion slotted into place. Anger. He'd lied to me. He'd made me believe *I* was his weakness—me, personally, not as a piece in a bigger whole. He'd made me believe I was his god.

Relief was next. I didn't have go through it again. I didn't have to share my darkest self with a set of twelve strangers and hope they believed me over him.

Finally, nausea arrived.

I jumped up and grabbed her trashcan, pulling it up to my face just as I puked into it. Pamela's presence beside me let me know she'd risen too, but she didn't touch. She just hovered. When I was done, she handed me a wad of Kleenex from the box on her desk. I wiped at my mouth, and then sat on the sofa again.

That's when I started to cry.

Pamela moved to the sofa beside me, a quiet presence. "May I rub your back?" she asked. "To comfort you?"

I nodded, and her hand drifted up and down my spine, centering me and letting me feel her care.

"You don't have to be so nice to me," I whispered.

"I want to be nice. Is that something you struggle with? Letting people be nice to you?"

My chin wobbled, and more tears fell. "Sometimes. Yeah."

Her eyebrows rose.

"But for a long time, I was better about it." I shredded the gross Kleenex in my hand. "I had friends that treated me well, and for a few years I felt happy, loved even."

"But something changed?"

"Yeah."

"What?"

I didn't want to tell her, so I motioned at my head. "In here.

Things changed. I started hating myself again."

Pamela was quiet a long moment before asking the next hard question. "Why?"

She wasn't going to let me get by without telling her. I took a shuddery breath, scrubbed at my face, and then slid away from her hand, saying, "You won't want to touch me once you know."

"I doubt that."

I shrugged, picked at the lace of my skirt, and wished I really was covered in fairy dust so I could magic my way out of there.

"Anything you say to me is confidential," she reminded me.

"I know. I've had therapists before. Court-appointed even." I smirked miserably. "Back when my dad raped me."

She didn't flinch.

Eventually the silence grew too heavy, and I blurted out, "'Things changed' when I found out I have HIV. I'm going to die soon."

Her long exhale let me know she'd been holding her breath. She didn't contradict me. She didn't try to placate or say scientists were working daily on a cure. She just let me have my feelings.

"May I?" she asked, holding her hand up above my back again.

I nodded, and the soothing rub started again. Tears started fresh, and this time I couldn't seem to stop them. She didn't pull away. She stayed right by me.

"Mitchell," Pamela said, when I'd *finally* stopped crying into the gross wad of tissues she'd handed me earlier. "I'm so glad you're here."

I couldn't say the same. Not yet.

But I thought it was possible I'd find a way to be glad one day before I died. Maybe I'd even be happy. With Luke by my side, maybe I really could be.

Chapter Thirty-Five

Late December 1991
Luke

I T WAS MY mother's idea to invite Nadine to Christmas at our
house. She'd also invited Rodney and his parents and had
insisted that it was absolutely a matter of "the more, the merrier,"
especially if it meant that Minty would be with us for the holiday
celebrations.

I didn't know if she really loved Minty as much as she
claimed—though he had been beyond charming the two times we'd
driven up to Johnson City to have dinner with her after that panic-
pancake morning—or maybe she just really wanted to make up for
all the times she hadn't supported me enough in the past. Whatever
the case, she had nothing but praise for Minty, and the first time
he'd turned up with me wearing a skirt, a woman's blouse, and eye
makeup, she hadn't even blinked.

Instead, she told him he had a knack for choosing colors that
complimented skin tones. That had set them off on a long discussion of color theory and Seasonal Color Analysis in choosing
clothes. Apparently, Minty was a Summer, like his mother, and I
was a Spring, while my mom was an Autumn. Whatever that
meant, I still didn't know. But they had a great time discussing it.

With my return to work at the shop, we'd been able to buy our
families halfway decent Christmas presents. If Minty got a part-time

job too, then we could start making plans for the future—however long or short that may be, given our diagnoses.

But that would all have to wait until we saw what happened with Minty's scholarships after his disastrous last semester. He was in danger of losing them and his place at the university.

Minty was still seeing Pamela every day, which was helping a lot. It was good for him to be in the presence of someone who was there solely for him. Pamela had no expectations beyond that he show up. So long as he did, she asked nothing of him in return, and it was clear Minty needed someone entirely dedicated to him that way.

He'd also decided to return to Aikido and Kickboxing classes three nights a week. Once, I went with him, not to participate in the class—it was far too advanced for a beginner like me—but to see him in his element. It'd been shocking to see him take down muscular men twice his size with ease. A sweep of the leg, and down they'd go. A jab of the elbow and boom, on the ground. I was impressed and mildly terrified.

Watching him do all the things he'd always claimed he could put Minty in a whole new light. I still wanted to care for him and protect him always, but it freed up something in my head to see that he could protect himself.

If he wanted to…

And that was a change too. Now that he had created his Your Majesty alter-ego for dominance play, he now saw a version of himself that was worthy—not only of my love, but of his own. Minty was determined to take good care of himself for the first time since I met him. He was eating well, exercising, studying his precious salamanders, cutting out photos from fashion magazines, and laughing over phone calls with friends.

With Kyle in jail awaiting trial on criminal felony charges, it felt as if a suffocating blanket had been lifted from our lives. I could see it in Minty's eyes, in his walk, and even in the way he hadn't asked to go to the basement even once since the night we returned from the police station. And, for now, I didn't miss it.

I was having too much fun playing his bodyguard, his service top, his devoted acolyte, and he was thriving and downright glowing with the change in our dynamic. He loved ordering me around. I'd become very adept in just a few days' time at painting nails and doing his makeup. He liked to call me into the bathroom, proclaim, "Valet me," and then sit on the closed toilet seat while I carefully applied glitter, eyeshadow, and lip gloss just the way he'd shown me.

Seeing him glow with confidence more than made up for not seeing him on his knees with red eyes after crying from a rough spanking or trembling from the intensity of the flogger. My inner sadist was happy to be hibernating. I didn't know how long he'd stay asleep, but I figured when he did wake up, we'd find out together if Minty was up for a game of pain. And if he wasn't…

Well, we'd cross that bridge when we came to it.

"What are you thinking about?" Minty asked. He was digging around in the glove compartment of my car, looking through the collection of mixtapes I had in there.

"The future."

Minty smiled. "Pretending we have a long one?"

I elbowed him lightly. "Hey, what does Pamela say about that?"

"She says acknowledging the reality of my situation is important."

"Well, fuck her then."

Minty laughed. "What about the future?"

"Just that I want you in it with me. No matter what."

Minty put his hand on my knee. "Me too." He turned the music up, singing along to "Closer to Fine" by Indigo Girls, and my heart rose.

I thought of my mother and how she'd probably felt this way about my father once upon a time. But now, here she was preparing for a very crowded Christmas Day without him. While he, through no real fault of his own, was sitting alone in a senior care facility. It was heartbreaking when I considered it. I still loved the man my father used to be. The situation was deeply painful and unfair, but I didn't have a solution for it.

That was something I was learning over and over with Minty. Life was often ugly and brutal. We had two choices—we could let it destroy us with guilt and shame, or we could be brave and save ourselves. I supposed there was a third option too. One I was desperately trying to employ today.

Forgiveness.

Now that was a tricky one.

As we pulled up in front of Nadine's trailer, Minty leaned over to the steering wheel and honked. We hadn't been back inside since the fateful day with the photo, and it seemed as if he had no intention of changing that now.

Nadine came out to the top of the small set of steps and waved us in.

Minty rolled down the window. "Just come on, Mama. We'll be late."

"No, please, sugarbaby. I need to show you something."

Minty tensed next to me. "What?"

"You don't have to go in," I said. "You're the prince, remember?"

He made an impatient gesture at me without even looking around.

Nadine went on, "It's just that I got a new sofa, and I put up the tree with your favorite angel on top. I thought you might want to see it all for yourself."

Minty went very still, and then slowly opened the passenger side door to climb out. I turned off the car and followed.

"Hi, Luke," Nadine called with a grin. I waved, but in my heart, I wanted to throttle her. "Come on, boys. It's a real pretty couch. I got it at Goodwill for just about nothing."

I followed Minty up the stairs, giving Nadine a closed-lipped smile and keeping a wary eye on her. If she pulled any crap, I wouldn't hesitate to grab Minty and leave without her.

She wrapped her arms around her son on the top step, pulling him into a hug. I stayed close behind.

Inside, the living room had been entirely turned around. The new pale green and gold plaid sofa was against the back wall instead of the front. She had bought a blanket in similar colors to throw over her recliner, and she'd taken down the wall of photos altogether, replacing it with a huge, terrible frameless painting of sunflowers. I half-suspected she'd done it herself.

"What do you think?" she asked, spreading her arms wide to show off the room and still grinning like she deserved a cookie for getting rid of the couch her son had been raped on.

Forgiveness.

Yeah, I didn't think I possessed enough of it to cover that.

"It's nice, Mama," Minty said, wandering over to the tree and tilting his head back to peer up at the angel, an old-fashioned thing in a gold tinsel dress. "She's so pretty."

Nadine enveloped him in a hug from behind, sniffing his hair and kissing his cheek. "Not half as pretty as you."

"Thank you. It's because I'm a fairy prince. Tell her, Luke."

"He's a fairy prince, Mrs. Arnold."

"Yes, covered in fairy dust at birth," she whispered with a happy giggle.

Minty relaxed in his mother's arms and nodded, never looking away from the angel. "Yes, thank you. I'm amazing, I know."

I nearly laughed, but I managed to keep a straight face.

Nadine said in a small voice, "I also took the liberty of changing up your old room."

Minty stiffened again. "How's that?"

She released him, clasped her hands together like a child, and explained. "I turned it into a sewing room with fabric and things for me to try to start up a seamstress business. What do you think?" She moved toward the door to the short hall. "Want to see?"

Minty licked his lips and looked to me.

I mouthed, "*It's up to you.*"

Putting up his chin, he took hold of my hand and led me past her. Together we walked down the hall to the room where he'd last seen his father, where he'd confessed his shame to me, and where, now, a big table with a sewing machine on top reigned where there had once been a bed.

The room was painted rose-pink, and it smelled like rose oil too.

Minty stared at the space for a long moment, his hand clutching mine, and then he nodded once. "It looks good, Mama."

"It does?" She stood behind us, wringing her hands and chewing her lower lip.

"Yeah. It's good. It's better this way."

She clutched him in yet another hug, and he let her, though he still held my hand. When she broke away, she wiped tears from her eyes. "So, you forgive me?" she whispered.

"Mama, I forgave you ages ago."

I grimaced. It was a good thing she'd asked him that question and not me; I'd have offered up a very different answer.

But it was Christmas. So, I gave them both the gift of keeping my mouth shut.

✦　✦　✦

Minty

THE DRIVE TO Johnson City could have been super awkward.

I knew Luke hadn't forgiven my mother for what he saw as her failure to protect me, and likely he never would, but luckily Mama was oblivious to that. She and I spent the ride up happily gossiping about people from her church and trying to remember the lyrics to "Grandma Got Run Over by a Reindeer" and then Olivia Newton-John's song "Physical."

Luke, for his part, was quiet, but occasionally he'd reach out to squeeze my thigh. His way of telling me he was with me and that he loved me. It made my heart melt a little more each time.

At Luke's mom's house, Mama got out carrying her green bean casserole, and Luke popped the trunk so I could retrieve the four pies I'd made to contribute to the spread, and he could grab the presents. We went in through the back kitchen door.

Inside, it felt as crowded as Tilt-a-Whirl on a Saturday night. Rodney's parents were there with not only Rodney, but his two sisters and their husbands. I forgot their names as soon as they were out of their mouths, but it was good to see that Rodney's family was so close and supportive.

Luke and Betsy's grandmother was there too, Mrs. Montgomery's mother. We'd met the prior week, and Mamaw gave me a twinkling smile and wave as we made eye contact across the kitchen. My heart warmed even more.

Betsy was smiling from ear to ear, clutching Rodney's hand and showing off her shiny new ring to anyone who walked by. It wasn't much, just a chip of a diamond really, but Betsy was thrilled all the same. And I was thrilled for her.

Next to me, Mrs. Montgomery greeted my mother warmly. "Your Minty is the sweetest boy. We love him."

"Your Luke is so kind too," Mama said.

With their mutual kiss-up over, Mrs. Montgomery took the pies from me and led Mama and the green bean casserole over to the table where she'd laid out the spread. Everyone was gathered around eating the appetizers and talking, and one of Rodney's sisters had Mamaw engrossed in a story about a scandalous romance in her workplace.

Luke juggled the presents, and I took a few, helping him carry them down the hall and into the empty living room. It was decorated to the hilt with garlands and mistletoe and red bows. Next to the fireplace stood an enormous fake Christmas tree with simulated snow flocking and blinking lights, and on the mantle hung stockings for everyone in the family—including me.

Placing the presents I was carrying under the tree, I wandered over to look at it. It was just a red and white commercial stocking, likely picked up at Walmart, but someone—Betsy, maybe—had written my name in gold glitter across the top.

"Come here," Luke said, tugging me closer to him. "I want to show you something."

"What?"

"You'll see." He laughed. I loved how his blue eyes twinkled. When I first met him, I never saw them twinkle with anything but sadistic lust. Now they twinkled with so much more: affection, joy, humor.

He circled me around to the back of the tree. Hanging on the hidden branches were all the homemade ornaments his mother had collected through his and Betsy's childhood. Mixed in with them were a bunch of small, framed photos. He took one off a flocked limb and passed it to me.

I gazed down at an image of little Luke, probably age six or so, wearing Christmas pajamas and a cocky grin. He was surrounded by discarded wrapping paper and wielding…was that? It *was*.

I gasped. "A crop? You got a *crop* for Christmas? No wonder you turned out like this."

Luke laughed. "No, a horse."

"What?"

"They gave me and Betsy a horse. Her name was Speedy, and she was anything but. She was a therapy horse for Betsy really. The crop was symbolic. I never used it on Speedy." His grin grew wicked. "But I used it on Joshua Jamison my freshman year of college. He appreciated it way more than that sweet old horse would have."

I licked my lips.

It'd been a while now since I'd felt the bite of his crop or any of the other rougher implements. I both wanted it and feared that if I submitted to him that way again, it might bring up all the bad memories. As it was, I was very happy being his fairy prince, his Your Majesty, and I was happy with him being my bodyguard, my servant, my very own man.

But…a touch of pain and submission would be so hot.

I licked my lips again, staring at the crop in little Luke's hand.

"I thought you'd think it was funny that my parents unwittingly gave me the gift that got me started fantasizing about sexual sadism," Luke said, pulling me even further behind the tree. "And, also, I wanted to do this."

He kissed me. His lips were so soft, sweet, and loving. I wrapped my arms around his neck. As his new beard tickled at my chin, my knees went weak, and my heart fluttered. His kisses did that to me now. I felt swoony whenever I was in his arms these days. But would he still want me if I didn't want him to hurt me anymore? Would I keep on making progress at loving myself it I let him anyway?

"Where's your head?" Luke asked, breaking the kiss.

"On that picture."

"The crop?"

I nodded. He took the ornament from me, hung it back on the tree, and then glanced around its big, flocked branches to ensure that we were still alone in the room. "Baby, talk to me."

"I don't know what to say."

"What are you feeling?"

I smiled and rolled my eyes at the same time. That was a question Pamela had suggested he ask me when I was all up in my head about something. "Nervous. A little horny, excited, and sad." I took a harsh breath and tacked on, "Scared too."

"That's a lot. What are you scared of?"

I squirmed, the bristling branches of the tree raking over my purple sweater and leaving pick marks. I started brushing at them. "What if letting you hurt me makes me get sick again?" I tapped my temple. "In here, I mean. Lately, I've felt almost like my real self for the first time in so long. And you seem to like me this way."

"I *love* you this way."

"What if I go back to how I was? What if the pain triggers something, and—"

"We don't have to do any of those scenes we were doing. The ones that were about shame and your…" He trailed off, clearly not wanting to mention my father.

"I know."

"And we don't have to do scenes with pain at all right now. I'm happy playing the way we have been."

"For how long, though? And what if I want pain too? I just think, maybe, I don't want to *need* it."

He pulled me in, dragging me tight against his body, and he rocked me back and forth. "We don't need to play that way for a long time, if ever again. If you want to try it in the future, we'll go slow. We'll talk it all out. We'll use yellow and green to negotiate during a scene. It's going to be okay." He nuzzled my hair. "I love you for more than the way you kneel for me. I love you for *you*."

"Your Majesty," I reminded him.

"I love you, Your Majesty, Minty, Mitchell, baby—all of you."

I curled against him, putting my head on his strong chest and listening to his heartbeat. I couldn't believe that only four months ago I'd been in McDonalds with Barry, arguing with him that I didn't need to meet his stupid Dom friend. And now I was so in love with Luke that the idea of living without him was unthinkable.

Speaking of…

"Luke?"

"Mmm?"

"I've got something else I need to tell you."

He pulled away enough to see my face, but otherwise held me tight to him. "What's that?"

"When I get sick…" My gut fluttered, and the expression on his face went dark with misery. "Like when my T-cells drop, and I get AIDS—"

"Baby—"

I put a finger on his mouth. "Don't interrupt me, please. I have to say it."

His jaw clenched, but he nodded.

"When it gets really bad, I need to know, will you be there for me if I don't kill myself?"

His eyes filled with tears, and he pressed his face to my neck, breathing me in. "I'll take care of you. I'll see you through it all."

I nodded. "Yeah, okay, me too. I promise."

And then, just like that, we were as good as married. I might not have a ring on my finger like Betsy, but I had a good man's promise to be by my side as I died a terrible, ugly death. That was a real vow. One I knew he'd keep.

"When we go to bed," I whispered, "I want you to try to make love to me."

"Yes, Your Majesty."

"No. To *me*. To Minty."

Luke squeezed me tight. "Yes, Minty."

Chapter Thirty-Six

Luke

OUR ALONE TIME behind the tree couldn't last, of course. Betsy was the first one to crash into the room with Rodney right behind her. "Present time! Present time!" she chanted.

The rest of the family trailed in from the kitchen too. There wasn't a ton of room to sit, what with just one sofa and love seat in the room. Chairs were toted in from the kitchen and dining room, and Betsy and Rodney happily sat on the floor by the tree.

Someone had opened wine and someone else had opened champagne, and without having to even ask, one of Rodney's sisters—Erica, I think her name was—had pressed a glass of each into our hands.

"I'll take the champagne," Minty said, relieving me of my glass of bubbly, and passing me his wine. "You take the red." Then he tipped the first champagne flute back and downed the entire thing in a few gulps.

I blinked at him.

"Nervous," he said. "What if they don't like my presents?"

"Don't worry. They will."

Betsy was already under the tree, sorting the boxes out by name. She read aloud, "To Betsy, from Minty." It was a long narrow box. She shook it. Something thudded back and forth.

My eyes flew wide, and my heart pounded. "You didn't," I

whispered.

Minty grinned at me wickedly. "Yes! Of course I did."

"No! But…it's…she can't…not here—" I sputtered.

Minty smirked. "I'm sure Rodney will be excited to use it with her."

"Betsy, don't—"

"Thank you, Minty!" Betsy cried out, holding up a beautiful Barbie doll complete with four extra outfits. "I love her."

"We can play together," Minty said. "I brought two of my own in my purse."

She grinned. "Thank you. And thank you for the other present. The one you mailed to me? It feels so good!"

"You're welcome."

I scrubbed a hand over my face. "Oh, God."

"Honey, hand that gift right next to you over to Rodney," Mrs. Montgomery interrupted. "He hasn't opened one of his yet."

Eventually, a small box made its way around to Minty. It was addressed to him from my mother, and I was anxious to see what she'd bought. She'd been fretting about it during a phone call last week, so I knew she'd tried very hard to strike just the right note.

"Open it!" Betsy cried from the floor.

Minty lifted his half-finished second champagne, downed it, and then put the flute aside. "All right. Let's see. What could this be?" He shook the box and then ripped delicately at the paper.

"Tear it!" Betsy cried.

A chant of "tear it, tear it" rose up, with even Nadine, who'd settled onto the love seat with my mother, shouting along.

Minty tore the paper, popped open the box, and stared inside with wide eyes. "This is…this is for me?"

He lifted out a beautiful necklace, a string of silver butterflies. "It's…it's…" I saw tears well in his eyes.

"Betsy picked it out," my mother said. "A fairy necklace for our fairy prince."

He glanced up at me, opened his mouth, and a weird little sob came out. I reached for him, but my mom was just as fast, jumping up from the couch to envelope him in a hug. "Oh, no. Don't cry. If you don't like it, we can return it."

Minty shook his head, clinging to her. "I love it. I just never thought—I never expected—"

"What, honey?" Mom asked.

"I never thought I'd be so accepted."

The whole room broke into a sweet awwww as I wrapped my arms around both of them. Nadine didn't want to be left out, and she joined the hug next, followed by Betsy and Rodney, and then even Rodney's sisters got into the ridiculously big knot of arms. Their husbands and parents stayed back, but the expressions on their faces showed that it wasn't because they didn't accept Minty—or me—but because they were reasonable humans with appropriate ideas of boundaries and personal space.

"I love it," Minty said again when he was finally free of arms except for mine. I helped him put it on. Once it was clasped, he lifted it up and ducked his chin to peer at it again. "It's so beautiful."

"Butterflies are my favorite," Betsy said. "And they didn't have a necklace with salamanders."

Minty croaked a laugh, and said, "I love butterflies too. They transform, you know. They start out ugly and then turn into something beautiful." He kissed one of the butterflies and looked to me. "They give me hope."

The moment passed, and more presents were opened. Nadine was given a scarf my mother had picked up from an arts and crafts sale the weekend before, and Rodney got another set of train tracks to add to the one he already liked to race his turtle on. His parents had brought us all bottles of white wine from the oldest winery in

South Carolina. Nadine gave out homemade candy she'd bundled into pretty little fabric squares from her new sewing room. And Minty's handmade glitter pinecone ornaments were a messy hit.

Once all the torn wrapping paper was crumpled on the floor, it was time for dinner, which was served in both the kitchen and the dining room since there were so many of us. We drifted between rooms, trading seats and talking. The food was delicious and accompanied by a lot of love and laughter.

It was a surprisingly perfect day. Even with Nadine there.

In my childhood bedroom that night, I curled around Minty and watched him study the butterflies on his necklace. "My mom said the guest room bed is really comfortable," he said after a few quiet minutes. He'd gone in to give her a goodnight hug and kiss before coming to get into bed with me.

"That's good."

"I'm happy for Rodney and Betsy. His parents are so nice to offer to pay for her to stay with him at Riverwoods. I didn't even know they had bigger rooms for couples, but it makes sense that they would. It'll be perfect for them."

"I hope so."

He placed the necklace on my bedside table and rolled over, facing me. "Hey, what about your dad? How are you feeling?" His fingers stroked through my chest hair. "It's okay to be sad."

"I'm all right. I've grieved him for years now. It's not like it'll ever be okay. It sucks that I lost him even though he's still living, but I'm learning to deal with it."

Minty's lips twisted up at the edges with a hint of pain. "Yeah. I get that."

"Oh, hey, you never told me. What did Pamela have to say earlier today?" Minty's therapist had called at our house while we'd been getting ready to go, and he'd never told me what she wanted. "Was it just a Christmas greeting?"

He shook his head and smiled bashfully. "No."

"Then what?"

"She wanted to tell me that she'd succeeded in pleading my case with the scholarship committee. She convinced them that due to extenuating circumstances, they *shouldn't* revoke my scholarships, despite my abysmal grade point average. So I can go back to school next semester."

"You'll be okay there?" I asked, remembering how he'd confessed that campus had become overlaid with too many bad memories.

He nodded firmly. "Yeah. I want to graduate. I want to get that internship with TVA. I want a lot of things, Luke."

I kissed his nose, my heart going soft and hot. "I want a lot of things with you."

He blushed, self-conscious again. "Yeah?"

"Yeah. I love you," I whispered. "I love seeing you excited about life."

"Oh, also, Sensei says that he wants me to help him teach the peewees on Saturday mornings. What do you think?"

"Will he pay you?"

"A little."

"I think you'd be great at it."

Minty nodded. "I think so too."

"Look at you, taking praise like a champ, Your Majesty."

"It's not as if I don't deserve it," he said in his faux aristocratic voice. "I'm a prince, after all."

"Fairy prince," I corrected.

"Who sucks cock like a dream," he said playfully, sliding his hand into my pajama bottoms. "Ever had your dick sucked in this bed?"

"Yeah. My junior year of high school. Anthony Hutchinson. A little nerd with a filthy mouth."

Minty frowned. "You were supposed to say no."

"Why?"

"Because that was my fantasy."

"I'm sorry, Your Highness, but it's just not the truth."

"Did you fuck him too?"

"Anthony Hutchinson?"

He nodded.

"Not in this bed. At school. Under the bleachers. Unbelievable that we didn't get caught."

"Well, then, tonight's your lucky night. You just happen to have a bona fide cock-slut here who's willing to let you fill his ass with your sweet, hot cum."

"A bona fide cock-slut, huh?"

"Yeah," he said, stroking me to hardness. "A slutty whore with a needy hole."

"Oh, baby, keep on talking to me."

"Get your tongue down there and get me ready."

"Yes, Your Majesty."

"No, not Your Majesty. Tonight, it's me and you."

"Yes, my beautiful, perfect, sexy Minty."

He laughed softly as I slid beneath the blankets and got to work.

Chapter Thirty-Seven

New Year's Eve 1991
Luke

N EW YEAR'S EVE at Tilt-a-Whirl was ablaze with joy. The dance floors were packed with queers of every stripe. Minty was out there now, dancing with his group of friends, twirling between Windy and a guy he talked less about called Antonio. Ryan was there too, but he was dancing off to the side, giving his Dom room to hang out with his friends.

I sat at the downstairs bar, keeping one eye on the drinks and the other on the clock. I didn't want to miss my chance to kiss Minty at midnight. He looked so pretty tonight, dressed in a silver tutu skirt, ballet shoes, and a loose, see-through, snow-white crop top. He was the fairy prince of my dreams. I was beyond lucky to have him in my life.

I hadn't thanked Barry yet for convincing me to take him on, but I would tonight. He deserved all the credit for changing both our lives for the better. He was working the upstairs bar, and Robert was doing his famous Renée DeShea drag performance a few minutes after midnight.

"Hey," a voice said near my right ear. "Buy you a drink?"

I shook my head, my eyes on Minty. "I'm good, thanks."

"Fair enough." The guy didn't take the hint, though, sitting on the stool next to me.

I swung around, ready to tell him to skedaddle. "Oh. Hi."

He was more handsome in person than in Minty's photos, which was saying something.

"Hi, I'm Daniel."

"Yes, of course. I'm Luke," I said, putting out my hand. "Nice to finally meet you. Minty says you're—"

Daniel rolled his eyes, a humble smile on his face. "The best guy in the whole world."

"Exactly."

"A sweet delusion of Minty's, but I have to admit I don't hate hearing it."

I got the bartender's attention, and he came over, taking Daniel's order. A Greyhound cocktail and a rum and Coke. When they were delivered, Daniel drank from the dark-colored one and put the pink one aside. It must be for Peter.

"So…" Daniel said with a heavy tone that warned me an inquisition about my intentions was forthcoming, and the storm clouds in his eyes told me Minty wasn't misrepresenting the situation. This guy really might be a party pooper.

"I love him," I said, cutting to the chase.

His eyes narrowed in evaluation of me. I might be ten years older, but I felt like a kid under his gaze. I needed to prove myself and make him believe in me.

I babbled on, "I'll do anything for him. I promise I'll protect him and keep him safe. Always."

After a moment, Daniel's lips tilted into a sweet smile. "Wow, you've got it bad. I recognize all the signs." His eyes shifted to the dance floor, and he sighed, "Ask me how I know."

Was that it? I had his full trust already? He'd been easier to win over than I expected him to be.

Suddenly, Daniel swung toward me, narrowing his gaze again. "If you hurt him, and I don't mean in the bedroom, I'll stop being the best guy in the world just long enough to ruin your life in every way that matters."

I wanted to laugh, but his dark eyes shone with a fierce seriousness that I couldn't even smile at. I raised my glass and tapped it to his. "If I hurt him, I'll help you do it."

Daniel nodded, satisfied. We turned our attention back to our men on the dance floor and drank in companionable silence until the little group returned, all of them covered in sweat, and all bright eyed and thirsty.

"Did you talk?" Minty asked, nodding his head at Daniel who now had his arm around a cute curly-haired twink who could only be the incomparable Peter.

"We did."

"And he approves of you?"

I put on a sad face and shook my head.

Minty's lips went flat, and he shot a glare Daniel's way. "How dare he?" He balled up his fists. "I'll give him—"

I gripped his arm before he could haul off and hit Daniel's bicep. "I'm kidding. He was fine. I promise. All's well."

Minty huffed. "It better be."

Daniel caught his eye then, smiling at first until he got a glimpse of Minty's irritation, and then his expression turned bewildered.

"Ah, now, don't be like that.," I urged, worried my joke would undo all the good will I'd earned. "He was nice to me, I swear."

Minty gazed at Daniel, jerked his chin toward me, and then lifted a brow in a "so?" gesture.

Daniel smiled again and lifted his drink to toast us.

Minty relaxed against my side. "Okay then. He likes you."

I laughed. "Yeah. He does. It's all okay." I sobered slightly. "What if he hadn't, though? What if the best guy in the world said he hated me?"

"Then he'd have to just go on hating you because you're my forever, and he's just my best friend."

I nuzzled his cheek, and he kissed me full on the mouth. The music lifted again, and Minty pulled me out onto the dance floor. I left my drink behind, happier to occupy my tongue with licking up his sweat and kissing his mouth.

As the big hand of the clock drew around toward the top, we all traipsed upstairs to the second floor where a stage was set up for Renée's drag show. Now that she was a bigger deal than ever, what with her show in Nashville, she'd drawn a big crowd. The entire upstairs was mobbed with people. We packed in around Barry's bar, and he brought out two Zimas, plopped Jolly Ranchers into them, and handed the bottles to Minty and Windy.

I waited until the others were distracted before turning to Barry.

"Thanks," Barry said, forestalling my gratitude with his own.

"For what?" I asked.

"For doing what I knew you could." He nodded toward Minty, who was laughing at something his pal Antonio had in his wallet. The little group was trying to grab it out and, unsurprisingly, Minty won. He crowed and held it over his head. It was Antonio's driver's license. "You brought him back to life."

"It was mutual. I was half-alive too, and now…" My throat tightened. "I just want to make him happy. Fuck me, Barry, but I'd do anything for him. I'd give him the moon if I could."

Minty glanced my way, blew me a kiss, and Antonio took advantage of his distraction to grab his driver's license back. A small shoving match began, but I knew Minty could hold his own. He'd taken down Sensei Junior two nights before, and I had as yet to hear the end of it.

"And, by the way, you're welcome," Barry said.

I laughed. "I did come over here to thank you actually."

"I figured." He grinned and slid a vodka tonic my way. "On the house."

"Fifteen, fourteen—!" the shouts of the countdown drifted up from the dance floor below.

"Here we go," Barry said. As if on cue, at the count of ten, Renée swept out of the dressing room behind the stage, making a beeline for the bar.

Minty ran to my side, his eyes gleaming and his smile broad. "Eight, seven—"

Peter and Daniel cuddled up. Barry and Robert started kissing and it wasn't even midnight yet. Ryan and Windy stood staring into each other's eyes, an intimate negotiation taking place silently between them.

Grinning, Minty took my hands, butterfly necklace glistening in the low lights of the bar, and he went up on his toes. "Three, two, one—"

He jumped into my arms. The room exploded with cheers from below, and my heart exploded with hope and the joy of Minty being safe and with me. The future was roaring into our present, and I had no idea what it was going to bring. Somehow, someway, we'd get through it together.

Because, against all odds, I knew love was on our side.

Minty

GLITTER FOLLOWED ME from the club to Luke's car and into the house. I dropped red, gold, and silver dust with every breath. It was in my hair, on my skin, and shining on my tutu skirt and clinging to my ballet slippers.

As I passed through the kitchen and the living room to the front hall to hang up my coat and scarf, I held back a small squeal at the surprise plans I'd made tonight for the basement. We hadn't been down there together since before Luke had gone home to help his mother with his father's transition to Senior Care, since before I started seeing Pamela, and before my last confrontation with Kyle.

I, however, had gone down two days after we got back from Christmas in Johnson City. While Luke was enjoying a post-leftover coma, I'd walked around the room, touching all the implements and contraptions, thinking about each one, considering whether—and more importantly *how*—it could ever be safe to use the room again.

A few days after that, while Luke was at work, I'd headed to Walmart with the gift card I'd gotten from Rodney's parents and some money I'd scrounged up from the back of my desk at the dorm when I'd moved out. After returning with an armload of bags, I'd prepared the space carefully, making changes both permanent and temporary. The fact that Luke hadn't mentioned it told me he hadn't been down there at all.

It was late—almost two in the morning—but I wanted him to see it now. It was time. Giddiness and verve made my stomach quivery, along with a glimmer of fear that Luke wouldn't like what I'd done, that he'd be upset about me making changes without him.

Entering the front hall from the living room, Luke slid his arms around me from behind, nuzzling the back of my head and breathing in my scent. I was sweaty from dancing, but he always seemed to love the way I smelled. I clung to his arms still encased in his winter coat and felt the scratch of the wool against my exposed lower back.

"Happy New Year," Luke murmured, squeezing me almost breathless.

"Hey," I said when he started kissing my neck. Fizzy anticipation raced through me. "Do you remember when I called you while you were staying at your Mom's house?"

"Hmm?" Luke pushed his erection into my ass and tried to walk me forward toward the stairs, making it clear that he was more interested in proceeding to the bedroom than in talking right now.

I turned around in his arms, stopping him. He tried to kiss me, but I lifted my fingers to block his lips. I asked again, "Do you remember the call?"

With a huff of disappointment at having his amorous ambitions thwarted, Luke released me enough to peer down into my face, searching my expression. Seeing that I was serious, he sobered too. "Of course I do."

I fiddled with the lapel of his coat. "Well, if you remember it so well, then you'll also recall that you promised me a New Year's spanking." I widened my eyes, bit my lower lip, and tilted my head toward the basement door.

Luke's brows went up, a spark lighting in his eyes. But just as quickly, he dampened it down, saying, "Are you sure you're ready to go down there? If you want me to tan your ass, Your Majesty, I can do that upstairs."

I licked my lips. Anxiety slipped through my bloodstream. I could do this. I *wanted* to do this. I'd gone to a lot of trouble to do this. "Not Your Majesty right now. Just me. Minty."

Luke cocked his head slightly. "Wait. To be clear, you're saying you want to go to the basement as Minty?"

I nodded and smiled up at him. "I've missed being your boy."

Now Luke's brows came down again, furrowing slightly. "What does Pamela think about it?"

I sighed, leaning my head against his chest. Thinking about my therapist, kind as she was, was not sexy, but given everything, Luke had every right to ask. I owed him an answer. I met his worried gaze, pulling lightly on his lapel again. "She said a consensual spanking in a sexual context from my loving partner isn't at all the same thing as what I'd been doing before, and if I feel ready to play like that, then I should try it. I have a safe word after all."

I went up on my tiptoes and gave him a kiss, hoping to soothe him with sweetness.

With a shuddery sigh, Luke drew me in, ducking down to kiss my neck and hug me close. He rocked me back and forth slightly. The press of his lips was distracted as if he were seeking comfort more than trying to arouse me.

"Just a spanking?" he asked.

"A crop could be fun," I said, breathlessly. "Like the one you got for Christmas when you were a kid. I could pretend to be Speedy."

He huffed a wet laugh against my ear, still holding me tight. "I told you, I never used it on her."

"Yes, just on some high school boyfriend—"

"Not a boyfriend, a guy I fucked."

"Right, and now I want you to spank me, maybe use a crop if things go well, and let me kneel for you as Minty, your boy."

He cupped my cheek, searching my eyes. "You think you can be with me like that as yourself? Your whole, gorgeous, perfect self?"

I started to lift my chin, ready to put on the Your Majesty persona to accept the compliments as my due, but immediately I knew I didn't have to. I could accept them as me. Just me.

"Yes. I want to try. I've thought a lot about it." I touched the necklace at my throat, feeling the butterflies. "And I'm ready."

He slid his thumb over my lower lip. "What if I'm not?"

I blinked at him. "What do you mean?"

"I love you. I don't want you doing this just because you think it's what I need. Because all *I* need is you—safe, happy, and here with me."

My heart went soft and hot at the expression of adoration in his eyes. "I love you too."

"Things can't go back to how they were, baby. They just can't."

"I know, and they don't have to." I took hold of his hand and moved us toward the basement door. "Let me show you something, okay? Maybe this will help you understand."

I led the way down the stairs and into the dungeon. He stopped at the bottom, his hand clenching in mine, and his brows lifting in shock and surprise.

"What do you think?"

His eyes swept all around, taking in the changes I'd made. My stomach knotted up with hopeful anxiety. What if he hated it? I should have asked permission. It was his home, his dungeon, and I was his sub, after all.

The twinkle lights I'd draped all along the wall holding the Saint Andrew's Cross glowed a reassuring gold color, and the glow-in-the-dark stars I'd painstakingly pressed to the ceiling over the bed in the shape of the constellations on the package shone green in the darkness. The soft, white voile fabric I'd gotten half-off in the fabric department draped on hooks I'd hung on the walls around the bed, giving it a romantic, soft look.

As for the center of the room, over the drain, I'd put down a big, multi-colored braided area rug that gave a warm energy to the area, taking away the stark, industrial vibe of before.

There were other changes I'd made too.

Pillows of all colors that matched the braided area rug were tossed on the bed, and on the chair, and even in a pile in the corner. I'd bought the majority of them at Walmart, but a few I'd picked up at one of the local charity shops.

On the horse lay another colorful braided rug, this one positioned to rub against my front if I were to lie down on it, providing friction. I'd tried it out when I'd placed it, by taking my shirt off and getting on. The difference in sensation was exciting and dissimilar enough to the feel of just wood and leather that I didn't think I'd lose myself to any past memories if I were to get flogged while buckled in.

All in all, the room was entirely different, and yet its function could be the same.

I bit my bottom lip, watching for Luke's reaction, but his wide-eyed gaze betrayed no emotion that I could decipher.

"I can take it all down, and we can use it elsewhere if you don't like it. I can give it all to my mother."

"No," Luke breathed. "It'll all stay right here."

I guided him to the bed, which had a new afghan thrown over the bottom of it. I sat down, and he remained standing, holding onto my hands and looking around the room.

"I want to be your boy again," I said. "But when I came down here the other day to see if I thought I was ready, I realized that to kneel for you and still be healthy in my head, I had to own the space more. I needed to change it so that what we do together feels different and doesn't feed any dark, hurt, angry parts of me."

Luke had stopped gazing at the room and started looking at me as I spoke. His eyes were gentle, and he squeezed my fingers. "Can it work?"

"Hit me and see."

Luke's lips curved into an amused smile, and he touched my cheek with trembling fingers. "I don't want to hurt you, baby."

"Not even a little?" I batted my eyes at him and pleaded. "But I've been *very good*, Sir, and I think I deserve it."

Luke's brows went up as he pondered me. "You think you deserve a slap?"

"Yes."

"And how about my dick?"

"Yes. And your kiss, and your spit, and your cum."

He tightened his fingers against the side of my face, and then drew his hand back and lightly smacked me. It wasn't hard, not like he'd hit me in the past, but enough for a sting to light up my cheek. I smiled. "See? That wasn't so bad, Sir."

He made a blustery noise, and then smacked me a little harder. I laughed, a burble of happiness.

Luke slid his coat off, tossed it onto the bed next to me, and then slapped my other cheek experimentally. "Do you like that?"

"Love it, Sir."

He did it again, harder. "Still like it?"

"Yes."

And the game was on.

"Your safe word is poodle." He pulled his sweater over his head, tossed it to the floor, and then kicked it aside. He toed off his shoes and stood in front of me in just his jeans and socks. I licked my lips, lifted my chin, and slid to the ground, kneeling between his toes. I tilted my head way back, gazing up at him. The green, glowing stars above the bed formed a halo behind his shaggy blond hair, and his eyes glinted.

Luke twined his hands in my hair, tugging lightly, and then he cupped his hands around my head and shoved my face into his crotch. I mouthed his jeans where his dick was pressing, kissing and lightly biting the tight material. He hissed.

"Fucking brat," he muttered, clenching his fingers in my hair more tightly, and then releasing me to undo his jeans. "Hungry for my dick?"

"Yes, Sir," I murmured, kneeling back and opening my mouth wide in invitation.

He huffed, cursing under his breath, as he wrenched his fly open and withdrew his cock. I waited as he tapped the tip against my bottom lip and then wiped the head over my tongue, letting me taste his pre-cum.

"Choke me with it, Sir," I whispered. "Give your boy what he wants."

"This is about what I want." Luke's lips twisted with a familiar sadistic smirk, and my heart rate picked up, thudding in my ears.

"Yes," I hissed, and then yelped in pain as he grabbed hold of one of my ears, hauled me to my feet, and pulled me toward the horse.

"Get naked, bitch. Get on it."

I laughed again, and Luke slapped my face hard. I hiccupped with a wild, gleeful joy that was laced with hot tears as I pulled my crop top over my head and started to carefully fold it. Luke snatched it from my hands and threw it aside. "Don't dawdle. Get your fucking ass on that horse, or I'll make you see stars."

I had to fight another grin, but I worked my skirt down and threw it to the side too. Climbing on the horse, I realized I was shaking. Was it with cold from the chill of winter seeping into the subterranean basement? Or was it with excitement that I was about to submit to intense sensations that I'd been too afraid to play with for the last few weeks? Both.

The braided rug dug into my dick as I got into position, ass up and straddling the bench. I placed my face in the donut head support as Luke latched my ankles and wrists, my head and waist, and then came around to run his hand into my hair. "Use your safe word if you need it."

"Yes, Sir." I giggled. I was giddy, and the rising hysteria in me was as much relief as it was anxiety.

"Something funny?" Luke growled.

"No, Sir."

"*Hmmph.*"

I jolted as a wicked slap landed on my ass, exploding sensation through my hip and haunch. I grunted, my humor drying up instantly and my pulse thudding in my ears. Another rough smack came down, and I cried out. Luke slid his hand over my back as he walked toward my head and knelt down. His mouth tickled my ear as he whispered, "Doing all right?"

"Yes, Sir," I answered. "Please. Treat me like your cock's slave. Your slutty little bitch. Your cum-hungry boy."

Luke hummed as he stood and moved behind me. He gripped my ass cheeks, spread me wide, and exposed my hole. "Gorgeous little cum dumpster."

"Yes, Sir," I agreed. "Use me. Now."

A harsh cuff on my thigh made me gasp. "I'll choose when I use you, brat."

I shivered as the spanking began in earnest. I twisted around as much as my restraints would allow. The steady blows from Luke's hand brought heat to my muscles and a sheen of sweat broke over my body. As the pain grew, I hunched against the braided rug beneath me, rubbing my hard cock against the uncomfortable friction.

"That's right," Luke muttered. "Hump that horse for me. Show me how greedy you are."

"Please," I grunted. "The crop. I need it."

The truth was, I just needed to prove to myself I could take it and not splinter into a million pieces of old shame.

Luke took me at my word. I heard him retreat to the wall of implements—which I'd only dressed up with a string of twinkle lights—and as he returned to me, I could hear the slap-slap of him striking the leather of the crop against his palm. I quivered with excitement and dread.

Luke ran his hand over my body, sliding from hip to shoulder, and then back down again. "Minty?"

"Yes?"

"This is gonna fucking hurt."

"Oh, God." I tensed all over before forcing myself to relax, trying to melt into the horse. "Do it, Sir."

Luke didn't hold back. I didn't know if he was testing me like I was testing myself, or if he just *really* wanted to see red welts on my ass, but the sharp sting of the crop was breathtaking on top of my spanked ass. I felt my muscles clenching and dancing under the blows.

"That's good," he praised. "That's my beautiful boy."

I groaned and refused to listen to the whisper in my mind saying that I didn't want to hear praise, that I didn't deserve it. "I'm your beautiful boy," I said aloud, combatting it. "I'm your gorgeous slut."

"That's right. My sweet, greedy cum hole."

"Your horny, needy cunt."

"Mm, yes," he agreed. The crop came down again. "Say it."

"I love myself."

"Yes, baby. I love you too. You're so hot."

As he struck me again and again, I play-struggled against the restraints. My cock rubbed on the braided rug, and I tightened my ass muscles, trying to release the burn.

"Unclench," Luke ordered, and as soon as I did, he struck me with the crop.

I shouted and clenched my fingers and toes. "Sir," I whimpered. "I want to feel you."

Luke massaged my ass, pulling it open and rubbing his fingers over my hole. "You're ready for my dick?"

"Yes, please. Anything. Your finger. Your tongue."

Luke laughed and went back to using the crop on me. Helpless, I sank into a hot and sweaty stupor, jerking with the blows. Time divided into two portions—being hit, and not being hit.

Luke was sweating too, and he dripped onto me as he continued to swing and strike, swing and strike. I melted onto the horse, surrendering, and only when I no longer tensed before the crop landed, did Luke speak again.

"Ready to fly, baby?"

I moaned.

"Let's fly."

I heard him walk back to the wall, and I knew without a doubt he'd return with the red whip. The sting of it had only ever been outshone by the heavy hurt of the rubber flogger.

"Got a word?" Luke asked.

"Yeah," I whimpered.

Luke knelt by my head, twining his fingers into my hair. "What is it?"

I couldn't stop myself from laughing as I said, "I've got three—hurt me, Sir."

The sound of the whip swinging through the air gave me the opportunity to feel the sharpness of fear before it was blotted out with pain. I laughed and cried and struggled away from the red-hot licks, and Luke started to laugh too when I shouted, "I fucking love this, Sir. I love being your boy."

He rubbed my flaming butt cheek, chuckling as he said, "I love hurting you."

"Don't stop."

The wires that had been crossed with the gift of his first crop when he was young, and which made him get off on hurting me, now twined with *my* crossed wires which made pain feel like power and pleasure. I writhed as the sensation mounted and grew to an ecstatic peak that made me convulse and cry out with a shattering joy.

"Did you come?" Luke grunted, as I came down from the splintering heights. "Did you shoot your load, baby?"

I gasped for air, unsure of what had happened, but then it didn't matter anymore. Luke was shoving lubed-up fingers into my hole, stretching me open before thrusting his thick cock in with a brutal swiftness that made me clench my fists, groan, and break out into a fresh sweat.

"Yes," Luke gritted out. "So tight. Look at you covered in my marks."

"I'm yours," I whimpered, as he began to fuck me hard and fast.

"Your slutty boy."

"Mine," Luke agreed. "Mine to hurt."

"Only yours."

I panted and whimpered as he nailed my prostate, and the strain of bliss began again, a rush of power that pulled through my whole body and made me shake. "I need you," I groaned. "Fill me up."

Luke bit my shoulder and grabbed at me as he climaxed. He unloaded into me, his hips stuttering and bucking against my bruised and sore ass. I panted, feeling proud, and silly, and sore as hell.

As soon as Luke finished, he dragged himself out my body and then bent to shove his escaping cum back inside my hole. "Hold it in," he ordered, and I clenched it closed to obey.

"Precious cargo." I giggled as he undid the restraints and lifted me from the horse. I clung to his shoulders when he picked me up to carry me to the bed.

"Yes, you are," he agreed.

"I meant your jizz."

His lips quirked up into a smile, and he lay down next to me. He was sweaty and flushed, and I knew I was too, but I couldn't stop grinning. I buried my face in his neck and started to shake with laughter. My skin was shouting with stinging pain, but my soul was easy about it.

"What on earth has gotten into you," Luke whispered, moving to kiss my cheek. "You're giddy."

"I'm happy. I just feel… *happy.*"

He tugged me close, and we kissed for a long time as I enjoyed the afterburn of his domination of me. I felt inordinately proud. I'd not only relished being hit like that, but hearing him call me dirty things had only made me ecstatic, instead of ashamed. I *wanted* to be his cum dumpster, his greedy hole, his dick's slave. I couldn't think of anything better. It was what I wanted most in the world right now.

I wanted to spend the rest of my life with Luke, playing thrilling games like this, and making love upstairs, and kissing on the sofa, and making dinner together, and *living*. For the first time ever, I was happy.

So fucking happy.

I'd finally won.

Luke

AFTER THE SCENE in the basement, I waited for Minty to fall asleep. Once he was out, I admired him for a few long minutes—he was still shimmering with the glitter that had clung to him from the club. He was also shining with all the red left behind from my strikes. He'd taken it all so well and with so much joy. It was almost as if I had a an entirely different boy here in bed with me than the one I'd originally ordered down those stairs months ago.

After I was sure Minty was asleep, I got up to do some cleaning. I checked the horse and found he hadn't spunked on the new braided rug after all, but there was still some mess to deal with. I handled it all, folded our clothes, and then walked around the room, taking in all the changes, big and small, that Minty had made.

It was different, that was for sure.

I'd set up the dungeon with Jerome's old tools without a lot of thought outside of making a boy sweat and suffer. In the past, I'd always sought sadistic sexual relationships that didn't involve my heart. The sex I'd had with those boys was fun, intense, and sometimes very intimate, but love had never tainted the experience.

Now, after our scene, I felt sure that love had not *tainted* the experience, but it had definitely changed it for me. I felt entirely different to slapping Minty now than I had when we'd started. Back then, it'd felt clinical to hit him. Prescriptive even. Sexy, but emotionally disengaged.

Now I felt so much *more* with even the smallest strikes. Building up to the whip had been an exercise in mental and emotional gymnastics. My desire to never see Minty hurting again had warred with the sweet joy of having him *beg* me for what I *knew* he'd allow only me to ever give him from now on. A way out of his head, a way to bliss through pain, and a shuddering, screaming orgasm.

The emotional tumult I'd felt during the scene had added to the intensity for me as well. The urgency with which I'd fucked him had left my legs shaking so hard that I'd barely had the strength to carry him to the bed. It'd been a terrifying rush. The scene was something he'd wanted and needed, and he'd trusted me to know how to give it to him without destroying him again. I was grateful to find his trust hadn't been misplaced because, even in the moment, I hadn't been sure.

My relief when the scene had left him happy, giddy, laughing, and breaking open with light had almost brought me to tears. We'd both changed since we'd started this journey together. It made sense that the dungeon would need to change too.

I smiled as I considered the sweetness of Minty using his Christmas gift card money on all of this. Returning to the bed, I straightened the soft new blanket over his body. I gazed around the room at the lights, the rugs, the voile draping, and tears came to my eyes. Minty was so honest with himself and with me.

He'd wanted this, but to have it, he'd known things had to change.

I wanted things to change even more. Speaking of…

I fetched the box from my coat pocket, having never found the right moment to give it to Minty at the club, and shoved it beneath the pillow. Heart thundering, I watched him sleep for another few minutes before I couldn't stand to wait another moment.

"Baby," I said, tapping his reddened cheek with my fingers. "Wake up."

"Mmm?" He came to with a drowsy blink, and when he focused on me, and then on the room around us, he grinned. "Oh. Hi. Want to play again?"

I laughed. "So greedy."

"Yes, I am. This hungry hole *needs* your cum," he said, giggling, wriggling around under the covers. "Want to do it here? Or in our bedroom?"

Our bedroom.

Yes, I'd asked him to move in, and he had. I loved that this was our home now, and his embellishment of the dungeon only emphasized that fact.

"Let's do it here," I said, grabbing lube from the nightstand by the bed. "Spread your legs."

Minty grinned, swanned back on the pillows, and did exactly as I asked, just as I'd known he would.

Shortly, I had him wet and open, and squirming on my cock with his legs thrown over my shoulders. As I screwed him slowly, lovingly, he tossed his head back in gratification, looking so beautiful and sweet.

My heart nearly burst with adoration. I loved him so much, and I was so damn *unbearably* proud of him. "You're fucking sexy, baby."

"Thank you," he whispered.

"I have a New Year's present for you."

His eyes lit with joy, and he shuddered, milking his ass around my cock. "Yesssss, give it to me. I want it."

I grinned. "Not my load."

Frowning now, he gazed up at me in confusion. I could see the green of the glow in the dark stars reflected in his eyes. "But I want it."

"Don't worry, you're going to get that too. I meant this…" I slid my hand under the pillow and pulled out the box. Fully pushed inside him, buried to the base of my cock in his hot, sweet body, I flicked it open.

Glinting in the low light were two rings side by side, one silver and one gold band.

"What's happening?" Minty panted. His pulse thudded quickly in his throat, and he squeezed around my cock. "Am I still dreaming?"

"No, this is very real. I know it's not legal, but this—" I thrust in again, lodging deep. "Us." I kissed his mouth and the tip of his nose. "I don't want us to ever end. I want the honor of caring for you for the rest of your life, Minty Arnold. And in return, I'll take anything you have to offer. Your darkest times, your sweetest, sunniest moods, your sweat and sex and cum. I want it all. I want you forever. Will you marry me? Here? Now?"

"Luke…" Minty's chest was flushed, and his cock leaked freely between us. He wrapped his legs around my waist, dragging me deeper. "I want that too."

"You'll say yes? You'll wear my ring?"

"Yes."

I placed the silver band on the third finger of his left hand, and then slid the yellow gold onto mine. As I tossed the empty box aside, Minty looked down at where we were joined.

"Luke?"

"Yeah?"

"Did you notice? You're making love to me, and I'm letting you."

My throat grew tight as the realization hit. I was absolutely making love to Minty and there was no artifice or story between us to make it safe for him. It was just me and him together. My cock in his ass, our love flowing between us.

"I love you," I whispered, rolling my hips into a fluid, sweet fuck.

A smile creased the corner of his eyes as he whispered it back, and added, "I love myself too. You help me do that. You show me how to love even the worst parts of me."

"Every part of you is good."

We kissed and fucked, and the sweetness stretched on and on. I focused only on him, enjoying his every shudder of pleasure. I whispered my adoration as we moved, and he didn't pull back or flinch at any of my declarations. When his balls drew up, right on the edge of coming, Minty gazed up at me, smiled and whispered, "I love you."

Convulsions gripped him and he shot a wet, sticky load between us. I drove in with a hard thrust, held and jerked, crying out as I came. He clung to my back, kissing my throat as I quivered and jerked.

Afterward, I collapsed on him, panting. "Baby, I love you so much."

"I know." Minty was boneless beneath me, letting me smash him into the mattress with my weight. "You married me twice this month. You love me a lot."

I shifted over, so he could breathe, but kept my dick buried in him since I was still hard. "Twice?"

"Beneath the tree at your mom's, when you promised you'd take care of me if…" He didn't go on. We both knew what he was talking about, and that reminder was enough for me to lose my erection. I slid out of him but used my fingers to plug his needy hole. He signed happily, and went on, "And now here in our special room with this beautiful ring." He held up his hand so that the ring glinted. "Given everything bad that's happened this year, I know this sounds silly, but right now, I feel really lucky."

He touched the necklace glittering on his throat. "I've got a new family and a husband who loves me. All mine for as long as I live."

"We've both been lucky." Despite all the pain, it felt undeniably true. We'd found each other against all odds. I kissed him sweetly. "And, hey, we got something else too. We made love as Minty and Luke, without a single Your Majesty, or even a nip or a pinch or a bite."

Minty preened like he'd just won a trophy.

"How do you feel about that?"

"Happy," he said, wonder in his voice. "I feel really, truly happy."

I kissed him again. "Me too."

"I've earned it," he whispered. "I *deserve* it."

"You deserve the world."

"I do."

His sweet smile gave me butterflies.

Butterflies and hope.

Post Script

In January 1992, Betsy and Rodney got married in a big ceremony at Riverwoods. Family, friends, and residents were in attendance. The cake was a three-tiered orange Creamsicle-flavored monstrosity that Minty ate three pieces of, and he was nearly sick in the car on the drive home.

In February 1992, Luke gave Minty a golden retriever puppy for his birthday. He named her Butter—short for Princess Butterfly Marmalade. She was the first in a line of four well-loved retrievers.

In August 1992, Kyle was sentenced to prison for drugging and filming the rape of three women. He was released in 2001 for good behavior. Minty never saw Kyle or sought out anyone like him again.

In June 1993, Minty started work with TVA in river ecology studying the salamanders he loved. The job provided him with the financial security he needed to buy his mother a small home, and to make improvements to the home he and Luke had made together. He stayed with TVA as a long-term employee until he started working for the US Forest Service in 2006. He was proud of being a "Pretty Boy in Hiking Boots," and he taught Luke to love camping and the outdoors.

In 1996, Minty received word that his father had died in prison. Luke was with him when the news came, and though he requested a longer than usual session in their now very posh basement dungeon, he didn't resort to past coping mechanisms. There were no tears shed, and he almost never talked about his father again.

In 1998, Minty and Luke began antiretroviral treatment with HAART, a revolutionary new drug which reduced their HIV viral load. As the years passed, they gained access to increasingly effective medications, and their life expectancy increased. With each passing anniversary of their respective diagnoses, they remained miraculously healthy. They felt they owed it to their friends who weren't as lucky to stay grateful and happy in their lives.

In 1999, Luke's father passed away from a second stroke. Luke had never been able to patch up their relationship, but his dad had been well cared for in the senior facility. That same year, they told Luke's mother about their HIV diagnoses, the effectiveness of the new medication, and finally allowed her to support them emotionally.

In 2000, Minty stopped his weekly sessions with Pamela Novik after almost a decade. He went to monthly sessions instead, continuing with her until 2006.

In 2002, Daniel and Peter spent a summer in Paris. Minty and Luke joined them for a few weeks, enjoying the romance of the city. But, on the flight home, Minty told Luke he'd missed his Appalachian rivers, and mountains, and salamanders. "Just call me your Appalachian Fairy Prince." Luke laughed and kissed his face.

In 2006, Minty and Luke moved to Asheville, North Carolina where Luke was invited to help a friend start a new brewery business. Minty began work with the US Forest Service in the Blue Ridge Mountains. Luke loved the new direction in his life, and Minty loved tromping through the mountains every day.

In 2015, after the Obergefell vs Hodges decision, Minty and Luke were finally legally married. Luke called Minty "Your Majesty" in the ceremony to make Minty laugh, and the minister insisted he repeat the vows properly. Either way, as far as Luke was concerned, he got married to a prince.

In 2018, with the help of the latest medications, Luke reached undetectable status with his HIV, and Minty's viral load was nearly so. Their life expectancy was assumed to now be the same as the national average. They started to see the dates of their diagnoses as anniversaries worthy of celebration instead of grieving. Another year well-lived!

In 2020, Minty discovered the term *non-binary* while clicking around on the internet and realized for the first time that a word existed to describe how he felt inside. Afterwards, he proudly wore a non-binary flag pin on his work jacket. Though, in the end, he chose to stick with he/him pronouns, saying that he still felt most closely identified to "a pretty man with the right priorities in fashion."

In October 2021, Minty and Luke celebrated their thirty-year anniversary with a trip to a cabin by Norris Lake. Minty fished and waded out into the water in his big rubber boots to examine the salamanders. In his sixties now, Luke paddled around in a canoe watching him do what he loved most. Later, they made love by a roaring fire. Even later, bent over Luke's knee, Minty received thirty anniversary strikes with his favorite crop.

In the end, love really was on their side.

Read about Daniel and Peter's love story now in the '90s Coming of Age trilogy! Available on Amazon and in KU.

Letter from Leta

Dear Reader,

Thank you for going on this emotional and tumultuous ride with Minty. I know we all loved him so much in the '90s Coming of Age trilogy and needed to see his story through.

I wanted to take a moment to tell you about my own history as a student of psychology in the early 1990s. At the time, I worked at a psychiatric hospital for children and teens, and I saw and heard about a lot of traumatic things. One child has always stood out in my memory—a twelve-year old we'll call Emmett (not his real name). Tender and sweet, with striking blue eyes and a kind heart, Emmett had been sexually abused and raped by his father.

While there was intense trauma to process for Emmett, the issue he had the most difficulty integrating into his concept of self was that, at times, he'd instigated the events with his father and that he had, at other times, physically enjoyed some of the sensations and the "closeness" he'd felt to the man assaulting him. For Emmett, the deep shame he felt, and his intense self-loathing associated with these uncomfortable facts, had led him to feel suicidal. His second suicide attempt was the reason for his stay at the hospital.

My time at the facility ended before Emmett's, and I have no idea whatever became of him. At this point, he would be a fully grown man, well into his thirties, and I ponder at times what his life might be like now. I hope that he found a way to forgive the child he was and the things he did to survive, and most of all, I hope he found a way to love himself again.

Emmett's situation was, of course, different from Minty's in very many ways, but that aspect of shame and self-loathing was something I felt compelled to address in Minty's narrative. It's an unpleasant concept that isn't typically tackled, nor is the way those feelings can drive a person to do dangerous things—drugs, drinking, self-abuse, sex addiction, violence—just to wrestle the feelings away. Having known Emmett, I couldn't just pretend those situations and the fallout from them never happen.

Should you or anyone you know need a person to talk with or should you need to report a sexual assault, the National Sexual Assault hotline at RAINN is 1 (800) 656-4673.

On a different, happier note, if you would like to know more about Peter and Daniel, you can read their story in the *'90s Coming of Age* trilogy. Don't miss out on a series that readers have called a masterpiece, the best they've read in years, and a new all-time favorite.

Again, thank you for trusting me to take you on this dark and harrowing journey with Minty. I hope I was able to keep your heart safe while exploring these hard narratives.

Love and healing to all,
Leta

Acknowledgments

Normally, I put acknowledgments at the front of the book, but I didn't want to distract from the important Content Warnings. So, I've moved them to the end this time. Let's get to the very necessary thank yous:

The Behind-the-Scenes Gang who edit, copyedit, proof, beta, and make sure everything flows just right: Jordan Buchanan, Willow Board, Kate Hawthorne, Scarlett Drake, Cecily Green, Enay, Kim, Brian, Paul, and Kirk!

My sensitivity betas for Down Syndrome and HIV in the 1990s: Miriam Porter, Bill Reid.

My family and friends: Brian, Cecily, Mom, Dad, and all my friends for the love and support. I couldn't do this gig without all of you. You make it all worthwhile.

My readers: You are truly the wind beneath my wings and the reason I keep writing. Thank you for trusting me with your precious time and even more precious heart.

My professors at the University of Tennessee psychology department, and my co-workers and fellow volunteers at Peninsula Lighthouse circa 1993. Most of all, my eternal gratitude goes to the children I worked with there. It was an honor to have been even a small part of your lives. May each and every one of you be living happily and well.

The authors of my Book Research:

The Loving Dominant by John & Libby Warren

Becoming a Slave by Jack Rinella

The Drama of the Gifted Child by Alice Miller

The Body Keeps the Score by Bessel van der Kolk M.D.

Perv by Jesse Bering

The Deep Psychology of BDSM & Kink by Douglas Thomas

'90s Coming of Age trilogy

"This series reminds the reader of what it was to be a teen, when every change was scary, every choice seemed right and also wrong, but discovery and hope were the engine of life."

~ Lara, The Reading Love

Peter Mandel is an 18-year-old private school senior who's passionate about photography and bent on keeping his attractions secret. Enter Adam Algedi, a charming, worldly guy who doesn't do labels, but does want to do Peter.

Swept away on a journey of first love and intimate discovery, Peter hopes for a future where he won't have to hide his truth. But as the web of lies he and Adam are weaving grows relentlessly tangled, can Peter find the confidence to do the right thing? Or will his crush on Daniel, a college acquaintance, put him on a different path?

Read *Pictures of You*, *You Are Not Me*, and *Only You* now!

The Difference Between
Standalone

"A very powerful book. Dark, gritty, raw. For an author to show us a humanity stripped of all its good and have the characters endure a Hell not many would survive and then turn it into a happiness we all wish we could feel just once in our lives? That's serious talent. I applaud the author and I do recommend this story."

~ Diverse Reader Reviews

"You're the strongest person I know."
Wade Maguire and Russ Paulson are in love. After a year of passion and happiness, they're buying a home and moving in together. Everything is rosy for them—until a jealous and insane ex from Wade's past puts all of that to the test.

"I need to figure out if there's a way to move past this. For both of us."
After being kidnapped and tortured by his deranged former lover, Wade loses his ability to engage with his own sexuality or with Russ. With the help of a psychologist, EMDR therapy, and a sex plan, they work together to overcome the damage inflicted. In the process, they discover wells of love they've never known before.

"You never deserved what happened to you. No matter what you've told yourself. You only deserved love."
As passion is reborn and their sex life reignited, Wade realizes a

need to re-experience certain events in Russ's loving arms. For Wade, the difference between pain and pleasure is love, and the difference between rape and rough sex is consent.

Dark, and yet ultimately hopeful, this story of true love and rape recovery contains **many emotional and graphic scenes of two men making love, as well as some intense scenes of torture.** *Proceed with care.*

The Difference Between is a 78,000 word steamy, graphic, intensely emotional novel with a strong happy ending. No cheating and no cliffhangers, just two men who fight for their love. STANDALONE.

Other Books by Leta Blake

Contemporary

Will & Patrick Wake Up Married
Will & Patrick's Endless Honeymoon
Cowboy Seeks Husband
The Difference Between
Bring on Forever
Stay Lucky

Sports

The River Leith

The Training Season Series
Training Season
Training Complex

Musicians

Smoky Mountain Dreams
Vespertine

New Adult

Punching the V-Card

'90s Coming of Age Series
Pictures of You
You Are Not Me
Only You

Winter Holidays

North's Pole

The Mr. Christmas Series
Mr. Frosty Pants
Mr. Naughty List
Mr. Jingle Bells

A Boy for All Seasons
My December Daddy

Fantasy

Any Given Lifetime

Reimagined Fairy Tales

Flight
Levity

Paranormal & Shifters

Angel Undone
Omega Mine

Horror

Raise Up Heart

Omegaverse

Heat of Love Series
White Heat
Slow Heat
Alpha Heat

Slow Birth
Bitter Heat

For Sale Series
Heat for Sale
Bully for Sale

Audiobooks
letablake.com/audiobooks

Discover more about the author online

Leta Blake
letablake.com

www.ingramcontent.com/pod-product-compliance
Lightning Source LLC
Chambersburg PA
CBHW031237310726
48971CB00004B/1050